MY
NAME
IS
YIP

MY NAME IS YIP

PADDY CREWE

THE OVERLOOK PRESS, NEW YORK

This edition first published in hardcover in 2022 by
The Overlook Press, an imprint of ABRAMS
195 Broadway, 9th floor
New York, NY 10007
www.overlookpress.com

Abrams books are available at special discounts when purchased in quantity
for premiums and promotions as well as fundraising or educational use.
Special editions can also be created to specification. For details, contact
specialsales@abramsbooks.com or the address above.

Library of Congress Control Number: 2021949394

Printed and bound in the United States

1 3 5 7 9 10 8 6 4 2

ISBN: 978-1-4197-6229-1
eISBN: 978-1-64700-711-9

ABRAMS The Art of Books

For Mum and Dad

and

In memory of Jean Ralph
1946–2016

1

AN IMPONDERABLE SPECIMEN

MY NAME IS YIP TOLROY & I am a mute. I have made not a sound since the day of my birth, October 2nd, 1815. I will say that my life has been something of a trial but such is God's wish & so I must tell my story here on the page.

Indeed I should thank Him for these 3 fingers left me, they might still hold a quill & feel the ink flow free beneath them. I did leave them other 2 where they lay & I have dreams still of the rains feeding them like greentip shoots where in that spot now stands a Hand, the wrist a smooth-barked bole & a Hundred Fingers wagging like branches in the breeze.

Answers have not ever come easy to me. By all accounts they is like teeth – you can try to pull them clean out but even then they will likely Splinter & Crack & there will be nothing but a palmful of dust at the end of it. Here is a lesson worth attending to – no One or Thing comes into this world whole & it is in the search of what is gone missing that our lives do find their meaning. That is the truth of it.

At one time a great many beardy doctors did apply their crude instruments to me though none was able to declare a reason behind my queer *afflictions*. I ought to make it plain I am not cut from the common cloth. Aside from my lacking a voice I stand at 4 feet & 8 inches tall & there is inexplicably not a single hair on my person.

Some have been willing to look upon my differences as mere eccentricities, though the majority have not been so generous with their opinions. I never did quarrel with them who chose to insult me & I did not simper up to them who chose to treat me with civility. It is not my business to decide how others wish to comport theirselves. Only know that I have growed to look upon my own reflection in kind, for there is no hatred more pernicious than that which is turned upon the self.

It is true enough though that most people are affronted in one way or another at the sight of me. I have had many strangers & even them I considered friends claim I should be caged & preserved for the general public to enjoy as Entertainment. I did not figure this a likely chapter of my days but much to my dismay their wishes was to come true & I did in fact spend a short spell under the dubious protectorship of Mr. Jim Coyne & his Traveling Show. Of this I will tell you more later.

As for them doctors I come to understand they are a breed what do not much relish a mystery. On meeting me they would work theirselves into a great lather of excitement & then after an hour of poking & prodding, looking down my throat & into my earholes, their faces would grow dark & irritable. More than once was I referred to as an Imponderable Specimen. I could not claim to have the understanding of such a remark back then but I had sense enough to glean it did not portend nothing good.

It is just my humble opinion that there is many stories writ beneath the skin what will not give up their meaning to no Earthly Eye. This I know troubles a doctor greatly. He will not confess to it but part of his studyment of all them long yrs was in the hope that he will somehow keep on breathing long past the rest of us have quit.

Well I am still here & still breathing. No one has figured me out yet. I have led a life filled with wonder & misery both. That is the way God intended it. If you do not suffer pain then you will not know what it is to Live & Love. I have to hope there is not so much pain from now on to the end though, I do not think any soul could claim me a liar when I say I have had my fill.

2

A CRUEL & UNUSUAL BEGINNING

IT IS AN UGLY TRUTH the day of my birth is fettered to an event for which there is no cause to celebrate.

Who knows how many others have arrived on the current of such cruel & unusual beginnings but I imagine us to be a Sad & Lonesome band, them who entered this Life & left the door ajar for their begetter to take their leave. Should I ever come across one such soul I would know them by their dark & cowled eyes, for like me they too must carry the weight of all that could have been.

My poor daddy did not get to hold me. He did not even get to take one look into my eyes. And I will not lie it has put a bitter twist on my lips to have wrestled with my portion of the blame. O yes that guilt is a Sour-Seeded Fruit what hangs from a man's heart, there is no dose of time what will bring him peace. Not until he is returned to the dark of the earth will he reconcile himself to all what come to pass in the light of his days.

It does seal my heart in Eternal Sorrow that to this day I do not know where his poor bones lie or whether they was not simply left for the wind to scatter or to sate the whiskered maw of some rooting hog. It does me no good to dwell on it but still I must tell you of how he met his end, for it was no accident or natural flaw what brung his heart to silence.

My birth it will not surprise your eyes to read was no simple matter. Death was busy that day trying to claim all he could. My own lifecord was snaked about my neck, a blue & slippery noose as if already I considered myself a weary veteran of life's many bewilderments. My Mama groaned & wept & bled. She arched her back & after a day of fret & toil expelled me on a blood-warm surf what ferried me to the Direful Shores of that day.

Pale & silent I lay atop the freckled slabs of her arms, only my hands what opened & closed in faltering bloom did attest to the putter of my troubled heart. My skin was like the finest vellum, it did not look fit to suffer a spring rain & my head was a frail & venous globe straddling my shoulders as an egg might the final stalks of a plundered nest.

It was no surprise then that Dr. Whit Parrick, our town's only practitioner at that time, should steer my daddy toward the cool shadows of the parlor & there inquire after the integrity of our spade, warning it would likely be put to use by nightfall. Dr. Parrick, he was not one to waste his words but spoke of my demise as plainly as of some turn in the weather.

But where an older man might have appreciated Parrick's candor & boldness of expression, my daddy – still young, still artless in the face of Death – could bear it no more. His eyes, so blue, so very piercing, assumed the dull & empty sheen of 2 buttons sewn into the head of a straw doll. Without a word he turned on his heel & begun to run.

3

COLD KNOWLEDGE

I WILL WASTE NO TIME in telling you that my daddy run right out that door & he did never come back.

No he did not return & night fell & my Mama was laid by lantern-light in bloodslick sheets while Dr. Whit Parrick soaped his hands & watched wide-eyed as she raged & cursed my daddy for a Weak & Gutless man. Dr. Parrick did think at first it was his own character come under siege until he realized it was her departed husband she so damned, O she did spare none of her characteristic rancor in her explication of him. She convinced herself that very night he was a coward of the Highest Order, I imagine now it did give her broke heart some comfort to think so little of him.

As for Dr. Parrick that dour man did surely tell every soul he come across in Peeper's tavern of my Mama's curses, for soon it was become common knowledge the lily-livered John Tolroy had lit off in favor of a childless life beneath the gaze of some distant spread of stars.

Of course you understand I had never knowed my daddy, he was gone before I got the chance. Some folk have told me over the years that you cannot miss what you never knowed, I never in all my days heard such Rot, it is a lie big enough to sink a ship. I do miss my daddy every day & through whatever mysteries in the blood is passed down from father to son, in all them yrs of my growing up I could not shake the notion that he had harbored no intentions of disappearing at all. Indeed I thought I knowed it for a fact he had not meant to be gone long, all he wanted was some air in his lungs, a moment to clear the clouds from his poor head after seeing his struggling boy. It did not sit true that he just upped & gone, I found I did have ideas of my own come to colorful bloom behind my eyes.

As I growed up like many boys I heard stories of men what wore masks made of sugar sacks & wagon canvas across their faces, holes poked in them for the convenience of eyes & mouths. They held up burning pine knots & went blazing through the black of night, roaming across Cherokee & White soil alike, not caring a bit for who they stole from or what brand of blood they let spill.

I heard them thundering hoofs & seen them ugly masks lit up near every night in my dreams & each time they was surrounding a man, their voices hollering out, their horses restless in the dust & their guns angled down from their saddles. Their mouths was always covered but somehow I always knowed they was smiling cruelly down at that man who was alone, frighted & cowering, turning every way only to find another mask looking down at him, another gun levelled at his heart. I never seen this man's face but them dreams did always end the same way, I woke with the echo of a gunshot in my ears & the Cold Knowledge that the cowering man had been my daddy.

I never told no one of them dreams, for when he never come back my Mama did her best to forget him. As is natural for any fatherless boy I would in time come to ask about him, though she was always well prepared. She was not the type to parry an answer with clever wordings or kindly distractions, as a fancy-dressed romancer might wear his heart upon his sleeve my Mama did wear her bitterness upon hers. She told me my daddy was a poltroon, her beliefs was stubborn as limpets, she would never say no word otherwise.

We do so like to think we is the writers of stories but they so often come to us fully growed, it is only for us to choose how they might be read. So it was the folk of Heron's Creek was happy to have their story as it was – John Tolroy had absconded his fatherly duties without a trace & that is the way it would be until someone did go digging for the Truth.

4
SILENT ROARS & SILENT HOWLS

ONE WEEK AFTER MY BIRTH I was yet to produce a single noise. Dr. Whit Parrick might have thought it curious I did not cry on my gushing arrival if he had not become so endeared to the belief I was set to perish. And so when my breath did continue to come in Thin & Stubborn threads he had assumed my silence was no more than the lasting effects of my arduous passage into this Earthly Sphere. He told my Mama it was only natural I should need my peace & quiet, she should not worry, I would turn out a healthy little fellow if she give me the chance.

So my Mama did what he said. She watched & waited. Indeed she thought me one of God's messengers, a wingless little emissary sent to bring down to her the white serenity of the clouds. In them quiet hours she could not help but imagine me in her store, handling her precious ledger & welcoming in her patrons. She would not have to want for nothing as I carried on her hard work & did polish the name of Tolroy to a High & Mighty shine.

But them imaginings was to be brung to ruin, you will soon see my *affliction* was about to announce itself.

Them October nights was darkening quick & my Mama did not like to leave me laid in shadow. Perhaps she was like me with my own childs, I have stared at them in darkness & they do lie so still & breathe so quiet it is too easy to imagine a tragedy has befelled them, their little hearts stopped & their eyes stared blank at the ceiling. Once in the light they look so very peaceable, you can see the trickle of their thoughts in their curling fingers, in the wet & bubbling little purse of their mouths.

That October the air was still mild, not yet bit by winter's coming & my Mama was carrying a lit tallow through the parlor. She wished to place one on the sill above where I lay wrapped in my crib. She looked down at me as she did so & seen my lips curled & reaching out, I thought myself suckling blissful in my careless dreams, not knowing I was soon to be woke & a Shock of Light sluiced down on a dark little Seed of Truth.

As my Mama had walked across the room she had not seen the flame was bent in the draught & not 1 but 3 pearls of hot wax was rolled along its length. They hanged there like pale & guilty men on the scaffold & so as she leaned above me admiring my sleeping face, wondering at the dreams behind the flicker of my eyelids, only then was it she seen them 3 drops fall & land on my left cheek.

For a moment I did not move. My Mama's eyes was wide & shimmering, she did not rush to wipe them 3 drops clear, something held her very still & as my eyes opened she could see them beads of wax was settled on my skin like boils once lanced & now risen into scars. She thought I must be the bravest boy in all the world & reached to pick me up when my face begun to crumple & tears come coursing down my cheeks. She watched then as my mouth did twist into all them shapes from which a roar or howl is bound to fly from.

But nothing come.

They was Silent Roars & Silent Howls.

My Mama could not take her eyes from me. She staggered back & fled the store with the tallow now extinguished in her hand & she left them 3 drops of wax to harden further on my cheek.

5

NO EASY JUDGMENT TO SHAKE

SHE FOUND DR. WHIT PARRICK IN Peeper's tavern, his cheeks gone ruddy with drink & his bandy legs all but turned to ash beneath him. She dragged him from his seat, he did not have no time to grab his coat but only his black bag of rattling instruments.

Dr. Parrick was what my Mama knowed as another Weak Man. She had a great eye for such weakness, tapping for where a person was stretched & hollowed as a deathwatch beetle knocks upon the joists & rotten rafters through the long summer nights. She only had to look at him & he would squirm like a maggot on the end of a hook.

The doctor followed her down the muddy road as she held her skirts in her bunched fists. As they hurried through the darkness my Mama did breathlessly explain to him what she seen, she tried to tell him but her words was each & every one lost on that drunk doctor.

I am afraid you are not making yourself clear, slurred Parrick.

Here my Mama did turn & slap him, she took him by his scrawny throat & nearly shook his head off his shoulders, she told him in no uncertain terms that if he did not sharpen up his wits she would cause him no end of pain & trouble & surely he did not want that. She made him understand what she had seen & Dr. Parrick nodded to confirm his understanding was now a good deal clearer.

Once back in our parlor Whit Parrick was give a gourd of water & a tin mug of coffee to help speed the return of his senses. My Silent Howls was come to an end & my Mama had knelt & very gentle she had hooked a fingernail beneath them 3 beads of wax to lever them off.

When they was pried away she seen beneath them my skin was scarred, 3 little white circles did remain & I will tell you they is here to this day, a queer constellation what never dims but always glows out like Orion's Belt. O I might have wore them with more pride if I had knowed they was redolent of that Giant Huntsman but my knowledge of such Celestial Affairs was very poor back then, I only seen them as another ugly flaw on my person.

Dr. Parrick eyed me very cautious from his chair as my Mama lit the fire, he worked his face to make it sit like it might in sobriety, he could not see how foolish he made himself look. He suffered a bout of singultus & his eyes did widen with each gust what assailed his chest.

When he thought himself recovered, he stood up & demanded my Mama place me on the sawhorse table for his consideration. His shadow was monstrous on the wall as he did perform some brusque examinations. My Mama watched over his shoulder, the smell of liquor what flooded from the doctor's nose & mouth did make her wince but she never took her eyes away as between his forefinger & thumb Dr. Parrick held my tongue. I could taste the yellow tobaccy stains on their tips.

It is true in sobriety Dr. Parrick was very firm with his words, his thoughts left his tongue straight & true as arrows. But like many after a drink the quality of his conference was much depleted, he did begin to mumble & murmur, O gone was his hour of advising & opining & now he let whatever luckless soul was in his company suffer from his palsied thoughts. Without warning Dr. Parrick pinched me hard upon that thin & sensitive skin on the back of my neck & again my eyes widened & the tears come streaming down & again my mouth twisted in all them shapes what surely presage a cry.

But again they was Silent Roars & Silent Howls.

Dr. Parrick nodded.

He turned to my Mama & declared with somber prestige that I was Dumb & there was nothing to be done about it.

You must accept God's will, said he.

Twice now he was wrong about me. The first time he said I would die, the second time that I was dumb. Perhaps he might be forgive for the first but I must confess it still does leave a bitter wash in my mouth when I think of the blithe pronouncement that my head be empty.

With them words Dr. Whit Parrick left to return to Peeper's tavern & once there he did tell everyone that the Tolroy Child would never be more than a simpleton. And like the lie about my daddy every soul in Heron's Creek took it for Truth, they thought me a halfwit & let me tell you that is no easy judgment to shake.

6

BOOKS OF HISTORY

MY MAMA WOULD NOT HEAR of her own child or indeed herself suffering such Ignominy. All them rules what told of a man & his mind being a Finer & Sharper tool was ignored & deemed by her as Nonsense. She did believe herself the superior of every other being she come across, it did not matter what hung between their legs.

That very night she shut her store & did take the lend of a buggy & horse from Elijah Langston's farm & set off to have me mended. She wrapped around her shoulders her favorite shawl and did sit atop the box-seat, her eyes was lit silver by the moon, her handsome nose fit to furnish the side of a coin. O she was one of them rare birds whose nature is somehow made manifest by the very shape & color of their plumage. She wore atop her noble face a bundled hive of flame-red hair, it did rest barely contained upon her head by a legion of pins which she was forever adjusting to suit her mood.

She snapped the reins & moved off in a plume of dust, she would not stop until she had me cured. She traveled each day through the harvest rains & brewing winds to every doctor within 50 miles. She stayed at boarding houses with lousy sheets & when she run out of money she slept in haylofts & at one point was forced to pass the night in the hollow of a lightning-struck poplar with me swaddled tight at her breast.

Every doctor that had time to see me was no different from the last. First their eyes would take in my Mama, she was broad-assed & ample about the hips & bosom, it was far from uncommon for her to liven the mind of a passing gentleman & if she cast a certain spell over their hearts then it was also over other less reputable organs.

These doctors was no different, my Mama must thrust me before them to keep them from their ogling. Looking down at me they was suddenly very interested but their curiosity & puzzlement did seem to countervail their wish to help me. They was happy to poke at me & turn me upside down & nip & pinch at me until my hands & arms was covered with the half-moons of their fingernails. Of course I cried each time & they did observe my Silent Roars & Silent Howls but none ever looked beyond them tears & into my eyes where they would have seen me plead with a right & lively intelligence for them to stop.

Their conclusions was always the same – I was Dumb.

Some did even offer to pay for my corpse when I perished so that they might cut me open & discover some New Wonder what would ink their names in the Books of History. A few suggested some salve or embrocation to rub into my throat, they was old potions from the curled & yellowed pages of dusty books, my Mama did spread on a cloth a bolus of conserve of melted mutton suet, rosin & beeswax & pin it from one of my ears to the other. I do not need to tell you this was Hocus, it did no more than make my nose suffer its wicked stink & make of us a pair of fools.

The truth was not a one of them had a single notion as to what was wrong with me. My Mama took me back home. She opened up the store again. At first it did seem as if nothing had changed. But then slowly there was some shift, Hope begun to leak from her soul.

Any tenderness in her dealings with me before was now begun to dwindle. She appeared to exhibit a grave mistrust of me, often I caught her staring at me with her head cocked & her eyes boring in mine. No she did not fondle me, she did not lift me up & offer sweet whisperings to my ear.

When I recall these yrs of my boyhood now I turn my mind to wonder what care she might have knowed in her own youth. The particulars of my Mama's childhood is mostly a mystery to me but I will say it is hard to imagine her enduring Fear or Lonesomeness, though it is possible she suffered beneath the penumbra of them 2 scourges as hopelessly as anyone else.

I will admit back in them early yrs I did not often think of her in such circumstances but again I feel I have reached a certain age & I have been inclined to revisit the past with my heart more Open & Forgiving.

Every so often I will see her now as clear as if she was resurrected like the Lord & stood before me in that long gray dress she so often wore, her bonnet hanging by its fastenings in her hand. I will see in her face then all them signs of Hurt & Pain I was too young to see as a boy but as soon as I move to touch her, she bows her head & will not look at me.

You do not know my Mama as well as I yet, she was so very competent in every way other than them feelings what lived in the service of her heart. It is only now I see she was so harsh because she was so hurt, it was them she loved the most what caused her temper to flare like the leaves of a maple in the setting sun.

7

MR. BARRE

SO IT IS YOU WILL now understand that when my daddy did not come home that night of my birth, my Mama did not pack all her belongings & retreat to some relative's home as any other might have done. The thought never come to her mind, if indeed there even had been anywhere for her to go. For she had set out already on the road she meant to travel & for such as my Mama there could be no turning back.

In the early spring of the year I was born my Mama & daddy opened a store on the edge of a town named Heron's Creek. I did not know it for some time but it was once a home built & owned by a Frenchman named Josue Barre. Mr. Barre had worked as a trapper along the Grand river & moved to Heron's Creek with his wife & child once he had growed tired of the stink of elk & beaver pelts & having to watch for Indians what wished to put an arrow in his back.

They did live theirselves a happy life in Heron's Creek until his wife & young daughter was took sick by a wicked fever. Their struggle was very quick as is the case when the body is pillaged by such cruel maladies, they died within an hour of each other, their hands was always locked to make that crossing together into the Next World.

Poor Josue Barre was then drove lonesome with Grief, it is a disease in itself & will see a man go mad if he does not escape its dark clutches. And so after he had buried his precious girls behind the house, he did then sell his property for a very low price & move off to some distant shores, it is not knowed where that heartbroke Frenchman went.

But I would myself spend a goodly deal of time tending to them 2 graves out the back of the store. They was marked with no more than saplings lashed together to form 2 awry crosses but with that little girl I felt a Powerful Kinship, not least because I would end up wearing all them winter furs she had once wore what Josue Barre had left behind in a dusty heap in the Top Room.

My Mama did often scold me that they was not mine to mourn. She warned folk is wont to become more possessive over the dead in ways they cannot be in life but I did not care, I often knelt in them long & swaying grasses & sent my prayers up for that lost little soul.

How it was my Mama & daddy had come to be in Heron's Creek & whose money they had used to purchase Barre's home with I cannot say. I am afraid that you too must suffer from my ignorance. Perhaps a day will come when I do seek them but I do not know what I will find & so have long surrendered them to the shadows.

8

THE STORE

THE TOWN OF HERON'S CREEK was small, no more than a hundred souls belonged to it. Its center revolved around a wide muddy street with 2 general stores & a blacksmith & a funeral parlor & a tavern & all them other small domiciles what sprout up & mark the beginnings of a Civilized Society.

The road was baked hard as stone in the summer months & in winter if the rains fell strong it was reduced to what you might call Sludge. Boardwalks was made & even before you turned the corner to see them you could hear the echo of bootheels on the wood & the chatter of them what did sit & smoke their pipes in the shade.

But my Mama & daddy's store was not in Heron's Creek, it did sit half a mile outside it down a pocked road lined with cottonwoods & other weed & scrub what in summer bloomed with the colors of nodding wildflowers but in winter was a tangle of brown & bitter creepers.

It was a 2-story building, clad in lengths of strong timber & the shakes of the roof made from poplar bark, a cunning practice Josue Barre had picked up from them local Cherokees what liked to keep the rain from their hillside huts with such ancient proficiencies.

All them who come across that store never entered it without giving some time to the studyment of it, it did boast certain idiosyncrasies only the mind of a Frenchman could be responsible for. It was not the more common low & thickset cabin of them parts but tall & thin like an old townhouse you might see on them cobbled streets of Europe.

O yes it was awful angular like a boy what had growed out of his clothes overnight. That is not to say Josue Barre was not a gifted crafts-man, the windows was high & very artfully fit, the wood around them scribed with delicate little curlicues what could have been the leaves of plants or wisping clouds. He had made for it too a deep & shadowed porch what my Mama could not ever keep free of leaves & dirt, her broom was worn to nubs by her daily efforts. If there is a sound what brings me back in my mind to them early days it is the Scrape & Itch of sorghum tassels against some dry & dusty boards.

Perhaps if anything did speak of my daddy's contribution & even as some measure of his character which I was always searching for, it was the painted sign what creaked & swung in them mountain winds. It read TOLROY'S STORE in dark green lettering, the outlines carefully shadowed in a bright & splendorous red. I took this to be a demonstra-tion of some poetic leanings on my daddy's part & for a while did fancy myself a blossoming artist.

Though the paint had begun to curl & flake by the time I was old enough to inspect it, I could still tell it was done with a loving hand. To hear that old sign creak & sway when I was drifting off to sleep was a great comfort to me, it was as close as I could get to him in them days.

The rest of the building remained a weather-worn gray, growed dark in some parts over the years & greenly darned with islands of moss & lichen. Them bits what clung to the lower quarters of the walls my Mama made me pick off with my own 2 hands. She had no doubt hoped I would grow tall so that I might put myself to use in keeping its windows clean but that time was never to come & so I was spared the degradement of that task.

The store itself occupied the front of the building & the parlor the rear. They had both been the one room in Josue Barre's time but I believe my daddy built joists & lengths of timber to separate the two.

The parlor was a neat & humorless room with a small circular window looking out onto a patch of scrub & the privy half hid by a mulberry tree. Its high ceilings made it seem far bigger than it was, it did boast a small kitchen & a sawhorse table with 3 ladderback chairs but the walls was kept bare & even when the fire was lit it did not seem to add no warmth but only created an army of rioting shadows which often frighted me when I was a young boy.

A narrow dog-leg staircase led up to a landing no larger than a stable door, one room was my Mama's & the other mine. My room had once belonged to that little girl & often was the time I heard her delicate weight upon them old boards as she went searching for whatever Unfinished Business she had left behind. I was not ever scared at such times, I listened out for her & willed her to keep looking until she found what she did so need. I had a straw tick on the floor but no other furniture to speak of, my Mama said she did not see a bedroom useful for anything other than sleep.

There was then another little staircase what led up to a room at the top, I come to name it the Top Room. The slant of the roof made a person any larger than a child stoop but I never had to, I could walk around easy as you like. It was in here that my Mama had discovered the heap of old furs & pelts left behind by the Barres, beaver hats & coats & blankets & a pair of moccasins what that little girl had wore & fit me perfect.

The store was a brighter affair with them 2 large windows what faced out onto the road. The dust my Mama swept up from the bootheels of her customers often turned & roiled in the light what come pouring in. My daddy's skills was not so advanced as Josue Barre's, my Mama did claim she had repaired the crooked shelves he had built what threatened to tip the rows of goods onto the floor. There was 2 great cabinets what displayed a mighty selection of liniments & embrocation what the sickly of Heron's Creek often sought.

The counter was a veritable fortress behind which my Mama kept Watch & Order. She guarded it with her life, there was a rifle kept on a rack & her ledger what she carried under her arm wherever she went.

You would be right in assuming it was my Mama's ruthless Assiduity what made the store a success. I will tell you more of that later. But it was also its positioning what she knowed was so very important which is why she did not feel herself to be at a loss not being on that main street.

She would have travelers, wayward & fancy types alike, tumbrels & carriages come rolling down the road & it was TOLROY'S STORE they would see & stop by to refresh theirselves or stock up on supplies for their continuing journey.

It come to pass between the lips of every man & woman for miles around, word did travel fast as fire even in them days with no telegrams or rails to carry them.

9

A MENACE

THE STORE WAS MY MAMA'S savior, all her dreams was holed up in there, but still it was no steep dig to learn of the sorry soil from which my own life was expected to grow or indeed see the path what would lead me to its end, so lonesome was it that it might have been carved across the moon.

Over the course of them first yrs I begun to develop most unusually. Long before any young bones is said to enjoy the act of locomotion I was begun to climb out of my crib & go walking about the room. And I will say they was not them little tottering steps what lead to a fall but small & quick & well balanced as a mountain goat.

I was not yet a yr old when my Mama come in & found me on my feet. We did stare at each other a long while & she looked at me as if I was the Devil himself. She come to pick me up but I would not have it, I hid beneath the table until she fetched the broom & prodded me until I did surrender.

She left me again like this but each time she returned to find me on my feet & carrying out my investigations, she would lament that she had give birth to such a Menace. Eventually she fastened me down with 2 of

my daddy's old belts, if I could have howled & screamed I would have
but you know by now I was silent as the grave.

Of course by the time I reached my second yr I still had not made a
sound. My Mama now allowed me to walk where I pleased but she had
realized I was barely growed any taller than when I had first set foot on
the ground, my head still reached no higher than the seat of them parlor chairs. My arms & legs was not abbreviated, they did not suffer from
no abnormalities, I was simply very small.

Not only was she become aware my height was not changed but
it had become quite apparent that no hair had growed upon my head
or anywhere else for that matter. No lashes or brows or even that faint
down you see catching the sun & glowing on arms & shins & the soft
slope of jaws.

Imagine then how I come to look beneath her Hot & Darting eyes.
I was her only child, a boy what weighed no more than a stook of corn,
who could not talk, who God had cursed with such strange & ignoble
torment. I could not help but reckon then that she must surely think me
the Worst Thing that had happened to her.

She did not bother to call on Dr. Whit Parrick ever again or any
other doctor for that matter. She tarred them all with the same brush,
she believed them a Great Scourge on the world.

She was not so fond of any other folk either, I do recall the first
day my Mama took me to town. She was awful anxious, grabbing at my
wrists & pinching me, she did take me to her room & plant me in front
of the large looking-glass propped beside her bureau. It was pocked &
discolored & cracked in places but she hovered behind me & smoothed
out the creases in my shirt & dusted the knees of my britches.

The great offense of my baldness was redressed with a broad-brim
straw hat of the ilk favored by them farmers what worked the rows in the
hot summer months. I do not know where she did acquire it but it was
a tightly wove piece with a misshaped crown & a blood-red band above
the brim. I had not ever wore a hat, it itched terrible on my skull but each

time I took it off my Mama thrust it back down. She warned me that if I took it off outside then she would strop my behind like never before.

It was the end of summer, all the leaves of the cottonwoods still green but fringed in brown, the last of their white fluffy seed drifting off in the breeze. I cannot have been but 3 yrs old, I was so small as I walked beside my Mama that I could not hold her hand without her having to stoop down.

But I did not want to hold it anyway, it was great excitement for me to see beyond them walls & the patch of scrub behind the store where there was nothing but the privy & the mulberry tree & them 2 sorry graves.

When we come to the town I had not ever seen so many people in one place. They was women & men & animals all milling about together, the dust of the road swirling about. I did feel my Mama's grip tighten as we kept on walking toward them but then we noticed many was begun to stop in their tracks to look at me. The nerves of all them eyes on me made my face grow hot, without thinking I took off my hat & begun to turn it in my fingers.

O yes that was when I first did see them recoil as though one touch of me might bring the Devil dancing to their door. I heard the whisperings & felt their ornery stares, they come rushing at me like cruel & sucking waves.

My Mama quickly seen I had removed my hat & roughly pushed it back down on my head so that it turned my ears down until they ached. She spun me around & we went straight home, all them people staring after us as we went. She thought perhaps Dr. Parrick had been right about one thing – that she must come to accept God's will & I would never lead no Ordinary Life.

10

BETWEEN OUR EYES

LOVE IS NO EASY CLOUD to catch, no feeling is as simple or as knotted but to most it is clear enough every mother must surely love her child more than the world itself. But it gives me no small quiver of shame to admit I thought back then my case did prove the exception to this noble rule.

As the yrs progressed my Mama begun to talk to me less & less. We did exchange some rudimentary gestures with our hands – I might point and poke at things I did desire, or when I was struck by hunger or thirst reach up to my mouth and make of my hand a pinching claw – but even these did seem to tax my Mama and stoke her temper. Only if some practical task demanded it would she seek to communicate fully. I will tell you it did little to brighten the shadows that crowded my heart and I could not help but feel I was not hoped or prayed into being like most other childs, but rather snuck like Odysseus in that wooded horse beyond the guarded gates of my Mama's womb.

It is in the Good Book – I believe Proverbs 1:8–9 – where it rightly says a mother's teaching *shall be an ornament of grace unto thy head, and chains about thy neck.* Not a day does pass where I have not took that book's blessed weight in my hands & turned its silken pages. I know there is much to be said for mothers & their duties in them long & wondrous tales, for it is spoke in clear & honest terms that a mother *openeth her mouth with wisdom; and in her tongue is the law of kindness.*

For all who is blessed with a voice it is of course the tongue what does the talking. For them what lacks a tongue by nature or has had it cut from their mouth in some gruesome turn they might make signs of their hands. But for me in them early yrs it was the eyes what served. They is fine tools to the likes of me. Filled with words what must remain unspoke they can still be read as they feed off light & shade & dart & dance. No, there is nothing they cannot tell you.

So I begun to think – & I do believe my Mama would agree if she could call down from her Saddle of Stars – our silences was not silences at all but a space that did occasion some intelligence to pass between us & our feelings was made clearer than if words had ever been spoke. It was not uncommon for her to spend entire days without saying a word & the day cannot be said to be any less full for the lack of them. How I do wish I could do the same with my Mama again now but she is gone. If you do not know it already Love might well be like a potion in a bottle but it can also be the cork what stoppers it, that is all I will say on that matter for now.

11
NO IDLE WHEEL

IN MY MAMA'S DARKEST MOMENTS, she did claim God had cursed me with a Great Genius for souring a person's countenance & loosing upon their innocent minds a storm of Black & Troublous thoughts. I did not have God figured for such a schemer but she thought she knowed His work as well as any & she had seen many of her customers – locals & wanderers alike – take a queer turn after seeing me.

So it was I found myself sent from the store most days to spend my time outside. For them first yrs of my life she would not let me out but now she could not have me in. It is fortunate for me that Mr. Josue Barre had left that great wealth of furs in the Top Room, some of which did once belong to his long-dead daughter. They was still far too big for me but once I growed into them they did come in handy in them winter months & I was kitted out like an old trapper with beaver hat & all the *accoutrements* as Mr. Barre might have said.

It was around this time the many injustices in my life begun to vex me greatly, for I knowed I did possess a Fine Intelligence even if I could not make it plain. When a boy's tongue is stone dead & he does affect no likeness to any other creature on God's earth, his brain must be no idle wheel but turning quick to score the passage of its own travel.

By no choice of my own I was forced to grow acquainted with the great virtue that is Patience. If folk no longer recoiled from me then they now chose to ignore me & I shared more in common with them risen spirits said to roam than I did with them what was made of Flesh & Blood. I would counsel that people do not know the value of Silence & how their lives would benefit from it if they was not so intent on filling it with sound.

But it was much to my wonderment that my other senses growed in their reach. I did begin to listen with ears pricked so sharp I could parse the words of a conversation 20 yds off & eyes so very lively & watchful I might count the nose hairs of a man sat astride his mule in the next county. To this day these eyes & ears is fierce instruments, undimmed in their mastery even if the light is growed thin & wintry or all them noises of the city are in full clamor.

But all that does not count for much if you cannot talk or so I then slowly begun to realize. For are not words the very mudsills on which our lives are built? How can a man live without his voice – that was the question that so often scampered around my brain like a dog with a taste for its own tail.

12

STOOL BENEATH THE ELM

SINCE MY MAMA HAD CHOSE to exile me from the store I had took to spending much of my time beneath a squat little elm that fed its ancient roots across the road. I was not so far away that I could not see the store & all the comings & goings along that particular stretch, busy as it was with wagons & drovers come rattling in from Gainesville.

Occasionally my Mama would stick out her head & scowl at me, she did not think it a respectable spot to linger. She was not content that I was out of the store but now wished to pass judgment on where I spent my time beyond its walls. I knowed I could not win but did not understand why she must make my life such a misery.

I must say that old elm would have served as no hatstand. It was a queer old specimen, its trunk stooped as an old peddler & its limbs pronged heavenward in abject supplication. I come to think it had a personality all of its self & that we was the pair of us united in all our losses & longings. It does strike me now as a sad reflection that I was resorted to the adoption of timber for a companion but in my defense they was desperate times indeed.

I was like a broke-winged bird turned loose & though I could not fly or sing I was free to roam as I pleased, which no young boy with a nose for trouble can say does not appear a most appetizing prospect.

That nose of mine led me on many an exploration of the town & during one such foray I did come upon an old 3-legged milking stool in a barn across from Tom Peeper's tavern. The roof was staved in & the weeds run tall & wild but I had seen its legs poking out & thought it a piece worthy of my attentions.

I carried it back through the town as if I had carved it myself & though I did not once look up, I knowed my back bore the brunt of many a piercing stare, I did not need to give folk no excuse to mock me.

I will not blame you should it amuse you but that stool did fast become my most cherished possession. My feet did not reach the ground but that was no matter, I thought myself at the height of sophistication to be the proud owner of such an appliance. If I had been ousted from the store, then I wished only to sit in relative comfort & dignity or such was my thinking back then.

13

BOAT OF JEWELS

NO HEAD WAS EVER DESIGNED to be corked & stoppered, soon my thoughts growed poisonous & the Black Mire of Melancholy begun to suck at my feet. Sure enough my Mama snapped at me plenty often. She told me that I was growed so slow with my duties that Susie – Elijah Langston's giant pig what was so fat it could hardly move but only wallow in the shade of an oak – could have worked her trotters faster than my dragging feet.

It is a devil to explain but when you is constantly hearing words & listening to the chatter of others all them words begin to enter your head, they did seem in my mind like little boats what went drifting out of people's mouths.

I did so often sit on my stool & watch folk at the store & these boats come along from their mouths regular as the sun does rise. But they was not empty & the sail did not snap & ripple with chancing winds swept down from the skies. No, they was loaded with heaps of glinting treasures, jewels or stones cut to wink with sunlight & steered by measured gusts or eddies what kept a course according to them who spoke. Sometimes I seen how they veered astray & did not come to anchor where they was intended. Others I seen them sail perfect through like smoke rings blowed from a wise old mouth & headed for the moon.

It hit me like a miracle that it was words what brung folk together. I could not take my eyes off their mouths & if they could my ears would have been pricked & pointed at the heavens. But I knowed I could not talk & it begun to feel at first as an itch but that itch was not anywhere on my skin, it was a tricksy little gadfly what hummed & rubbed its scheming legs deep in my head where I could not reach it. How I wished to scoop it out & nip its life between my fingers but I could not, it was a torment what had me clutching my head & shaking it as if I had been for a dive in the creek & was plugged full of water.

The truth was all them words I heard I had been gathering like fire-wood & stacking & stacking & stacking until I had a mighty pyre what was fit to burst out my earholes. But they could not be lit. I needed them I now knowed for the light & warmth they would give off but no matter how I tried I could not strike no spark.

Sunk in mystery of how it was folk made these words in their throats, I begun to blame myself. I thought if I kept my mouth open all the time then they might come flying out like bats at dusk from their sleepy cave.

Sometimes I even found myself coveting the trills from the birds in the branches above me, I knowed them sweet notes not just for pretty song but messages & needling birdtalk. Several times I admit I made myself vomit by trying so hard to force something from deep inside me, I hoped each time I might cough out a word & the rest would come pouring out after.

But nothing ever come.

And so as time went on that great heap of words I had collected begun to rot & give off a foul stink. They was too many to sift & sort through, they was like creeping vines clumb up a window, they begun to block out every other beauty in the world & there was no light to see by. I begun to grow very weak & the skin beneath my eyes darken like smudges of charcoal left in them long-dead fires. It was the Great Weight of all them words in my head & the poisonous whiff they give off what felt they was lulling me toward a deadly sleep.

14

STILL SHE DID NOT BLINK

HOW CAN A MAN LIVE without his voice, O this was the question what begun to haunt my every waking & sleeping minute. Then something what give me Hope did occur, it come to me one morning, with winter about to commence in earnest, the sky gray & quilted & fixing to snow.

I was sit beneath that crooked elm draped in all them old furs & on my stool, when I looked up & seen a girl coming down the road toward me. I should say that perhaps this would not have struck me as so unusual was it not that there was no wagons or tumbrels to be seen or any other soul present, the road was emptied of all but her as if she had won some Special Privilege to travel it alone.

You would not think one as young as she would carry such poise, her step was steady & even as a senator's. All them roughbarked cottonwoods what lined the road did shake & clack their naked branches in the wind, as if she was being applauded for some great war she was returned from wreathed in the Spoils of Victory.

Now that heavy sky chose to unburden itself & the clouds did shed their own soft & heavenly flesh, with flakes sifting down fine as flour &

darting in little squalls along the ground. Snow is a great menace for a fellow of my stature but still I think it a thing of wonder & did so then as it clung to the girl's hair like stars in the dark & tangled firmament.

From somewhere she had acquired a fine length of buffalo robe & wore it wrapped about her shoulders in the style of a cape. I did not have her picked for a hawker & nor did she impress on me any sign of secret wealth, for if she had any currency rolled up & sewed into the folds of her dress, she surely would not be out in such weather but tucked up by a fire with a belly full of hot food.

Where she could be headed in such drear conditions & with no companion – man or beast – I could not know. I thought she might be lost, my only other notion being that she was seeking some succor & hoped TOLROY'S STORE could be relied upon to serve her in this her hour of need. But if this was her thought then she had not met my Mama.

My own furs was laid heavy across me, that old beaver hat of Mr. Barre's daughter would not keep from slipping over my eyes & them fleece-lined boots fit so snug it felt as if I were floating when I walked. You would think a body as small as mine to be vulnerable to such weather but it is another quirk of my constitution that my blood does appear to travel so quick & hot that I have been knowed to break out in a sweat even in the Dead of Winter.

Perhaps this does explain why I so well remember the queer chill what spread across my chest & clumb my neck as the girl did not head for the store but steered my way. She was not tall, her hair was lopped short & hung in knotted curls above her shoulders.

She come to stop direct before me, her face was thin & pale, her nose pinched red, her eyes big & round & flecked with notes of green & gold. O it is true her skin wore an honest layer of filth but this did not do no damage to my conclusion that she was a beautiful creature. Had you held a hand atop my heart you would have thought I kept a wild & violent bird locked inside it.

For some time we did nothing but stare at one another.

Finally she said, You got yourself any food?

In the company of any stranger it was my practice to point at my tongue & shake my head to signal its lifelessness. This was then generally followed by a period of confusion before they slunk off casting troubled glances over their shoulder. But the girl before me wore no expression of surprisement across her poky features, her eyes did narrow & she cocked her pretty head.

Your tongue gone dead? said she.

With a nod I admitted this was indeed the case.

That is a shame, she continued. My Mama was the same though my daddy told me it weren't always so – she had once been a fine singer with a voice like honey, only God stole it away from her. I know He don't need to offer us an explanation for His doings but sometimes would it not be more agreeable if He did?

I had not ever heard of any others sharing my affliction & nor had I ever had God's powers questioned so brazen before me.

She looked at me as if she had forgot my affliction & did expect an answer, her sparse brows knit close, her thin lips turned down.

Said she, I'll bet all them thoughts can get to be a burden on you.

Her eyes was unblinking, the pair of them a-glisten like the shells of some winged insect & beneath their steady glare I nearly did topple from my stool. She was evidently not well schooled in her Social Graces for she was oblivious to my discomfort & instead of taking her leave as I had hoped she did sit down beside me in the gathering snow, her legs crossed & the soles of her ruined boots flapping in the wind.

If she felt the raw & burning sting of the cold beneath her rear she did not say. She looked up through the snow's busy drift & turned out her palms as if they was a fertile plain from which some seed might make its bold beginnings. She held them out & did not say a word but sit with her back pressed firm to the bole of the tree, her eyes closed & still beneath their lids.

Several minutes passed & I thought she was Deep in Dream but I could not have been more wrong, for it was then she begun to talk. She opened her eyes & did not look at me but stared straight on as if what lived in her head was now come walking into the world.

She told me of her life, where she had come from & all what had come to pass to bring her here. It was like a great spigot had been turned & her words ran like a river, which did in turn split into a dozen more rivers that each then bled into one another & coursed into my head in free and flowing chapters.

Of course my daddy died, said she, but that were not an unexpected turn. He had been sick for some time though it weren't the sickness what took him in the end. It ought to be the queerest way a man ever did lose his life but I met myself an awful learned fellow in Missouri some ways back & I told him how my daddy got hisself kilt & he then told me square it weren't so uncommon as I thought.

I was so accustomed to my solitude that I could not help but wish she would be gone but there was something also in her voice what I did not want to stop, my mind could not choose between them.

And so on she continued.

He told me that in them Ancient Times somewheres cross the sea there had been an old Greek fellow who had been done for just the same as my daddy. What happened was an eagle come flying over him & mistook his big bald head for a rock on which to drop a tortoise he caught. He wanted to crack open his shell & peck out his soft belly but of course it weren't no rock but the top of my daddy's head.

Have you ever heard of such a thing? she asked.

She did not turn to look at me but stared ahead, again I thought she did expect an answer from me even though she knowed I could not speak.

But on she went.

Well that was how he got hisself kilt. I seen it with my own eyes that tortoise come down out of the skies. It made a queer whistling noise as it fell, my daddy was just stood there lighting up his pipe when it landed straight on his head & split it open like an apple.

Here she paused again & I believed her story over but she only reached into her pocket & brung out a thin & curved sliver of what I took to be a broke-up pot. She turned it in her fingers, still her eyes stared straight ahead.

See this? asked she.

I looked at it.

This here is a piece of my daddy's skull. I kept it & I reckon it to be the most precious little thing I do own. I picked it up after I looked down at him & seen all that blood come running down his face. I did not have to hold a finger against his lips to know no breath escaped them. I thought, here is the man from whom my life was sprung. I owed him the feet I was stood on, the fingers that gripped the hem of my dress, the hair what fell across my eyes. I did not cry, I had lost my brothers & my mama before him, I knowed Death was no stranger to me but still I could not keep from puzzling how quick & brutal Life can be took from us, how we do carry ourselves as if we have forgot it must come to an end.

He was only a small man but still he was no feather as I dragged him for a day across the earth, his blood was black & alive with blow-flies by the time I found the road again. There I waited by his side until the dust of a wagon bloomed up on the horizon, its driver was most surprised to find us there. He helped me bury my daddy but I knowed I should not have let him, there was Evil in that man's eyes, I had seen it straight away. He offered to take me into town, his grip upon my wrist was too firm, I could not get away.

Suddenly her words was dried up, she did sit in silence, the snow falling thick & feathery as a plucked fowl. Still she did not blink. Them flakes landed on her lashes but she did not brush them away, she let them balance & melt & run like tears down her cheeks.

I did not know what to do but was reminded then of her original request for food & gestured for her to wait while I went to fetch her a poke of cornbread & a cut of salted pork. But before I could move off toward the store she did reach out & grab me by my wrist, now her eyes looked into my own, they was so very green I thought them pulsing with the currents of the highest creekwaters in the land.

It will find you, said she.

I looked at her, I did not know what she was talking about.

It will find you, said she again.

I thought perhaps hunger had drove her mad, I made sure she was to stay where she was & turned to run & get food. I was not gone long, perhaps no more than a minute is my reckoning but when I returned with the victuals wrapped in muslin the girl had upped & vanished, she was nowhere to be seen.

15

IT WILL FIND YOU

I CUT THE SNOW FOR sign of her but there was no single track to follow. It did not seem likely that they should have been covered up so quick by snow but what other explanation was there?

I did consider at first if she was indeed the returned ghost of Mr. Barre's daughter. Perhaps she was growed tired of her nocturnal wanderings & was come to visit & instruct me in plain sight but her story spoke of other lives & other times far away from here, I knowed they did belong to a different person entire.

I could not parse any meaning from her Tall Tales but I could not deny something in them had got me thinking. And what had she meant by them final words?

It will find you.

It will find you.

No matter how I tried I could not rid myself of them, they was like a piece of gristle what becomes lodged between your teeth. I had no answers but still they chased me.

That day she vanished I had spent the remaining hours of light stumbling through the snow looking for her. Everything was silent, I

have never knowed a silence like it, so thick & dreamy it did seem as if
I was the only soul left on earth.

I did keep my eyes open for her but also for whatever it was she said
would come to find me. But nothing could be seen but for them white
flakes come sifting through the dark bare branches of the trees from a
sky stretched so blank & pale it was as if God did wish to point toward
some much necessary Renewal.

But as with so many things in life, there is no use in looking for
them things what will always come looking for you, you will never see
it until you is no longer watching.

It will find you, she had said.

I figured that girl to be right in one vital sense – my thoughts was
indeed a burden on me. It was possible that was her only message to
deliver, simple as it was. If the head is suffering, then so too is the heart.
They are like quarreling brothers who will not leave each other be.

Months did pass & still I could not rid her from my mind. Finally
the warm breeze of summer begun to arrive & I thought I had put that
queer episode behind me. I had even part convinced myself that it had
been so very cold that I had summoned her from my own mind & she
was evidence of no more than what the bitter cold could make a man see.

But in fact it was in these summer months I finally come to understand what them parting words of hers did mean. And O how true she
was. And I will tell you now our paths did cross again & it was then I
discovered she was no more a ghost than a fish is a bird.

16

SHELBY STUBBS

THEY IS CERTAIN MOMENTS IN a soul's existence what do not arrive under any bugle or banner but sidle up as Innocent & Meek-mouthed as a short-horned cow. Only they is not so ordinary as they hope to seem but loaded up to the gills with all manner of Meanings & Implications what will play out in their wake.

It was in this the early summer of my sixth yr my life did take a turn I could not have foreseed.

So it was on this most unremarkable of days I was sit out in the blue shade of evening beneath my tree. The road was busy still with foot & hoof, the dust turned & spun by the wheels of a cart, 2 mules & the music of its traces chimed clean through the still & sundrunk air. Perched atop my trusty stool I watched on lazy as a lord, chewing on a sweet stalk, its green tip dry now of its juices but still rich with all them nourishments of the earth.

Through the dust then I did see an old gentleman approach from a distance, his pace slow & stately. I had not ever seen him before & I considered myself a Great Authority on such local knowledge for I did enliven them long days by keeping track of all the customers & their purchases. I come to know their routines as well as my Mama did know the numbers & sums in her ledger.

This man was to become to me so very dear but then he was a stranger & no more. I am sure he would not begrudge me saying that even then he was a ripe old age, I never did find exactly what number he reached but it would not surprise me to learn he had achieved his eighth decade.

A horseshoe of gunsmoke curls encircled his freckled pate & he had took to supporting his anxious footing with an ivory-topped cane, the tip of which he did drive into the hard earth & use also to smite at the flies what whined in a black halo about his head. I do not believe he once killed a thing but that is often how I come to know of his impending arrival, for he did grunt & curse as he attacked the air with his murderous swipes.

So it was he cut a queer figure indeed as he picked his way toward me, he paused & appeared to scratch at the dirt with his boot like an embittered quail. The loose skin hanged down from his chin like wattles & I did then think him like a great bird what had had its wings clipped & deemed a citizen not of the skies but of the land.

He did not look to me as if he had changed his attire for several decades, which is not to say I thought myself a Beacon of Refinement in them days but even that dreadful heat could not persuade him to remove his old cocked hat & green frockcoat, the sleeves & hem of which was in need of much repair. There was a flower cut & threaded through the buttonhole of his lapel, its petals was a violent shade of purple. I would come to learn he knowed his flowers & herbs very well, they was a great passion of his & though I have since always wore a flower in my own buttonhole, it is of no matter what its name is so long as it is quick to please the eye. He did always lament this streak in me what did pick & choose between my areas of knowledge.

The front of his shirt was stained about the collar & cuffs & the weave of his britches was growed so thin at the knees that they showed through like some shelled creatures overturned, their pale bellies give up to the light.

His head would not stay still, his eyes seemed so very greedy to take in every detail of the day. When finally they did land on me them eyes of his I could already see was blue & watery little pools behind the circled panes of his eyeglasses. He slowed a little & I watched him tend to the sweeping gray fronds of his mustaches, smoothing the errant hairs with thick & square-tipped fingers.

My first thought was this man is as rude as every other soul, he has learned of my reputation & come to have his fill. I did not care for his scrutiny one bit, I begun to squirm on my stool until something did shift in his face & there struck me then a different quality to the slant of his attentions.

I presumed him headed for my Mama's store but he did come walking over toward me.

Fine day, said he, planting his cane before himself & resting his hands one atop the other.

The late sun was not so far from dipping behind the blue slopes of the mountains, its last quartile shined off the gold rims of his eyeglasses.

I eyed him very cautious but with a nod I ceded it was the truth he spoke.

He used the tip of his cane to point at me.

That looks a muscular little stool you have yourself there.

He was not a tall man but broad about the shoulders & chest. His left eye had narrowed as it observed me & his lips was constantly moving, puckering very gentle as if to plant a kiss upon the brow of a sleeping child.

I nodded again that I could not find fault with his estimations.

You are not a natural conversationalist, said he.

He cocked his head then, the muscles in his neck straining at the collar of his shirt.

Or is it that you cannot? added he.

I could not see how he knowed so quick or what had give me away. It was clear now he had not seeked me out, no one ever come up to talk to me before. I might easily have felt fear in my heart then but there was something in them eyes of his what could see beyond all them defenses I had built & so treasured.

As was my habit I pointed at my tongue & shook my head.

The old man nodded.

Well that is no bother, said he. My name is Shelby Stubbs.

He extended his large hand. No soul had ever introduced theirselves to me before, I was not sure what to do.

It is customary to take the hand proffered to you & gently shake it, said Shelby Stubbs.

I did as he said & placed my hand in his. He smiled & begun to shake it, the skin of his palm was warm & rough as maple bark.

You are a natural, said he.

I dropped my hand then & he placed his own back atop his cane.

He said, I suppose your name must remain a mystery for now but I have a keen nose for such things.

Though I could not see his lips for his mustache I could tell he smiled, kindly lines creased at the corner of his watery eyes.

He turned away then & headed for my Mama's store.

17

A BOOK

FROM THAT DAY SHELBY STUBBS come to visit me beneath my tree without fail & each time he now addressed me by my name. I never found out where he had learned it. My Mama never mentioned she had give it him but I suppose it was her what disclosed it.

It never did seem to bother Shelby Stubbs that I could not reply to his questions, he did ask them anyway. There was no hint in his honest eyes he thought what every other soul thought. He knowed I understood him as well as any & he did not shy from seasoning his talk with great long words I did not know the meaning of.

But I was so happy to listen to him, no one had ever talked to me so much in my life. He told me he had himself been a doctor in that distant city of Washington, indeed he even seen that Historic Moment it become our fine Capital. O yes in his youth he had enjoyed the splendor of serving all them with money & wine & Grand Entertainments where women did walk in their whalebone dresses beneath glittering lights & sweet moans of violins was never far from your ear.

Now he was growed too old he had picked himself a spot where he might live out the rest of his days in Peace & Quiet. I never heard nobody describe Heron's Creek as Charming before but Shelby Stubbs thought it so, he could not keep from staring off into the blue hills & breathing in their lovely scent.

I cannot say whether he knowed how much my spirits was lifted on them occasions he visited me. You may now think it queer that with such a span of yrs between us we should fall into such comfortable & convivial routine but I will say it did not ever enter my mind, I was so very happy.

Perhaps 2 months after our first meeting, with the leaves on the turn from green to yellows & the first Chill of Fall sweeping in, Stubbs come over as usual, wearing his old cocked hat & frockcoat buttoned up to his wobbling chins.

I did think him come to speak his usual few words but he did then a most peculiar thing. He stopped short of me several steps & I watched much puzzled as he dipped into the pocket of his frockcoat & from its musty depths produced a book. It was bound in smooth black leather, its spine tooled & inscribed with gold lettering of considerable opulence. I thought of the sign my daddy painted & wondered if he had ever seen lettering of such beauty.

Shelby Stubbs held up the book as if he was taking an oath.

Said he, I have a notion you might like to read, boy.

Disbelieving, I pointed at myself.

Enough of all that pointing, boy, said Stubbs. You will not need any such poxy signs once I am done with you. If you are to mark your permanence and have yourself heard in this world, then there is only one way to do it.

I looked at him a good while, no doubt my face wrestling with itself to make sense of his words. The truth was I never had give a thought to such a thing. The only books I had seen before was the Holy Bible & the fat spine-split ledger what my Mama kept behind her counter & used to keep her accounts in order. If I had ever thought of books I had not imagined they would ever offer up their lessons to me directly but that I would forever be reliant on them more learned to deliver them to me.

I did sit & stare up at that book he held as if it was a star unknowed to God's design. I knowed it was no Bible because it was a slight & fancy volume & I knowed well the simple heft of that other book like an old friend, for even though I could not read my Mama kept it by her bedside always & I was an occasional visitor to that room. Oftentimes I would pick it up & feel its bulk & was comforted in the knowing that the Voice of God did weigh so very heavy.

But of this new volume I could not imagine what it did contain. The old doctor smiled down at me, his eyes alive with some cunning I could not take the measure of. Of course he was no fool & could see the intrigue printed upon my brow. With forefinger & thumb he stroked his mustaches.

It would appear I was correct in my thinking, said he.

18

A GREAT UNTAPPED POTENTIAL

SHELBY STUBBS THEN LEFT ME sit beneath my tree. If his aim had been to see me hopelessly bemused then he should be congratulated, for as he hobbled off for his twist of tobaccy & cuts of salted pork, I did stay in the deepening shade looking out toward the snow-capped mountains, my mouth a pulsing O of confusement.

This reverie was broke only when I heard the door clack shut & the old doctor tottered back down the steps of the store. He did not look my way, his head was bowed like a dozing mallard, his hands burrowed deep in the pockets of his motheaten frockcoat. I thought him headed for home without another word on the matter when he suddenly turned, his unruly brows was hoisted high onto the furrowed plain of his forehead.

He held up the book once more, its gold lettering gleaming in the setting sun.

Well, said he, what is it you are waiting for?

I had not knowed I was waiting for anything but Stubbs's voice was edged with impatience, I thought I had better follow him before he used that cane like a switch & took it to my behind.

As we walked along the dusty track past Langston's farm & through the sap-sweet clouds of dust from the sawyer mill, he explained to me that it had long been his fervent hope to have me as his Student. He claimed to have sensed in me a great Untapped Potential, a word I did not know but was led to understand it was a terrible sin not to have thoroughly excavated.

I did not much care for the sound of this *Potential* & wondered for how long I had been its unwitting host & if it had not already done its damage.

Stubbs suddenly turned & crouched low before me as if I were a squat little crown of wild garlic he wished to cut at with his clasp knife. My straw hat lifted off my head & skittered through the dust, I was not sure if it was the evening breeze or if it was not the great gale of words what then begun to blow from the doctor's mouth.

I tried to turn & fetch my bolted hat but he thrust 2 fingers down the collar of my shirt & yanked me back to face him.

It was a necessity, cried he, his eyes wide and nostrils flaring like the bellows of an organ, that since I did not have words at my disposal I must commit them to the page & have them speak for me there. Then & only then would I be free to live a life worth living.

A life worth living.

I had not heard them words before & you will not believe this was the first time I did ever consider such a possibility. My hat had continued on its merry way & was now floating in a ditch of dirty rainwater but I did not care. I had long been resigned to my fate of Eternal Silence & did not think anything save a miracle of God would allow me to add my voice to the world. But now here I was being told I might be taught to apply these words to a page myself & have them talk for me there.

And so as Stubbs skewered my hat with his cane & offered it to me, I took it from him very slow as if it were not my hat at all but some well-sprung snare. I hoped for him to see in my face a Serious & Discerning scrutiny, that his words had better be honest or I would make him suffer for it.

But for all he could be kind to me, he did not have time for foolish-ness & of my suspicions he took no notice. I took my hat by its dripping brim & as we continued to walk he placed a splay-fingered hand atop my skull & allowed his fingers to drum & roll along it as if it were the ivory knob of his cane.

At first I did flinch, for I was not used to that shamed & snowy expanse of skin being touched. O but how I had longed for my Mama to caress me so, to have her hand linger & her warmth travel down into my lonely frame. It is my opinion there comes a time in a person's life where they know theirselves to be in the right place, that they could not be anywhere but where their feet was set. That is how I felt there & then. That is how I felt with Stubbs's fingers idly drumming on my head, no I did not ever want to wear my hat again.

19

NO BETTER PLACE

I HAD NOT KNOWED WE was headed for his home but it was there we arrived, a short walk from the road down a chalky little track. He told me he had been staying at Mrs. Cripps's boarding house while he was having himself a cabin built in the woods, that did explain the *pock pock pock* of wood being cut & nailed what had rung out for the past few weeks.

It was a neat little cabin, the timbers hewn & planed & caulked between the slats with pails of blue clay fetched from Heron's Creek. It did sit on a patch of cracked earth beneath the dappled shadow of a willow, whose low-hanging branches idly stroked the shakes of the roof as a master's foot will stroke the belly of his hound as it sleeps beneath the parlor table.

I would not enter the house that first night for the weather was still warm enough to sit out on the porch & with the addition of a lamp hung from the door there was light enough to see by. The porch was still covered in little heaps of sawdust from the fresh-cut timbers & would have benefited from the sorghum tassels of my Mama's broom but it was a quiet & peaceful spot there is no doubt.

No better place, said Stubbs, as he bid me sit down on one of 2 wicker chairs set out there as if they was awaiting us.

He opened that book he had brung in his pocket & without pausing to tell me its title or the subject, he begun to read & from that day I abandoned my post beneath the tree each evening & when the sun was sunk low & the sky growed pink, this is where I would come.

O them first months was slow work I will not deny it. I took my seat beside Stubbs & pulled it close enough that I could smell the mustiness of his coat & dampness of his sweat-soaked hair. He lit a lantern & hung it from its nail. Then he read & I would follow his finger as it drifted beneath the words.

Slowly slowly they did begin to offer up their meanings. Night after night after night we would read until the air growed chill & the moon begun to silver the smooth-grained handrail of the porch & creep along them boards toward our feet. By the time it had reached the straps of my dangling boots my eyes was growed heavy & Stubbs would send me home, my sleepy steps kicking up clouds of dust what stained the cuffs of my britches and my boot-ends white.

20

THE HABIT OF WASTING TIME

AS THE MONTHS WENT BY & the weather was begun to turn, we could no longer sit on the porch but was forced to retreat inside. I had worried this change would somehow disrupt my learning, I did live at that time in constant terror them words would somehow be took from me. I would sometimes dread falling asleep for fear I would be woke & the words would have been stole from me in the night, as if a soft pale hand was able to reach inside my head & filch them like apples from an arbor.

Inside Stubbs's cabin there was only 2 rooms, one of which was his bedroom & the other a room like no other I had seen before. The first half of it was as you would expect. It had a small kitchen with a sink & a stove & a table draped in a frayed white cloth & 2 ladderback chairs propped against the wall. A window looked out onto the porch & the old willow what swayed in the fenceless yard.

But the rear half of the room was different entire.

O it was a small marvel to my eyes, its walls lined with books & curios, vials of mysterious liquids illuminated by green-shaded lamps, a drop-leaf desk which did pin to the floor a red turkey rug, the patterns of which was so complex it made me dizzy to look at it.

The first time I set my eyes upon this spectacle I could not pull myself away. At first Stubbs watched me with great amusement, he thought me like a fish in a bowl the way I gawped. But as was always the case he soon growed impatient & barked at me to take my seat and continue on with our work.

On them cold winter nights we would take our seats by the fire, the light of the flames dancing swift-footed across the page. I would feel its heat warm my fingers & dry out my cold & sodden toes if it had been raining or if snow was falling from the black night sky. I cannot sit by a fire to this day without feeling the bulk of Shelby Stubbs beside me, smell the musk of his clothes, hear the bristling of his mustaches as he combed his fingers through the long & wiry hairs.

My Mama you may not be surprised to hear did not so much as question me as to my whereabouts. When I would return late & find her sit staring into the flames of the fire, she would not look at me but only thrust her strong chin in the direction of the kitchen table where she might have left me a plate of pork & biscuits.

I was growed well used to her silence. I feared she did not think me worth the effort & so the secret knowledge of them words inside me was loyal things what come to serve me as armor against her Indifference.

Still for all I was used to her ways, I was not prepared to hear her conversation with Dr. Stubbs one day late in that same year. The sky was growed dark & the wind tore through them naked trees with a wicked howl what presages the beginnings of a Fearsome Storm.

Stubbs was in the store making his regular purchase of tobaccy at her counter. Both he & my Mama believed me to be beneath my tree but the turn in the weather had drove me inside.

Since my Mama had banished me from the store I was forced to enter through the back door. As soon as I entered I seen the door what led to the store was ever so slightly ajar. It opened up directly behind my Mama's counter & as I neared I heard the low rumblings of Stubbs's voice. I pressed myself firm against the skirting & through that gap I could see & listen in on their conversation without myself being seen.

Your boy out there is no different to any other, said Shelby Stubbs.

He was standing with one elbow rested on the lip of the counter & the other leaning heavy upon his cane, his eyes old & milky-looking behind the steam what fogged the lenses of his eyeglasses. A volley of rain hit the window like a handful of pebbles & then the wind yowled once more.

My Mama looked very calm out through the rain-tracked window & then back at Stubbs. I had not ever seen them together before but I knowed when my Mama did not like a person & I seen it in her face now, she turned them fierce green eyes on him, they was hard as stones.

That is nonsense, said she.

Her voice was flat & even, her hands was rested on her counter also, the fingers delicately interleaved.

Said she, He cannot talk. There is no denying his *difference*, Mr. Stubbs, & only a fool would say otherwise.

Stubbs brushed some invisible crumbs from the lapels of his frock-coat & studied her just as intently as she had done him. He was a man who would not be so easily cowed. His eyeglasses was slipped down his nose & he looked at her from beneath his wiry brows.

That does not mean he is *different* in here, said he.

At which point I seen him give his temple a poke with his blunt-edged finger.

He *cannot talk*, said my Mama again.

Two small pools of blood was rushed to her cheeks. A strand of hair had escaped one of her pins at the back of her head & she brung the flat of her palm down against her neck as if it had been tickled by a blowfly.

She lowered her hand to the counter again & smiled at Stubbs, not unkindly but not warmly either. She was a mistress of such subtleties, never allowing a person to feel theirselves at ease.

I happen to believe that such a thing makes a very great difference, said she.

Shelby Stubbs nodded. His mood was suddenly turned somber. His feathers was at times easily ruffled but now there descended upon him a sadness I had not seen in him before. His eyes was large & watery behind his eyeglasses & he looked so very old I thought him surely not long for this world.

He looked at my Mama & shook his head of curls before slowly collecting his purchases in silence. With his cane, he shuffled toward the door & I thought him to be defeated when he turned.

I am teaching your boy to read, said he.

My Mama did not express no note of surprise. She would not be outdone & remained as composed as he, her eyes unblinking, her hands as still as stones atop the counter.

Well, said she, if you are in the habit of wasting your time, Mr. Stubbs, then I cannot stop you.

At that, Stubbs turned his back & left. They was the last words them 2 adversaries exchanged, for the old doctor did not return to my Mama's store. From then on & for the rest of his days it was John Wexley's DRY GOODS STORE in town what enjoyed the old doctor's business. Of course, my Mama made no comment on it. She would not allow a fool such as he to alter her ways of thinking.

But if she remained unchanged, then I did not. I believe that to have been the first moment I allowed a Seed of Revolt to be sowed into my blood. If I had not already been committed to Stubbs's leadership, then I now offered up a silent vow that I would be his most faithful student.

21

GUSSIE

OVER THAT WINTER MY MAMA had made the surprising purchase of a horse, a fine buckskin mare by the name of Gussie. Why she had bought her was a mystery to me. She did not ever travel & was often very bitter about the steaming cairns of dung she had to shovel from the road outside the store. Even so I had woke one morning to find Gussie nibbling at the grasses around the 2 graves, her tail swishing against the mulberry tree.

If my Mama was impatient with people you can well imagine how she was with animals, she was of the opinion God had not properly considered their inclusion on earth. They was greedy & foolish & no sooner had she introduced me to Gussie than she was cursing her for all the chores her existence did demand – the feeding & the brushing, the sweeping & the raking, the shodding of hoofs & portioning of oats what must be done to keep her Loyal & Happy.

I believe it had been her plan to have Gussie stabled & cared for on Langston's farm but Elijah Langston was a proud man & I do not believe he cared for my Mama's presumptions when she approached him. I so well recall him gently rolling up his shirtsleeves & folding his arms, his face purple & creased like a sun-shrunk plum.

Them first nights then poor Gussie was left out in the cold, teth-
ered to a picket drove into the hard earth outside the back of the store.
I could not sleep for fear she would perish. From my window I could see
how her moonstruck form shined the ghostly blue of a blinded eye, the
fine hairs of her sleek coat a-glisten with frost.

I was forced to sneak downstairs & standing on my stool I did tie
the sleeves of my coat around her neck. She shivered & tossed her noble
head in gratitude. There is no bond forged so close with a beast as with
a boy & his first horse, it is a kinship only death can sever.

In the morning I caught my Mama looking at me, one thin brow
raised & arched like the haunch of a bridge. She had seen me in the
night, I thought I was to be punished but her mind was to my surprise
elsewhere.

Said she, Might we not keep that beast in the place you found that
awful stool?

To this day I do not know how she knowed where I had acquired
the stool but it was to the old barn opposite the tavern that I led Gussie
who was only too happy to be freed from that picket.

Tom Peeper agreed to fix the shakes of the roof for a small fee &
also construct a corral from the discarded timbers of Eason Claire's coo-
per shop in town.

Here Gussie made herself at home. The drunkards' midnight cries
& dawn revelries did not startle her, she was dreamy as an artist, her
long-lashed eyes took in the world in slow blinks, her pink nostrils sniffing curiously at the ingredients riding on the air.

It is just as well she was a kind & fair-tempered creature, for even
with my stool it was a great struggle to mount her. I used the girth strap
& the stirrup as a sailor will use the rigging of a ship until my hand found
the smooth curve of the cantle or the pommel & I could haul myself up.
Gussie did not mind one bit, I was light as a gnat once I was up there, sit
so low & close I could not be shook off. I do believe even once or twice I
caught my Mama cast my horsemanship an Admiring Glance.

22

A GIFT

IT WAS LATE APRIL BY the time the snows had melted. The sun shined weak through the fresh-budded trees & the birds trilled down from the branches, their feathers preened & glossy. I realize it is common in the telling of tales in which some Great Change is in the offing that the speaker will spend some time detailing how very Ordinary the beginnings of that day was appeared to be. I do not wish to suffer from that same dreary impulse but I cannot help myself, the scene must be set.

I had read through them late summer months & on through fall & winter. O I had read so much I had begun to dream often of writing, of the delicious shapes of them letters across the page & their little black bodies marching with the industry of ants through my mind.

I rode Gussie into Stubbs's yard that day & though I say the sun was shining there was still a chill in the air, it was not yet warm enough to sit comfortably on the porch. I set Gussie to graze on the small patch of grass what had greened the earth beneath the porch & I rapped my knuckles upon Stubbs's door.

When he answered he was usually very gracious, often inquiring about my day & musing on his own affairs. But now he appeared distracted as he took me by the arm & pulled me rudely inside. I had not took off my boots before he gestured for me to sit down. I looked at him very quizzical but he waved away my concern.

Come, said he, we do not have all day.

I was about to oblige him when I seen there rested a parcel on the seat of my chair. Brown paper did conceal its contents with 2 neat bows tied with green twine. I looked up at the old doctor & he smiled a Secretive Smile, his pipe tucked in the corner of his mouth.

Said he, I think it is time.

I did not gather his meaning but I was as happy as any young fellow to receive a gift. I picked it up & assessed its properties, it was hard & flat & by no means light. I looked up at him again & he cursed me with that barbed tongue of his for my *damned irresolution.*

It will not open itself, cried he.

No sooner had I begun to tear at the paper than I was greeted by a dark smooth surface. Deep purples & blues of such I had only ever seen up in the clouds when a storm was shaping to pour its contents down upon our sorry heads. I laid my palm flat against it & felt its chill suck the warmth from my fingers.

It did not take a mineralogist to recognize it for a length of slate what had been cut & buffed so that it was no flimsy flaky piece but thick & strong & hard as iron.

I could not deny its beauty but I also could not help thinking: what use am I to get from a rock?

Give it to me, said the old doctor, who had seen the dark spire of puzzlement parse my bald brow. He thrust his fingers greedily out toward me.

Still sit in his chair, Stubbs begun to root about in the pockets of his frockcoat. When he could not find his quarry he hobbled irritably into his bedroom. A moment later he did return holding aloft what I took to be his prize, it was no more than a knurl of chalk. I thought Stubbs to be excessively pleased with himself. As you know I had never entertained the notions spread so by others that the doctor was enfeebled but I will admit it did cross my mind for the first time now that he was perhaps suffering some Queer Episode.

Of course, you will have long ago understood his intendment but I remained shamefully ignorant. At no time had my Mama thought to send me to school, I would gladly have gone & even once walked there only to be turned away. The schoolmistress & them other childs in the town had been warned against me, they did not want my kind there.

Stubbs took his seat once more & without delay set to scribbling away with the chalk on the slate. I stood there looking at him dumbly as a fish. I thought he had give me a gift only to take it back & ruin it before my very eyes. Perhaps there was a lesson in this cruel act that I was supposed to learn from, I did not know.

The heat of the fire was oppressive on my face, I felt a worm of sweat burrow down my back. Stubbs then lifted the slate & as soon as I seen it I did realize my foolishness. He had writ on it and this is what it said:

My Name is YIP TOLROY

I looked up at Stubbs & I am not ashamed to say tears did spring from my eyes. It is a queer thing to say but I do not recall ever having wept before that moment but now I found them tears streaming down my face until I could taste their salt on my tongue.

Gently, Stubbs set the chalk to my fingers & laid the slate on my lap. It was no small piece. It was heavy & awkward to hold, I knowed even then I would have to craft some apparatus if I was to carry it on my person.

I did not know then what it was I felt, it would be easy to say it was joy but I do not think it quite so simple. What I do know is I held that slate & held that finger of chalk as if they was living things.

I rode Gussie to her stable that night beneath the bright map of stars. Smoke billowed from the chimney of Peeper's tavern & I could see the firelight spilling out & hear the thumping feet & singing of the men but I did take no notice of it. I had stowed the slate beneath my coat & shirt where I could feel its cold pinch, I pressed my hand to it the way I have seen a woman feel for her unborn child.

When I arrived home & my Mama turned to me from the fire, I did not look at her. I did not sit & eat the cold plate of bacon & biscuits left for me on the parlor table but headed straight upstairs where I took the slate very gentle from beneath my shirt & the chalk from the pocket of my britches.

It was there I did sit on the hardwood floor in my room until them first salmon-streaked clouds of dawn drifted by the window, forming with that piece of chalk them same letters over & over again. The soft whispering & occasional whimper as it glided & turned across the slate. The crumbled white skirts of dust what formed around the tip. The way it clung to the sleeves of my shirt & the knees of my britches. The smeared clouds after I had brushed the letters away like the fog my daddy lost himself in.

O but I was not lost. I was only just found.

My Name Is Yip Tolroy.

My Name Is Yip Tolroy.

My Name Is Yip Tolroy.

It is no accident I opened this account with them very words. They was the first I ever learned to write, I could not have knowed I would come to be sit as I am with so many more to go. But this story will not tell itself, I must not slow now even though the night does steal upon me.

23

SLATE-SLING

WITH A LARGE SQUARE OF wagon canvas & a length of old leather I fashioned what I come to affectionately call my Slate-Sling. As I have said that piece of slate was a bastard to hold, its edges was very sharp & after a while my arms growed tired to the bone. I knowed there must be some easier way to convey it & to have myself look very proper as if I was a fellow of Considerable Learning.

My Mama had long ago taught me to sew, since my eyes was so good she would often have me mending in the flickering light of the fire. But now I was to use that Quiet Pursuit for my own purposes, I did fold that square of canvas in half & stitch up its sides with strong black thread.

Next I done poked a hole with my clasp knife in each top corner of the canvas & stitched an eye to thread through the leather, it was a very soft & pliable piece what I had snipped from an old bridle in Elijah Langston's tack room. If he ever did miss it he did not say, it went on to live a long & happy life in my service.

I have since had several designed & made to suit different occasions but still I have kept that first one I ever made, it would break my heart if I could not touch it every now & then & see them old days rise & fade like smoke in my mind.

Once the leather was run through & measured even all there was to do was tie a knot. The slate fit very snug inside the canvas & I could wear the leather like a strap across my shoulder & chest with the slate held at my back. When I wanted to write I would simply turn it to my front & take it out, it was one swift movement I savored every time.

I completed the design in the secrecy of my room & only once my Mama had gone to bed. If she had found me I do not know what I would have said, I still had not showed her I did want to improve & try and master all them words before she found out. There was no use in only being able to write a few, you might think me cruel for it but I wanted to shock her was the truth & to see in her face that she had been so wrong to doubt me.

24

FARTHER THAN ANY EYE COULD SEE

IT HAD BEEN A LONG hot day, the sun never dipping behind a cloud for there was not one to be seen in the sky. Most times some could be found scudding around the crest of Blood Mountain but that blue did stretch on farther than any eye could see.

Me & Stubbs was so close now I did on occasion realize I had begun to let slip them Nagging Dreams of my daddy from my mind. His mystery was begun to fade & Stubbs come to assume the dimensions of the hole he had left. Not only did we continue our lessons but now I could write a little we was able to sit out on his porch with the warmer spring winds come wafting in & that new-leaf scent what is hot on its heels.

I got a chance to ask him some simple questions about his life & he was very generous with his answers. He told me of a son he had, they did no longer speak, I seen his eyes well up with tears. But he always had some wise words to say, he had that habit I learned to love & admire in a man where he was in no hurry to talk, it seemed he plucked his words from out of the air as if they was ripening on some ghostly vines what hanged down from the sky & could not be seen.

Here I was now sit beneath my tree & dozing with the hum of insects & songs of birds & chatter of customers & travelers filling my dreams. I had come to sit on my slate for fear it was ever took away from me, such a thought was unbearable to me now. I had dozed with it on my lap before & the sun had baked it too hot to touch, when I had reached down to pick it up my fingers was scalded like it was a skillet.

I took it out from underneath me now & did decide to write something for dear Stubbs. It was a simple little passage, I wrote only what I seen about the cloudless sky & the birds in the trees & how I was looking forward to visiting him. I did not want to make no mistakes, I imagined his face then if I managed to write them words without fault, his eyes would surely crinkle with delight.

When I got to Stubbs's house I seen that his door was shut. He did usually like to keep it wide open, even if it did mean inviting in all of them droning critters what will feast on your skin every chance they get. There is no use in shutting the world out, he would say, that is where Life does its Living. Even if his pate was a bit raw & giving him grief, still he would not shut it.

I thought perhaps he was working on some particular delicate task inside & must not be disturbed, on occasion he would become so spellbound by his books that he become closed off to all that was outside his head.

I knocked at the door but he did not answer.

I knocked again & after there come no response I did open the door myself.

O that is when I knowed something was not right. There is a breed of silence what tells of tragedy, it is a sound so empty of sound I could only hear my fearful heart. Normally he would have cried out in joy to see me.

Young Yip, I thought you must have got lost on the way, he might have said.

Or even if he had not cried out, I would have heard his heels upon the floor but now I did hear nothing.

I walked very slow into the parlor.

Dust motes sifted down in the fading light from the window. I seen them willow branches stir outside & could hear the caroling of the birds. But when I turned to look at Stubbs's desk & hoped to find him writing there, I seen his chair was empty. No candles was lit. Them shelves of books looked dark & suddenly as if they had never been opened, as if they was not filled with words but every page was blank & empty.

Each board seemed to creak or groan as I trod on them.

There was only Stubbs's bedroom left to look in, its door was slightly ajar, I seen through the crack a pale sliver of light. I did stand there looking at that crack until I found my feet begun to move for me & then I was knocking on the door & praying to God above that old Stubbs would bustle embarrassedly to the door, woke from a doze with his hair on end & muffling apologies that his age would at times get the better of him.

But that silence did continue & as I stood there in the hall that light in the crack of the door begun to dim as I could not bring myself to open it. I waited for so long that it was near dark before finally with the tip of my finger I prodded it open.

As soon as I had I wished I had not ever done it for I seen my old friend lay twisted in the sheets of his bed, his mouth hung open, his eyes wide & staring at the ceiling. I had once found a dead fox behind my Mama's store, its body growed stiff & dark eyes lifeless but nothing could ever have prepared me to see this life so thoroughly extinguished, all the warmth leached from he I loved the most.

I did not want to get no closer but again I found my legs was in control, I crept over to his bedside. I was still so small that I was not so much looking down on him as at him. I seen his skin was growed white & papery, there was a darkness around his eyes I had not ever seen before. Even the hairs of his mustaches seemed to have growed stiffer, never again would I hear them bristle.

And then there come that Sourness off him what I had noticed but tried to ignore.

But it was them blue & watery eyes what hurt me most, they had lost all their light, I could not bear to look at them. My own legs was suddenly growed so heavy I thought they could not move & as I turned to leave I did trip on a black case, its handle poking out from under the bed. I sent it skidding out across the floor but I did not care, I could not be in that room no longer. Like a spooked horse I went crashing out through both doors & stumbling down the steps of the porch.

It was the last time I ever set foot in that house, I wish to this day I had stopped & took one last look around, between them walls my life was changed, I owed them some measure of thanks, even if they was deaf to any such offerings.

I do not remember how I got back to the store but it did mark the beginning of my affair with Death & the knowledge that like them blue skies above Shelby Stubbs had gone farther than any eye could see.

25

NOT FROM THE HEART

I HAD NEVER KNOWED WHAT it was to have someone you loved so dear took from you with no chance for Goodbyes or Reparations. I never got to tell Shelby Stubbs what it was he had meant to me, I know it is not such a Manly Practice to express them feelings but Love is of no use if it is not heard or felt by them you know.

Perhaps I could have guessed at the sadness what would flood my heart but I was not prepared for the rage what come along with it. Them 2 did bitter battle inside me until I was so exhausted I could not leave my bed. I lay awake for hours & hours & could not shake from my mind them sour scenes from his bedroom, the sight of him laid so deathly still.

My Mama thought me ill, she brung bowls of weak & watery soup up to replenish me in my room but I did leave them all untouched until a skin formed across the top & I was haunted afresh by the skin of Stubbs & how it had turned so very thin & gray.

At first my Mama did not complain, it was only after the second day she begun to feed me herself. She visited me between her customers & though she could not ever be described as Tender she was not so rough as she cupped her palm at the back of my skull & brung a steaming spoon up to my cracked lips. Most of it did dribble down my chin & chest but some I did swallow & could feel its warmth spread through me.

Grief can make a body so very tired, it feels as if you have worked a full day ploughing acres of stubborn sod. Your bones ache & you is unmoored from the rhythm of Time & at the mercy of sudden drifts of sleep what have you drowning in memories of the dead.

One time I woke gasping from one such doze, it was late for the light come slanting in a wash of lonely blue. I thought myself alone but then I seen my Mama sit at the end of my tick. I did not know if she was some living sliver of my dream come to life but she was holding something in her hands, I realized it was my slate. I still had not ever showed her it, she did not know I could read or write.

I seen then it still had on its brooding surface them last words I had writ for Stubbs. I watched her read them, she then looked up at me.

Did you write this? asked she.

Her voice was soft, the contours of her face made soft also by that light. I could not look at them words I had writ without tears filling my eyes & streaming down my face. I seen again poor Stubbs lay twisted in his sheets, what foul & fearful visions had come before him to make him look so very pained?

Well? said my Mama. Did you?

Her voice was no longer soft, she did suddenly appear angry.

I nodded.

She looked back down at the slate & then without another word she left immediately. I longed to run after her. I wanted to tell her about my friend Stubbs & how I had found him but when I tried to swing my legs from out of my sheets I was so weak I could not do it, even that small effort brung such a weariness into my heart that all I could do was lay back down & fall into one of them sleeps tinctured by fever, again that kind where you is always just beneath the surface sifting through what is Real & what is Dream, there is never no knowing between the two.

When I woke the light was gone, my room plunged into the near black of night. Sleep is a Wicked Trickster when it wants to be, I thought my world was unchanged & Stubbs was still alive. But all them truths of my new existence soon come crashing down, my grief was born again afresh & the nimble beast what is Grief set to burrowing heartward once more.

Perhaps I slept again I cannot say but there come a time when I did wake & find myself staring at some shape leaned against the wall. Not a moment come to pass before I knowed it for that same case what I had tripped over in Stubbs's bedroom.

Hear me now when I say that case now haunts my darkest dreams, I do not see it in my mind how it was then, its fragrant leather yawning open to reveal a trove of wonders but all a-smolder with the flames what would bring Death & Destruction in them distant days to come.

Now it was propped near the door, I could not think how it had come to be there, I did then think perhaps I had been visited in sleep by my old friend's ghost & he had delivered it to me out of some duty what could not be ignored even in death.

I turned back my sheets & swung my feet to the floor. Them shadowy boards was cool on my hot soles, my legs shook as I tried to rise from my tick but they was stronger than they had been, I stepped slowly over toward the case.

Even in that dim light I could see the 2 gold clasps what kept it closed like the carapace of some winged critter stilled for All of Time. They was cold as ice when I laid my fingers on them & they come apart with a soft clicking what sounded like my Mama's tongue against the roof of her mouth when she was deep in thought over her ledger.

Then just as my Mama had come into my mind the door did open beside me & there she was standing on the landing & holding out a lantern so that its glow come shining over me & onto the case.

I had not heard her footsteps, her hair was unpinned & hanging in soft curls around her face, it did always make her face look softer, her eyes kinder.

You could not call it a smile but some movement danced across her lips. She had not said nothing about my learning to write, I knowed then she would not ever. But she must have gone to Stubbs's house, she must now know he was dead, her voice was softer than I had ever heard it when she spoke.

I believe he wanted you to have them, said she.

She pointed down then & I seen that the case had folded out & revealed small little boxes stacked atop one another so very tight they was like the bricks of a townhouse.

I picked one up, it did let out a small rattle as I held it. I pulled it open & there I seen 9 sticks of smooth white chalks. That whole case was filled with them, it was my friend speaking to me from the Other Side, he wished me to keep on writing.

26

LIGHT EVERLASTING

LIKE ANY HEART WHAT HAS suffered the dark & aching hollow left by Death, there does come a day when coins of sunlight come dappling the walls & the birds chime gentle notes of peace & condolement behind your weary eyes. O it is a light not innocent of Sorrow or Despair for that brightness will go forever unseen by the earthly eyes of them who did depart but there is comfort in the knowing they have gone to their final rest in Light Everlasting.

Shelby Stubbs was laid to rest in the graveyard of the chapel. There was not many single graves as most was family plots but dear Stubbs had no family here other than me, he was lowered down into the dewy earth beside the Waltons.

The Final Words was said over him by the Reverend Alexander Strill, his pale face awash in early morning light. His words come as usual in fits & starts, how he did seem to fear every word what come out of his mouth, he was the most skittish man I ever knowed. My Mama did lead me to that fresh-dug earth but she did not stay, I believe she did not think it her place. She watched them somber proceedings from the humming shade of an oak at the corner of them grounds, her black dress swaying gentle in the wild grasses what needed to be scythed.

As she walked me back toward the store, we passed the track what led to Stubbs's home. I took my Slate-Sling out & asked what would happen to it. I had to stop to write, I had not yet acquired that skill what allowed me to walk & continue to put words accurately to my slate.

My Mama stopped also. She had took very quickly to my slate in them few days since she had discovered it. If I ever did look up between my writing I often found her not looking at the words I writ but at me, there was always a look of mild surprisement on her face, I could not ever put my finger on what it was she thought.

My Mama then told me his house had been cleared. A man had stopped by the store, she did not know how he had come to be informed of Stubbs's death but he had claimed to be his son.

At first this news did trouble me & I walked past that track feeling like I had lost something what was owed me. Perhaps I thought I would have his books or I might even get to keep on with my studies in that empty house. But perhaps deep down that son felt as bad as me, I could not say, I only hoped he would treat his great father's possessions with the respect they did deserve.

As Shelby Stubbs had been lowered into the earth I did vow to carry on his work. He had made me a Stronger & Braver boy, if he could not guide me all the way to manhood then I knowed he had give me enough of his advice to let me get myself there.

He had left me them pieces of chalk for good reason, they would last me many yrs, they was not to sit gathering dust in my room but to be used. He had always believed every thought in my head was worthy of putting into words, there was no end to what I could say with them. There was hundreds of them & each one would be added up at the end of my own time here on earth & they would tell the Story of my Soul.

27

A GRAVE OFFENSE

THERE WAS NOT MANY WHO COULD READ & it was these unworldly souls what come to dislike me even more than they already did. All them bright & pleasant visions I had had about sharing my thoughts & entering of the Realm of Discourse was at first made to seem a small & foolish dream indeed.

Many who had lived in Heron's Creek & knowed me my life entire did see my knowledge of the writ word as an affront to their own intelligence, they had for so long thought theirselves a station above me they did not like it when they was made to contend with their own shortcomings. For a lunkhead such as me to come out & know the meanings & secrets behind them wriggling lines was a grave offense indeed.

O yes it struck them as some dark interference of Order, an aberration they could not quite place. I suppose it was a great shock to them, not many times in your life is a belief reversed entire but even if that be the case it does not excuse the cruelty what some seemed to think it fit to deal me. I was either ignored or rebuked, I did not mind which it was after a while, they was both the same in a way.

And so them yrs went on & how strange Time does become, shrunk & made so lean only a paltry score of days will surrender theirselves to your keeping. There is no knowing which of them days will remain loyal & which will run wild like a dog what has forgot its own name.

Yet despite the scorn I often seen in faces & heard in voices I did my best to fit in, for since Stubbs had died I did yearn for friendship. There was a group around my own age, William & Elijah Wullum & Nancy Browntack & Dickie Wallace & Senora Lee. I would approach them girls & boys I often seen capering about by the creek or sitting upon some fence, their legs scissored & dangling.

But the girls did shy away & the boys puffed out their chests like brave little birds, they was the protectors of them girls. Or sometimes they did make of my approach a Game, they would run & hide & cry out for help any time I got close. But it was no game I knowed that well enough, eventually they would chase me away with stones & cried that I was no more than a varmint, they told me if I come back they would break my slate in half.

As I got older I watched them boys as their bodies begun to change, their britches become too short so that there was a flash of white flesh beneath their cuffs whenever I seen them walking through town.

Next time I seen them they was newly fitted with a pair of their daddy's old britches or a new pair of boots, their toes no longer pinching but room enough to lengthen. They growed a dusting of hair on their upper lips what soon begun to thicken until they was forced to wet a blade each morning & their jaws shined blue beneath their skin.

As for them girls, some did grow very timid & abashed at every turn, Nancy Browntack's cheeks would redden when she come slippering by her mama's side. They begun to fill out their dresses about the hips & bosom, they was simple dresses of course, no fancy materials but still they could be made to look very pretty.

And yet some of them did possess a calmness & a poise what made the boys Tremble, the likes of Senora Lee had done their maturing in Secret Darkness & come into the light with no horn to announce her arriving & no frills to adorn her neck or sleeves but there was something different to her steady gaze, her movements was slow & deliberate, she did suddenly look fit to bear her own childs.

But for all these folk I had become a silent fixture of their lives for so long that they could not see beyond what was already formed in their heads. At the age of 13 yrs I reached the height I stand at today. I never growed an inch beyond it & I barely come up to some of them boys' & girls' waists. No hair ever growed on my head or nowhere else, no dark shock nested in my armpits or lined in bristling ceremony upon my upper lip.

Only if you had opened up my chest would you have seen the toll of them yrs, my bruised & battered heart, it did look as if it had lived a hundred lives. Had any soul thought to ask me what was held in my future for me I would have writ it plain & simple, I thought I knowed exactly how my life was to unfold. I would still be sit on my stool beneath that old elm, my Mama calling me in for my feed until I was an Old Man & life had done burned a hole right through me.

But of course you know as well as I things will not ever stay the same forever. Some change is always hid around the bend, it has been waiting for its Time to Strike.

And that time was come for me too. It was in the year 1829 & all I knowed come to an end & everything I thought was to be would never be. I was 14 yrs of age in the dwindling months of that yr but I would not stay so young for long.

28

THE HEART OF MAN

THE SERPENT IS A SAINT when set beside the heart of man. The organ that does beat inside our breasts is a thing of wondrous complexity, author of our greatest Kindnesses & Cruelties both. Who knows what details of love & nature you might find should its chambers be opened up but such secrets belong to God & only He might apply His bright & sober eye to them.

We is each of us born in sin & so they is no heart on land or sea innocent of darkness or temptation. But perhaps there does dwell a more dangersome cast in some than others is my thought, God knowing them whose faith must be tested. These is the ones in which Evil is give its chance to thread its black roots & take its whispered orders from the Devil.

They is many things in this world what will excite such Black & Desperate greed in a man but it is my opinion there is none such as Gold to bring it so feverish to the surface. I have seen men go mad with the longing for it. They left their wives & childs with promises to return but the yrs did pass as quick as days & them men could not mourn for they had lost even any recollection of what homely treasure they had once had. Them they did love most with their sweet & innocent faces, faded like ghosts in the empty vessels of their hearts.

DO NOT THINK I know these things from watching alone. That would make me a liar. I was there the first night that Gold was discovered not so far from my own front door & I knowed well enough my blood to be poisoned by the need of it as soon as I seen them shimmering flakes held in an outstretched palm. I too turned my heart away from God & took a turn down the Road to Ruin.

29

BURL

WILLIAM T. BURL WAS KNOWED TO all in Heron's Creek simply as Burl. It was no secret that his mind was a broke gourd from which some vital serving of sense had escaped, words spilling often from his wet & fishy lips in a stream what could not be halted but for the trickle of corn-liquor down his noisome throat.

There was nothing he would not repeat if he had heard it nor nothing he would not tell if he had seen it, even if death should be the consequence. No menace was intended for not a soul could deny his nature was sweet as a babe's, there being no Violence living in his bones or in his slow & ponderous heart. Should Tom Peeper reach from behind his bar & remove his drink he might grow sullen & balky but never would he lay a finger upon he who was so often his guardian & protector.

Burl was knowed best for the peculiarities of his voice. What I mean is that his was a tongue governed by no territory in particular but disposed to drift across any number of them, so that at one moment he might speak the dark & somber tones of a dignitary from our Capital & the next the harsh brogue of a Scotchman.

To hear him talk was to travel the world or so that is what many said & plenty was the time he would stand upon a ladderback chair &

perform in front of an audience at Peeper's tavern. Even I cannot claim to have envied him though for his garrulous ways did come with its own troubles. Them details are incidental but I suppose I am trying to say his was a distinctive presence & not easily mistook for any other. Indeed that is how I knowed it to be he when I was woke one night late in the October of 1829.

30

THREE MEN ON THE ROAD

I COULD NOT BE SURE how long I had slept but the moon was sunk in a reef of cloud & my room as well lit as a grizzly's den. I went to my window & followed the sweep of road leading toward town for I was sure I had heard them wild words of Burl echoing in the night.

But when I did scan the path I was rewarded with no sign of life but for a sleepless fowl what pecked dreamily in a patch of Timothy grass.

My eyes was closing & my bed calling for me to return when I then discerned a lantern lit & held aloft come round the bend, its light made smoky by a fine weave of rain. Black & pleated shadows made him who held it a mystery, though I could see Burl clear enough, his large & drunken frame staggering afore.

All I could say for him who held the lantern was that he favored a dark dress & had Burl held by his cocked elbow, steering him down the road as if he was a bolted pig being returned to its pen.

Burl was chattering away, a great volley of words slurred by drink issuing from his foolish mouth. The man did not seem to mind & might even have been amused but when they drawed level with our store he

growed suddenly straight & nervous & my sleepy eyes then seen him deal
Burl a sharp blow to the side of the head what brung him to a stunned
& wounded silence.

He looked up then & studied each of our windows in turn but I was
well hid, only my one eye observing them from the shadows.

Now that they had stopped, the man's lantern swept beneath his
hatbrim & his face was suddenly lit & aglow. He removed his hat and
held it gently to his chest as if he was about to bestow some fine & schol-
arly words upon his audience. I had not seen him before but I will say I
did not care for the look of him. O it is a strange feeling when you come
upon a stranger & as you take in their features you is rushed by feelings
of Anger & Dismay as if they had wronged you long ago. That was the
case with this fellow with his cold & empty eyes & the long thin strands
of hair what hung from his rain-slicked scalp.

I had thought this to be the extent of their party but I was wrong.
There was a third who then come from behind to step into the lantern's
flare – a tall gangly figure with a crop of hair what the rain had plastered
to his short forehead. He wore a riding jacket what was too small for
him & britches cinched about his narrow waist with a length of whipcord. Even in that weak globe of light I seen his queer Indian buckskin
boots, fastened to their fringes was wild turkey spurs & metal trinkets
what gently glistened in the light.

I had seen him only once before but knowed his name to be Dud
Carter. He was only recently arrived in Heron's Creek, he did hold himself back from the others, his face a great tangle of hurt as if he had just
had his backside stropped raw.

Burl was still rubbing at his head very peevish, he had dug his heels
into the mud like a stubborn old goat. I thought he would not be budged
but it was the Stranger who leaned into his ear & looked to whisper
something, I could not imagine what. I would remain ignorant of them
particulars but only a fool would wonder at the nature of the exchange

as I seen then Burl's lamplit eyes widen in fear & a fire was lit beneath his heels as he hurried on in silence.

Do not think I don't know it for truth, they is many what would have witnessed such a scene & repaired to their beds without a thought. But just as a bluegill nosing through the shallows cannot resist a mealworm dangling from a hook, Yip Tolroy cannot stand on the fringes of a mystery & turn to it his back.

So before I knowed what I was doing I had pulled on my britches & boots & was creeping down the stairs.

31

A FOOL'S PURSUIT

THE STRIKE OF A BLACKSMITH'S SLEDGE could not wake my Mama from her precious sleep & I was out the door with her none the wiser.

The sky was furled in cloud but should the moon show her face I knowed my head would be a victim of her lovely shine & sing out like a beacon for all to see, so I took with me my Mama's black shawl what was draped upon the stair & swaddled my bald head in it as if it were a mourning veil.

No sooner had I stepped out into the night than the rain begun to fall as fat as coins, the mud beneath my feet pulsing like the song in a frog's throat. My Mama's shawl growed heavy as an anchor & my neck did ache beneath its sodden weight. No doubt the rain would turn the roads to slurry & render them impassable by morning with wagons stacked up like forgotten timber-piles & men shin-deep in mud & digging away to free the axles. O yes I imagined my Mama to be cursing in her sleep.

You would not think it a complicated business to stalk a group but there is a delicate balance to be found, it is not unlike the flavoring of a broth, you must know when to add some ingredient & when to keep some secreted away. I had give that band of men a lead of no more than a minute but there was now an urgency to their movements, that lantern was growed dim & hazy in the slanting rain.

A fellow of my size is easily left behind, he must be light on his feet like a cat stalking a sparrow the way it will sneak & then dash, sneak & then dash until it has the fluttering little body between its paws. Slowly but surely I caught up with them until I could smell the sour reek of liquored tongues & the rank drift of their sodden clothes.

Their formation was unchanged. Burl was at the front, the Stranger guarding his flank & Dud Carter lurking at the rear like a coyote hoping to pick at the bones of whatever prize it was they hunted.

There was something in their progress what brung to mind some ancient migration or pilgrimage though I knowed even then it was no journey in honor of any good or noble act but drove by a Derelict & Injurious force.

There was something to the gait of the Stranger in particular, his shoulders was set square, his fist clenched by his side, his boots meeting the earth with the beat of a soldier marching for war. His eyes did seek no contemplation of his surroundings or recognize them as God's Good Work but it was as if he himself had laid their foundations & would now build upon them what he pleased.

The bend of the road led out toward Gainesville & I thought their business might lead them to its wide & busy streets. That town was a deal bigger than Heron's Creek, filled up with them what thought their lives bound for Grander Things. I would come to pass through it in time but I now understood it would not be this night, for I seen them then peel off & cut through a field of dried-up cornstalks & follow a stubbled furrow what pointed toward the dark swatch of woods.

And so it was I kept as close to them as I dared, weaving in & out of the stunted trees what bordered the cornfield, their boles left open to fierce crosswinds what was bent & doubled over as if hungering for an honest meal. Every so often I would leave my cover & swoop as low as a swift along the ground, the lip of Mama's wrinkled shawl dripping rain down my brow & stinging my eyes.

I will admit the prospect of entering them woods did not fill me with joy but as I watched from behind my cover the Stranger step forward & part them fronds, I knowed it was where I was bound. Only a halfwit would go in there with no light to guide him or a gun to defend his life. I had myself neither, my clasp knife was tucked in my belt but that would not count for much if a catamount or a bear was to decide upon me for the purpose of their refection.

And yet despite all this I did hurry after them & plunge into that dripping scrub & undergrowth, my brain empty of everything but the need to discover what it was they sought.

32

TO SEE IT, TO FEEL IT

THE AIR WAS CLOSE & the rain drummed a mournful tune upon the thatched & tangled awning of the wood above. Now that they did consider theirselves to be beyond the threat of prying ears & eyes, their voices was raised & I heard Burl whimper like a dog in dream as the Stranger struck him once more.

That Stranger did suddenly appear in very boisterous spirits, his merriment bolstered by a flask he kept stowed in the waistband of his britches. He sung an old ballad then, it was a haunting sound what floated back through the rain & sent a shiver run up & down my spine.

Poor Burl was silent as a stone, whatever the Stranger had said still turning in his mind. Who knows if a person can sense their end coming, perhaps they feel it in some secret organ what delivers a dim & fractured vision of what is to come? I think now there was some such feeling trapped inside him but what can a man do to alter his path when it is so clearly carved by the hands of another?

Their pace was slowed as they navigated a tall stand of hickories & the lantern throwed up a halo above them, the rain-dark boughs rimed & wincing in its light. I was as careful as I could be with where I put my feet but it is not easy to move quiet in a wood, its floor laden with traps, scattered as it is with twigs & acorn shells what crack beneath a person's soles.

I was no more than 10 yds behind them when I thought disaster struck a Cold & Brutal blow, my Mama's shawl snagged on a branch & as I turned to unpick it some roosting bird was frighted from its perch & lit off in a bloom of feathers & drumming wings. Its cry echoed throughout them woods, not even the rain could smother its terrible reach.

Burl cried out in fright & dropped to the floor, his knees tucked up to his chest & his arms wrapped about his feeble head. Them other two spun on their heel, their lids narrowed to slits as they stared into the black. I had no time to find cover & could do no more than crouch & stay stock still. Raindrops fell, I heard each & every one tick away as if they was the Timekeepers of them dreadful moments.

I thought myself surely caught as the cold eyes of the Stranger traveled over me not once but twice, pausing on me each time as if in quiet reflection of some distant memory. But for all they stared they must only have took in the dark for he hauled the quivering Burl off the ground & ordered him to continue on his way.

Just as Heron's Creek was filled with many voices, so too was these woods, all of them clamoring to be heard. Nighthawks cried & owls flew low in search of their prey so that you might at any point feel the rush of their wings above you. There was no single step I took what I did not think could be my last, for fear is never made more real than when the imagination is in full flight, it is a curse & can ruin a man before he has even got himself out of bed.

I found myself strangely relieved when I could hear the hushed trilling of Simmerstone Creek. It was down a steep declivity what I watched them 3 men descend with the lantern bobbing & reach the bank overlooking the water.

It was no simple task to follow them, one stumble would alert them to my presence. I had to then slither down through the damp leaves as if I was a snake disturbed from his slumber, my chest was greased with

old leaves by the time I reached the bank & took my shelter behind a
cluster of river birch.

I could not put my finger on any reason in particular but there was
suddenly some shift in atmosphere, the smell of the creek wafted up &
the trees arched over from either side of the bank & leaned into their
tangled embrace. I had knowed such moments when an unnatural quiet
does settle, I thought of poor Shelby Stubbs. The world does appear not
like the stage on which the drama will unfold but like one of them seated
in the darkness & listening in.

I watched on as Burl waded into the water. He let out a girlish tit-
ter as it rose to the gusset of his britches, his round face suddenly bright
as a boy's. Then his face growed very serious, he stared down at them
currents what foamed white as they rushed around him as if they might
offer up an answer to some long-sought question.

I seen it around here somewheres, he said.

His voice was softed by them currents but I could hear him still,
what he was referring to I did not know. I watched the Stranger very
close now, he seemed to be bristling with a queer energy, his dead eyes
peeled & come to busy life. I seen his hand was rested on the long handle of a hatchet blade what was tucked in his belt. I had not noticed it
before & perhaps I would not have thought it so unusual if there had
not been what looked to be strands of long black hair fastened to it &
hanging down.

You ain't lost it have you, Burl? said the Stranger.

Dud Carter was growed silent as a monk in the way that only drink
can do to a man. His eyes was turned glassy, he looked out from the shadows of the bank, they did shift between the pair of them. He brung one
hand up to worry the frayed ends of his sparsely bearded chin, it was a
habit of his I would come to know very well.

I swear I seen it around here somewheres, Burl said.

He turned his great head downstream toward a willow thicket, their
sad limbs looming over the water. Suddenly his moist round eyes was

ignited by Hope & he went hurrying toward them willows so quick that he stumbled & fell & more closely resembled a frolicsome hound than any growed man. His shirt & britches growed dark & sodden with the water what lifted & sprayed around him.

I seen it over here, cried he, his chin dripping water. I seen it by these here willows!

The Stranger leapt down into the water & so did Dud Carter, whose face was suddenly transformed, his considerable nose sniffing at the air & his small & rheumy eyes no longer glassy but burning with desire.

Burl scrambled ashore & parted the willows. He did it ever so careful like the drapes in the parlor of some exalted personage. The Stranger & Dud Carter was quick behind him & though I could no longer see their faces they was a quality to the silence what ensued what told me they had come upon their quarry. I could not know what it was their eyes beheld but how I did so long to see it.

That lantern set the leaves of them willows ablaze as if each possessed some small engine of light. You might have thought it home to some magical & sweet-natured creature, you would not have knowed Great Evil was brewing & soon the dirt would run red with Innocent Blood.

33

THE STRANGER'S HAND

YET FOR ALL MY LONGING them weeping willows was spoiling my view, I could not see a wretched thing. I would not be denied the beauty of whatever their eyes beheld & so it was I then spied a windblown ash tree on the opposite bank.

It did lean out beneath the tangle of other boughs, the angle of its trajectory very kind to one who might wish to climb it. O my heart did protest at such a notion but once it was there it did root itself strong & would not be moved.

I have said before I do not much feel the cold but I had never stepped into a creek on the cusp of winter before, my poor heart was nearly stilled. I had hoped it might be shallow enough to cross on foot but as Dud Carter would later point out I could drown in a puddle never mind a creek.

Where I had chose to cross I thought the current tame enough but creeks are filled with Deception & Lies, their murderous truth runs beneath the surface. The creek run no wider than a stone's throw but as soon as I pushed out I felt its deathly tug & knowed myself in trouble. My Mama's shawl growed so heavy that my pockets might have been filled with stones, I could have sworn hands growed like reeds from the riverbed & was pulling me down to my watery grave.

With one hand pushed down to keep myself afloat, the other I used to unwind the shawl from my head & surrender it to the current where it briefly bobbed before sinking into the depths. Even though I was near death it was my Mama's voice what then come into my head, cursing my name for the loss of her precious shawl.

Choking & spluttering now I knowed I would soon draw level with the men & should one of them have been so inclined to look they would have seen my bald head as clear as any star needling through the night sky.

But I could not keep myself from being dragged under once more & knowed this time I would not surface. But it would not be the last time God did reach down & pluck me from the Jaws of Death, there come then a nudge in my back & I turned to face a handsome log what burrowed its nose into my chest. All I had to do was take a grip of one of its stubby branches & use my trailing legs as a rudder to steer myself to the other shore.

I arrived at the opposite bank & found it to be alive with mud crabs, a shifting mosaic what crunched beneath my boots, God forgive me I had no choice but to extinguish their little lives.

Now that my Mama's shawl was gone I could not be out in the open, my bald head was plain for all to see. I did dive for cover, now was the time for Stealth & Slyness.

The old ash tree was a scarred & knotted specimen, some ancient storm had felled it long ago & now it was to serve me in my quest. On the other side of the creek I seen the men was still huddled in the willow thicket. The lantern was placed on the ground & I could hear their whispered voices, deep murmurs of approval from the Stranger. If I did not hurry I feared I would miss whatever delights they had discovered.

I felt the tree's rough bark, my hands stroking & prodding as I imagined my Mama might have prodded at Gussie in considering her purchase, checking for any weakness or flaw in flesh & bone.

The bole was too thick for me to straddle & so on my hands & knees I did crawl, the bark biting into my skin, up & along its length until I reached the middle of the creek. Though I had not knowed it, my size did lend itself to such an endeavor, had I been a little heavier it would surely have begun to bow & I would have been in danger.

Laid flat I clung to that limb like a piece of fruit what would not let itself be picked. It was most precarious but I had myself a clear view into the heart of the willow thicket what now stood no more than 10 yds away from my nose. The rain had let up & fell soft & quiet as muslin so I could catch well enough the upshot of their talk.

Well you was right, Burl, I heard the Stranger say. By God you was right.

All 3 men was crouched at the fringes of the thicket where the lantern showed the upturned roots of a stricken tree. I could not yet see what fixed their attentions so rapt for their shoulders was knit together as men will do when thawing out before the flames of a fire.

No, sir, said Burl, I in't no liar. I told you what I seen & now you set your own eyes to it. I in't no liar.

Burl stood up, his face beaming with pride, all of his woes forgot. He danced a disheveled jig & took a step back to admire his work further & it was in this moment I was give my first look.

The Stranger was knelt by the roots, the lantern held in one hand above the other which was filled with dirt & as he moved it I seen his hand wink with little darting specks of light.

I had not ever seen Gold before but there was no soul on earth who would not have knowed it for what it was. My heart galloped as if whipped & spurred & I did nearly slip from my perch. I did not summon them but pictures of wealth & luxury come flooding into my mind, that is the danger of Gold, it stirs longings in a man's soul he thought he never owned.

Of all things it was then the nasal tones of Dud Carter's voice what cut through the night & brung me back to my senses. He had stuck to the shadows all night but now he stepped boldly forward so that he loomed over the Stranger.

How is it you suppose we go about the sharing of all this? said he.

The Stranger turned sharp to him & fixed him with them cruel & brooding eyes. He stood up & let his great weight settle before the reed-thin boy before him.

You ain't got no say in this, Carter. You is only here since you wasn't taught the manners to tend your own affairs. If your daddy is any tell on your character then you ain't to be trusted any more than a rat in a pantry.

I ain't any like my daddy or any of his doins, said Dud Carter.

Every man got his daddy held up inside of him, in't no use in the denyin of facts like that, said the Stranger.

I cannot say it with no certainty for them was tricksy lights but I do believe I seen Dud Carter's eyes grow shimmery with unspilled tears. His voice turned high & sharp with the unfairness of them accusations.

I ain't seen my daddy in near 2 years, he cried.

Don't matter if he sleeps in the same bed as you or he's a hundred years underground, said the Stranger. It is likely his character's dug into you like a worm in a apple.

Dud Carter's lips was now all aquiver. He rubbed the sleeve of his riding jacket across his puffy eyes & spit into the dirt. Without a word then he parted the fronds of the willow & stalked off into the night along the bank.

Don't you be goin nowheres, growled the Stranger.

He watched Dud Carter go & then turned his back & begun muttering to himself in a voice so low I could not hear.

Burl was now standing over his shoulder, his eyes was bright, there was a wide smile on his face.

We gunna get rich ain't we?

The Stranger did not answer him, he kept on muttering to himself.

Burl then poked him in the back, his eyes blinking, his smile still wide as a slice of moon.

We gunna get rich ain't we? said he again.

The Stranger now rose to his feet.

Open up your hand, he said.

Burl looked at him, he was still smiling but his eyes showed the shadows of his confusement.

Go on & open up your hand, said the Stranger again.

Burl did as he was told & the Stranger poured the clod of glittering earth into it.

This here is all yours, said he. You & me is going to be partners. You & me is going to be so very rich we won't know what to do with it all.

Burl whooped with delight but the Stranger put his hand on his shoulder to calm him, he brung his dirty finger to nearly touch Burl's lips.

But you got to be quiet about it. If we is partners then we got to keep it a secret. You understand?

Burl nodded, his face suddenly serious again.

A secret, he said.

That's right, said the Stranger. You got it now. We got to keep a secret.

I heard then the jingling of them buckskin boots & turned to see Dud Carter had come along the bank until he was near enough beneath me. He stumbled down to the creek where he did make a basin out of his palms & splash them dark waters in his face. Strange thing to do, thought I, considering he looked to be wet enough from the rain already but no doubt his thoughts was tangled & his temper high, so it was to the natural gifts of water he went to soothe himself.

The tree I hewed to was long dead & I had myself only a sparse covering of cord-thin branches. I looked down near directly onto the top of Dud Carter's sodden head. Some light from the lantern still reached him & picked out the sharp angles of his bent knees & the side of his long & mournful face.

His was a face I had seen only once before. I had heard talk that he & his daddy, Ewald Carter, had lived a queer kind of life & had spent some time in & around Heron's Creek over the years.

I had not ever set my eyes on Ewald but I knowed he was a drunkard & had seen no stretch of regular work to keep them in food & shelter. Dud was half wild in his ways because of it. Word was he had spent a good spell of time living in the Cherokee Nation, learning their tongue & other such oddities which no doubt owed to them queer moccasins he wore on his feet.

He sniffed loudly beneath me & fiddled with his wispy mustache. The water surged past, he set then to cursing God & all He had created.

He found hisself a heap of Gold & he got plans to keep it all to hisself as if I ain't got no say in it at all, he said, grinding his boot-end into the mudbank.

That is how he went on, cursing this & cursing that until his rage begun to ebb & a great lassitude washed over him. He stood back up & looked set to make his way back over to the willows where the Stranger was still standing & talking with his arm around Burl.

Now I do not know if you have ever spent much time up in the canopy but they is a good reason why it is only birds do spend their lives up there. I had growed so cold & stiff laid flat against that grating bark that it was come to feel as if I was entirely weightless.

I moved slightly to find some comfort & shift the blood along my limbs but as I did so my bootheel caught a knot in the wood what sent a small shower of woodchips down into the water.

Dud Carter looked up, his lids narrowed to inquiring slits. Without my Mama's shawl there was no place for me to hide, his eyes was well adjusted by now & he seen me clear as day.

Goddamn, he said, there's someone up in that there tree.

Goddamn, he said again, much louder so that I seen the Stranger now look over toward him.

Dud Carter was so very shocked I thought I might use this time to make my escape. I tried to slide back down the length of trunk but my arms & legs was growed stiffer than I thought. I felt the burn of the rough bark across my shins & in my hands as I slipped & knowed myself plunging down toward the creek.

34

WORDS

THE WATER HIT ME LIKE a mighty punch, I was tossed & turned, my nose & mouth was rushed with water & when I opened my eyes it was Dud Carter's pimply face I was looking at.

He did not say nothing to me as his strong & wiry arms carried me to shore & dropped me there in a heap. I gagged & vomited up half the creek & lay there shivering like a Newborn Foal.

When I opened my eyes I could see I was laid like an offering at the feet of the Stranger, it was he who got down on his thick haunches to look at me, his face burning orange with lantern glow like a mask of the Devil himself.

You have brung us a plucked owl, said he.

He run a thick dirty finger down my cheek. His breath was rancid, the leather weskit he wore was torn at the shoulder & through its split seam I could smell the sharp tang of his sweat.

That ain't no owl, said Dud Carter.

The Stranger turned & looked at him, his damp brow furrowed & greased with lamplight.

You know him?

Dud Carter nodded.

I seen him in town before—

He was about to continue when the Stranger did rudely interrupt him.

You is a very queer-looking creature, said the Stranger to me, his voice slow, his bloodless lips turned down.

What is your name, boy?

I stared him back very plain, I did not even point at my tongue.

He slowly tilted his head to one side, his thin hair resting on his right shoulder.

I asked you a question, boy. Or is you deaf as well as bald?

I looked at him again until his nose begun to twitch in anger. He was very still but then he reached out & wrapped his fingers tight around my throat, I could smell the wet earth off of them.

Dud Carter then spoke up.

You will be waiting a long time for an answer, he said.

And why's that then? said the Stranger, his hand still gripped around my throat.

He is a mute, said Dud. He can't talk any. I seen him in town walkin about & people say he is dumb as a fencepost.

The Stranger looked at me. Slowly he relaxed his grip around my throat & the air come rushing back into my grateful lungs.

Well well, he said, is that so?

He patted me roughly on the arm & offered me a smile. His teeth was no more than Yellowed & Mossy pegs.

That is just as well, said he. I do not know what he thinks he seen here tonight but if he knows what is best for him, he won't get no notions of spreading any talk about it.

He then let out a bark of laughter, spit clung to the hairs of his beard & glowed in the lantern light.

But I don't suppose that will be a problem you got, said he.

There was a moment in which our eyes met & through his all sorts of Evil was communicated, the Devil was sit right behind them on his black & burning throne.

But if I hears you have somehow, said the Stranger. Well. You will be getting a little visit from me.

He looked up then from me & brung his eyes to rest on Dud Carter.

What I say is that you go on & take this ugly little fellow home.

He put his arm back around Burl who had come over & was smiling down at me.

Me & Burl will have ourselves a little talk about what to do here.

Dud Carter looked about to open his mouth & complain some more but the Stranger stood up & let his hand rest again on the handle of his hatchet.

You just remember what we had ourselves a conversation about on the ways over here, Carter. You just remember that.

No doubt Dud Carter had seen the same look in them eyes as I had, for he did not say another word but took me by the arm & led me away.

35

LAID OUT FOR THE CROWS

ALL THAT LONG WALK BACK through the woods we was a sorry-looking pair. We carried no lantern between us & we was both soaked to the skin, our shirts & britches sucked to us like they was after a taste of our blood, our boots belching very rude through the dripping brush.

Dud Carter said not a word to me.

His face was blued by shadow but more than once I did catch him looking down at me out the corner of one gray & searching eye. So it is a man will reveal his Nature, he would not hold my gaze but set to muttering recriminations under his sour breath & pulling on the threads of his poxy beard. It appeared the fool was to hold me accountable for his empty pockets & it was his great ploy to convey his grievance through the Powers of Sulking.

By the time we left them woods the clouds had broke up & the moon was silvering the flooded furrows of the cornfield what led back toward the road. Soaked as we was we took no notice of them pooled waters but waded through them, some was risen up to my knees, others was deep enough to bathe in. My clothes would have to be hid from my Mama, there was no yarn I could spin what would save me from her wrath should she find old rainwater dripping through the boards of the floor.

Down come that moon & I knowed I was not alone in feeling exposed beneath its fulsome glare, for Dud Carter did also throw his long jaw over his shoulder more than once to see if we was being trailed. But the farther we went the more the Stranger did seem contained in them woods, as if its tangled boughs held a different world entire.

I was foolish enough then to imagine them trees was great Secret-Keepers & my life would continue on as it always had. But them trees was always whispering. O no it would not be long before my thinking was revealed to be that of a Boy who was now entered into the World of Men. And it is a rule with no exception that once you have crossed that threshold there is no turning back.

As we waded on across the field I turned my attentions back to Dud Carter & since there is no light purer to see by than the moon I thought to give my surly companion a more considered valuation.

Let me say firstly that neither ELEGANCE nor BEAUTY was high up on my list of descriptives. His hair had dried out some & it was clear he had took a blade to it himself. The front was crooked as a cricket's leg & cut straight around his ears so they looked like they was boxed in the shadows of their own little doorways. His eyes was small & gray & secretive, bedded either side of a great nose. O that nose it was a cragged slope what looked to have warranted much doctoring over the years, its bridge & tip shamed by pocks & scars aplenty.

Some illness he must have suffered in his youth was no doubt to blame & yet for all this he carried his awkward frame as though he thought himself a Saint who trod upon Holy Ground, walking with his hands clasped behind his back, his chin tipped imperiously to the night sky. He sniffed frequently at the air as if it was flavored with some wafting note he considered an insult to his Worldly Sophistications.

I would not have cared to admit it then but these was all signs of some common thread spun between the pair of us. Strangers we was but our lives was marked by the same indecencies, them cruel words & looks of others had dogged us both but now we carried our skins as if no bruise or cut could mark them. We did not want others to see our hurt & so we acted as if hurt was no acquaintance we ever come across in our lives.

I would come to learn Dud Carter did not care much for reminiscences on them days of his boyhood & I would find him to be very quiet on the topic of his own mama, only once did he speak of her. She was an awful clever lady, he said, she had give her heart over to designs on setting up a school of her own to teach in. But them dreams of hers was dashed when she did succumb to a sickness what could not be cured by nothing other than Death, though like all them blessed with the most generous souls, she did not depart before giving her boy a gift to own & treasure.

Now the sky hung high & black above us, how many stars burned their lives up there we had no right to know. But the Not Knowing is a blessed space in which to live. People do so love to forget it, they want nothing hid from their greedy eyes. But they forget that these hidden glades is what keeps their brains burning, their hearts beating, their lives filled with all them necessary longings. No we cannot claim to be owed anything in this life.

These was my thoughts as we reached the road & turned toward the store when Dud Carter suddenly stopped mid-stride, one leg raised. He stood looking down at the earth as a marsh bird will stare down its lancing beak into the mudflats. He looked mighty puzzled & I thought he had lost his bearings before he then spoke.

I think I seen that man before, he said.

I did not know what man he was talking about, for I looked around us & we was clearly alone. But I seen his eyes was growed misty & his nostrils flared, the whiff of some old memory come drifting back to him.

Said he, I swears I seen him before.

His voice was brung low to a whisper, his lids half lowered & sleepy as if in the grip of a dream. He stayed like this a good while, turning over that mystery behind his eyes before he shook his head free of whatever it was had held him & stalked on without another word, one hand scratching at the crown of his head. I thought him a strange creature indeed & getting stranger by the minute.

We reached the store with its wood rain-dark & my daddy's painted sign dripping steady into a moon-blue puddle beneath it. I had not ever been out so late & it had to it a quality of stillness & quiet I had not knowed before. The wet shakes of the roof was shining but its front – the windows & the porch & the door – was consumed by shadows.

As I had expected there was no light lit in the windows, the porch banked in black. I do not think I had ever been so glad to see that old place, I yearned for my bed & sleep to steal me away from these Strange Events & let them become a thing of the past.

But then I seen a quiver of movement on the porch, no more than a flutter of some cloth or lace. I thought it an animal of some kind but then there she was, my Mama, stepping out from the shadows with my daddy's old rifle braced against her shoulder & its barrel aimed directly at Dud Carter.

Do not touch him! cried she, her voice shrill & wild in the night.

Her hair was unpinned & hung twisted about her shoulders. Her face was washed white, her eyes round & fixed, her mouth a grim & furious line. She was stood in her long white nightdress with her feet bare & when she walked slowly down them steps & into the mud I seen that dark slop rise up between her white toes.

A dog barked from somewhere in town & a faint roar of laughter carried from outside Peeper's tavern but not one of us turned to heed it.

Dud Carter held his long arms aloft, he did look like a spider what had been shook off its web, his eyes was bright with fear as he watched my Mama inch forward, one foot creeping over the other like a hunter what does not wish to spook his quarry.

Do not touch who? stuttered Dud Carter.

My boy, said my Mama.

O I can still hear them words now, for I had not ever heard her refer to me in such a way & I would not hear them again. But there was no chance to savor it, it was Dud Carter's death she appeared to desire, his soul she was eager to claim.

I do not intend on touching no one, said Dud Carter. I just—

Who are you? snapped my Mama.

She was now only a yard away & still holding the rifle braced against her right shoulder she grabbed me by the wrist with her left hand & pulled me behind her so hard I fell & lay writhing in the mud like an eel.

When I sit up I seen the barrel of the rifle pressed against the breast of Dud Carter's riding jacket. My Mama's head was still, her hands steady. Should she pull the trigger his chest would be blown open & his innards laid out for the crows.

Dud Carter swallowed & his Adam's apple was hoisted like a flag up & down his long neck.

I saved your boy, said he. I saved him from drownin hisself down by the creek—

My Mama jabbed him with the rifle.

I asked you who you *was*, said she.

Dud Carter. My name is Dud Carter.

My Mama cocked her head & narrowed her eyes slightly. I seen her toes curl in & then stretch out again.

Ewald Carter your daddy?

Dud Carter paused, it was plain he could not tell if admitting such a thing would benefit him or hasten his arrival to an early grave.

Yes, ma'am, said he finally.

My Mama's grip on her rifle looked to slacken slightly.

You do not look a bit like him, she said.

Dud Carter's face darkened, a line of confusement passed his dusty brows.

He tells me it is my mama I take after in the particulars of my face.

He is a liar, said my Mama, & he always has been. You do not look any more like her than you do him.

Dud Carter lowered one hand slowly to his face & dabbed at it with his fingertips as if he was suddenly a stranger to himself.

How is it you got any notions on what my mama looks like?

How is it you got any notions askin questions with a gun bearin down upon you? I believe it is me who ought to be doing the askin. Now. You say you was savin him from the creek?

My Mama jerked her head back toward me.

That's right, said Dud Carter, pulling on his lapels proudly. I don't deserve no gun pointed at me by some crazed whore—

O my Mama did not care for them words, she struck him then with the butt of the rifle across the brow. He howled & fell clutching at his head & my Mama planted herself firm over him, I seen in her eyes then a Wildness, such insolence was a Terrible Crime to her. I had seen a man dare to use such language against her in her own store and she had took the bristles of her broom to him & swept him whimpering & cursing right out onto the road.

She tightened her grip on the rifle & took her aim afresh then, I had seen her shoot a squirrel through the eye from 100 yds, there was no doubt Dud Carter was a Dead Man.

It don't bother me none to put an end to you, said she.

She cocked the hammer, I thought her about to fire. I did not know this man now cowering in the mud no better than any stranger but he had plucked me out of that creek when I was set to sink & so I reckoned I owed him in return.

I picked myself up out of the mud then & run to stand in front of him. It give my Mama a turn to see me there, her eyes was hotter than the coals of hell.

Get out of the way, said she.

I shook my head.

I won't ask you again, cried she.

We was both stubborn as goats, I seen her pale feet sucked at by the mud as she took another step forward.

Yip Tolroy. You move yourself right now. You know I mean what I say.

But there was nothing my Mama could say what would make me budge, it was a matter of Honor now what I could not abandon. I could hear Dud Carter breathing awful panicked behind me, he had believed himself a Goner. Now his trembling lips was alive with contrition, he had the quivering tones of a Saved Man. He clumb slowly to his feet.

I did not mean no offense, ma'am, I got a foolish tongue in my head in times of distress. I swears I saved your boy here, he would have got hisself drowneded without me.

My Mama breathed in deep through her nose, she was no less disgusted by the sight of us but fading was that murderous look in her eye. She turned to me then, my hands & face was black with dirt & rivermud.

That true? He save you from drownin?

I turned & looked at Dud Carter, blood was running down his face, his eyebrows was both raised expectantly.

I nodded that it was indeed the truth he spoke.

My Mama turned back to him. She did not lower the rifle but I could see the fury was ebbing from her some more. She looked at him long & hard, there was some light working across her features what I had not seen before. Twice she opened her mouth to say something but seemed to think better of it.

Finally she said, I don't believe a word of what you told me. I can smell the drink off the pair of you & I'd ask you what you was doing but you're a Carter & I know well enough I won't get no sense out of you. I want you gone from here now.

Dud Carter lowered his arms & stood looking at my Mama. His face was of that mold what could compass many feelings at once & now he looked wounded & scared & curious, dipping in & out of each one as an artist will dip into his colors with his brush.

What you waitin for?

My Mama jabbed at the air with the rifle again.

You better get gone in the next few seconds before I empty this thing out on you.

I thought Dud Carter on the brink of some half-witted remark but he appeared to enjoy a rare moment of restraint & he turned & stalked off through the mud, looking over his shoulder only once before he rounded the bend.

My Mama watched him go till he'd gone from sight & then she looked down at me. I thought she might whip me there & then but there was that look on her face again, that light what crossed her features & did briefly resemble something close to contentment.

I could not predict her no better than the weather, just when I thought the clouds was set to gather in dark & unruly bands they growed lighter & parted & allowed the sun to come slanting through.

36

STRANGE FLAMES

AS YOU WELL KNOW ME & my Mama had never forged ourselves a bond beyond the necessaries our arrangement did require. We was not like mother & son but more like a boarding house owner & a lodger, each had growed accustomed to the other's quirks & usages & did not wish to disturb them.

Since I had learned my letters as a boy we had of course conversed but for my Mama to see me with my slate & chalk was an insult, I did then believe it depressed her spirits to be so reminded of my *affliction*.

But my Mama was far from ignorant of my change after I come back that night when she wanted to shoot Dud Carter to pieces. O yes she did sense in me some unease as I kept my eyes lowered & left my slate hanging in my Slate-Sling by the door.

But you also know that in her manner she was not aimed toward subtlety or some slow propitiation but to have whatever irked her quashed with all them blunt & reasoning tools what originate in the head & not the heart. And yet still she trod very soft about the house after that night & when we took our seats to eat I observed some shift in her disposition though I could not name it.

The next evening after we had et she took her seat as she always did by the fire. In all our years together she had not ever expressed no desire to be joined there, she would stare into them flames & I would retire upstairs to my room. I had long assumed she took her place by the warmth to mull over the store's Business Doings, such dealings being as restful to her busy mind as prayer is to most others.

But that night she did sit & pull up another chair from the table beside her.

Come, said she, I want you to sit.

I was so confused I could only stare at her for a good few moments, my mouth agape.

I said sit not stare, she added impatiently, smoothing out the creases in her lap & picking up the poker to tend the embers slipping through the grate.

I did as I was told & clumb up onto my seat beside her. She did not turn to look at me but placed the poker down & kept her eyes on the fire. The flames – orange & red shot through in parts with greens & blues – leapt & darted & licked the wood to cinders. A log split & cracked & then rolled down into the bowl of heat & give off 2 great wings of sparks. I turned my head away from the gust of heat but my Mama did not blink.

These is strange flames, said she suddenly. I have not seen flames like these for some time.

I looked at the fire but I could not see nothing strange about it. It was a fire & that was about all I could think on the matter. But my Mama did not see it that ways in the slightest, she was frowning now, the lines on her brow growed deeper over this past year. I had noticed some of them fine red hairs of hers had turned white also, some of which did now escape her pins & glow in a unruly nimbus about her head.

You know on the night you was born, she said with her eyes still on the fire, when your daddy had took off & left me – I lit me a fire down here & I come & sit just where I am now, with you in my arms & I stared into it & you was staring into it & it was the most peaceful I ever did feel in my life. Even with your daddy gone I felt filled up with Peace.

She turned to look at me, still frowning. Her eyes was shadowed & dark but softed somehow, their secrets was always stubborn things but I did sense in her a change, some fresh weather blown in to do its work. O yes it was a volley of warm winds come to thaw out a clutch of cold & froze up memories & here they was now come to slow & cautious life. I could not believe it but she then begun to talk about my daddy. I had never heard no words on what he looked like but now she give me all the particulars of his appearance, of how his dark eyes was just like mine, how his brown curls lapped at his collar, of his long & slender neck & thin face, his fine-cut nose & pointed chin. I seen him clear in my mind as if he was standing before me, the man in my dreams was to have a face from now on.

She did then pause again but there was some other detail what worked its way to the surface, I seen what I took for a smile chancing across her lips.

Your daddy always wore hisself a Red Kerchief tied around his neck, she said. I thought it an ugly thing & the smell it give off was like to bring tears to your eyes. He had it on the day you was born & I told him to take it off but no matter how I told him he would not give it up. That was the only thing he ever spoke up for. Anything else & he would roll over like a dog.

She looked down into her lap & when she looked back up at me, her eyes was shining wet.

You won't remember them days, said she, but I used to sit with you down here every night. You would look into that fire & soon you was asleep & then soon I'd be asleep & we was both dreaming together.

She looked at me a moment longer & then she turned back to the fire once more & shook her head slightly at the sight of it.

But these is strange flames, she said. They growed stranger & stranger of late.

Then without looking at me again & without mentioning anything more on the fire or her old memories, she ordered me up to bed & did implore me to get a good night of rest.

I looked at her & brung out a nub of chalk from my pocket. I was preparing to encourage her to continue for she had never talked so plain to me before but she raised up her hand to stop me.

Bed, said she.

I could do nothing but make my way upstairs.

I lay awake a long time that night picturing myself wrapped up in my Mama's arms & the pair of us looking into the fire. I thought on the pair of us sleeping there, my skin against hers & how queer it would be to touch her skin now. I wondered if she had been a different person back then to the one I had come to know.

When I finally fell asleep I dreamed of her. We was both sit by the fire as we had been but we was looking at only ash & old blackened logs long gone cold. But when I turned to look at her I could see her red hair waving about beside me, only it was not hair but flames raging wild licking the ceiling above us. She looked me in the eyes, she did not cry out or writhe in agony as you would expect but whispered very quiet, so quiet I almost could not hear.

These is strange flames, said she, these is strange flames.

37

MISSING

THEM DAYS AFTER THAT NIGHT by the creek & my Mama's words by the fire, the world did seem to fall quiet on itself. Each morning I rose to a songless dawn, the birds was flown to warm their feathers under a distant sun & our lush country was suddenly locked in ice, the air so cold it stung your teeth to breathe it.

This weather come as a shock to all of us. We was used to warm winds taking the leaves off of the trees as late in the year as November but now they was dropping in red & burning squalls. I remember well that time the air was filled with the sound of wood being split day & night, for fires was kept burning without relent.

When Elijah Langston found one of his cattle froze bone-hard his curses could be heard across the county, he had to haul it out with rope tied about its neck & a team of mules with their breath come steaming out as they pulled it stiffly onto its side.

I did not sit out beneath my tree but stayed in my room like a man jailed & sentenced to Hang. I thought about the Red Kerchief of my daddy's but more often I admit my thoughts was drawed to the Gold & the Stranger & them eyes of his what was lit like none I had seen before.

I could not eat & yet more than once I was took by surprise by my bowels. O yes they was turned to water & I could be seen running beneath the moon across the frozen ironware of the earth where I did sit shivering in the foul dark of the privy.

Since that cold snap people had come out in their droves to the store. Corn cribs had shriveled up & they feared they would starve if they did not stock their pantries full.

It was on the third day that I might say events did begin to unfold with a force I knowed I could not stop.

I was there standing & gazing dreamily out my window when I seen Tom Peeper & Dud Carter come riding down the road. They wore their slouch hats low, they had scarves wrapped around their mouths but still their breath was hung in clouds before them. Even from that distance I could see the cut & lump on Dud Carter's forehead, he did wear it like a badge. Steam rose up off the flanks of their beasts, the horses' forelocks was damp & flat with sweat. It was clear they had come from thundering across the fields, up & down the hills, worked so hard they could barely stand.

I watched as Tom Peeper dismounted & tied his piebald mare to the hitching rail outside the store. He turned & motioned for Dud Carter to join him but that lanky fellow appeared to refuse. He offered some muffled excuse through his scarf & stayed sit atop his mount, taking out his clay pipe & stuffing its bowl with a wad of tobacco.

I had not seen Dud Carter since that night, I thought on the words of the Stranger & prayed Dud had kept his foolish mouth shut.

Tom Peeper was a quiet & troubled man, he had fought in them Indian Wars & his mind was plagued with memories of them ensanguined battles. His skin was pale, his eyes was black & serious. He had a beard what he kept cropped close to the skin on his cheeks but allowed to grow full & thick around his mouth. As he took the steps up to the store, he took off his hat & raked his fingers through his straight dark hair.

My head was pressed against the glass & I felt that cruel cold burrow beyond my skull & turn my thoughts Wintry. I did not much care for the feeling what was hunkered down in my guts either. I listened to Tom Peeper's bootheels on the puncheon floor & his deep voice travel up through the timbers as he greeted my Mama, though his words was soon lost to me.

I looked down at Dud Carter.

He had lit his pipe though he did not look like a man who was in no position to savor it. By that I mean his mood was not Contemplative, O no he was not musing on Life's many quandaries but in a state of muzzled agitation. His eyes was a riot of red & yellow, I could not smell his breath but knowed it could have drawed a cloud of flies away from a dungheap. I had not got no taste for liquor then but you will need no guesses as to who it was introduced me to it.

Dud Carter watched the blue smoke from his pipe tunnel skyward & as he did so his eyes found me in the window. Them small blinkers of his growed wide & after flashing a glance over each shoulder he motioned me down to him with a lively wave of his gloved hand.

With my hat on & Slate-Sling looped over my shoulder I snuck down the stairs & out the back door where I could peel round to the front without my Mama seeing me.

I had no chance to write nothing down before Dud Carter spoke up.

I reckon I got to thank you for the other night, said he.

His eyes was lowered, he was awful sheepish. He did idly take the hairs of his horse's mane & run them through his fingers. That beast did not belong to him, I reckon he wished it did but he had only took a lend of it from old Tom Peeper. Dud looked down at me then, I could see there was a great torrent of feeling in all them crooked features of his.

Your mama is quite a woman, he said.

He did then seem to suffer from some sudden spell of Dreaminess before he sniffed & shook himself awake & continued on.

We both got ourselves in a spot of bother & we both helped the other out. In old Dud's book that's God's way of sayin you got yourself a partner & you don't turn your back on no partner who put their life between yours & death. Not ever.

He did mean every word of what he said, of that I was sure & I reckoned he was right. I must admit I did like the sound of such a Pact, my blood run quick to hear it.

What do you say, Old Salt? he asked.

No words did need to be writ down, he seen in my eyes I thought the same, I give him a firm & soldierly nod to make sure.

Good, said Dud Carter.

He then extended his hand down toward me & I shook it as firm as I could, dear old Stubbs had schooled me well in that regard.

But now I seen him glance around again, his nerves was suddenly returned, he did not want whatever come out of his mouth next to travel far. He leaned down from his horse.

I'm afraid to tell you we got some more trouble come our way, he whispered. Burl ain't been seen since that night we was at the creek.

I took out my slate & fished around in my pocket until I found some chalk. I had not been out there thirty seconds but my hands was already numb & my writing a mess.

Have you told him?

Dud's eyes narrowed as he slowly read my untidy words.

I think now on the fact that these was the first words of mine he did ever read, I cannot say why but I was not surprised to find he could. This was the great gift I spoke of earlier that his mama had left him with, she had owned a single book & had give him enough schooling to have him read.

Told who? said Dud Carter.

I jutted my chin toward Tom Peeper's horse.

Course I ain't. We can't have no one go sniffin around that creek because it will be us what gets it in the neck.

Dud sucked on his pipe & looked at the windows of the store where we could see Tom Peeper leaned on my Mama's counter nodding & stroking his stubbled jaw.

Tom is grown very suspicious, he said. He drunk hisself into a stupor that night we was at the creek & can't remember a lick. But he knows Burl well enough that somethin ain't right. He knows somethin ain't right when Burl don't show up at the tavern these last 2 nights.

I was about to write & ask where it was he thought Burl had got to when the door swung open & Tom Peeper stepped back out onto the porch. He put his slouch hat back & adjusted its brim before looking out across the still meadows toward the mountains. The sun was risen up high & billeted behind peels of scudding cloud what turned it the color of an iced puddle.

He looked down & seen me stood beside Dud Carter's horse.

Well, said he. Little Yip Tolroy. I see you still ain't grown.

He walked down the steps, the thumbs of his gloved hands tucked into the waistband of his britches.

I just bin asking your mama about somethin. I just bin askin her about Burl – you know Burl?

I nodded that I did.

Well nobody seen him for a coupla days. His daddy says he ain't bin home. He ain't so sharp at lookin after hisself & I got me a bad feeling that he's run into some trouble.

Tom Peeper looked out toward the mountains again. He pinched his nose between his thumb & finger & sniffed very loud. He turned & looked at me, his eyes was sad & full of something I could not put no name to.

Your mama ain't seen him & me and young Carter here bin up since dawn scourin the country for him. No sign.

He spit & ground it into the mud with his bootheel.

I think it's awful strange myself, he said. I don't suppose you've seen him, little man?

I did not have time to pull out my slate before Dud Carter butted in.

Well, Tom, that is just what I was askin him, said he.

His horse moved forward a few paces until he tightened the reins & brung it to a halt. His clay pipe was still clenched between his teeth as he spoke.

He just writ it out on that little board of his there. Says he's as clueless as we is. Ain't seen hide nor hair of him.

Tom Peeper looked at me & sighed heavily & shook his head.

That don't surprise me, said he.

He moved over to the hitching rail & petted the white muzzle of his mare.

These horses'll be plumb tired out. We'll get them well watered & rested tonight but they got a little left in em. Might ask around in Gainesville & see if anyone's seen or heard anythin down that way.

O, said Dud Carter, that sounds like a fine idea. I think we might get lucky down there. Might just be Burl'll be dead drunk in some cathouse, his prick bout ready to drop off.

Tom Peeper nodded but there was no hope in his eyes that this was true.

Maybe, he said.

It was when he turned his back to mount his horse that Dud Carter then give me a queer look, I could not read it. His eyes was rolling & his head was jerking toward the mountains as if he was suddenly come down with a case of Lockjaw.

Tom Peeper hauled himself up & gathered the reins in one gloved fist.

Come on, Carter. We best get goin if we want to make a day of it.

He pinched the brim of his hat between forefinger & thumb & looked down at me.

Thanks for your help, little man, said he.

Dud Carter wheeled his horse round but not before he pulled that same face, hauling his chin toward the mountains again. I could have swore he said something but the hoofs of them horses was like thunder on the froze mud & they left me in the middle of the road watching after their billowing coats.

It was only after I had returned to my room & lay down on my bed, with straw poking at me & keeping me tossing & turning that I knowed what it was Dud Carter wanted from me.

38

THE REST OF MY DAYS

THE ICE HAD FROZE THE mud so it was reared up like a mountain range shrunk down by God & set before some tiny race of travelers. Gussie's hoofs did not take to it, she slipped & tossed her head in dismay, casting longing glances back toward the frosted grasses in her corral. I stroked her neck & smoothed the coarse hairs of her mane but it did little to sugar her temper. She would be needing some oats if we was to make amends.

I was myself slickered up in an oilskin & my daddy's old sou'wester with its gutter front-brim. Dark clouds was gathering again above the mountains, the sun gone & the sky bruised & hurting to rain or snow I did not know which. I could expect fierce nightwinds to come riding down the slopes & all they carried with them, raindrops like bullets what could likely blind a man.

Several hours had passed since Tom Peeper & Dud Carter had ridden off toward Gainesville. I knowed they would be gone till past nightfall. But I had been left with my own task, for now I found myself heading back to them woods & Simmerstone Creek. O yes that is what Dud Carter had in mind for me I knowed it, he wanted me to go looking for Burl.

My slate jostled around my waist as I rode back from Gussie's stable toward the store, the leather strap rubbed across my shoulder. Who could say what waited for me in them woods but Death seemed as likely a suitor as any. It was the eyes of the Stranger what lived in my head as 2 eggs live in the darkness of a nest, they was waiting to hatch & then they would be watching watching watching.

As I come up to the store I seen my Mama was stood sweeping the porch, her head bent to her work. The sorghum tassels scratched away an ugly tune as she made her neat little mounds of leaves & dust. The sleeves of her dress was rolled up & the muscles in her arms was shifting beneath her pale & freckled skin. She looked up. She stopped her sweeping but she did not beckon me over. No her face did register no feeling, no thought appeared to cross it, only her eyes followed me. I could not let her read the fear what was wore plain across my face, I nipped Gussie with my heels & we sped off where them eyes of hers must content theirselves with boring into my back.

I rode on toward the cornfield, the furrows froze over, the sky gray & flat above it. In that band of trees what picketed the border a dozen crows was perched & cawing out. Some of them lit up & turned idly before returning to preen their glossy apron of feathers. I felt them stare down at me as if I was indeed one of their own, dressed in black & drawed like them to Death itself.

It was then as I was about to turn off onto the field that I heard a cry of such a kind sunk in grief & terror, the kind what does bring your heart galloping up into your head to set your ears a-ringing.

I looked on down the road, coming toward me was a woman, her bonnet askew, dark curls escaped & pouring down the length of her back. I seen it was Burl's wife, Mary. Her voice was strained & cracked & her eyes was red, the skin beneath them the color of clay. I seen then that she was not alone, for trailing behind her with their heads bowed in confusement & shame was a little boy & a little girl. They was twins of no more than 5 yrs, their hair was dark like their daddy, for they was the 2 childs of Burl.

I brung Gussie to a halt & waited. Mary was not knowed well, she was a quiet woman & though I had seen her any number of times we had not ever conversed. You would not have thought any woman inclined to hitch up with Burl but she doted on him, she believed he was the kindest man on earth & she did treat him no different to them childs she reared.

She held 2 fistfuls of her dress as she approached, tripping & stumbling over the froze-up mud. I had seen her always very plump & rosy about the cheeks but somehow she did now look thin, her face growed pale. When she reached me she clung on to Gussie's bridle & looked up, her eyes was dark & shining.

Have you seen my husband? said she.

Now her voice was quiet & pleading, my blood did run cold to hear it. My hand shook as I reached for my slate & chalk. It did break my heart to tell such a lie but I wrote that I had not seen him for a week or more, not since he was last in my Mama's store.

Mary looked at my slate & then at me & her brows knit in hopeless confoundment. Them words was a mystery to her, she could not read. I shook my head as the 2 childs each took a handful of their mama's dress as it turned & lifted in the wind, their small faces mooning up at her. Their hearts was still too young to know the cold spread of fear what was scrawled so clear across her face. How would she survive without him, Burl's daddy was lame in the leg, her own people was miles away & she could not work to earn her keep & look after them 2 young childs all at once.

Again she asked if I knowed of Burl's whereabouts & again I shook my head but now she was not looking at me, she was turning this way & that, her eyes gone loose & wild.

The young girl then stepped forward & looked up at me, so too did the boy. Sometimes young childs like that will have a better read of a person than them who have lived a lifetime longer, I felt their eyes on me & was forced to look away across the fields. I thought they must surely see the truth I kept from them. How could I who had been denied my own daddy keep hid from them such secrets?

I did not want any more part of this tragic scene, to my shame I tried to pluck Mary's fingers loose from Gussie's halter but her knuckles burned white & would not let go.

Where is he? she said again. Where is he?

O my face does redden to recall it even now, I swear I did not mean to but in my panic I pinched Gussie with my heels & she took off across the field toward the woods. Poor Mary was dragged a yard or so through the mud before she let go, her pale face looking up after me, her 2 childs crying out as their mama lay twisted on the earth. Gussie's hoofs beat across the ice, my heart was going too & I could not look back though I knowed the picture of them 3 faces was burned in my mind for the rest of my days.

39

GOD KEEP HIM

THEM OLD TREES WITH THEIR old bones & their old bark-rough tongues. They was creaking in the wind & the sky picked through their branches above, pearly white & grading into ash. It was no place for an unsettled mind to linger, O yes trouble was a-stirring now good & proper.

I thought of Dud Carter riding along the rows of stores & warm lamplit windows in Gainesville & I cursed him for sending me out into this gray & desolate country alone.

Still I was not without some luck & it was not long before I seen beneath me them blurred outlines of our old prints. They was not perfectly preserved by the cold & a stranger might have seen nought in them but I thought I knowed well enough they was mine & Dud Carter's.

Gussie weaved in & out of the trees after them, my numb hands gripping the reins & steering her with little fingerturns as my eyes was locked on our old tracks. Gussie's ears was pricked sharp & her eyes bugged so wide they was fit to burst, her mellow nature had been disturbed there was no doubt. Something in the air she did not trust & I too could not sit still in my saddle, blowing hot breath into my bunched fists & twisting in my seat.

The sky darkened as we went on & there was 1 or 2 distant peals of thunder. How much it does sound like the Devil trapped & raging at the bottom of a well, raking the black tines of his fork up & down the walls. I felt the wind riffle my oilskin & frisk the cuffs of my britches, they was a sharpness to it I imagined to carry some warning or retribution I could not say which.

Our old tracks had been rubbed clean in some places & I was forced to seek them out again & again & so it took over an hour to reach Simmerstone Creek. I had expected to hear its sweet trilling but of course when we arrived it was froze over, the waters held in perfect stillness.

There down the way was the willows gathered, their mournful limbs cased in ice. As Gussie trod careful along the bank I stared down into the creek. I had hoped to see some shimmer of Gold but the ice was gray & dusted & would not reveal no such secrets to me now.

I clumb down from Gussie & tied her up on a stiff switch of river birch & hoppled her with a spancel I kept in a saddlebag. Normally she would root about & savor her rest but she stood stock still, her flanks all aquiver & her ears & eyes alert.

She watched me as I walked over toward the willows & slowly parted the fronds what were heavy & stiff with ice, rattling & shaking theirselves free of their little silver bodices. It was awful gloomy inside, the light like that of an empty room in a house what was long abandoned but still held on to some ancient note of the lives what had lived there. That queer sense that there had been someone in there not long left. I did not like it one bit.

I was about to part again them iced fronds when I then seen a patch of earth at the rear of the gnarled trunk had been churned up. The frost what had remained in them shadows was tinctured a queer shade of pink & 2 faint grooves led off out of the willows & I followed them out onto the creekbank till they veered back into the woods. They was only faint but they was something about them. Let me tell you they was not made by no paw or hoof I knowed that much for sure.

I went back to Gussie & untethered her & soon we was following the tracks as they snaked through the dense brush & then straightened as that timber growed strangely sparse. Most was the ghostly frames of river birch but there was also other trees, old veterans what had been there since creation begun & so old I could not name them.

You cannot help but feel yourself watched in them spaces, you do not know whose eyes are out there. There was so much stillness & so much silence, the sky so flat & white, the trees naked & unmoving. Each step Gussie took & the crunch of brush beneath her hoofs struck like a great offense to some permanent order laid down by God Himself & yet I did not sense Him there.

Just then something struck the brim of my sou'wester. I thought myself under attack & looked down to see a white stone veined with blue & shaped like a teardrop. It was pinched at the end & growed fat through the middle, as big as a good-sized egg.

Then they was falling all around me, drumming off the trees like a barreling herd of buffalo & striking my head & arms & legs & making Gussie rear up onto her hind legs in fright. And what a queer scent it woke in the sleeping earth also, all the ancient metals – arrowheads & blades tipped with the sour iron of blood – risen up & out into the world again.

My hands was so stiff with the cold I could not hold on long before I was bucked off where I lay in the dirt covering my head for fear I was about to have my skull split open like the daddy of that queer girl I met all them yrs before beneath my tree.

A minute passed & when I looked up the woods was returned to perfect stillness, though it was as if the sky had broke itself into pieces & now lay strewn across the ground. Small as these hands of mine are, when I picked the nearest to me up it was big enough to fill my fist. I felt its cold weight & smelled the freshness of the sky in its meltwater but beautiful as it was it is in every boy's heart to wish to see something so precious shattered. Do not ask me why but that is how a man's heart works, whatever is built must be brung to ruin & so it will continue until my bones are turned to dust beneath your feet.

I stood & turned & picked out one of them ancient trees, it was a sickly looking thing, its trunk fat & rotted but still somehow standing strong. Aiming I throwed & it struck the lower quarter of its bole. The hailstone popped in a spray of glittering ice but also skittered a great many logs what had been arranged around its base like stones around a firepit. They all of them fell & to my surprise there was revealed a hole in the trunk, a black & splintered hollow what reached from the ground to perhaps a little taller than myself.

A less loyal beast might have cowered away but Gussie had remained close & looked on again as I slowly approached the tree, my feet crunching on the hail. There was them crows again roused by that celestial dispatch & circling above, their sump-throated cries ringing out.

The hole looked to be bigger than I had thought, filled with nothing more than leaves & timber. I could have fit in there with ease, I thought if my Mama was ever to banish me for good I might return here & make from it an Honest Home.

But I was no more than a yd away when I was suddenly halted, my heart leaping like a frog on hot coals. I thought at first my eyes was deceived or the cold had drove me mad for what I had took to be leaves & timber was now a pair of brown boots poking out from the darkness. And now my eyes was adjusted they was visited by more horrors, I could see 2 legs leading up into the tree before they disappeared.

I looked & knowed it then they was the brown boots & corduroy britches I recalled Burl had wore that night. I could not bring myself to touch them, for I could not move & I am not ashamed to admit I did fetch up the small breakfast of eggs & grits I had et that morning.

After I was recovered someway I begun to pluck at the fabric of his britches afraid that he might move, afraid that he was living still even though I could see there was no life left in him. I then took hold of his shins & they was cold & hard as iron. I pulled but the legs would not bend though when I got a firm hold just above his heels & leaned back there come a noise from up in the tree as the body begun to slide down & the legs shot quickly out & I was throwed backwards.

When I looked up there was Burl sit before me, looking out from that tree. How he had found himself in there was a mystery to me. His face was black & swolled & frostbit & down the center of his skull there was a terrible cleave from which black blood had flowed.

O it took no Lawman to know it was that hatchet of the Stranger what had done the gory deed. Burl's eyes was still open but they was frosted over, looking out toward Icy Eternity.

I tried to stand but my legs was turned to air beneath me. I knelt & lowered my head long enough to breathe some life back into them & did find myself at prayer.

God Keep Him, thought I, before I staggered to my feet.

Mounting Gussie was not easy in the best of times but the shock had turned me flimsy as a doll & it was as if her tack was greased by some cunning trickster, my progress was like a sailor clambering from the ruins of a shipwreck. It took me no less than 5 good minutes to get a firm foothold on the stirrup & haul myself onto the saddle.

Finally I did wheel that faithful beast around & we was headed for home, my mind set on nothing but the whereabouts of Dud Carter.

40

THE LIGHTS OF PEEPER'S TAVERN

BRANCHES SNAGGED AT GUSSIE & drawed blood from her sleek coat but there was no time to let her poor heart rest.

Darkness was near upon us, them clouds I had seen brooding above the mountains now rolling down & the first shells of hard rain singing through the air. I lay close to Gussie's neck, my eyes narrowed & straining for my old tracks until I could see them no more & must rely on God's Helping Hand to guide me good & true.

The memory has no master or so I have heard it said before, in my opinion no truer word was ever spoke. Even that grudging rain could not drive from my mind the sight of poor Burl & still I see him now as these words are writ. The black blood froze down his face. The eyes frosted over. How queer Death did seem preserved like that as if it was only a Temporary Station, as if I could have lit a fire beside him & his life would have returned to him like water to a dried-up creek after the rains.

But you must always have faith in Him above & His timely blessings, I tipped my sou'wester in thanks after I finally come upon the fringes of the woods. Only a stretch of thorny brush separated me from the road.

Gussie had no choice but to nose her way through it, she tossed her head but boldly persevered & come out the other side with her soft muzzle bloodied & some wisps of her forelock snatched from her brow & left hanging from a thorn like a ward against Evil Spirits. Them thorns was a merciless bunch, I did not escape their wrath either, they left my poor shins pecked & torn as a fighting cock's.

As I had rightly presaged that weather was a menace to me & all living things in general, I was forced to ride with my forearm held up before my eyes, peeping every now & then to check my passage. The rain run off my gutter front-brim like a stream sluicing down the foothills, O me & Gussie was far away now from them gentle plods we used to take to Shelby Stubbs's, them was innocent days I longed for with all my heart.

The windows of Mama's store glowed with lamp & firelight as we passed, my Mama was no doubt cooking, her hair damp & curled in the steam, her cheeks flushed red. How she then seemed a beacon of all things Safe & Good in the world. But we could not stop, we was threading between the icy puddles, under the great wind-tossed cottonwoods & when I looked down at my hands I seen they was spotted with blood as if decorated by a war-bound brave.

The lights of Peeper's tavern shined out as we arrived at Gussie's stable. I made her comfortable, freshening her water & feeding her so well I believe she thought her Horsey Dreams was come true. She nickered & bowed her head appreciatively though I could not help but note a haunted look in her eye, for had she not also looked upon Burl's broke body? Who is to say a horse cannot suffer from the agonies of memory just as keenly as us? I have long suspected they is very well versed on the subjects of Pain & Sadness, they wear it so plain in their eyes.

On leaving the stable & eyeing that simmering glow across the road I had me a strong suspicion Dud Carter was in Peeper's tavern. I had seen that place near every day of my life but never set a foot inside it. It was a squat log-house sit atop a small muddy incline & surrounded by tufts of witchgrass what bowed very stiff in the wind. The glass of its windows was cracked & dusted & patched up with greased paper, the steps & porch yawed like the deck of a half-sunk boat.

I was still unsteady on my legs as I approached, my slate heavier than it had ever felt around my neck. Now it was my own black & bloated face what sprung to mind, the same yawning wound atop my skull as Burl's, my own cold & lifeless eyes what stared back at me. Perhaps the Stranger was inside & Dud Carter already dead, do not think that notion did not occur to me.

I paused in the rain at the bottom of the porch. I could hear the voices of them men inside, it seemed to me they was raised in Merriment & Anger both, I was not yet versed in the vacillations of character that devilish drink did induce. I did not know how it might bring a man to his knees in anguish one moment & have him leaping for joy the next.

41

BRUNG TO SILENCE

WHEN I DID OPEN THE DOOR it was my nose took the first offense, all them rude vapors what flower full-bodied from sodden furs & sweat-rimed hats was partnered up with pipesmoke to hang in ghostly ruin above my head.

You might have mistook the origins of that stink for a shovel of Farmhouse Shit but it come from a crowd of half-drowned men, they was hunched at their tables before me, their backs steaming like a herd of shorthorn cows, their beards ambered with drops of liquor come weeping from their plump & wetted lips.

O how quick their wagging tongues was brung to silence as the door swung shut behind me. Rain dripped steady from my oilskin to the boards, I fancied it did echo in all that stillness loud as grapeshot. My own face was chaptered with streaks of dirt & blood, no doubt they took me for some woodling creature come to damn their Earthly Doings & curse their souls with ruinous spells.

I should say not a one of them was a stranger to me or I to them but that unnatural weather & the queer play of shadow & light from a fire burning in the grate was conspired to fray the faith of any trusting man. Their eyes was set hard upon me, O it is easy to forget how well a lively blaze might turn a friend to foe, all them wise & kindly lines upon a face soon scored deep as Death.

So it was I had no chance to take off my hat before several of them had laid a hand upon their weapons, they might have blown my head clean off had Tom Peeper not looked up from his doings behind the bar. He had himself a clasp knife, he was working on some lump of wood with shavings like snowdrift upon his sleeve when he did recognize me for the innocent I was.

Well, little man, said he, his voice come booming out across the room. If it ain't Yip Tolroy.

Them men blinked in confusion as old Tom stepped out from under the 4 lengths of rough-hewn timber what was generously considered a bar & put his arm firm around me. His manner was much changed from the morning, vanished was his somber tones & hangdog expression, his eyes was now loose with drink. Had I not just seen Burl laid dead in the woods I would have thought him found.

To hold such tremblesome news in your heart & keep it from them what ought to know is a Great Weight to bear, I did flinch like a fox in a trap at his touch & could not look him in the eye.

Ain't no need for nerves here, said he. I do reckon I am right in sayin this is your first time settin foot in my establishment is it not?

He spread his arms wide & looked about as if it was a Palace of Wonders he did present before me. It was no bigger than the store, the tables was bowlegged & the chairs a sad affair indeed, it was a wonder they held any weight at all. The roof was patched in places, a dinted pail collected the steady drip from a split shingle. As for that bar it was as simple as they come, it did boast no mirrors or rows of polished glasses as you see in them fancy saloons these days, it looked more like a mule's stall than anything I seen.

Tom Peeper stared back down at me, he was expecting a more excitable response than the blank look I give him, his brow was suddenly knit in concern, spittle did fleck the corners of his mustaches.

You is looking very hard done by, little man, said he. Put that slate of yourn away. You do not need no single word writ down to tell me you is in need of a good drink.

He clapped his hands & dipped back under his bar & set to preparing me whatever it was he spent his days brewing.

All them men was staring at me still, there did sit Wesley Peck & brothers Amos & Ned Seagrave. There was Vaughan Bilpin & Jack Keeves & Brody Waghorn also. Now my character was revealed they each did offer me a somber nod or tilt of their glass, though I could tell they was still disgruntled by the interruption. That was my first lesson in the habits of a Drinking Man – his fervent hope is to return to his own problems, he is not there to concern himself with the troubles of others.

But where indeed was Dud Carter?

I searched every shadow for him but he was not there & soon my eye was drawed to the walls, how queer it was to see them bedecked with shelves & them very shelves lined with so many dark & skillful carvings. Many I seen was horses so artfully crafted in their poses of majesty & triumph, some was risen on their hind legs & others was stilled by some timeless breeze, their strands of mane all a-riffle & well-muscled necks nobly twisted with stony eyes set upon some Distant Glory.

I had not knowed Tom Peeper for such a craftsman, he must have been hard at work upon another when I come in, there was little piles of dust & shavings I seen now upon the floor what skipped & jumped to the whistling of the wind outside.

Perhaps, thought I, this might in time come to resemble a merry scene but then I begun to see nailed to that same wall some rows of shallow & leathery bowls or so it looked to me. They was sprigged with a shock of dark & dangling fabric, at first I took it for some finespun cloth or lace.

But it was not long before I realized what they was, they was no delicate enterprise like the carvings but the wrinkled scalps of all them Indians what had fell beneath Tom Peeper's blade. The hair hung down,

I fancied I still seen the blood gone to brown, it fringed them scalps like woodworm.

How strange to think they was the tops to people's heads who had once walked & thought & lived out their lives. Where was the rest of them now but surely no more than bones laid out beneath some cold & distant sky, I cannot imagine any soul resting in peace in the knowledge their missing parts was made a trophy of & nailed upon a tavern wall.

42

TIME IS A PECULIAR THING

THAT OLD BLOODTHIRSTY SOLDIER WAS now come back &
in his hairy fist he carried a tin mug, it was brimful near spilled over
the rusted sides.

He handed it to me & without asking proceeded to remove my hat
& oilskin, he shook them out like bedding for the line & pegged them
on a trunnel drove into the wall by the fire.

Now, said he, bending down so that his face was level with my
own. Your daddy never come visit me in here but I always had a notion
you might, I seen that hunger in them eyes of yourn. I want you to
try that there in your hand & tell me it in't the finest thing to ever
pass your lips.

I will admit even the smell brung water to my eyes but all them faces
was again turned upon me, my Pride I knowed was in this moment at
stake. I had had no father to guide me in these Matters of Manhood but
I knowed well enough this was some rite I must perform.

I had no appetite for it with all I had just seen but I had less appetite
for ignominy, it had for so very long been my aim to be seen as nothing
more than a man in the eyes of my fellow men.

I swallowed & found that smell was no warning for the mighty explosion what burst in my chest, how I could trace every drop of its fiery passage through my innards! I opened my mouth & gasped for breath, I was sure I would burn the place to cinders with the fire what come roaring up my gullet. But that same fire was suddenly quelled, who could have guessed a taste so foul would lead to the spread of such wondrous warmth, it come drifting slow & lazy across my breast like a late blue shadow on a summer's eve.

Tom Peeper looked down at me, his eyes was crinkled at their corners. He clapped me hard on the shoulder, his hands was the size of rackets the old trappers wore & hard as them rawhide lacings. My drink did nearly leap out my grip but he did not notice, he only tipped back his head of dark curls to throw a great laugh to the ceiling.

Well, said he, dabbing at a tear in his eye, I do believe we have another convert.

It was then there come the slam of a door & in come Dud Carter from some rear entrance, he was awful unsteady on his feet, buttoning up his britches with 1 hand & holding a tin of liquor with the other. He did not see me right away, his eyes was half lidded as if he was just woke from some nourishing doze.

He did sit himself down low on a ladderback chair pulled away from the fire & them other men, his long legs was crossed at the ankle. He looked up then & seen me but did not seem in the least surprised, he watched on lazily as I clambered up onto the seat next to him from which my legs did dangle a good few inches off the floor.

His hat was tipped back on his head, his hands was steepled atop his little paunch.

Evening, Old Salt, said he. I must admit I is feeling about as handy as a pig with a musket.

He bowed his head until his chin was rested on his chest, it lolled there for several seconds before he snapped it back sharp & blinked at me like some varmint come into the day from his Dark Winter Rest.

Weren't no sign of Burl down in Gainesville, he said, so's we had ourselves a drink in them handsome taverns they got down there & now we come back here to finish up what we got started.

I was not interested in his stories, I wanted only to tell him of Burl's cruel end & have him understand the danger we was in.

We need to talk alone, said I.

He watched with a half-smile as he followed them letters I formed & once I was finished he looked up at me with his sparse brows raised as if he was the victim of a Great Surprise.

He let out a sharp bark of laughter & slapped the table so hard our tins leapt up as if woke by reveille.

We need to talk *alone*? spit he.

Amos Seagrave & Vaughan Bilpin turned in their seats to take a look at us, their brows was darkly furrowed, their mouths wreathed in pipesmoke. Them older boys did not care to be so disturbed but Dud Carter paid their reproach no heed.

What is it you have in mind, Old Salt? said he, his mouth & eyes was turned on me suddenly very cruel. Is you after gettin me to pucker up under the moon? Or now you had your first taste of that there liquor has you got a little horn on what you want to put to use?

He slapped his knee & his hat fell from his head onto the floor. He stared at it dumbly & then picked it up & placed it back at a devilish slant, grinning at me like a madman.

Or is it, he said, straightening a little, a little secret you was hoping to share with your old friend? Because we got ourselves a little secret don't we? We got ourselves a little secret that we need to keep secret or it won't be a secret no more will it?

How my blood did boil then, I was not so far from bringing my slate down upon his brainless head. If he could have seen Burl as I just had he would not be gabbing so very brazen, he would be quaking in his boots.

But I knowed then I could not talk to him, it would not end well of that I was sure.

And so with no other ideas come to mind I notioned I would behave the very same as he.

And so I did nothing but stare back at him & smile.

What is it you is smiling about? asked he.

I did not answer him.

He asked me again & demanded I tell him but still I did nothing. I did sit & smile & after a while this seemed to suit him very well. He smiled back at me & we begun to drink from our mugs until a feeling stole so quick upon me what I had not ever knowed before, it was as if I wore a sun-warmed crown balanced atop my skull & then that crown begun to slowly melt & fill my head with Bright & Golden thoughts.

Time did grow into a peculiar thing. I could not keep a hold of it, it did slip through my fingers & refuse to be held until I begun to feel as if no other people in the tavern existed but myself & Dud Carter.

To my shame I will admit I no longer thought of Burl. Like one of them old potions the Cherokee was said to stir, that liquor did act to rid me of my memories, I thought I was become a new man entire. Folk come through the door & traipsed their sodden selves across the boards toward the bar but I took of them no notice. I did hear voices grow loud & ever more boisterous but of them I took no notice either.

Me & Dud Carter was sunk in our own private pool we did not dare surface from, we stared & smiled & then we was laughing until we was near falling off of our chairs. I had not ever knowed the likes of it, all them worries inside my head was ripped clear & I was no more than water slipping through the hands of God Himself.

43

PISS LIKE THUNDER

HOW LONG THIS WENT ON I cannot say but I was finished 1 tin & a good way through another before I become aware of a deep burning beneath my waist, my bladder was fit to burst.

When I did drop down from my chair & my boots touched them old & sagging boards the room swum & swayed, I tried to take a step but my limbs was under the impression I was battling the currents of a fast-flowing river. My vision was narrowed to that of a blinkered horse, for all I knowed I might have been hauling timber in them northern woods of Canada.

O how Dud Carter did laugh, he brayed like a mule & stomped his feet to the rhythm of some Mad Band playing in his head. Drink can bring the meanness out of a man like rain will bring the rot out of a joist, he cares much more for cruelty than he does for kindness, that is until it is his own woes come for him in the dead of night & kindness is all he begs for.

I had left my slate on the table all dark & slick with liquor, several knurls of chalk was scattered wildly about. It did cause me some considerable disquietude to see my most valued property in such disarray but when I tried to reach to collect them my arms & legs was fallen deaf to my commands.

Slowly I picked my way across the room, all the roars & laughter of them men did rush my ears like waves upon a rocky shore. Once I reached that door it did tower over me, the handle was long ago wrenched from its moorings, you was obliged to hook your finger in a splintered little hole & pull it open in that way.

For some time I did apply myself to this delicate task before I was forced to admit defeat, I did not know who it was come to open it for me but he also put his boot to my back & shoved me good & hard onto the porch like I was a dog what had been whining for its freedom.

Outside the sky was wicked of cloud, the wind softed to a low & simpering moan. Hovering up over them distant mountains the moon was turned out very pretty, how I did wish to elect a corner of Her chalked & hollowed turf for my own keeping, it did look so calm & peaceful.

I breathed in deep & found myself somewhat revived, that bitter cold did act a tonic & returned to me a portion of my senses but still I could not unbutton me my britches, they was suddenly the most confounded & mysterious contraption ever created.

My poor fingers did grope & blunder, I thought I would piss down my leg until by some grace my member was sprung from his confines like a cuckoo at the strike of the hour & I was relieving myself onto the boards.

There will be hell to pay if I find myself slipped up in that, Old Salt, said Dud Carter.

The rogue had followed me out to savor my humiliation, he was propped up against the door with his clay pipe dangling from his mouth. He had brung out a lit twig from the fire, he held its burning tip up to the tuft of his tobaccy until it begun to smoke.

Goddamn, said he, you piss like thunder for such a little peckerwood.

Dud Carter thought his tongue the deliverer of many a Tremendous Quip, he doubled up wheezing thinly as if the journey from inside to out advanced 40 yrs on his body.

I paid that fool no mind but thought on how the sound of my piss did more resemble the drumming of hoofs upon the earth as it splashed my boot-ends. This I deemed one of my finer observations of the evening & vowed with great earnestness to correct Dud Carter.

I expelled them last irksome drops & was fumbling once more with the cursed buttons when I paused, the sound of drumming hoofs still in my ears. I looked down to see if by some queer turn I was still pissing but I was safely tucked away.

Now do not ask me what seized me then, perhaps God was once again looking down on me as He had been in the creek, but something did make me grab Dud Carter by the sleeve of his jacket & pull him sharp around the corner of the porch.

What in the holy hell are you doing?

He cuffed me across the head but I leapt up onto his back & clamped my hand over his mouth. He tried to buck me off but he was soon become stilled when I did point down as 2 horses come thundering up to the hitching rail, their nostrils streaming white & wraithlike vapors behind them.

I could not then believe my eyes, I seen that moonlicked hatchet blade tucked in the belt of the Stranger, it did flash with menace as he dismounted from his beast. No other sight could have turned my blood so cold, my hand was still clamped tight over Dud Carter's mouth, I felt his breath come hot & quick upon my palm.

We watched as they moved toward the porch, Dud Carter was pressed flat against the tavern's weathered logs with me still clung to his back like a barnacle upon the prow of a boat. Luck had it we was both still able to peer around the corner, my head stacked atop of his like 2 melons on a fruitstall.

We heard then the tavern door swing open, someone did step out onto the porch singing soft to theirselves with a voice as fair as a lady's. Only when they noticed that fresh company come trudging through the mud did they curtail their sweet serenade.

If you boys is come here to wet your gullets then you come to the wrong place. I 'spect old Tom gone & run dry of his potion by now.

It was Amos Seagrave's younger brother, Ned, who was come out onto the porch. He was a small fellow who liked to dress himself smart & offer up his opinions very ready, he was stood looking down at them men with his thumbs tucked into the pockets of his fancy weskit.

We ain't lookin for no liquor, come the gruff reply, it was the voice of the Stranger there was no doubt.

Well this ain't no hotel neither if that's what y'all are after, said Ned Seagrave, he did not know it but his spiteful tone would cost him very dear.

We watched then as the Stranger clumb up the steps, I knowed his lumbering gait well from down by the creek, it did belie his frightful speed. His companion appeared to have a dread of the mud, he did not want to dirty his boots & so skirted them steps looking for one of them timbers to tread what was not full-sunk beneath the muck.

Meanwhile the Stranger come up to Ned Seagrave, he made him look a little boy but Ned would not be cowed.

What you—

Ned Seagrave was bravely begun to protest but them two words was all what got said before he was silenced by the mighty fist of the Stranger, he did drop to the floor as if garroted from his horse, blood was soon pooled darkly about his head.

I regretted I could not minister to young Ned's wounds but we was far from nurses in that moment for the thinner man had found himself a route up. The Stranger opened the door & held it for him as if he was his beloved & in the glim of the tavern there was indeed some womanly quality to his frame.

I had not ever seen a man like him, his face was sharp & delicately lined, his eyes deeply shadowed, his hair long & graying at the temple but combed so thorough he wore it proud as a crown. Tucked beneath the band of his hat was a feather of some description, it was too dark to see its coloring but his face was lit well enough to reveal a queer shadowy stain spread behind his ear.

They walked into the tavern then & the door swung shut behind them.

Time for us to bolt, said Dud Carter.

Time indeed, thought I.

I dropped down from his back & we was both loose on our feet, our bodies was not our own but belonged to whatever furious flow of liquor & blood & fear what did course through our veins.

A roar of laughter come from inside as we spotted ourselves a gap where the porch railings had rotted & Dud Carter squeezed his thin hips through & dropped down onto the hill. He slipped in the mud & slid down a yd or 2 on his rear, cursing as he went.

I was about to clamber down & join him when it struck me like a mighty blow I did not have my slate. I was so used to carrying its weight around my neck I did feel its absence as if it was an amputated limb.

What the hell you waiting for? whispered Dud Carter.

No sooner was he standing than he was down again, it was like he was doing battle with some Vengeful Spirit. His face & hands was covered in muck, he resigned himself to remaining on his hands & knees & looking up at me.

I pointed back toward the tavern & waved my hand as if to write on the very air but Dud Carter only scrunched up his face in confoundment.

What in *hell* are you doing? he hissed again. If you is wanting to get yourself kilt then that is your own business but I ain't waitin around.

I watched him turn then & crawl & slide down the rest of the hill until he reached the road. He stood & motioned for me to join him once more but I would not leave that slate, I knowed I could not live without it.

44

SLATE

I CRAWLED ALONG THAT BUCKLED porch, its wood was soft with rot & moss beneath my knees. Back to the window I was come, I had to stand so's to look through its broke & blotted glass.

Most of the men was now hushed up, they had turned their dripping beards to them outsiders what was now leaned heavy on the bar & engaging Tom Peeper in a conversation I could not hear.

No one seemed to have noticed poor Ned Seagrave was not returned, he moaned soft in the shadows like a newborn kitten searching for some titty. If he growed any louder he would give me away, I hoped he would shut his mewling for now.

I watched the thin man with the feather in his hat as he took in his surroundings, O he did strike me as a Keen Observer indeed, his eyes looked to make familiar every face & detail, I seen them linger on my slate & chalks before moving back to study Tom Peeper. That stain was like red wine spilt down his face but he did not try to cover it, he did look a hard one to shame.

If it was not for that cursed pair Jack Keeves & Brody Waghorn I might have been able to hear what was been said but them boys was talking very heated between theirselves at a table near the bar, their faces red & fists clenched white before them.

They was still young, their blood easy made hot, they had took no notice of the newcomers & was arguing about the color of a bonnet on a girl they had seen earlier that day. It was White, claimed Jack, It was Blue, insisted Brody & before I knowed it they was on their feet. The color of that bonnet could not be settled & I thanked their ruined eyesight for it as they begun to butt heads like 2 old goats & beat at each other with their tin mugs.

Soon they was on the floor rolling around & every man was on his feet & roaring. I knowed this then for my chance & was through the door, crawling over them sour boards & through falling ash & swinging legs until I reached my table.

I made it easy enough & my fingers was but a second away from touching my slate when I was laid flat & breathless by a blow to the ribs & was forced to roll beneath the table before I was trod to death. A great hail of mugs then come raining down after me, chairs was split & the table was lifting & jolting & dancing a murderous jig above me.

I was sure I would see my slate fall & shatter before my eyes, I do not know to this day how it did not. So many writhing bodies was now on the floor, they was all bloodied & wild, I could not tell who was fighting who.

It was then I glimpsed through the great forest of legs a muddied face at the window. To my surprise it was Dud Carter, the old devil had come back, them small gray eyes was searching the room & when they found me crouched beneath my table it was no more than a moment later the door opened & there he come crawling toward me, his crooked fringe hung over his eyes, his long nose near touching the floor.

I knowed I was then rescued & was about to seek Dud Carter's helping hand when I felt someone took a hold of my leg. I turned & looked down to see it was the Stranger, he was laid flat on his belly, his beard was thick with blood & sweat, his cold & desperate eyes bored deep into my own.

You ain't goin nowheres, said he.

I did try to pull free but them fingers of his clung to my shin as if it was a cliff face he dangled from above his death.

Dud Carter now arrived, he seen I was snared & tried to tromp upon the fingers of that brute but it was as if they was not made of flesh & bone but some unearthly root what could not ever be broke.

Dud gripped me by my lapels & pulled & heaved, mud fell away from his face like scales but the Stranger would not let go. I seen him then reach for the handle of his hatchet. Dud Carter lost his grip on my coat, he did trip & stumble to the floor where he did sit staring dumbly as the Stranger raised up that blade, he was set to cut through my leg as if it was no more than a stick of cane.

Queer how it is sometimes when great violence is come your ways that time does appear to slow.

I seen my slate on the tabletop. How peaceful it did look waiting there for my words, like a friend what did sit well quiet & listening to your troubles. I reached out & took it in my hands. It had been warmed by firelight & was wet also with liquor so that its color had darkened to near black rather than them purple & blue notes of thunderous skies what was so often cast upon its face.

How strangely weightless it was become, it did feel no heavier than a feather as I raised it high above the Stranger's head. It had only ever been used for such quietness, I cannot say what Shelby Stubbs would have said to see it poised amid such Violence. What come into my head then I could not say but nothing could have prepared me for what would follow, I did not know it but my life was balanced on the edge of a Steep & Terrible drop, I was about to tip myself over.

I brung down my slate with all my might, it was the sharp edge of its corner what dug into the Stranger's bald & glistening skull.

That skin & bone was opened up like a keyhole, the darkness of his final thoughts faced me back before it did fill with blood & then begun to dash my face, its warm spray was iron-rich as it wet my lips & found its way into my mouth.

The Stranger's grip was turned suddenly slack, his hatchet dropped to the floor, the handle rocking slowly until it stilled itself, never to feel his grip again.

I had by then seen 2 dead men, poor Stubbs took by Time & Nature & only hours before Burl laid out froze & bloodied in the woods. O yes I had seen what a body looked like with life blown clear out of it but you must understand there is a very great difference between the look of a man who has let his life drift away & one who has had it snatched from him.

Yes Stubbs's eyes was cold & empty but Fear & Fright did not linger in them the way they did in poor Burl's, it was as if that sweet & innocent soul could not believe it himself that his life was come to such an end.

But let me now add it is different again to see a man dying by your own hand, for that was what I now looked upon.

O I looked into them eyes of the Stranger I had once seen so busy with life. He did look up at me still, his eyes was filled with confusion as they found mine but how strange it was to see the light start to leave them, how strange it was to know it was me what had vanquished it. How simple it was to end something so vast & complicated as a Life. It did end in a moment & the warm blood what had moved it through the yrs now leaked out on the floor.

Then them eyes went Still & Cold, they was no longer staring at me but I now think they held in their gaze the flaming Gates of Hell.

It was then that slowness was ripped away, I come to noise like I was sunk under water & shot bursting back to light & air. A great roar went up from somewhere, a gun was fired & a part of the ceiling come tumbling in on itself. Curses come flying like arrows from all directions but still I stood looking down at that body made lifeless by my own doing. I do swear I might have stayed there for the rest of time if Dud Carter did not grab me & we was then out the door & tearing down the steps of the porch, Dud near enough carrying me along with his great strides, the slate still held dripping & bloodied in my hand.

45

THE ENDS OF TIME

AND HE THAT KILLETH ANY man shall surely be put to death.

Them words was visited upon me with thunderous tumult, their echo strung like black bunting above the flight of my wicked soul. O yes rot set in my pith the moment I dealt the Deathly Blow, soon dark clouds was gathered above me like hooded saints, their sad & restive eyes did flash & dart as a flurry of bolts was pitched earthward by God Himself.

I hope you never took a man's life though if such a foul act beleaguers your spirit you will know the terrible cold what floods your very Blood & Bone. It is no wind what chills or rain what wets, no you cannot touch it & there it hopes to lie until the Ends of Time.

But it was done & now I found myself beside Dud Carter in Gussie's stable. How it was I got myself there I could not say, I could barely walk my legs was turned to air beneath me. But Dud was in a fearsome hurry, I had heard him curse them 2 beasts they had rode to Gainesville for being either spooked or stole, now he was kicking through the piss-sour straw & knocking over Gussie's bucket of water, she was our only choice.

That poor beast was shocked to see us, her lips did curl at the untimely intrusion but she did not have time to complain before all the sodden & creaking leather of her tack was once more heaped upon her back by Dud Carter. He then did lift me into the saddle & clumb up behind me, he took them reins in his hands & steered us out into the night.

Still Peeper's tavern blazed across the road with the wild cries of victory & defeat, now smoke did billow from its door & windows. As God is my witness I seen a man hold aloft a flaming chair & bring it down upon another's back. Did the Stranger's blood still slowly pool about his head & might it be brung to a simmer by them creeping flames?

Dud Carter was in no mood to tarry & find out, he dug his heels so hard into Gussie's flank she tore off at speeds I never knowed she could move. It is only because I was so small I stayed in the saddle, his wiry arms flecked with blood & ash wrapped around me, his sharp & jolting chin knocked against my hatless head.

All was a blur but still out the corner of my eye through Smoke & Shadow I seen there stalked a figure upon the porch. He was tall & thin & held a leg what had suffered some wound & caused him to limp. But his eyes was bent upon us of that I was sure, when we rounded the bend & headed toward town I seen that feather in his hat was singed & glowing like the plumage of that flaming bird they call a Phoenix.

46

OUT, DAMNED SPOT!

SOME YEARS AFTER SHELBY STUBBS'S death I had come to notice the tips of my fingers on my right hand was permanently stained white so often did I hold a piece of chalk. Even when I was not writing it could not be scrubbed away, a fine dust was made part of my skin & it is still so to this day.

But I will say I do so well recall looking down at my hands as we rode away that night, with Dud Carter's arms wrapped tight around me & his breath sour & heavy as a pig's in my ear. I recall how they did jounce limply in my lap & there was no tincture of white to their tips for they was sleeved in blood, so sticky & warm that no matter how I did wipe them across my britches it would not leave.

Come out, damned spot.

The famous words of that murderess did not strike me then for I was ignorant of the Arts & all them fine words writ down so long ago on that Damp & Windlashed isle. But my position these days after so many yrs gone by & age crept up on me like a catamount has afforded me such luxuries & when a traveling band did perform that dreadful scene not so long ago, I did sit in my seat & stare at my hands, I could have played that part better than any for I seen that blood besmear them just as it had done that night.

Later that very evening I could not sleep, I did sit at my desk & stare at the shutters closed in front of me. Bars of moonlight come slanting in & ribbed across the lacquered wood, it touched them many fancy things – bottles of ink, the timepiece I kept safe, scrolled in silver in its plush velvet case – what privilege had allowed me to own.

I heard then a stirring behind me, I looked & seen my wife was woke, her short hair tousled from sleep. But even her touch & whisperings could not tempt me back to bed. Her own hands was often cold, she could not help it, her past she said had made them so. She too had faced her trials, I knowed that well enough & so it did not fright her to see them ghosts trapped behind my eyes.

She often teased how little the yrs had changed me though I had seen the lines what now lingered upon my brow & the stiffness what had entered my joints & made me creak to rise on a morning. It was also the mornings when I lay most vulnerable to them memories, most think it is the nights what summons them but the dim glow of dawn through the curtains does always seem to call them forth.

I looked up at her from my desk, her curls was long since cut, she had give herself a boyish trim with scissors kept well silvered by her bedside. It had confounded some but I loved her more for it, she had not ever been one to listen to the opinions of others. This I had learned from her.

What is it? said she.

I shook my head but she was never so easily dissuaded.

You got no need to keep them thoughts to yourself.

The country lilt to her voice caused so many to wince but it only ever made me smile. I dipped a cloth in the bowl of water & rubbed clean the slate I always kept at my desk. She placed a hand upon my shoulder as she watched me write.

I am tired, I said.

She looked down at me & stroked my cheek, she knowed me for a liar but I have long knowed you must not lay the troubles of your past at the feet of them you love & expect them to be righted. There are some sorrows what must be Borne Alone.

47

LIKE A BABE

THE BOARDWALKS & BUILDINGS OF town come to view & Dud
Carter took a sharp right & followed a path of trampled brush through
a stand of scrub oak. On we went until eventually we come upon a small
clearing where there stood a structure the likes I had not seen before.

I had not knowed where Dud Carter lived, I thought perhaps he
took a room in Mrs. Cripps's boarding house but certainly I could not
have imagined this queer design before me.

It was a hut of sorts, its walls comprised of all manner of wood &
moss & reeds, all them scraps of nature wove together as if he was some
species of wingless bird who must build his nest upon the ground. The
roof was pitched on all sides, it was a crooked thing tilted skyward as if
in search of heavenly favor, though I knowed well enough God would
not confuse it for one of His own. Nor surely would He recognize the
condition of my own blackened soul, I had never felt so keenly His Eye
upon me.

Dud Carter pulled me down from the saddle, perhaps he feared I
would fall from my seat. As it was he was right to do so for when my
feet touched upon the earth, my legs was stole from beneath me and I
toppled over like a spire of ashes.

Here I lay so very cold, the wet earth pressed against my cheek.

Come on now, said Dud Carter. Get on up.

He tried to pick me up but my body was turned stiff & unyielding as a corpse, I must admit I wished I was one. So it was he propped me up against Gussie's leg like an ornament you might arrange on a lintel. Had Gussie moved I would have resumed my communion with the earth but as you well know by now she was the most loyal beast that ever did live, for all her moods there was no horse more kind-hearted than she.

Propped as I was I watched on in something akin to a trance as Dud Carter yanked at a short length of rope what attached to the side of his hut and a door – it looked to me like the headboard of a bed lashed to an array of other broke-up household articles – swung open on rope hinges. He had to stoop somewhat to enter, I watched him go in very furtive like a beast will its burrow.

I do not know how much time did pass but he come out with a gust of dark & fragrant earth, leaves must surely have served as his carpet in there. He had with him a mound of blankets, some was frayed & tattered but still he looked to have made good use of them.

He then returned inside but soon he come back out again & so it went on, he did swipe & grab whatever he could make of use.

Finally he was done, he had stacked a tin plate & a mug & a sheathed knife & 2 dinted pans what was near rusted through. I seen also a book, I could not read its title but it was a dog-eared piece, the pages was yellowed & folded as if he wished to return to some particular passages. I knowed it for the one his mama must have teached him to read with.

All these he did bundle into an old weather-worn saddlebag, his blankets he rolled up & fastened with a length of whipcord similar to what kept his britches up. That precious book of his he fit snug in the pocket of his riding jacket.

I seen then the effects of the liquor had been burned off by fear & fright & now sweat was run down his face & that mud what had caked his face come down in dark streaks.

Come on, he said again. We ain't got time.

Still I could not move, I did not want to.

He reached down then & took me in his arms like a babe, my nose was briefly buried in the smoke-sweet bouquet what lifted from his blackened collar. He placed me in the saddle & took his seat behind me, he gathered up them reins & snapped them in the cold night air as we sped off beneath the risen moon.

48

GET THEE BEHIND ME, SATAN!

I HAD TOLD DUD CARTER of how I found Burl & we had come to no agreement but in truth we both knowed there was no choice left us but to leave Heron's Creek.

Poor Burl lay froze & bloodied in his hollowed trunk & the Stranger lay felled in Peeper's tavern. How quick a life can be made to look a stranger to he who lives it, the map he once followed now inked & blotted with ugly shadings & misdirections.

So it was me & Dud Carter left that land behind, we fled through the town, past the blacksmiths & the boarding house & all them softly glowing lights of cooling fires in silent parlors. No doors did open or curtains twitch to see us go, we was no more than ghosts.

Behind me Dud took a flask from his pocket, he swigged long & hard, breathing fire back into the night. As we vaulted a branch what had come down in them howling winds he tilted his face heavenward.

Get thee behind me, Satan! cried he.

I come to learn these was the times Dud Carter savored most, when his life was imperiled & all he knowed upheaved so that the Unknowed once more lay spread before him.

He offered me the flask but I could not stomach it. I wish I could have shared in his thrill of escape but what I found come unbid to my sight as my bones was shook by Gussie's hoofs was no longer them images of death & ruin but of my Mama sit by the fire.

There she was, her eyes looking into the flames as she had the night before last. How long ago it did now seem, how quick Time had been twisted & wrung of all its logic.

Was she sit staring into the fire now? Was they still them same Strange Flames she spoke of last time? Why now did she suddenly strike me as a Lost & Lonely creature who had never give her heart to the under-standing of another? Why was it now as I rode through darkness away from her – an Outlaw with the blood of a man on his hands – that she no longer seemed that fierce tyrant but a broke little thing?

It may seem strange to say that it was in this moment I come to for-give my Mama for any wrongs she had commit against me & that when I was a young boy & thought she did hate me, I was wrong. I knowed it then as I know it now, she could not love as she wanted to, she did not have the words even though her heart was filled up with feeling.

O how the tears did stream down my face only to be dashed away by the wind as we struck out across fields & meadows unknowed to me, I thought never to return again.

49

HOW SMALL WE IS

GUSSIE HAD NOT EVER RUN so long or hard before, we did not slow until them Blacks & Blues of night was begun to wash away & the day come in unspoiled above us.

All that night I had kept my eyes on the skies & the infinite sprawl of stars did pour down their wondrous light. But I was not moved to see them, no indeed gone was the days where glory might reach me by their distant glow. I had once imagined them to be the eyes of all them had lived Good & Honest lives but here they bore down with white-hot malice, they was an accusive pack what heaped guilt upon my Murderous Heart.

God had surely designed the dawn so pure an expanse to further wound me. Or such was my thoughts, perhaps a pattern is now come to your attention I was myself too blind to see. There is nothing like Tragedy & Despair to drive a man into such violent solipsism, he thinks himself the center of all the world.

How unfair it all did seem.

O it is so very hard not to turn to pity & ride all them bittersweet rivers what naturally flow from such ugly pleasure.

Beneath that dawn sky as we rode along a dusty track where spindly pines struck skyward from the mossy earth, I begun then to bemoan all the hardships of my life: If I had not been so small, if I had a head of hair to run my fingers through & a tongue to deliver my thoughts, would I be here now in this state of Fallen Grace?

Such thoughts is a worm with the Devil's wriggle in his tail & your mind no more than a rotted apple for it to gorge on. And so it was my sorry selfdom was turned to rage against the World & He who made it.

I did then pull out my slate from its sling & throw it upon the passing earth hoping it would crack & that crack would well mark my commitment to a life of Silence & Saintly Reflection. If I had remembered my pockets was filled with knurls of chalk I would have throwed them too.

But that slate did not crack.

Dud Carter pulled Gussie to a halt & walked her back to where it lay. We both of us looked down at it in the mud of the road, its corner still darkened with blood. We looked at it a long time & I was only stirred from my reverie when a breeze did blow through all them canted pines around us & the clouds scudded pink across the dawn sky & I felt Dud Carter's hand rest gentle upon my shoulder.

I knowed then all of life would continue on as it always had. O no it would not stop to take my woes into account. How small we is, thought I, in the scheme of His great plans.

50

THE GREAT SMOKIES

DUD CARTER HAD CLUMB DOWN from Gussie & picked up my
slate, his bootheels was clot with mud. He had stared into it as one might
a looking glass or windless lake, who knowed what he seen there but my
Good Companion had not said a word all that long night & there is no
words I have what can describe my gratitude toward him for this kindness he showed me.

With the sleeve of his riding jacket he dusted off its face & handed
it to me. I took it sheepishly, my eyes lowered & filled with contrition.
He did not judge me for my lapse, he only smiled before he clumb back
onto Gussie & I did feel the fold of his arms around me as he took up
the reins & settled us once more into a gentle walk.

Even if Dud Carter had talked I would have had no answers for any
questions, I would not have had the strength to put my chalk to slate. It
was silence I had needed & he had knowed it all along.

Looking back I will say now that perhaps this was the moment me
& Dud Carter begun to form ourselves a Bond like Brothers. You may
be surprised to hear me say as much, me & Dud had not knowed each
other so long as all that. But if you is lucky in this life there will come a

time when all your own Hopes & Hurts & Fears & Joys & Longings is reflected back at you from another, you know they have kept stowed in the dark of their head them very same secrets as you.

That don't have to be no woman you bed down with, often as not it might be a boy you growed up by or in my case a young man you happened across at the Right Time. This Right Time is a mysterious thing, it don't mean nothing to no one who was not a part of it, again words must on occasion fail you, they only got so much room in their small beating hearts.

Let me only say I spent near all of my life feeling so very uncomfortable in the presence of every soul I come across. Shelby Stubbs proved to be a wondrous exception but even in his company I could not ever truly be myself. Me & Stubbs was friends no doubt but we was also Teacher & Student, the span of yrs between us never allowed for that Easy Feeling what comes between 2 souls setting out on their lives together & looking at the world from the same position.

If this sounds to you like a marriage then I don't mind admitting to there being some resemblances to one, Dud Carter was like no other I ever come across, O it was in them eyes of his, not in how they looked at me but how they did not.

Everyone else seen my Differences right away but Dud didn't hardly take no time to consider them. Perhaps you might argue he was too busy working on his own Thoughts & Problems, selfish ass that he was, but I knowed we had both spent Hard & Lonely yrs fending for ourselves, a part of it might be so simple as to have your life bore witness to. A witness can just stand & watch but already we had stepped in the river & changed its flow if you might allow me to put it that way, we had no choice but to ride it together now.

I turned then & he seen a smile on my face, it was no flashy grin but quiet & simple, directed at Nothing & No One in particular.

What you thinkin on? said Dud Carter.

He was looking down at me, his own lips was curling in amusement. But he did not need me to answer him, he knowed very well what was behind my eyes.

We is quite a pair, ain't we, Old Salt? said he.

I nodded. O yes we was. That is the connexion I is talking on now, our thoughts did travel back & forth like birds along a branch. My wife may one day read these words but I cannot lie, I do not know her mind as well as I did Dud Carter's then.

All them hours of hard riding was brung us deep into the wilds & all had begun to shift around us, the hills steepening & the bends sharpening as we wove between dense woodland, the branches overhead now draped with old hanging moss & alive with the caroling of the woke birds in the treetops.

So to speak the onset of day had returned me to my Corporeal Self. For a good many hours my body had all but ceased to exist, it was a numb & empty vessel. But now I realized my legs was aching like never before, the cold & my saddle was in cahoots in their cruel hopes to make me weep. Each of Gussie's steps was an agony, if I could have cried out every second I gladly would have done so.

It appeared Dud Carter was a more seasoned rider than I, if he was in pain he hid it well. Since I had throwed my slate down he had slowed Gussie to a walk. I felt them awkward bones of his ribs expand as he breathed in long & hard through his mighty nose.

Said he, Soon's we get beyond these woods we'll see us some mountains what I heard called the Great Smokies. You cross them & you find yourself in Tennessee.

I had not ever imagined I would cross into any other state, I must admit this news did hurt me afresh. How far did we have to go before we was safe? How far did we have to take ourselves before we shed our old lives & was give a chance to start anew?

I turned to face Dud Carter but he did not look at me, his eyes was red with Drink & Weariness, his hair was windblown & his cheeks still grimed with Dirt & Blood but he looked so queerly peaceful I thought him then almost holy in his aspect.

We walked on in silence & watched as the sky continued to brighten, the clouds reddening on their undercarriages & the woods furnished with an ashy light, the earth steaming in places & stirring up a low-lying fog.

I will not say my spirits was raised but something in Dud Carter's face told me my core was not blacked & burned all the way through, I would not ever find my way back to the boy I had once been but there might be hope for me yet.

51

SILENCE GRIPS THE TOWN

THE ROAD WAS BECOME CHOKED with trees as we clumb to the top of a crest & there we come upon the beginnings of something resembling a small town.

It had been some time since we had seen any sign of such life & I felt Dud's arms stiffen & seen his fingers worry the reins, that damp leather did squeak out like a starved little nursling chick.

We was slowed to a plod as we come upon a chapel but there was no soul present, no noise what spoke of lives in the living. It was a simple enough build shaded by tall & silent oaks with dry & brittling beards of hanging moss swaying from their branches.

To my eyes that chapel looked no older than a day or 2, there was still the sharp scent of fresh-cut pine in the air, the wood yet to be treated or stained but drying out in patches from last night's rain.

The road did then broaden & next we come upon a string of little log-cabins lined up alongside each other. There was a large hog-pen fenced around with good strong lengths of timber though it was most curious to see no hogs enjoying its great bounty of mud. There was some stables here as well, also newly built but the gates was left open & empty, straw scattered about the entrances & white dust & siftings whisked off in the breeze.

I ain't come across this place before, said Dud Carter looking suspiciously about.

We walked past more empty cabins until we come upon a store of sorts. It did not boast no wooden sign like my Mama's but only STORE was writ in crude letters painted white above the door.

Dud Carter brung Gussie to a stop, he tried to peer through the dusted glass of the windows but them shadows was too thick to make sense of its insides. Perhaps there was a face looking out at us, we would not have knowed if there was.

We could use ourselves some breakfast, said Dud Carter. I am hungrier than I ever been in my life.

I looked down at the road & noticed the earth was become lighter than I was used to. The dark brown mud of Heron's Creek was now replaced by a fawn-colored loam what looked to me more like sand. Gussie shifted her weight & little spirals of dust clumb up off of her hoofs.

Dud Carter then swung his legs from the saddle, all the warmth was leached from my back as the cold come rushing in his place. He stretched his long shanks & rubbed some heat into his thighs before walking on over toward the store.

There was no porch nor any such sophistications added to that structure. Its wood was not so fresh as the chapel or them stables but it was new enough to see its bands of grain run smooth & clear along its width.

Dud Carter stepped right up to the door & knocked. His feet shuffled impatiently when there come no reply & so he knocked a little louder & then louder again but it was no more than silence what greeted him.

He looked back at me & shrugged & then turned the handle, the door did swing open most obligingly & he thrust his long neck inside.

Got yourself some customers out here, he said. We ain't eaten for a good stretch & we was looking for some refreshment.

Again there come no more than silence. He turned back to me & then looked down the road at the other dormant cabins, his pale brows hoisted high.

Don't seem to be a soul here, he said.

I watched as he marched into the store & disappeared from view. I did not know how he could be so brash, I clambered down from Gussie & hobbled with my sore legs over to the store & looked around me again before I followed the devil inside.

52

NOTHIN AIN'T HARDLY EVER WHAT IT SEEMS

I FOUND DUD CARTER CHEERILY helping himself to some salt pork & cheese & he had found himself a great big cooked ham what he had clutched to his hip.

I hurriedly got out my slate & tugged at Dud's sleeve.

They's people living here, said I.

I know that, said Dud Carter with his mouth filled up with cheese. But they ain't here now is they?

I had just murdered a man & now I was turned to thievery also, how heavy my heart did weigh inside my chest.

Dud Carter moved behind a low wooden counter, he knelt & set to rummaging about. A moment later he come back up with a crock of lard in his hands. He took off the lid & dipped his finger in & tasted it, nodding his approval.

Now, said he, leave this to me & you just go on and keep a-watch at the door an let me know if you see anyone comin along.

I seen him eyeing up the shelves of other jars. He flashed me an ugly grin & patted me on the head.

God has chose to bless us, he said.

This don't seem like a good idea, I said.

He scoffed so that he spit out a bit of food.

You don't think much of any of my ideas so why don't you jus go on an do as I say.

I knowed my remonstrations was useless, I left the store & looked anxiously about. My stomach churned at the thought of some folk emerging bleary-eyed from their homes & finding their store being ransacked. But all was silent save for a whippoorwill's sharp notes needling down from the trees somewhere near the chapel.

After a little while Dud Carter emerged from the store, his pockets was bulging with stole goods, he looked mighty pleased with himself. I shook my head in disgust at his thievery but he was shameless.

You know, Old Salt, you will have to eat at some point. You will fall off this nag of yours if you don't indulge in these here vittles I bought us.

I took exception to his calling Gussie a nag & I told him I knowed he had not bought a thing.

Well I suppose that is correct but that don't mean you shouldn't be thankin me right now.

I watched as he distributed some of the goods in his saddlebags. He wrapped the cooked ham in his bundle of blankets & tied them up again & then he was wafting a piece of cheese beneath my nose.

You will not last long if you do not succumb. Starvation is a powerful force indeed, said he.

I am proud to say I did decline, I did not need more Sin heaped upon my soul but I will say that sour & empty knot inside my stomach told me I could not hold out forever.

We left the town behind us & continued on along the road, it was of a kind what could not make up its mind. It snaked along, clumb up & then sloping down, them woods growed thicker as we went. We sometimes had to part the hanging moss like drapes if the branches leaned over the road above us.

My stomach ached now as much as my legs as I heard Dud Carter bite into an apple, I turned to see the juices run down his pimply chin.

He winked at me when he caught me watching him, that Old Mischief was returned to the corner of his eye. I seen he had a sizable chunk of salt pork wedged between his teeth, he looked a most disgusting specimen.

You ever think God got you to kill that coot back there? said he. You bin sulkin now for long enough I reckon an it occurs to me you ain't proply thunk this whole thing through.

I felt him looking over my shoulder as I wrote, his eyes fixed on my slate. By now he had come to know my writing as well as any, even if my hand was cold & numbed as it was & gone awful slanted because of it.

I said, Since when was you an authority on what God wants?

I could not see him but I felt him shrug & could well imagine him raising his foolish brows.

If you do not think me an authority then it would appear you must think yourself one, Old Salt.

He took another bite of his apple, I felt a drop of its juice upon my head.

If I do not know God's meanins, he continued with his mouth full & gesturing with the core of that apple, then I don't see why it is you think you know. Unless you is reckoning I am the more stupid of us an you the great Wise Man? I sure ain't seen any evidence of it. Let me remind you I is the one sittin here with a full belly.

He then belched loudly with great relish & blew it so that I smelt the sour contents of his stomach. Still I did not rise to his goadings.

A full belly is more a sign of greed than it is of any wit, I said. Especially when them fillings is stole, I added with what I thought a smart little flourish.

Is that so, said Dud Carter. There was me thinkin a full belly was jus Common Sense. You ever think you spent too much time with them thoughts of yours an you got em all goosed?

You ever think you spent too little time with yours?

He scoffed.

You would not think I done rescued that piece of slate after you throwed it down a ways back like a babby tired of his toys. Now here you is usin it to insult me. If it was not for me you'd be back to pointin & noddin & clickin or whatever it was you used to do to have folk understand you.

I did not say a thing but I knowed well enough Dud Carter did need no reply to keep on talking.

You just remember what I was talkin on earlier, he said. You ain't always got to figure His ways straight off. He likes to have them lessons of His revealed slow sometimes, jus so you really learn em good.

He tossed that apple core into the woods & begun rummaging in his pockets for his pipe.

Remember, Old Salt, said Dud Carter, I done lived a few more years than you on this Earth & I can tell you nothin ain't hardly ever what it seems.

53

MR. EDER

WE HAD BEEN ON THE MOVE again for around an hour when in the distance a little cloud of dust was risen up & a crowd of people come trudging our way. We was hemmed in by woods on either side, the only way to avoid them was to turn right around & head back the ways we come but that was no option either of us knowed we could take.

Some was on horseback but there was a good few women & young girls walking along besides. Surely these was the residents of that Empty Town, some communal calling or pilgrimage had roused them from their beds & now they was returning.

Dud Carter shuffled in the saddle behind me, I felt the coarse weave of his riding jacket against the back of my head. We was both struck by that unease like your guts is give the wings of a turkey or fowl what could not fly but will flap & beat about in panic.

Dud wrapped the pork & cheese in a square of muslin he had acquired & tucked them in his pocket.

Well, said he, it looks like we got ourselves some company at last.

It was an old man we seen leading the group, he was not on horseback but striding with a long staff held in 1 hand & I could see the strap across his chest what held an old flintlock fast against his back & a powder horn slung across his shoulder. Them men on horseback around him was also carrying their weaponry very brazen laid out across their saddles for all to see.

We moved on very slow, Dud Carter begun to whistle a lively tune like he thought it any ordinary day what had found him in particular Good Spirits. When we come within twenty yds or so that old man raised up his hand in greeting, he let it linger there a good long while like he was sworn some kind of Oath or Promise.

Dud Carter brung Gussie to a halt, he had deemed it best we wait until that party of souls was come to a stop before us.

The old man sported a forage cap of sorts with a rusty buckle above its blunt peak & he had growed himself a long white beard what was shot through with streaks of gray & yellow. He was thick about the chest & his staff was planted firm in the ground. I did not care for the look of him, he had what you might call a Disagreeable Mien.

He looked up at Dud Carter & then paused to study me a long while. Who would not be insulted by the scrutiny of such a dirty man, he was shameless as a pig as was all of them behind him – 2 young men, 3 women & 4 little girls – they all did the very same. How my face did burn to have so many eyes fixed upon me.

The old man then cleared his throat and took to talking. Somehow his mouth did barely open when he spoke, his jaw was near rusted shut. But still them words come out at a great volume, it was as if he spoke through cupped palms. He told us his slave done run off, a man under his own command what had a rare nerve to defy the terms of his proud ownership and in these words he spoke I seen the hatred of his heart & the yrs that it had run wild & took away any goodness like a flooded river will its banks.

I did pay a handsome price for him, said he, he's a damn fine specimen & we can't find him nowheres. But if that warnt enough he stole hisself a sum of my own hard-earnt money to boot.

He shook his head & spit out a yellow streak of tobaccy juice onto the road. He continued to Curse & Condemn the soul of which he spoke, O there is no occasion fit to serve the wickedness what left his lips, them words he did use to heap heavy shame on already bruised & broke backs & I will not have them sully these good pages now or ever.

No I had never heard no man talk so hateful of another before. Of course you will know there has since come & gone our good President with his face carved from such Sad & Lonesome stone. O he brung down God's Good Word for all to see, yes indeed each man is created Equal & by this One & Only measure I reckon I can hear that old man hotfooting it about on the coals of hell beneath me now, his staff no more than cinders in his hand. But this weren't about to enter his mind now, set firm as he was on what he deemed his Property.

So you boys ain't happened to see him? he asked.

I am afraid we ain't, sir, said Dud Carter.

The old man shook his head & smiled, his eyes blinked slow & rueful.

Well, said he, I thank you for your time.

He pinched the peak of his cap & was ushering on all them other folk he led when he looked up at Dud Carter & something caught his eye, I knowed then it was that pork I had seen stuck between his teeth earlier. I ought to have told him but now it was too late, suspicions had been woke.

The old man stopped & I seen his fingers did tap out a little dance upon the stem of his staff. Suddenly he turned to address 1 of them riders behind him.

Why don't you get everyone back to the town, Lyle? he said.

He smiled down at a little tow-headed girl & placed his palm on her silky head.

These young girlies is gettin restless, said he, smiling up at us.

The man named Lyle might well have been his son & everyone else there some relation or other, now I looked close they all of them did share the same sharp nose & thin bloodless lips. Lyle eyed me with a dark &

brooding glare before he begun to herd up the others & took them on down the road back toward that cluster of dwellings.

The old man watched them go with a smile, he did look briefly enchanted by some Sunny Vision he was conjuring for himself though when he turned back to us his mouth turned down quick at its corners & the sag of skin by his left eye twitched like the wings of a trapped moth.

My name is Charles Eder, he said, and I run that store over yonder. You boys must have passed it by I'm reckonin?

I felt now one of Dud Carter's knuckles dig hard into my back.

Can't say we seen ourselves a store, Mr. Eder, said Dud Carter, shaking his head sadly. To be honest, sir, we been in somethin of a hurry ourselves. You see we have ourselves a similar problem to you.

Is that right? said Charles Eder, pulling thoughtfully on his long & foodstrewn beard.

Yessir, said Dud, we also lookin for a runaway. He taken us on a right wild chase up & down these mountains. He is a crafty one like yours but I got me a feeling we is hot on his heels now.

Charles Eder nodded slow & then spit on the ground again. He looked at it for a time & when he looked up I seen his eyes was banded black & gold like some taloned bird's.

Tell me, where is it you boys is come from?

O we come a long ways, Mr. Eder, said Dud Carter. A long, long ways indeed.

Charles Eder nodded again. Them eyes of his was uncommon quick as they flicked between us.

You boys got yourselves some names? I like to know me who it is I'm talkin with.

I felt another knuckle dig into my back.

You is just like mine own daddy, said Dud Carter. He was a man of proper manners also & I can well imagine he would have liked you a great deal, Mr. Eder. He's dead now of course but I reckon he's lookin down now & admirin your many qualities. His name was Henry Brooks & he give the very same to me & this here is Wendle Jones.

Charles Eder looked at me again. He took a step closer so we was not so far from face to face, I swear I could smell his foul breath.

Wendle Jones? said he, grimacing a little.

Yessir, said Dud, Wendle Jones is correct. And let me say you is quite right to pull that face. Wendle here is a strange-looking critter & it takes a while for the eyes to adjust.

Charles Eder stroked his dirty beard some more.

Don't he talk?

Yessir he does, said Dud, but he is very select with his words, he does not like to waste them. I would be surprised if you was to get a word out of him now but I must admit I have not been able to shut him up this last hour.

A genius could not have figured what route Dud Carter was aiming at to take us out of this situation, though I do not say it to suggest Dud Carter was a genius himself. If I ever doubted his lying nature I would no more, not a single thing what left his mouth was true, it seemed to me he was saying the first things what come into his damn head. Still his mind was working awful sharp, I would be a liar myself if I told you I was not impressed.

So there's 2 of em loose in these hills, said Charles Eder.

Them's the calculations, said Dud.

That they is, said Charles Eder, that they is.

He reached over & stroked the long barrel of his old flintlock. His powder horn was a cracked & mottled piece the color of old bones. Them eyes looked quick between us again & then suddenly he was smiling so very cordial & gamesome that he might have been our great cohort.

You boys look like you could do with a bellyful of edibles, he said. Would you care to join me & I'll get my Bessie to cook you up a plate of good eatin? My Bessie is a angel & I swears you will be glad to be acquainted with her cookin.

For the first time Gussie did shuffle nervously, her ears was fine points turned up toward the sky. I have said before a horse is no Ignorant Beast, she had seen Charles Eder's queer smile as clear as I & did not care for it. I looked down at my hands & seen my knuckles was near bursting out of their skins but still Dud Carter's voice come even & knowing. He smiled down at Mr. Eder as a preacher might from his pulpit.

That is awful kind of you, sir, said he, & I do not doubt for a second your Bessie is a angel come straight down from God's Good Kingdom. All them ladies was here but a minute ago looked like fine creatures of God also, I bet you is proud of each an every one. But I do regret to say we got our orders & our employer would not much care to find us with our buttons fit to burst off of our shirts.

Charles Eder let out a little wheeze of a laugh.

I understand, son. Ain't nothin like a rested mind after you done finished what you set out to do.

You're right there, said Dud Carter, who was himself now laughing away also.

Charles Eder wore a long brown coat, the sleeves was decorated with some queer red piping & he run a dirty thumb up & down a row of silver buttons what just then begun to glint in the rising sun. He then looked up at the yellowing sky.

Sun comin up nice today, he said. Reckon it will be comin up nice everywhere.

His eyes then returned from the skies, still creased with cheer and goodwill it seemed.

Now just remind me where was it you boys said you was from again?

For the first time I felt Dud Carter shift in the saddle, it was a question he did not care much to answer.

Well it's so far away, Mr. Eder, that we can barely 'member it ourselves, said he. But it comes to me now, it is right near Plummer Mill. Mr. G. W. Bates owns the estate that way & it is that good & noble man who we is to report back to.

I ain't heard of no Plummer Mill before, said Charles Eder, all his smiles was now turned to ash.

I 'spect you haven't, sir, they do not like to draw attention to theirselves over that way. They is a quiet people & do not much care for any disturbances.

Charles Eder stuck his thumbs in the waistband of his britches & rocked back on his heels, them dark eyes of his dancing between us all the while.

Is that so, said he.

I turned to see Dud Carter nodding & smiling & then felt myself do the same.

There then come a great pause in which we did nothing but look at each other. Charles Eder appeared to be making some calculations in his head, I could not help but think he knowed us for the caitiffs we was. How long that pause did last I could not say but a sweat had snapped out on my brow by the end of it. Dud Carter though was still unruffled, I thought his blood must have run cold.

Well, said Charles Eder finally, if you git your hands on what's mine then I trust you 2 will apprehend him. He got hisself a mark here just below his left eye & he answers to the name of Solus.

O yes, Mr. Eder, you can rely on us for that. We'll be keepin an eye out for your Solus.

Mr. Eder nodded & then pinched the peak of his cap again. Without another word he walked past us, his firm stride & staff rucking up the dust of the road.

Only a guilty man does tear off & so it was we plodded very gentle on. But when I turned to look back behind us I seen Charles Eder standing in the middle of the road, his staff was rooted firm in the ground, them banded eyes watching us as we went.

54

REST FOR THE WICKED

GUSSIE WAS BONE-TIRED. SHE HAD run all night with the promise of rest but now she was back thundering up into them hills, her hoofs all gaumed up with mud. How she must of craved a good watering & an honest feed but Dud Carter would not relent.

It was not out of cruelty he drove her so hard but since departing the company of old Mr. Eder Dud had admitted to having some misgivings on the Humor of that fellow.

Twice we had hid in the woods & seen that man on horseback named Lyle go galloping past us down the road.

That old goat back there does not strike me as a man who is very regular in the practicings of forgiveness, said Dud Carter. I do not believe he would hesitate to put a bullet in us.

I turned & searched his face for some sign of remorse but there was none to be found – we had rode to escape death & danger in Heron's Creek & now here we was in the thick of it again as a result of his wretched thievery. But Dud Carter was one of them souls what refused to see such links, he would always be the Innocent Man.

This was all most unfortunate, Old Salt, said he. A man given to such strong suspicions is not fit to build a town in this good state. Mark my words it will no longer be standing soon enough. It is no wonder that group he led looked so goddamn miserable under his command.

He shook his head & sighed.

When will our winds change, Old Salt?

I did not answer him, to indulge them musings of his was to sign a good portion of your life away.

We rode on until the sun was risen full & slanted through the boughs & moss. It was warmer than it had been for some time though what at first felt pleasant soon made my head feel awful heavy & my eyes burn with all them hours gone unslept, my head did keep drifting back to knock against Dud Carter's chest.

I tried to keep my eyes open but them passing trees was all begun to blur & spin, I snatched Gussie's reins out of Dud's hands & brung her to a walk.

What is it? asked Dud.

Wearily I took out my slate.

We need to rest, said I.

Dud Carter looked up & down the road, only the birds called out & a cool breeze blew little eddies of dust into the woods. Sweat did drip from our faces, he would not have cared to admit it but Dud was in no better condition than myself.

They's likely a creek runnin through these woods, he said. We'll get this girl watered an fed an take an hour of rest ourselves an then we'll get goin again.

We peeled off into the woods, the sun did battle to sluice through the tangle of branches, it was so dark & damp the reek of wet earth was enough to make me bury my nose into my shirt. I will admit that did not smell much better neither, how I then longed to have my Mama ordering me about with a pail of fresh water to get scrubbing. When you leave home it is awful queer what things you miss.

But what Dud Carter had said was soon proved to be true, we come upon a creek, its waters was slow but clear & Gussie bent her head to it

& quenched her terrible thirst. We did not wait to fill up the flask but did the same, them waters was frightful cold & near burned your throat to drink but we was not complaining, that water was a heavensent balm to caress our dry & scratching innards. O there is no feeling like it, we drunk at that creek until our bellies was fit to burst.

Once we was done I thought we would get to our resting but just then Dud Carter begun to strip off all his clothes, before I knowed it he was naked as the day he was born.

I never seen a man wear just his own skin before, his pecker was a shriveled fellow what poked out from a tawny bush of hair. He took his member by its end & begun to stretch it out.

You ride long enough in a saddle hard as that an you will turn yourself into a woman, said he.

It was the first time I ever seen another Man's Parts, I had not knowed hair was meant to grow there. I watched with a dark fascination as Dud crouched low in them waters & begun to scrub at himself, he hooted like an owl at the chill of it.

After a while he turned to me.

Ain't you washin yourself?

I had took a seat against the bole of a tree, I shook my head & he eyed me like I was no better than a rat.

I ain't havin you stinkin up the place. Come on down here an wash yourself.

I shook my head again, I was afeared I did not look as I was meant to.

I is deadly serious, Old Salt. If we is sharin that horse then I ain't havin you give my nose grief the whole ways. I'll come up there & strip you off myself if I has to.

So it was I found myself pulling off my shirt & trews, I knowed well enough Dud Carter would do it & if I was to strip then I would be doing it in my own good time.

Dud Carter watched then as I walked on down to the creek.

There really ain't a hair on you, said he, his eyes was wide with wonder.

I stopped & covered myself with my hands, I should have knowed it was his aim to shame me.

Now now, Old Salt, I ain't teasin you. There's plenty of folk what is built different in this world, there ain't no use in hidin it away. Come on in the water & git yourself clean.

I hurried into that water to save him staring at me any more. That creek was surely the coldest on earth, it took away my breath, my ribs shrunk up & caged my pounding heart. But I could not deny it was a great relief to feel it cool & soothe all them hot & bothersome places what a long ride does cause.

Nice ain't it? said Dud Carter.

He had sit himself down & was scrubbing at the sole of his foot with a creek stone. He looked up at me, there was the beginnings of a smile upon his lips.

I don't suppose you put that thing of yours to use yet?

My slate was over by the tree, I could not ask him what he meant but he seen my confusement writ plain enough across my brow.

I means you ain't pleasured a lady yet with that there danglin between your legs has you? said he.

Aside from such conversation I had overheard as a boy, I will admit my knowledge of such matters was very poor, I had not had a soul to discuss such things with in them yrs when such thoughts come unbid to your mind. I had been forced to reach my own conclusions but there was plenty what remained a mystery to me.

I shook my head.

Well, said Dud Carter as he carried on scrubbing at his foot, there ain't no shame in that. You is still young & now you has old Dud with you it won't be long before the girls is all lining up to have a ride upon your pole.

This did sound promising enough to me, we finished washing ourselves & walked back up to the tree to dry off with Dud's old blankets.

They smelt of ham but that was no bother to us, we was in high spirits suddenly.

We changed back into our clothes & did sit down against the mighty bole of the tree, Dud Carter took out his knife & sliced up some of that ham.

I suppose you ain't eatin, Old Salt?

He dangled a strip of tender meat before my eyes, he knowed well enough I was too hungry to protest. I took it from him, I never tasted anything so good in all my life, it was salty & sweet & I chewed it till it was a rich & meaty paste what slid so easy down my throat.

Well look who got his appetite back.

Dud Carter then buttoned up his coat & folded his arms before closing his eyes.

Now I reckon we get ourselves a couple of winks & when we wake, Old Salt, we will be back on our way.

55

I SEEN THAT FACE BEFORE

I WOKE WITH A TERRIBLE START, a gunshot ringing in my ears. I thought we was under attack but I knowed it then for one of my dreams, them masked men circling my poor daddy. And had I not seen the face of that man with the feather in his hat, had I not felt his wicked eyes searching for my own & seeking vengeance for his fallen friend?

O dreams can be terrible brutes, stirring trouble at every turn. I did look around & there was that feeling what comes after someone's eyes have stole upon you without your knowing but when I looked about me I did not see a soul. Gussie was grubbing about for roots by the creek, dust did roil in silver shoals about her fetlocks as the sun come slanting down soft as butter across the earth.

Dud Carter was still asleep, his mouth hanged open black as a rabbit hole. Only after I poked him did his eyes snap wide & he looked about him with the fear of a man what had woke from a bad dream. He followed them shavings of sunlight upon the dried leaves & old moss of the forest floor.

We been sleepin too long, he said.

He quickly upped & walked stiff & groaning to the creek where he washed his face & filled up his flask with water. He poured a measure over his head & then filled it up once more for our drinking.

I swatted at some flies what hovered about the ham & wrapped it back in the blankets. We both of us then relieved ourselves against a stand of willow & then we was back up on Gussie, my rear no less sore than it was before I was gone to sleep but we was back on the move & there was more comfort in that than staying still.

You might think it queer that the murder of a man might slip your mind but the farther we strayed from Heron's Creek the less them thoughts bothered me. Perhaps Dud Carter's Queer Logic was growed on me without me knowing but I had not thought on the Stranger for a good while, there was peace in the distance what we had traveled.

We journeyed the rest of that day beneath a cold & pale blue sky, the road so quiet at times I could hear & feel the dull beat of Dud Carter's heart against my back behind me.

You often hear from Travelers & Drifters alike all them stories of strange folk they meet, but they all do neglect to mention them great stretches of time where they see not a soul for mile after lonely mile.

So it was with us until near dark when we heard the creaking wheels of a wagon in the distance. Dud Carter threatened to steer Gussie back into the woods to hide but we did not have chance, that wagon come round the corner at a fair clip, a bobbing lantern was lit & suspended from a pole.

There looked to be just the 1 body sit on the box-seat, a dark figure well swaddled in furs & holding the traces of a spirited mule. As it come closer I seen the wagon bed was loaded up with all manner of possessions, they was lashed to the back of it in a great unwieldy mound – chairs & a bureau & a couple of rolled-up rugs just to mention a few.

I had supposed it was a man but as it come closer still I seen it was no man, the shape was too small & too slight. Yes it was a young woman who held them reins & cracked the whip, she was perhaps no older than I.

As she passed she lifted her beaver hat in greeting to reveal a head of cropped curls. A boy with no hair is wont to apply his eye very close to the hair of others, it was a mystery to me then but I reckoned I knowed them curls & how they fell just above the nape of her pale & slender neck. But she was in no mood to stop as a great cloud of dust billowed up so that the contours of her face was all become a haze. Still I thought there was some life to her eyes what I had once knowed, I twisted in my saddle, I swore I had seen her before.

Something about them eyes I was sure brung back an old memory to me what would not reveal itself & I was left with that disquieting feeling what comes when Time begins to tie itself in knots.

Dud Carter took my agitation to be no more than fear of being pursued by Charles Eder.

He ain't comin for us, Old Salt, said he. No need to get yourself so worked up.

56

SOLUS

DARKNESS COME UPON US QUICKER than we thought. The sky greened at the fringes before them first stars showed above us in that quarter what first purples into night.

Still we went on till the moon was risen. We had slowed to a walk again, Dud Carter was looking for a spot where we might light a fire for the night when he suddenly begun to talk.

You know, said he, I got somethin I must confess to you, Old Salt. I suppose that girl we passed back there got me thinkin. I bin meanin to tell you my own thoughts about a particlar woman we is both familiar with.

I could not think of no woman we was both familiar with. I turned to him & shrugged.

I do not know why you is lookin quite so puzzled, there is one you know very well, said he.

Still I could not think, Dud Carter had promised there would be plenty soon lining up to ride my pole as he so put it but I was sure there was no women we knowed now.

Again he shook his head & sighed.

You is a prize dope, Old Salt, he said. You know that night your mama was pokin that gun at my belly & hollerin that she was goin to have me kilt might have been the best of my life.

He paused then & sighed again.

The truth is I do believe she is the finest example of a woman I ever did lay my eyes on.

I am sure the horror was writ plain in my face, to hear him utter them words was such a shock, it was against a unspoke law what men kept between theirselves.

Dud held up a placatory hand.

Now I know it don't make for easy listenin to hear your own mama praised in such terms but we is both growed men now & even you as her son must acknowledge God endowed her with certain qualities what shine & make most others of her sex look awful humdrum. You is her son but I ain't & I think you ought to remember that before you go judgin me.

Dud Carter breathed in deep & searched the sky with longing eyes.

Yes I been thinkin on her a good deal & I reckon I am in love. It has broke my heart to leave her.

In love with my Mama? I had not ever heard such a thing, I hoped this was no more than horseplay & he was about to laugh himself off Gussie's back. But when I turned to look at him his face was gone soft & mournful, perhaps I even seen a tear shimmer in his eye.

Still I had no pity for him, I was about curse him for the slimy bastard he was when there come some whisperings of movement from a Pine Grove by the side of the road & me & Dud was stopped in our tracks. Dud took out his pistol, all was silence then we could not hear a thing.

There come a sharp crack again & the fronds of them pines was parted & out stepped a man into the middle of the road. His skin glowed blue beneath the moon, he was dressed in filthy ripped trews & a white cotton shirt what hung limp about his narrow waist. His feet was bare & the whites of his eyes did pulse in the dark steady as a flame. He had a high forehead & a broad nose & lips what was parted ever so slight to reveal the neat bite of his teeth.

There he was like a deer haunted by some dangersome scent, his back very straight, his arms hung loose, his thin shanks planted close & feet splayed like a marsh hen's. I had never seen so timid a creature in all my days.

I turned to Dud Carter but his sympathies was flown far away, gone was thoughts of love for my Mama, he held his pistol trained firm on that moon-stilled figure.

Don't you move, boy, said Dud Carter.

That nervy soul seemed to nod as if he understood but he was quick to renege on this gesture, he then raised his arms & like a cat what stretches the life back into its bones he lowered himself onto his knees.

I do not tell a lie when I say his movements was so slow & ponderous it was as if the air about him hung thick as honey. I watched on as that tranced & luckless fellow pressed his forehead to the road, it was a slow dive of the soul as if he longed to plumb the Depths of Perdition.

Get on up off the road, said Dud Carter.

His face was terrible stern but his voice traveled the scales of a warbling bird, I knowed uncertainty beat strong in his breast.

I did then wonder why this fellow had chose to offer himself so freely before our path when he might so well have kept himself safe in the shadows. But such a thought did not appear to have crossed Dud Carter's mind, he was not one to consult his companion in the midst of an Event. His temper was high & clumb still, I feared he would shoot him dead.

Don't you got any sense, boy? Quit your kneelin & stand yourself up.

There was no movement from his stilled & craven form. I thought perhaps he had presented himself before us expressly in the hope that we would execute him. Perhaps it was his plan to spring his broke body upon some unsuspecting strangers & behave so insolently they would be left no choice but to trample him beneath their horse.

But it was then I watched as he reached slow into the pocket of his trews & pulled out a small bundle. He held it out in the palm of his hand & pushed it toward us. It was a misshapen thing, lumped & awful irregular in its dimensions though my ears did pick up the little jingle of its contents as it sagged in the dust.

I seen Dud Carter narrow his eyes, they was turned hard as they flicked over this mysterious offering.

What you got down there, boy? asked he.

O he did not raise his head but prodded the strange little parcel toward us some more. Perhaps he was like me, thought I, & God had chose to strip him of his speech.

He then raised his head a little from the road, his brow was paled by dust & his cheeks streaked silver with tears. In them eyes of his there did seem no room for anything other than sorrow.

I got me some monies, said he suddenly.

His voice was so quiet I could barely hear it. Dud Carter leaned over his saddle & offered up his ear a little closer.

What's that? Speak up so's we can hear you.

Again he pushed the bundle closer.

I got me some monies, he said, his voice a little louder now but so high & reedy I wondered if he was not a girl.

Money? said Dud Carter. That what you got there?

Dud Carter scratched at his hairline with the muzzle of his gun.

You ever encountered such a sorry-lookin specimen in your life, Old Salt?

He looked back at our captive & then back at me again.

I tell you what. Why don't you hop on down & take a look at what he keeps pokin toward us there. I'll keep this pistol here on him though I reckon this one don't need no more frightenin, Old Salt.

57

BY FIDDLES AND DRUMS

WAGGING SHADOWS DAPPLED THE ROAD as I clumb down from Gussie. My feet was numbed as I walked & I cannot deny my heart did quicken as our wary-eyed guest from the woods watched my approach from his fawning crouch. Still his eyes was like a babe's, they showed no sign of calculation & even if he chose to fling himself at me I believed what Dud had said was the truth, even I might have matched him.

I come closer and he nudged the parcel forward, I could now smell the sharp sweat what had soured his clothes, I seen his hair was filled with burrs & broke-up bits of leaf & twig, there was no doubt he had spent a goodly spell in them woods.

When I come upon the bundle rested before him, it was a canvas pouch with twine wrapped tight around the bunched excess at the top. It did look to me a considerable weight, I crouched down as I once seen a hunter do to inspect the tracks of his quarry.

What is it, Old Salt? called Dud Carter from behind me. He tellin us lies?

I did not pay him no mind but still keeping a careful watch I reached out & picked it up. Immediately them coins chimed out, O it was the truth what he had spoke for sure & it was no small amount I held in my

hands. I stepped quickly away & carried it back for Dud Carter to see
for himself.

Dud swung his long shanks out of the saddle & took the bag from
me. He weighed it quickly in his palm. He then begun to unfasten the
twine & when he had twisted it loose he looked down inside, it was filled
with Silver Quarters. Suddenly his brows was hoisted high onto his forehead, he shook his head in disbelief.

Well I'll be damned, said he. Lookit that.

Without another word he strut over & put his pistol beneath his
captive's chin so the sorry creature was forced to tip his head up & surrender to a closer studyment.

That a brand you got yourself there? said Dud, poking at a hollow
circle above his right brow.

He nodded his dark head very slow.

Dud Carter turned back to me, his teeth was bared in a knowing grin.

You know it don't take no genius to guess this is the one that old
Charles Eder would not stop his crowing about, he said. There ain't no
doubtin it. Looks like we stumbled upon his runaway, Old Salt.

Your name Solus ain't it?

Our New Discovery give no answer, he only lowered his head back
down to the road again.

You a sorry critter, said Dud Carter, weighing the parcel in his hand
again, but you is awful generous.

Dud then come back toward me, he pinched the ends of the sack
& jiggled it about so them coins chattered away. His face was suddenly
glowing, his eyes was lit, O he could not help himself & he begun to perform a little dance. He waved that pistol of his in the air in 1 hand & shook
the sack of coins like a tambourine in the other, his bootheels kicking up
little bolts of dust what glowed thinly in the moonshine.

I am no dancer myself but I had felt nought but Misery & Fear for
so long it was a great relief to see a glim of happiness. I could not help

but smile & before I knowed it Dud Carter had bent low & linked his arm through mine, spinning me around & across the road.

We danced then as if we was accompanied by Fiddles & Drums, as if we was admired by ladies whose eyes shined bright with longing for our spry & limber bodies. I was suddenly empty of all worry & concern, the mind is no fortress on receiving such gusts of Sudden Rapture.

Yes we was so caught up in our celebrations that we did not see the one we thought our Prisoner rise to his feet. We did not hear as he walked slowly toward us wielding a snub-nosed cudgel. And it was too late to stop him as Dud Carter was struck & dropped like a stook of threshed wheat to the floor & them coins was dashed across the road where they shined like the wavetips of the rolling moonstruck ocean.

58

A VERY FINE ACT

SOLUS COME TOWARD ME, HIS limbs did not seem so frail as before, his feet was not splayed & his eyes no longer filled with sorrow but bright with menace. I knowed then his little show in the middle of the road for a very Fine Act, he had outfoxed us, O how easy we was become players in his Cunning Design.

So stunned was I that I had not even thought to reach for the gun before he grabbed the collar of my shirt & threw me roughly to the floor. He snatched up Dud Carter's pistol & then with the quiet precision of a doctor palpating his patient's flesh that crafty slave patted down my clothes & took from me my blade & slipped it into the waistband of his own soiled trews.

Could Dud Carter still be counted among the living? He had took a fearful club to the face & blood did run free & dark from his nose & mouth. I feared he was killed deader than a stone.

Solus looked down at me.

Stay by your fren, said he.

So too was his voice now changed, no more a pathetic whimper but even & measured as if addressing a Court of Law. His pronunciations was coarse but I sensed it was a tongue what had been shaped by some measure of learning. Who knows where he had acquired it, I cannot imagine Charles Eder very likely to school his workers but some Secret Knowledge was stowed in his mind.

I was now crouched & cowering like he had been only moments ago, how our roles was so suddenly reversed was an astonishment to me. I placed a hand on Dud's leg & shook him gently but his body was limp, only a faint gurgling did issue from his nose & mouth. This I did not dare hope to be him sucking air, I feared it may be no more than his soul departing for some Other Realm.

Solus gathered up them spilled coins. What a queer sight it was, I had not ever seen a man so unhurried, it was as if he was picking a posy for his lover.

He then went rummaging through Dud's saddlebags & begun to help himself to our amenities. I know they was not hard won but still it hurt to see them depleted as he applied his teeth to a generous wedge of salt pork. Soon his lips was suckling from the neck of our flask, the water did dribble down his chin & all this time I will tell you he did not once take his eyes away from mine.

When he come back over to us, he looked down at Dud Carter. I tried to discern some suggestion of his Intent but his features was unmoving. He then kicked Dud Carter hard in his ribs, Dud moaned & after a moment his eyes blinked slowly open.

He was alive.

Solus said, You listenin?

Dud nodded weakly, though I do believe he did not know where he was, his senses was all deserted him like a army fleeing from a battleground.

An you too, liddle bald man?

He had Dud Carter's pistol trained upon my head, what more could I do but nod.

Good, said Solus. Now I wants you to keep listenin.

He stared down at us & there was then a quality to his eyes what brung to mind my own Mama's. They was awful dark, there was no lick of color but it was a certain hardness to their shine what summoned her into my thoughts.

If I was seen walkin along this road on my own, said Solus, you both knows it well as me that I wudden get so far before somebody come clap some irons round my wrists & have me strung up from 1 of these here trees.

He looked up at 1 of the overhanging branches as if he seen then his own broke neck swinging above him.

Thas why I got you 2, he said. See I got a sister what got took away from me. She my only family & I got to fine her even if it kill me to do it. You see I know where she gone. I seen the man what took her. I seen them letters writ on the side of his little old bundlin wagon an I heard him says they was on their way up t'ward Tennessee. An this here is the road what leads me to her.

Dud Carter had closed his eyes again & Solus give him another little kick.

You keep on listenin to me since what I'm s'posin is I keep a hold of this here gun.

He pointed the pistol at the both of us.

And then what I do is I ties my own binds on my own wrists & the other end to you, liddle bald man.

Here he stopped to look at me. The moon did disappear behind a cloud & then come drifting back out again.

You will lead me along the road. Just like you caught me an you was takin me back to the post to have my back opened up in the name of Justice. You understandin me?

Dud Carter was still dazed, he looked at me & then back at Solus.

You see, liddle bald man?

I could do nothing but nod again.

An if you think to call out to any passin man or cart or spur on that there beast or do a single thing to muss up my plans I will fire this gun & you will feel a ball rip through your back & your blood come drippin all over this road.

He now crouched down & looked at us both in the eyes, I swear I never seen a man so set on dressing his wild thoughts & have them march out into the world.

He begun to poke at Dud Carter with his dirty foot.

Come on now, he said. Get up & get you on that horse.

59

THE FEAR OF DEATH

I AM SURE YOU HAVE heard many stories from men who had at 1 time or other found theirselves staring Death in the eye, they is often filled with high ideas of Courage & Daring. The truth of course is very different, only the Godless desire to see theirselves buried, when Death does shadow your every move you learn how you do savor your life.

So it was all that long night & into the next day neither me nor Dud Carter made any attempt to escape or alter our fortunes. You might claim us white-livered or yellow-bellied or any other colored organ for that matter I do not care, for I will wager you have not looked into the eyes of a Desperate Man who has all but lost his mind. If you had you would have done the very same & sit in your saddle & thanked God for each breath of air you took in your lungs.

Poor Dud slept them first few hours after our capture with his head slumped on Gussie's neck. Our positions in the saddle was cunningly reversed, Solus had us arranged so I now did sit behind Dud Carter & he had tied a lariat & knotted it high up my back so I could not pick it free. The other end of the rope was looped about his wrists, of course it did not bind him so even if Dud Carter tried to speed off it would be me what got hauled from the saddle & no doubt shot where I lay.

Dreams was Dud Carter's constant torment that night, a fever of sorts had locked him in its grips as his brow growed slick with night-sweats & he moaned soft nonsense to the stars. The blow delivered to his head had swolled his jaw up so he looked like some wintering cottontail what had stowed its food in its cheek.

When he woke just before dawn, blood still run free down his chin & matted Gussie's dark mane. The sky was graying in the east, the only sound to be heard was Gussie's hoofs & the sad shuffle of Solus's steps behind us. Dud Carter slowly raised up his head, he felt tenderly about his mouth. The memory of what had happened was slow in returning to him but he had not forgot entire, he turned & seen our situation, I never seen him look so down.

60

AN OLD MEMORY

NOW AS WE RODE ON with Dud Carter once again succumbed to his tortured sleep, I stole a few glances at Solus. With the light of morning arrived I seen he was not aged much older than myself. There was no lick of hair on his upper lip, he was not so menacing a figure without all them shadows, his eyes no longer hard & mean but somewhat Boyish in their aspect.

He did not take kindly to my attentions, he said nothing when he caught my eye but placed his palm atop the contour of the pistol what showed through the thin weave of his shirt. Still it was time enough to study him & it was them scuffed feet he dragged through the dust what brung to my mind a memory I had long forgot.

I will admit I had not come across many slaves in my time, they was too costly for any in Heron's Creek to afford. All them grand plantations of Cotton & Tobaccy did reside farther South where the breeze come bearded with salt & the sun shined fierce & true & the winters did not bully the earth with frost & snow.

But from my stool beneath the old elm I had seen some on occasion. Sometimes they was sit in the back of a wagon watching idly as the world passed them by & sometimes they appeared free to sing or chatter amongst theirselves, I had no thought then of what Burden & Constraint such as they was under.

It was a warm summer's day when I was in the thick of my tutoring with Shelby Stubbs. As was my habit I had been waiting for his arrival beneath my old tree when I seen a very fancy buggy come to a halt outside the store, it was painted & polished, the horse what drawed it a gleaming pinto.

A tall and black-skinned man was sit atop the box-seat & handling the reins, he was finely dressed in livery, a blue frockcoat clean of dust & mustard-colored leggings what clung to his shapely thigh. I had never seen a white man so well attired as that, consider how my eyes did widen to see his frame complimented with such Finery.

He clumb down then from his seat & opened the door for a corpulent man to step out. This man's face was obviously gone unshaded from the cruelties of the sun, it was burned & blistered, he dabbed at it very light with an embroidered kerchief. He wore his whiskers very thick, a roll of fat dripped sweat at the collar of his shirt, I would later learn his name to be Mr. Bajoleer.

The coachman escorted his master toward the store but it was clear some pain in his leg ailed him for the slave limped along & near dragged that foot behind him like it was Something Dead. He was a young man, it could not have been age what had crippled him so but some other injury he had sustained.

Quit your hobbling, snapped Mr. Bajoleer, his small eyes peered out from pinkened rims.

He did his best to hurry his pace but he could not hide his pain, he did wince with every step.

Now it was I noticed that old doctor Shelby Stubbs was walked round the bend, it soon become clear he had studied this pair's progress as close as I. With his cane he made his stately advance toward the store, swatting at them flies as he come. But he did not come to greet me as normal, instead he headed for the store & when he reached the hobbled coachman he looked him hard in the eye. Mr. Bajoleer was gone inside, I could see him jabbing at my Mama's shelves with the tip of his cane.

Said Stubbs, Take off your boot.

The coachman looked at him as if he were quite mad.

Take off your boot, said Stubbs again, his voice was raised & very firm. I well knowed myself he was a man near impossible to deny.

That fellow's eyes was wide & fearful but slowly he knelt & begun to unbuckle his left boot. He peeled off the stocking very slow, his face was etched with misery.

What I seen then was a long wound, it stretched from his smallest toe to his heel, it was black as night & wept a terrible pus the smell of which did reach me even on my stool.

Stubbs did not appear to notice that woeful stench, he crouched & begun to dab at the wound with a kerchief he had removed from his pocket.

Just then Mr. Bajoleer come out, he looked down at the stinking wound & recoiled, he dropped his purchases & brung his gloved hand to his nose.

Get your hands off him! cried he, his voice was strangely muffled through his hand.

Your man will die if he is not treated, said Stubbs.

Treated for what? inquired Bajoleer.

His foot, said Stubbs. You can see it as clear as I.

Mr. Bajoleer looked back down at the foot & recoiled once more, he was very Theatrical in his manners.

What concern is his treatment of yours? asked he, the sweat beaded thick in the creases upon his indignant brow.

I am a doctor, said Shelby Stubbs.

I do not care what you are, said Mr. Bajoleer. He's mine & I decide what treatment he is to be offered.

Your man will die without it, said Stubbs, his tone was plain & his face very calm.

But Mr. Bajoleer would not listen, he now grabbed his slave by the sleeve & hauled him from the porch, he did pull him so fierce that the fabric ripped and gold buttons went spilling onto the boards. But there was not time to fetch up the boot or them buttons, there was nothing his man could do but hop after him, his foot dripping its rotten blood.

Dr. Stubbs looked on, I seen then a sadness was crept into his eyes as he watched Mr. Bajoleer bustle up into the buggy & the bleeding coachman take the reins & drive off in a cloud of dust.

The doctor turned then & seen me watching him from beneath my tree across the way, he collected up that boot from the ground & held it like it was a living thing come to the end of its days.

He was a man I thought always spoke his mind but I seen him hold something back then, whatever it was he would not say it.

Now I seen them bare & broke feet of Solus's that look upon Shelby Stubbs's face come back to me & I believed I knowed what thoughts was turning in his head, O yes I do share the very same now.

61

A MOST PARTICULAR BREED OF INSOLENCE

ALL THAT LONG WAY THE road had been hemmed in by thick woods but now we was come upon a ridge of sorts what took in a fine view of a shallow valley below. A track led down to some log-houses, some of which plumed smoke finely from their chimneys, by all accounts it was a pleasant view.

Earlier that morning Solus had done himself some thinking, he had tugged on what I come to call my Leash & I had knuckled Dud Carter in the back to wake him. Poor Dud had tried to talk but he could not muster a single word without having to lean out over the road & let pinkish spit dribble from his mouth. I thought he would need a slate of his own now, I do believe he tried to offer me a smile but by the black gaps at his gum it was plain to see he was missing a good many of his teeth.

Dud brung Gussie to a stop & stared round in bewilderment & fear as Solus come walking up to his side.

Get down off your horse, said he.

Dud Carter looked at me & back at Solus, he did not move.

Solus put his hand atop the handle of the pistol.

Through grit teeth he said, Get on down off that horse now.

Dud Carter did as he was told, wincing as he got off, he believed his days was come to an end.

I did not know myself what Solus was about to do, perhaps I was to witness my friend's execution. But when Dud was standing before him I watched Solus take off his shirt & take the canteen of water from the saddlebag. He then poured some of the water on the shirt & begun to dab at Dud Carter's wounds, he did wipe away that dried blood & cleaned him right up so only the bruising did remain.

At first I thought it a kindly act but then to my shock I seen Solus took the pistol from his waistband. I thought he had cleaned Dud Carter up only to shoot him down. But I watched as Solus took the butt of the pistol in his fist & then struck himself a fearful blow across the brow. He struck himself again & again, he did not stop until blood run down his face, I had never witnessed so unnatural a act in my life.

Dud Carter looked on but there was no horror writ in his eyes, he knowed what Solus was up to, he knowed that slave did not want to attract no Unwanted Attention to us. A white man with a beat-up face is likely to cause some suspicion but a black man with a bloody face tells a story every white man knows & likes to see. Dud clambered back up onto Gussie.

Now Solus tugged hard on my Leash again & I knuckled Dud Carter just as I had them hours before. Dud pulled on Gussie's reins & we both turned to see Solus was looking down into the holler, his eyes turned very hungry. That blood had dried & crusted on his face, them cuts still open & weeping a steady gleaming rill.

He begun then to mutter to himself, he had not seen where the road bent away from the track & continued into the woods there stood a large cottonwood, the bole of which 3 young boys was leaned against.

Me & Dud Carter had spotted them, they was all belonging to that age where Idleness & Anger share the same quarters & a most particular breed of insolence is born. They is fearful & fearless all at once, it is a combination what does not lend itself to no good.

It took no special wisdom to see one did clearly occupy the position
of Leader, his eyes was slit with intrigue, he was sucking heartily on a
pipe though he looked as if the smoke worked too harsh in his young
throat, it did putter from his nostrils in fits & his eyes was much irritated.

Them other 2 was smaller, they looked like brothers with the same
dun-colored hair & soft blue eyes. They turned to their leader to study his
reaction at such a queer band of travelers come into their Small World.

Me & Dud turned again to see which way it was Solus wished us to
go & we eyed each other very anxious. Solus had by then espied them
boys, he muttered as low under his breath as he could that we was to
take the track down into the valley but this was not so subtly done as
he might have hoped. That pipe-smoking little devil had sensed something odd about our procession, our indecision was like a hot meal set
before his hungering eyes.

He offerin up his opinions? said the boy, poking his pipe at Solus.

He was just a young shrimp himself but it did no doubt stoke the
coals of his pride to address a man his senior so very brazen. He had a
mealy mouth replete with yellowed teeth, he tapped out the bowl of his
pipe & stowed it in the pocket of his coat. The sorry beginnings of whiskers on his cheeks did catch the sun & glowed like spidersilk strung out
in the morning dew.

I did not dare turn to look at Solus, I imagined his hand placed
firm on the handle of the pistol. With no other instruction Dud Carter
then nudged Gussie & carried her on walking, his eyes was fixed on the
track ahead, he hoped as much as I that the boy would soon lose interest.

But this boy was of that ilk what appears to relish a Cold Shoulder,
he left his post beneath the cottonwood & begun walking close behind
Solus. Solus's head was bowed but the boy stooped & craned his neck
to look him in the eye.

What was it you jus said to these here men? asked he.

Solus kept his head down, he would not answer him.

Gone quiet now has you? You look like you already took a good beatin but maybe you still short on sense.

The boy looked back up, he then hurried round to the front of Gussie & begun walking backwards so he could address us as we moved.

Ain't you 2 got time to stop & chatter? We is awful friendly round these parts.

He looked back & forth between us & smiled.

You is a strange pairing. God ain't give no words to describe a fellow like you, he said pointing at me.

And you, he said, looking at Dud Carter, your face is so swolled up I can't tell whether you is man or beast. What happened? You ain't been takin beatins from this one as well as orders is it?

The boy thought himself a grand exponent of Dry & Clever witticisms, he laughed & so too did his friends what now trailed behind us like a pair of sulking coyotes upon the bloodnote of some carrion.

Well? said he. Neither of you gunna talk?

He shrugged though indifference was far from an acquaintance of his, not a single thing could pass before his eyes without the flames of his ire being fanned.

I ain't offended, he claimed, his tone was most churlish. That is alright with me. You boys ride on an I'll just go & take care of this right here.

So it was he begun kicking about the roadside scrub until he found himself a long switch. He whipped it through the air so it sung out a wicked tune what pleased his ear so much he looked down at it like it was a living, breathing hireling of his own.

You boys won't mind if I work him over a little bit for you?

He walked now alongside us, turning that switch over in his grubby hands.

Nothin to say still? Well alright.

There was nothing we could do, we did not know what rules might be breached if we tried to talk back. Solus had laid down them rules

awful clear that we should not draw attention to ourselves, we would
be shot if we did.

I turned then to watch as the boy raised his switch & brung it down
across Solus's back. Solus's back was immediately become spotted with
blood & I heard them 2 boys behind laugh & jeer.

Ain't you bad, said that boy, ain't you just the worst I ever met. The
boy's lips was turned red, his eyes was alive with the longing to test his
own limits & them of a growed man & see himself come out the Victor.

He then raised his hand to bring the switch down again upon Solus's
back when Solus suddenly turned, there was a moment where that boy
looked down, his mealy mouth did twist in confusement as he seen them
slave hands was unbound & free & holding a pistol.

But that boy did not have no time to make no sense of it before the
muzzle flared & there come a deafening roar. The boy sprung back so
high it was as if he had been dropped from the heavens, he landed with
a sickly thud in the dust, his switch flung from his hands & come to rest
by the side of the road.

He was shot through the neck, he now used them mean hands of
his to clutch at the blood what pumped through his pale fingers, his eyes
was wild & filled with the Fear of Death.

Spooked by the shot Gussie bucked & throwed me off, my Slate-
Sling was loosed from my shoulder & my slate slid down the slope & into
the brush. She bolted & went galloping off down the track toward the
town with Dud Carter crying out through his swolled mouth & wrestling
with the reins to halt her. He disappeared around the bend in a cloud of
dust, I tried to run after him but still Solus had managed to keep hold
of me by my Leash.

Them brothers was turned & running also, they seen their leader
laid writhing upon the ground with his warm blood leaping between his
hands. Solus then raised his gun once more & I thought him set to load
& fire upon their young fleeing bodies when some exhaustion come over
him, he lowered his weapon & sunk to his knees.

I watched then as Solus crawled over to that boy.

The boy's eyes was wide & darting still as he took in his last breaths, his blood was pooled all around him, his britches was darkened about his crotch where he had pissed, it also come snaking out along the road.

Solus stared down at him, his own eyes was filled with anger but they brimmed with tears also, them salty drops rolled & fell onto the boy whose movements now growed slower by the second, his feet no longer kicking but flopping from side to side, his hands not clutched at his neck but placed on his heaving chest.

As if I had not witnessed enough death that boy's eyes was then stilled, his life come to an end. Unless you have no heart there is no getting used to that sight, you do feel your own blood work hot & fast though your veins, very grateful it is still carrying your life along.

O you know I had done the killing myself also, I done felt them Dark Desires & I knowed that ache in the bones what warns you is breaking apart & soon won't no longer be Whole. I seen Solus then & just like I had knowed I had got to run from Heron's Creek, so did he feel that pull to bolt & never look back.

That ragged hole in the boy's neck pumped out the last of his blood & Solus then stood up. His eyes was gone blank. He wound my rope about his wrist & begun to pull me up the slope away from the town & away from Dud Carter & back toward the woods. I looked around & seen my slate laid in the brush, I cannot tell you how it broke my heart to see it left behind.

62

SOMEONE HE LONGED TO MEET

WHO HAS EVER BEEN HELD AT GUNPOINT & bid to roll theirselves in creekmuck? I must surely have been the first as Solus ordered I cover myself in a layer of filth what turned me black as tar like himself.

Deep into them woods we had gone.

Solus had clawed his way through the trees & scrub, he did not care if he cut himself or me to pieces on them wicked thorns, his shirt was ripped, it hung limp & bloodied from his back.

Sweat was dripping heavy from our brows when we had come upon that muddy creek & I watched as Solus begun to wallow in the shallows. He cried as he did so, moaning & cursing, I did fear some other dark invention of his with which to mire my helpless soul.

But he soon revealed his true purpose, it was to veil his scent & if he had done so then so must I. Mud dripped from his arm as he aimed that pistol at me. God alone knowed he did not need to brandish it no more, I had seen him kill a boy stone dead, I would do anything he wished but his eyes was wild, his hand shook with fear & fury, I did know both coursed through him.

How quick darkness was begun to fall in them woods, I thought, as I writhed in them shallows & the sky spun above me, them first stars stippling the blue between all them branches wove black & leafless.

I felt then a splayed hand atop my head & I was held under, I thought my captor aimed to have me drowned & the blood of 2 souls on his hands. I struggled but he was too strong & as darkness closed around me & I did hear the slow beat of my heart, it was as if them cold waters had entered it & brung it to a plod. It pains me now having lived so rich a life that I did feel myself ready to Meet my Maker.

Imagine then the rush of light & sound as Solus pulled me out by my Leash, that rope did slice into my skin as I was dragged this way & that. It was the barking of dogs & the cries of men what reached my ears, we turned & seen their distant lanterns pricking the gloom between the trees. Branches cracked as them dogs bent their noses to the ground & howled out their Lust for Blood, they growed by turns distant & loud then distant again as we rose to our feet & cut through the brush once more.

We run until darkness was fallen & the birds in the blue stillness of the trees above turned their song to silence & all I could hear was the breathing of me & Solus. By some chance or luck if they cannot be said to be 2 heads of the same beast we did lose them dogs & men, they took theirselves a wrong turn along the way, but if we lost them then I also knowed we lost Dud Carter.

What if I never seen him again? What if we was lost from each other for the rest of our lives? No I would not let that happen, I vowed there & then I would not ever stop looking until I found him.

Now we was come upon a clearing, tall & sere grasses ringed about a great black bowl of water, its surface so very still there was not a ripple or pleat to be seen across it. It breathed out its own wet & ancient scent, Solus pulled me to its edge, I thought we was to quench our thirst.

But we only stood & our breath come ragged as we stared down into its surface, the sky ripening above us, 2 birds drifting aimless through the darkling clouds. How queer a pair we looked, our black faces mirrored back at us.

You lost that piece what you write on, said Solus.

He did not turn to face me but spoke into them waters.

I nodded.

I knows how you feel, he then said, though I did not then see how this was possible. I could see only my own woes stretched out before me, I reckoned we was no way similar.

Solus seen my nose wrinkle in dismay.

They is many kinds of silence, added he, breathing in heavy. He then begun to laugh very quiet to himself & shook his head as if the meaning of some Fine Joke was suddenly revealed to him.

You know, he said, there's some things in this here head what I'd like to tell you.

He run his hand through the tightly wove springs of his hair & bits of leaf & twig dropped into the water, thin ripples spread & then died. He then beat hard against his skull as if it was a door what would lead to someone he longed to meet, his young face begun to crumple, his cheek twitched, his words come out all choked as he tried to hold back his tears.

Charles Eder dint own me no more than you do, said he. A man stoled me away & sold me to him & then took my sister with him.

He wiped his nose with the back of his hand & let out a breath what shook as he tried to reel it back in.

I did not then take in what he had said, my mind was too busy with problems of my own. As far as I seen this was no time for Stories, we should be running as far as we could get. Only as the yrs did pass have I had ample occasion on which to ponder what words & stories & secrets of our hearts we might have shared together. O but we could not then & it is just one more sadness what comes for me in them same Blue Hours when I can well imagine myself still in them woods & crouched beside him.

Solus begun to talk again.

I say these things to you cus—

But he did not finish his sentence.

There come then the barking from them dogs & cries of them men suddenly very close, their lanterns held high & swinging light between the trees. Solus wiped the tears what had fallen down his dark cheeks & wrapped my Leash tight around his bunched fist.

63

A SINGLE DARK CLOUD ON THE HORIZON

THEY IS MANY KINDS OF SILENCE.

O the wisdom in them words was only revealed to me many yrs later but at that time I thought Solus addled in his brain, I thought Death did seem no more a worry to him than a single dark cloud on the horizon.

I thought perhaps something deep inside him was snapped, I got to reckon now it was no muscle or bone but them Invisible Strings on which thoughts & feelings can travel freely along without no Guard or Gate to block them. But whatever had kept him anchored to them was made so light as to be took with the winds, for now he begun to tread the black waters of that pool.

I seen his feet go so very light & slow, I could not take my eyes from them, them black waters parted as if they knowed him well. I turned & seen them flickering lights, the dogs & men come closer still. Should I break free I could not help but see myself killed, their rage run so high that I would be shot or them dogs rip out my throat.

Just as gentle then I followed Solus into the pool. I did not have to be told as he took me on his back, my arms was wrapped around his neck, my nose buried in the musk of his hair. I could not see if he still held my Leash as the water begun to deepen, I watched it clumb up his leg thick & dark as oil.

Hold on, said he.

That water did creep up & I felt it trickle in my boots first then rush them full. I was still wet from the creek but this water felt heavier somehow as if it was itself alive the way it snaked up my britches, as if it wished to know my body what had dared to stir its Holy Waters.

Solus was as calm as a saint, his feet & hands working unseen & unheard beneath us, only our heads was sticking out, our noses tipped up to take in the air as we seen then all them dogs & men come crashing through the trees, some held knots of pinewood flaming, their light lapped at the edges of them dark waters we was sunk in.

We heard their yells echo out through the woods, seen their faces lit like masks of the Devil. But our scent was lost to them. We stayed there until the cold begun to seep into my bones & finally Solus spoke.

We is goin back to that town, he said.

64

THE TOWN

IT WAS DEEP INTO THE night by the time we had found our way back to the road.

We was very fortunate them winds was dry & warm as I knowed them possible to be, I do believe the pair of us would have froze to death otherwise. Still I feared my feet would succumb to rot they had been wet so very long & that rope had burned a Bloody Ring around my chest, it did feel like a noose of flame would burn there forever more.

Blood was soaked deep into the earth where that boy had laid. Solus had stared down at it as we passed but he did not stop, there was a look in his eye the very same I had seen when he cast his eyes across that valley before.

My slate was nowhere to be seen. We had walked past that spot I knowed it had laid but it was gone. I cannot tell of the shadow what crept across my heart then, I knowed if I was to get myself free of this trouble then I could not be without it.

I would have scoured that slope for the rest of my days even if it was shattered & broke into a thousand pieces, I would have crawled until my knees was worn to bone to find it. But Solus would not relent, he kept me still by his side as we wove between them crooked pines what had made that scabrous slope their home.

When we reached the bottom we took our cover at the back of a large wooden building, the nature of its use was not clear until there come shufflings & snortings through the chinks & a sharp stink what told us it was a Livery home to dreaming horses.

Heron's Creek was Lilliputian compared to this town, as we crept around the corner we had ourselves a fine view down the main street, it was wide as a river & lit by rows of lanterns what dangled from the eaves. It was eerie quiet, no doubt owed to plenty of its men having offered up their services in our pursuit.

Still when the wind quieted there come drifting the muffled voices of some chattering folk, there was a rowdy note to their exclamations & there come also the faint drift of music, I took it to be some kind of tavern.

I prayed there & then I might see Dud Carter, that he would suddenly appear but there was no sign of him. Poor Gussie was so frighted she might have bucked him off & cracked his head upon the slope or perhaps he had had his fill of disaster & set off for some far place to start his life again without me, I could not know.

We clung to the shadows of the livery a long while as Solus seemed to make some calculation in his head, he made a queer ticking noise with his tongue. Soldiers have been knowed to take their sleep on the battlefield beneath musket fire & cannons & so it was with me, I felt my eyes begin to lower, sleep was finally come for me & I was ready to welcome it.

Suddenly Solus did rise to his feet & I was being pulled across the street to the other side, my chest alive with pain once more.

We crouched down in the shadows beside a clapboard building, it was painted green, the words NEWSOME'S FUNERAL PARLOR was writ bold in buttery yellow. There was a single candle lit in an upstairs window, the rest was dark. Now we looked out toward the other side of the street, all them buildings was adorned with wooden signs creaking in the breeze & windows polished & glowing merry with firelight. Long sloping shapes of light stretched out onto the road, I had never seen darkness dressed to look so fine.

There come again that music in my ears, the keys of a piano played by a lively pair of hands. It wafted out from a large tavern with a mighty veranda down the way, each & every window burning bright.

Solus looked down the street toward the tavern, I would not have put it past him to march straight in there but he turned away & next we was weaving our way behind the backs of them stores & houses.

We was lucky no man had took his Evening Pipe outside but Solus was crouched so low, his feet so soft upon the earth perhaps he would not have seen us anyway. We took a stop by the reek of an outhouse as Solus worked his eyes & ears until he was sure our presence was still unknowed & then we was off again.

Now that music was growed louder still. We settled by an old broke-up wagon, its wheels gone to rot, it had not been put to use in years. Still it had a tattered tarp over it & when the wind lifted it, it did give off a wicked stink of Piss & Shit, many had dropped their britches near it & done their Dirty Business.

But its cover did afford a fine view of that tavern which I now seen was clear become the focus of Solus. He watched it with his eyes unblinking, I never seen a man's face stay so still for so long.

We waited & we waited, that piano player was a skillful fellow, he had himself a mighty repertoire. Still we listened out for them barking dogs & wailing men to come charging back through town but they never come, instead several men then come stumbling down the steps, they had scantily clad ladies draped about their necks like furs.

Them ladies laughed very High & Dainty as the men set their hands to wandering in the secret folds of their dresses. There was then much rude & boorish talk, they begun to weave in drunken circles on the road, they growed so close that when their backs was turned Solus lifted me into that old wagon & clumb in himself & through the rips in that tarp we spied on them.

Them men soon returned inside to continue their carousing but we remained in the wagon, the smell was foul beyond belief, the wood was gone so soft I felt my bootheels sink into it like clay. But in that stinking wagon we did wait some more, I thought we was to sleep in there all night, again I felt that tiredness work a slow dance around the fringes of my eyes.

I had just nodded off when there come a tension in my Leash what had hung slack for some time. I did writhe as my chest burned but Solus's body had gone stiff as a board, his eyes was wide as a man come staggering out of the tavern. Piano still played out behind him as the door swung shut & this man did himself a little dance down them steps & took a bow at the bottom as if a audience was blessing him with applause.

65

JIM COYNE

WE WATCHED HIM FROM THE wagon then as he come down the road toward us. Even before I seen him close or he opened his mouth I would have declared him the beneficiary of some Astral Charm, he had to him the look of a man what commanded all the elements around him, the winds & rain & sun & stars did seem to look down on him as if he was their own child risen from the earth.

He begun then to whistle & dance, his feet was very nimble over the earth, his fingers rolled across the air as if there was a piano floating before him. Then just as quick he seemed to sadden, he slowed & did plant his feet firm in the road, he closed his eyes & tilted his head skyward. A song was come to his lips, one I had not heard before.

> *The girl who sings from the mountain top,*
> *Dressed in airs of green and gold,*
> *She is the girl rose fair as the crop,*
> *She is the girl I yearn to hold.*
>
> *The girl who sings from the edge of the sun,*
> *Her hair to fall like flame and fire,*

She is the girl so hard to be won,
Of this bold girl I will never tire.

The girl who sings down from her throne,
She is the girl who holds the reins,
The girl who rides forever alone,
She who has my heart in chains.

His voice I must say was far from beautiful but still them words come out wrapped soft & warm, he delivered them into the air as if they might be so easy broke as glass. It was as if he had no choice in the matter, that song was visited upon him & he was bound by some unspoke pledge to have it enter the world. There is no more mournful sound than a man singing of his love-trod heart beneath the night sky, he looked much moved by them words & so was I, I could not take my eyes from him.

But not everyone was so fond of his performance, we heard then a window crack open from the building nearest us & a woman cried down, she did implore him to quit his Caterwauling & shut his God-damn Trap. She throwed some object what landed with a dull thud in the road, it was intended to strike him but he only picked it up & bowed as if it was some token to savor from a member of that imagined audience of his.

Thank ye, Madam, cried he. My name is Jim Coyne & your blessings is much obliged.

The window slammed shut & he bowed low again, I noted there was an accent to his voice, a certain lilt what had traveled far to be here but I could not then have said from where. He pocketed the object & continued on his way.

Now it was this man who called himself Jim Coyne come level with the wagon. We watched him stop & pull out a bottle from his pocket, he took a healthy swig & then paused, I thought he must have seen us cowering beneath the tarp for he come walking right for us.

I seen now he wore an old beaverskin hat, the fur gone thin in places as if drove by some wincing nerve he had plucked it bald. He was thin & tall, a long greatcoat swept the length of him to his boots, his gloved hands was wove together & rested behind him at the small of his back.

Solus gripped me hard about the wrist so's I would not move but the man only unbuttoned his britches & begun to piss a long hard stream so that it come flooding through the chinks in the wood & pooled steaming at our feet.

That piss did seem to wake all them other Sleeping Scents up until I nearly gagged but still Solus clung to my wrist, he would not let me move a muscle.

Through a tear in the tarp I could study the man's face, his features was sharp & narrow, his brows was a dark & lively pair as they jigged above his eyes. I could not see them eyes so clear but they looked very light in their shadings, I would later know them for the bluest I ever seen. He wore long sidewhiskers & a close-shaved lip & chin, his hair come down spooling from his hat in loose & oiled curls.

As he shook his member dry, I swear he looked through that hole in the tarp & our eyes met but he said not a word & I thought he must have seen only darkness. He continued on his way then, he was headed toward a stand of trees what I now seen dimly glowed in the distance.

When he was a good stretch away from us, Solus begun to look up & down the street once more. He then clumb out & lifted me after him & we was stalking after him away from the lights of town & back into the shadows.

Surely I thought this runaway slave should seek the shadows as much as possible but Jim Coyne had roused in Solus something I had not seen in him, it was clear it was him he had been looking for. But Jim Coyne did not once look behind him, his hands was again wove at his back, he walked as steady as a judge on his way to the Bench.

Solus brung us to a halt & pulled me down into a low crouch as we watched him disappear into that ring of trees. We was now close enough to see that glow did belong to a good-sized blaze, we could see a feather of smoke risen up above the treetops & sparks come dancing before they died in the dark of the sky.

Solus turned to me then, he looked as if he was committed to telling something but then thought better of it.

He stood up then & walked over to them trees the man had just parted, it was only then I seen he held clasped in his other hand the gleaming blade of my knife.

66

A DEAL

THAT FIRE BLAZED HIGH & wide, it was surrounded by towering tulip trees, their branches was met in tangled & flickering congress above us.

Jim Coyne was nowhere to be seen but arranged in a horseshoe around them flames was some adzed logs to seat those who wished to skewer their meat above the fire.

Solus begun to move through that empty camp when to my shock 1 of them logs stirred, I thought my eyes was mistook but beneath the crickling of the fire there then reached my ears the ebbing tide of sleepers breathing, they was not just logs but Bodies laid curled around them.

Who knowed if they was awake & looking at us, they was swaddled deep in blankets but none moved & I turned to see Solus's eyes was lit & roving from 1 body to the next, his breathing shallow as a man who run himself to the moon & back.

Suddenly he bent down & shook a body. It was a young girl, her forehead high & her lips full & slightly parted. There was no doubting she was Solus's sister, she was the spit of him, she rose up & flung her arms around his neck, she tried to cry out but Solus clamped his hand over her mouth.

It was a moment before I realized that in his embrace Solus had dropped my rope. I was free to run & turned to do so but found myself charged into the legs of a man, it was Jim Coyne who towered over me.

Yous two did well to endure the stink of my piss, said he. Very admirable indeed the way yis squat in there like 2 hens at the laying & made barely a sound whilst I give your boots a good wetting.

His hands was placed upon a brace of pistols in his leather belt, but he smiled down at me, I must admit I thought it the most generous smile I ever seen.

And I seen yis both come creepin in them shadows behind me. Yis was ever so quiet but my mammy would tell you I come out the womb with the ears of a fox on me.

He looked then at Solus who was still crouched by the girl.

Now now there's no need for them evil eyes, yis will burn a hole right through my innards & it would be a dreadful shame to see all the drink come spillin out of me just as soon as I'd poured it in.

Solus said nothing, his fists was tightly balled at his sides, his eyes was wide & his nostrils flaring.

Jim Coyne was smiling very warm still, he turned then & got down on his haunches, he removed his beaverskin hat & run his fingers through his long hair. His pale eyes was level with my own, they was brimful with unspoke kindnesses.

I am familiar with your fellow journeyman over there but I don't believe we is acquainted, is we?

He reached out his hand, I thought it was to shake my own or so I had hoped but instead my Unlikely Savior took up the rope what Solus had dropped & begun to turn it in his fingers.

I seen him pulling you around, said he, & I thought to myself, That ain't no way for a fella of such unusual qualities to be tret. He ought to be looked after. He ought to be looked after very special like & not drug around like an old dog.

These was very flattering words from such a man as he, I did not know what spell his character had cast but I longed to hear him speak more niceties. I was so glad to hear he knowed how ill I had been tret, I thought no doubt he will be very eager to help me & have me reunited with Dud Carter as soon as possible.

Now them other sleeping bodies was begun to stir, they turned their faces to us but still I could not see them well, the shadows of them flames worked to obscure them. Jim Coyne looked at them & tutted sadly, he turned my rope in his fingers & looked me again in the eye.

I'll forgive yis for waking up my friends here because I know well enough it was not you who is such a Thoughtless Brute.

By now the rope around my chest was a running sore, my shirt was damp with blood. I tugged at it so he could see.

You want it off? asked he. Well that is only natural, why did you not say so before?

I pointed to my tongue & shook my head.

Jim Coyne frowned.

Yis haven't a tongue?

I stuck out my tongue to show it was not lost but only lame.

I seen then a look in his eye, I did not have the measure of it but he smiled again, it was so warm & tender a expression I could not help but smile back.

I'll take this rope & have it burned, my little friend, but yis are to promise to not go running off. It isn't safe for one so Special as you, you stay with Jim Coyne & yis will be well looked after.

Jim Coyne now bent down & begun to unfasten the rope what Solus had tied at my back. I have never knowed such relief, my ribs stretched theirselves out, there was a painful throb but it was a fine thing to feel the air reach the wound.

Better? asked he.

I nodded & he winked at me & then turned back to Solus.

Yer know when all them fellas dropped their drinks & was sayin an *escapee* snuffed the life from 1 of our boys I had a notion it might have been you. But I must admit I am surprised yis found me here. I bet it is a grand old story to tell but I sense yis is in something of a rush, am I right?

He cocked his head & frowned most solicitous.

Well? Is it something of a rush yis is in to get away? Because I won't be stopping yis. I am as fair a man as they come, I don't think there's many would begrudge me in the sayin so. And I ain't the mean sort to turn the hard edge of me heart toward another man when he worked so hard to earn his prize. There is nothin worse than a man who don't recognize when another man is due his reward.

Still Solus did not say a word, he & his sister's eyes was so wide they looked like cornered beasts at the point of a spear.

And there was me thinkin yis would be armed & ready but unless yis keep that gun up your jacksie then it is no more. I seen that knife on yis but that ain't no good to you now.

I had not noticed but gone was Dud Carter's pistol from the waistband of Solus's trews, perhaps it had sunk to the bottom of the pool or fell in the scrub as we run, I realized then he had not wielded it since we was by the creek.

If yis still had it I bet yis would have put a bullet in me would you not? said Jim Coyne, his smile returning to him.

Yis already killed 1 fellow today & I've knowed plenty of men that see no difference between 1 dead man & 2. But here yis are come into my camp & I must admit it is a great admiration I have for ye. So if yis is proposin that you & your sissy run off an you leave me here with this little fella then I see no reason why I should decline your offer.

Solus stood up very slow & pulled his sister up with him. Still they could not take their eyes from him.

Well go on with yis, said Jim Coyne, shooing them away as if they was no more than a pair of pesky crows. Old Jim won't stop you.

Solus looked at me. I could not read that look upon his face, perhaps in that moment he too did think on all them words we might have exchanged in a different time but then I was only glad to see his back as he turned slowly with the girl & they stepped out of the ring of light from the fire & vanished into the darkness of the trees.

67

A GENTLEMAN

AFTER SOLUS & HIS SISTER was fled into the darkness, Jim Coyne had took me away from that blaze, he told me he did not wish to see me overwhelmed by the attentions of his friends. O I was a delicate little so & so, said he, and not to be ogled after such an ordeal as I had endured.

Was there no end to this man's kindness, I thought, as he took me beyond them poplars to a small painted wagon what was still dimly lit by the fire's glow. I heard the shuffling hoofs of a mule nearby, the chiming of his tack reached my ears as I seen the graying mantle of his jaw & oil-black eye swing into view.

That is Mr. Johnson, said Jim Coyne. He is spoiled rotten though he earns it for his hard work taking us from place to place. I'm sure yis will soon be introduced to him proper, though it is well advised yis carry a treat of some description to sweeten his mood.

Mr. Johnson eyed me with great suspicion, he bared his row of crooked teeth, they did remind me of Dud Carter's. I was sure now me & Dud would find one another, O yes Jim Coyne would see to it that we was reunited there was no doubt.

There was something writ in fancy lettering aside the wagon though
I did not have chance to read it, Jim Coyne went unhooking various little clasps until that whole side folded out.

Inside I had not ever seen no wagon like it, its walls was draped
with queer shags & tapestries, there was framed pictures also of men &
women, their bodies mingled with them of animals. There was a turkey
rug & a table & chair, I did not know it then but they was all nailed to
the floor as they would be in a ship.

Jim Coyne then pointed beyond Mr. Johnson to a large black shape,
I took it for another wagon.

That is the more commodious of the 2, said he, but this I think is
more suited to your needs. I'll fetch yis some stew & a drink to calm the
nerves, I reckon yis is in need of it.

He left me then sit on the lip of that wagon. It was more like a parlor, I thought, it smelled of some scented smoke like candied flowers. Jim
Coyne returned to find me running my finger along the maze of color &
pattern of them tapestries.

He smiled & handed me a bowl of stew, I had never had no stew
like it, it did put my Mama's to shame. It was thick & rich & so very
flavorsome with game that I did long for more & that generous soul
did oblige me. This time he returned with a tin canteen of liquor also,
that too was a fine improvement on the Potent Swill Tom Peeper did
serve.

I drank & ate greedily as he watched me.

Can yis write? asked he when I was finished.

By some queer miracle, I still had that single piece of chalk left in
the pocket of my britches but it was no use to me now.

I nodded, stew was dribbling down my chin & he reached out with
the sleeve of his greatcoat & dabbed it away. As far as I knowed my Mama
had never done such a thing, it was a Great Intimacy & it spoke of that
man's fine talent for Friendship.

He then looked down by his feet & bent his long legs, he come up with a stick.

Would yis write your name for me?

I hopped down from the wagon & carved it deep into the earth. The stick did nearly snap, it was a great struggle to make them lines clean & it was a bastard to read, the light from the fire only just reached it.

Yip Tolroy, said Jim Coyne, squinting down at it.

I nodded & extended my hand.

Very pleased to meet ye, Yip Tolroy, said he. Yis have a very fine writing hand there.

O this did please me no end, I did carry on writing then & Jim Coyne read along.

Now who would Dud Carter be? he asked.

I scratched away with my boot at my name in the dirt like a dog after it has done its business. I then wrote a little easier in the powdery earth I had churned up & my new & high-minded friend did continue to congratulate me on the quality of my hand, O I did blush to hear it.

He looked down at them words once I was done & took my stick back up, he was not so disrespectful as to presume.

A friend is it? said Jim Coyne. Well, old Jim will do his best to find you some writing tools & see if he can find that friend of yours as well.

That word FRIEND was still writ as I shook his hand again, I could not thank him enough for his hospitality.

He rose then to his feet. I had expected he would stay with me but he suddenly looked anxious to be off.

I'll be back with you shortly, Yip Tolroy, said he before he went.

I seen him then eye that darkness into which Solus & his sister had slipped.

My friends have their eyes on you & Mr. Johnson also, I advise yis get yourself some rest, yis will find many a blanket in there to warm yourself with. And remember it isn't safe for one so Special as you, you stay with Jim Coyne & yis will be well looked after.

I watched him then as he stalked off back toward the town, my plan was to wait for his return but I stayed awake only long enough to scrape out the dregs of my stew before the warmth of the final swallows of whiskey & the winking light of the fire lulled me into a deep & dreamless sleep.

68

THE COTTONWOOD

NOW I HAD WOKE TO the rock & sway of that wagon, all them pictures jostled on their nails, the shags & tapestries shook out their fragrant smoke & bars of early light come slanted through the chinks & kneaded the motes in delicate folds.

I knocked then on the wall & soon I felt it come to a halt. I heard the trappings of that hatch then being undone & it was pulled open, I was near blinded by the sunlight what poured in.

I shaded my eyes & there was Jim Coyne, his beaver hat atop his head, a clay pipe hanging out his mouth & smoking idly. He smiled at me.

Now yis are awake I reckon I will have yis ride up with me, said he.

Once I was sit on the box-seat, I seen it was not long past dawn, the sky was pale & ashy above. Mr. Johnson toiled as he pulled us up a slope, I did not know where we was until I turned & seen the town behind us, its street was already busying with people & chatter & following us was the unharmonious honking of a goose what a Chinaman carried in a wicker cage.

Jim Coyne seen me looking back.

I asked about for yer friend this mornin whilst yis was still restin, young Yip, & there was no sign of him I am afraid to say. But don't yis worry, we'll be findin him in no time.

Behind us that larger wagon was on our tail, it was drove by a dark-skinned man, he wore himself a black slouch hat, a scarf was wrapped around his mouth though I did not think it cold enough to do so.

I did not want to wake you, said Jim Coyne, turning to me then. Yis was much in need of a good rest & there is many an eye in towns like these that like to make other people's business their own. I thought it best I keep yis under wraps for fear they find somethin out they needn't.

I thought this all most considerate of him, he was a man of outstanding moral rectitude was my summation.

Mr. Johnson strained as we headed back up the slope. My eyes did scour the scrub but again I could not see any sign of my slate. I longed for something to write on & was about to make such a request in the same way I had done before, hoping Jim Coyne had found me some in town when I seen that old cottonwood come into view where we had first seen them boys.

I looked at it & reckoned there was something changed about it as Mr. Johnson brung us over the crest & onto the road, I thought then it had growed 2 extra limbs but my eyes was yet to come to terms with that light, they was still misty with sleep.

Mr. Johnson slowed, his gray rump swayed & his black-tipped tail flicked as I seen a cloud of flies circling his rear, I thought it most unusual to see so many in these colder months.

Jim Coyne then brung the old mule to a halt, I thought him offering Mr. Johnson a chance to rest but when I turned to him I seen he was squinting up at the tree.

I did then turn myself & that is when I seen that hanging from the cottonwood was 2 black bodies twisting & swaying in the morning breeze.

Well, said Jim Coyne, yis can't blame them for the trying.

He tutted & shook his head as he took off his beaver hat & held it in his lap very respectful indeed. His long hair was tied in a scrap of ribband at the back.

It was Solus & his sister dangling, they was stripped of their clothes & their shit run down their legs in a stink what made me bring my sleeve to my nose. Solus's face was swolled & bloodied, I thought of us then crouched in the woods & his eyes pulsing with life, now they was bugged open & stared lifeless at the ground, their color already soured to a queer gray.

It took me a moment to notice he did not have his hands, they had been hacked off, only bloody stumps what was being paid very close attention to by a bevy of flies. His poor sister, her eyes was open also, she had done no wrong but still she shared his fate.

I must admit I felt that stew rise up my gullet. I had crouched by Solus in them woods & seen his tears, I had felt his beating heart in the pool, I had seen his eyes light up with joy when he seen his sister. Now with each passing second come another detail I seen of the damage inflicted to them both. I seen that where Solus's sister's breasts was meant to be there was now only rags of flesh & Solus had had his own parts hacked clean off also, they did not look like no bodies what ever took a breath or walked around or ever had a thought or dream in their heads.

There come then a cawing from the woods & I seen the branches filled with crows, their dark eyes counted the drops of blood which I seen slowly drip into the dust.

Listen up, young Yip, said Jim Coyne, he was cocking his head & putting a finger to his lobe.

At first I heard only them hungering crows & the distant murmur of the town but then I begun to hear the soft moan & creak of the bough as it sagged beneath the weight of them 2 bodies.

Yis would think them still alive would you not, the way that moaning comes on now? But if yis had seen them drop last night yis would know there's no life in them left. If yis had heard the snap of their necks yis would never be mistook.

Jim Coyne shook his head & sighed. He looked down at me & seen the look upon my stricken face. His face did soften, that smile come creeping back across his lips.

Yis must remember that Justice has been done, said he.

He pointed with a gloved finger up toward the sky.

It's what He would have wanted, young Yip, He don't care to see a crime go unpunished down here on His good earth.

He put on his beaver hat again & took up the reins.

I am afraid we must be leaving them for the crows, said Jim Coyne.

69

ON DISPLAY

THEY IS NOT A SOUL ON EARTH who has not done the reading of another man's heart & come away with a different story to the one truly writ there.

Jim Coyne was all Charm & Chatter in that wagon, I had never knowed a man with such a silken tongue, how I did admire his fancy wordplay & great glossary of compliments.

He did promise as soon as we reached the next town he would personally fetch me some Writing Materials, he would inquire with every single soul he come across as to the whereabouts of Dud Carter, there was nothing he would not do to keep me happy. And I did believe every wretched word what come out of his mouth, I had not ever been so well spoke of before & he could not seem to say no bad word about me.

At a store we passed he stopped & come out with a new hat for me, it was a beaverskin just like his own, he said we surely did look like Father & Son.

I want yis to keep that hat on & only take it off when I says so, young Yip. I think it suits yis so well it would be a shame to not make use of it every moment yis can.

I did agree, it was my Pride & Joy. It was so very different from the one what had once belonged to Mr. Barre's daughter, the fur was dark & glossy & did smell of Man & all his Triumphs over them busy little beasts.

We reached a new town before nightfall but before we rolled through that busy street Jim Coyne took me down from the box-seat & shut me back up in the wagon.

I don't want yis getting *overwhelmed,* young Yip. I know as well as any yis has had a rough time of it & I want to keep yis safe that is all.

He give me one of his smiles then & I thanked God I had been rescued by so caring a man. The rattle & bite of them bolts & clasps was not to my ears the sounds of imprisonment but the chimes & peals of Protection.

We rolled on then & I seen through the slats of the wagon many faces come gathering around as we come to a stop. Above me I heard Jim Coyne's boots as he stood up & begun to address them milling crowds what was turned toward us.

Ladies & Gentlemen, said he. I am Jim Coyne. Yis might think yis have seen my kind before but let me assuage yer creeping suspicions & give them stale & wilted thoughts of yours a kick up the arse.

There come then a few disgruntled cries from the crowd but Jim Coyne knowed what he was doing, he was a man what knowed his role through & through.

I mean that as no insult, Ladies & Gentlemen, & yis should not take it as one. Yis cannot be blamed for thinking me a mountebank or a charlatan, I know there is plenty to come through these parts claiming all kinds of lies to be truths. And what do yis get when yis give yer hard-earned money?

Again that crowd did cry out, he did treat them like a grate of dozing embers, stoking & stirring until the flames come licking back to life.

That's right, Ladies & Gentlemen, said Jim Coyne. Yis is right. They is cheats & scoundrels & they don't show no respect for honest folk like yerselves.

He did pause then & let them flames simmer down again.

But now is the time yis should open up them very pretty eyes & ears of yours to look & listen well. I am no fraud but an honest man who has come to learn there is no need for lies & deceit in this life. Yes I am a purveyor of Great & Mysterious talent, an agent to them souls God chose to bless with Queer & Wondrous secrets. Yis do not need me to tell we is ruled ourselves by powers unseen & not always heard, our God does not reveal all them forces He did bless us with on His earth. And so it is there is so much we do know but here is a chance, a Golden Opportunity, to have some of them Unknowns made plain, to see beyond what the humble eye can see.

I could hear how very spirited his oration was, I wanted to tell that crowd to trust his every word, he did speak the truth when he said he had no need for lies & deceit. O yes I knowed that as well as any.

The thunder of his boots above me did shake loose all them sleeping motes & ancient shavings what fell fine & soft as the first snows of the year. I did have to brush them from my bald head & rub them from my eyes but I did not care. O my cowardly half did think it like being in the dark belly of some Raging Beast, but that other half was filled with Excitement.

That is not to mention there will be the finest Acting & Dancing & Singing yis have ever seen, cried Jim Coyne, his boot stamping out each cast of entertainment. Come & find me, Jim Coyne & his Traveling Show, this evening & yis will all go home with yis jaws dropped to the floor!

He did sit himself down then, he did not wait to answer no questions & all that reached my ears was the excited chatter of the crowd as Jim Coyne snapped the reins & Mr. Johnson lurched on. Jim Coyne had them a-dangling on his line.

I knocked on the ceiling of the wagon so that I might now be let out but Jim Coyne did not stop, I heard him shout above the din of clopping hoofs & grinding wheels.

All in good time, young Yip, cried he. All in good time!

70

A TRAVELING SHOW

I HEARD JIM COYNE CLIMB down, I waited in that darkness for them bolts & clasps to be undone, O I did have so many questions I wanted to ask.

But he did not let me out right away, I supposed I could not blame him, Jim Coyne was a busy man barking out orders to that following wagon. Finally I seen his bewhiskered jaw clenched through the slats as he undone them bolts & clasps but he did not greet me with no smiling face this time, he turned very sharp away & set about the business of Making Camp.

In my fervor to have his attention I did tug at his sleeve but he did not take kindly to that, he whipped round & near knocked me on my rear.

Yis will have to wait! snapped Jim Coyne.

I will not lie I was very shocked at this change in his manner but I reckoned he had his work to do & did surely suffer from them same petty frustrations as the rest of us.

I was then forced to try & make myself understood to him by subtler means but suddenly Jim Coyne begun to claim my every gesture was incomprehensible to him.

How them old feelings from my youth then come surging back, my voice was lost & I felt that gap begun to open up again between me & my Fellow Man. O it started off as just a crack but it did widen & widen until it was a gorge, shadows fell across me & you could not see me standing at the edge of the other side.

There is no use in yis makin them signs, young Yip, said Jim Coyne.

He had sit himself down on his own personal stool he had fetched from the wagon. He lit his pipe as he stared out across a small creek what run through a stand of willow & a dark meadow stretched out toward a distant bank of trees, the last light of the horizon glowed dim above the reach of their black branches.

I am no trained reader of them signs yis are makin, continued Jim Coyne, yis will have to wait.

His cheeks went briefly hollow & gaunt as he sucked hard on the stem & breathed out a great plume of smoke.

I told yis I will get yer as much paper as yis want & yis can write until yer heart is content. I am a fair man, there is not many who would begrudge me in sayin as much. But yis will have to trust me. Now how does that sound?

I nodded. I could not wait to get to writing again. I would ask Jim Coyne what town we was in & I would write a fine description of Dud Carter & show it to any what could read & I imagined then the sight of my tall & gangly friend come toward me, his small gray eyes searching for mine until we seen each other. How I longed to be reunited with him again.

If I had suffered any doubts about Jim Coyne's Nature I was back to believing him the most benevolent man alive.

The weather had suddenly took a turn again & I was glad of my new hat, how very generous Jim had been to buy it for me. The air was bitter cold, our breath come misting out of our mouths & the nostrils of Mr. Johnson still dressed in all his tack & waiting very impatient to be released.

I seen that old mule eyeing me then, I had tried to feed him a apple what Jim Coyne had give me when we had stopped at that store some hours earlier but he showed no interest in it, he only tried to take a chunk out of my coat with them wicked teeth of his.

Just then a man come walking past with an armful of firewood, he had already gone skirting about the creek. He was small, a very industrious little fellow, I realized he was the one what had drove the bigger wagon behind us. I could not see him so clear in that darkling light but I took him to be old, his hair was gray & his cheeks flecked with tight little coils of hair what made up a patchy beard.

He stacked up that first load of wood & then he took Mr. Johnson down to the creek for his watering, he talked to that beast in soft & deferential tones as if indeed it was Mr. Johnson what did own him.

He give that cantankerous beast his nosebag of oats before tying him up beneath the soft & sorrowful rustlings of them willows & then I seen Jim Coyne call him over & whisper some instruction to him. His driver set to nodding like he never heard anything so truthful in his life, he begun then to collect more wood & pile it up in a clearing.

That there is Joseph, said Jim Coyne, pointing at him. He was striking a flint now & sending a shower of sparks into the kindling he had gathered. Shyness or fear did prevent him from looking up, he kept his eyes lowered & set on his task.

I found him & Mr. Johnson some yrs back on the side of the road near Chillicothe, said Jim Coyne. They was both whip-thin, their bones pokin through their hides. Yis can believe me when I say they both would have perished if I had not give them a home.

Jim Coyne shook his head sadly.

I suppose yis can say I have made a habit of it ever since, picking up strays like you, young Yip, & giving yis a second chance. Life wouldn't be worth the livin if yis didn't have a second chance now would it?

I shook my head.

Good boy, said Jim Coyne, he did begin then to very carefully adjust my hat to make sure my ears was well covered. I knows yis has some sense in that head if yis agrees with old Jim.

He winked & set to unloading the wagon.

71

THE PERSON HE CLAIMED TO BE

THAT WOOD SOON TOOK HOLD & Joseph was lit up, I seen his eyes was most unusual, they did sit pale as marbles in his dark face as if he was struck by Blindness. But even if he had not looked at me, I did sense somehow he had took in my measure.

Only now in the light of them flames was it I seen what was writ on the side of the little wagon I had rode in.

It read:

JIM COYNE'S
TRAVELING SHOW
PERFORMING TWICE DAILY
The LIVING DOLLS
The PIG-FACED LADY
The Famous FORREST and BENJAMIN QUICK
Plus:
SINGING and DANCING and ACTING from
the FINEST SHOWS

I had no idea who these people was or what it was exactly they did. Bits of Jim Coyne's fine speech earlier then come back to me, he had talked about mysteries & God & performing artists, I now realized he run some kind of Entertainment.

Joseph had brung that other wagon along & now that the fire was lit I seen there come 2 girls from inside it, at first I thought myself gone mad for they was 2 of the very same, they was dressed in the same blue dresses, their faces & eyes & turned-up noses was the same, their bonnets beneath their chins tied in the very same little loop. I could not tell them apart.

I will not lie I thought them very beautiful, their eyes was blue as their dresses, their young & supple lips seemed to me like them soft & tender things what Shelby Stubbs had told me lived in shells in the salted darkness of the ocean.

I had heard of Identical Twins but had not knowed if they was just fibs told to confuse me when I was young but now I seen them to be real. They did introduce theirselves as Lorrie & Esther Challip, their voices & mannerisms was also the same, I stared at them in wonder as each word did flow off their darting pretty little tongues.

O I did not mean to be rude but I did find I longed to touch them, fastened about their pale white throats was thin velvet ribbands of the kind a jeweler will use to dress the case of some precious stone, they did adorn their thin wrists also as if they was the joins in a china doll. It did strike me then that perhaps these 2 was what was writ on the side of the wagon, The Living Dolls.

Then come along 2 young men, they brung them adzed logs with them from the previous camp & arranged them around the fire. The Challip twins took a seat & once them boys did introduce theirselves as Forrest & Benjamin Quick, they was jugglers & equilibrists & musicians all at once. They was talented & nervous souls, their eyes never still, their hands always worrying at some loose thread or lock of hair.

Jim Coyne had excused himself to commence his Nightly Ablutions in the meadow & now he emerged from them long & whispering grasses. He crouched by the flames & rubbed his hands. I seen him look over at me & give me one of his Famous Winks, they did never fail to warm my heart.

He come over then, he did rest a hand on my shoulder & begun to steer me out of earshot of them gathered around the fire so that the cold come rushing at my face & set my eyes to watering.

Now, young Yip, said he, since I has been so kind as to take yis into my care, I think it only fair yis offer something in return. I have not had the pleasure of meeting your dear mammy but I expect she did inculcate in yis an honest desire to work & earn your keep.

I nodded, having resented them duties for so long, I was suddenly proud that this had indeed been the case.

Good boy, said Jim Coyne, he did pat me on the head. Yis will be able to do all the writing yis want soon enough, I will make sure of it after yis has been so generous to offer your services.

I did not know what services I had offered but I would do anything to start writing again & to please my new friend.

I picture my young face now all these yrs down the line & I see them Bright & Innocent eyes staring back at a man who was so very far from the person he claimed to be.

72

MISS VIVIAN RAY

AFTER WE HAD ET A SIMPLE meal of mush & cornbread by the fire, I listened to the Challip twins & Forrest & Benjamin Quick. They talked about towns I had not ever heard of & things about the routine of their days I could not then take the measure of but would find out soon enough. I fingered that knurl of chalk in my pocket, how I wished I could write & join in their conversation.

Joseph did sit on his own on the ground, his pale eyes did rove over them flames, every now & then he added another log before going off in search of more.

Jim Coyne had et his plateful in a great hurry & he had headed off toward that town. It was not so big as the last but it was still lit very bright, voices was risen now & come echoing across to our fire.

Jim Coyne had fetched me from somewhere my own little stool, it was not so different from my own with 3 sturdy legs, only it was a good bit taller & my legs did not hang so agreeably. I looked at them strange faces around me, perhaps it was the simple feel of that stool beneath my rear but it was then there first come a dark little knot tied in my insides. I had been so grateful to be rid of my captor, I had not took the time to think on the situation I found myself in now, I still had no notions as to where Dud Carter was, I did find myself wishing I was back home in Heron's Creek & beneath my old elm.

My mood growed darker & darker until I heard Jim Coyne whistling on his way back to camp.

He come strutting back into the circle of light, he looked very spritely, he clapped his hands together & demanded everyone's attention.

I believe we will have ourselves a fine audience tonight, cried he.

There was a strong whiff of whiskey on his breath, he had found his time to stop in at a saloon & take a drink.

He smiled down at the Challip twins.

Girls, yis are lookin very beautiful tonight. And boys, he said looking down at the Quick brothers, I want the pair of yis to gloss up the horsehair on yer fiddles. I want yis to play some lively tunes for this lot, they is fond of a drink here & I can only imagine they is fond of a dance as well.

Finally he looked down at me, he smiled his Gentle Smile.

I am glad yis have all met with young Yip Tolroy here.

Now he got down on his haunches again, he took my hands in his & locked his kindly eyes on mine.

I have asked around & this town has everything yis need to get that hand of yours flowin across the page. Like I say all yis need is to do old Jim a favor & yis will be in my Good Books for the rest of yer days.

He looked about him now, he did look very furtive indeed.

Now, young Yip, you is a man as much as me & every man on this good earth does like to hear the jingle-janglin of money in his pocket.

He smiled, he shook the pockets of his britches & I heard the cheerful chatter of some coins.

Are you a man as much as me? he asked.

I nodded, I thought I was.

Well, Old Jim here has heard rumors of some Gold found in Old Virginny & that's where I is headed. Now I know yis want to be getting back to yer friend but if we don't find him – but yis know I think we

will – then yis would be welcome to join & we might consider ourselves
a little partnership, how's about that?

O I thought this a most generous offer, I did not know how he ever
spared a thought for himself. It was Gold what got me into this trouble
but I cannot say my heart did not quicken, he seen me then pick up a
stick I had found, I did want to write in that dry dirt & ask some questions but he snatched it from my hands.

Not now, young Yip, I is very busy, said he.

He patted me on the back of my hand.

Take a little time to think on it, he said.

As it would happen I would soon have good reason to forget all
about that offer & see it for what it was but I marveled at him then as he
went about his business, he sent the Challip twins back to their wagon &
Forrest & Benjamin Quick to fetch their fiddles. Soon I heard the lonely
cries of them instruments as they was tuned.

I watched Jim Coyne move about the camp, he was awful restless.
He paced back & forth & did keep checking on his timepiece before he
suddenly lit off for the town again for another drink.

I stayed by the fire & mopped up the rest of my mush with a wedge
of cornbread. Joseph was begun to smoke himself a very long ornate pipe,
the smoke billowed thickly from the bowl & his light eyes was stared at
the shapes gone drifting up.

That fire was so warm I could not help from dozing off & when I
woke Joseph had gone & I could hear something above the crickling &
popping of the flames.

I turned & seen it was Jim Coyne, he was returned from his second
visit to the town & along with Joseph he dragged behind him something,
a sweat was broke out on both their brows, it did make a terrible noise
on the frosted earth.

I could not make out what it was, only when he come into the ring
of the fire did I see it was a large cage of sorts. It was made of thick green

lengths of timber & sharp iron wire what glinted in the light. I could not yet see what it was home to, it was hammered together awful crude with rusted nails, I did think it looked the kind you might keep a cur in what was foaming at the mouth.

Jim Coyne seen my fear, he smiled down at me.

This here is our Porcine Princess, said he.

I did not understand them words of his, I only seen his queer firelit grin. Jim Coyne & Joseph did push the great cage closer to the flames, I could not believe what I then seen inside, it was a small & withered old bear sit on its hindquarters. Only it did not look like no bear I'd ever seen out in the woods, its face had been shaved of any hair & it was dressed in a yellow frock & gloves & shawl & a dark wig with a bonnet fastened beneath her hairless chin.

Her jaw was slack & teeth near all rotted out, her eyes gone milky-pale. O yes gone was any of that Muscle & Power endowed them fine creatures, her shoulders was slumped & she let out a volley of weak grunts & groans, her bald snout raised up & sniffing at the air.

There did come a dreadful stink from her, her fur was alive with all them creeping critters, I would have thought any soul in their right mind would have recoiled.

Yis are to do a little acting for me, young Yip, said Jim Coyne.

I did barely hear him, I could not take my eyes from that cage, he seen the worry at work beneath my skin.

Not to worry, said Jim Coyne as he then begun to untie a knot of rope & slide open a hatch.

Miss Vivian Ray don't bite no more, she is a very Respectable Lady.

With a bowl of cornmush he had saved he now temped that old bear he called Miss Vivian Ray up from her seat to come sniffing & blinking her old eyes, she trudged through a slick & foul map of her own scat & piss, the hem of that frock was besmeared & frayed.

She dragged a noose what was tied about her neck along & Jim Coyne took it in his hands & pulled her out.

Now you could see very clear her fur was all et up in parts, skin bit by bugs & nipped raw & them bones of her shoulders & ribs come angling through like old reed fishing poles through her hide.

I seen many a bear in my time & they is normally the most powerful beasts God put on this earth, their pelts glossy & thick, their eyes sharp & their noses black & wet. Their paws could likely take a head clean from its shoulders but Miss Vivian Ray did look so very weak, her own claws did leave a print in the dirt what looked no bigger than a dog's, they was brittle as cinders.

She followed Jim Coyne & the cornmush over to that stand of willow where he tied her up. Mr. Johnson did not balk as you would expect but Miss Vivian Ray did sit down then in her frock & commenced eating, not with the wild & savage lunges you would expect but quite refined in her style, she had obviously took her lessons.

Jim Coyne left her to eat, he then come back over & clumb into the wagon & went rummaging through that oaken chest he kept in the back.

What do you make to old Miss Vivian Ray? he said over his shoulder. Awful pretty gal ain't she? It is a great mystery she ain't yet been fixed up with a suitor.

Again his words was mostly lost on me, I heard him chuckling to himself as he then produced an old sheet, he held it up & begun to slice at it with his knife. It was filled with ragged holes by the time he was done. Then I did watch unmoving as he went down to the creek & come back with them strips dripping & lathered in mud.

He smiled at me again as he smeared it around & then wiped his hands on his britches.

We are all of us performers here, young Yip. We are a family & we all must play our part. Don't yis want to drink in the Praise & Wonder of all the town? Sure & yis will be doing old Jim a fine favor & in the morning yis will wake up & have yer pen & paper waiting for yer.

73

A FIRST PERFORMANCE

JOSEPH HELD MY ARMS & LEGS DOWN, his pale & icelocked eyes looked into mine as Jim Coyne stripped me of my clothes & all them sodden & filthy rags was draped over me. Them remaining globs of mush in the pot by the fire Jim Coyne then daubed around my mouth, they was turned bitter with ash.

O I seen he aimed to make of me a Wildling, a creature what had no knowledge of humanity, captured & brung for civilized eyes to take their Lordly Pleasure.

Just as I had knowed it was no act when I was a young boy & them other childs would flee my company, I knowed now this was no act neither. O I did try to escape, sprung & coiled like an eel I wrung myself out but they was too strong, they dragged me kicking through the dirt & throwed me in that cage.

That same hatch Miss Vivian Ray had just walked out of was now slammed shut behind me, my Savior was now my Jailor, Jim Coyne had no key but tied that thick bind of hemp rope so I could not get out. I slid through the old bear's foulings, there was no inch of skin what was not covered, the smell so strong I did then fetch up my dinner & add it to the wreckage.

The wood was old but strong, that wire sharp & rusted, I tried to pull on it but it did bite into my hands, they was spotted with blood like I had picked up the glittering little dustings of broke glass, I now knowed what had tore at Miss Vivian Ray's fur & left her coat like a threadbare rug.

Now yis promised me yis would do a little acting, young Yip, said Jim Coyne, he was crouched down now & looking at me through the wire, his face split into a dozen slices of skin & eye & mouth & nostril.

Remember how old Jim here saved yis from that wicked slave, without me yis would be laid somewhere with your own knife buried in yer heart & cold death come upon you.

His breath was pungent with the sour heat of liquor, his teeth like flotsam washed up on a rivershore. How I had ever thought him charming I did not know, now I seen there did live in him a Conniving Devil what did not leap or lash but purred in them corners of his heart, stalking horned and cloven-footed.

Joseph then begun to pull that cage along the ground, the skin on my bony rear & legs was torn on the cold earth beneath me as we went, splinters of wood come stabbing at me, each & every pain did have its own particular song what cut through the skin & let loose a chorus of Howling Fear in my heart.

I could not see where we was headed, I clung to them timbers of my cage as Forrest & Benjamin Quick then begun to play their fiddles, it was no lively tune to a dance but Short & Violent stabs, you might imagine a cat with its tail snipped & knotted & yowling out to warn folks that they too was in danger of being visited & tormented by their Worst Fears.

Indeed it was a large crowd what awaited us in the town, Jim Coyne was right, they was all of them merry with drink, I could hear their lively & excited chatter as we growed closer, it did appear the Great Stink of my cage did indicate some Exotic Presence, they suddenly had the minds & hearts of flies.

When we reached them they did part like a river around a stone, some was brung to silence & some did cheer, a tin of ale was tipped over me & dripped through the slats of my roof, even above my own foul dwelling I could smell all them commixed fluids squeezed from their Hard Lives.

At first I could not see anything but legs, dusty britches & dresses & boots what scuffed about but then folk begun to crouch & stare. Cries went up among them that the cage did contain a Filthy Beast, I shrunk away from all them peering faces, lit by lanterns they loomed & glowed with Devilish Menace, I had not ever been so frighted.

They begun to jeer, boots kicked & rattled the iron wire & shook it so I was tossed about as if in them salt winds of the sea. I cowered in the corner until childs begun to run alongside me & jab at me with sticks, they too pricked & pierced my skin.

I could not see Jim Coyne but now I heard his voice, Joseph dropped the cage & Forrest & Benjamin Quick silenced their fiddles, I seen their bows held slack in their hands, the horsehair glowed with light.

Ladies & Gentlemen, said Jim Coyne, I present before yis a creature that has not knowed anything but the wild woods & sky & mountains of this vast land. He come out his mammy's womb with a full head of teeth, it was not her milk he was after but Flesh & Blood.

If I was to open this cage then he would not walk on his 2 feet like you or I, Ladies & Gentlemen, but he would scurry away on his hands & knees, he would howl up at the moon & slink into them shadows of the world that we people of the light would not dare enter.

Jim Coyne paused then, he waited for them whisperings to stop.

So long has his tongue gone unused, continued he, that he cannot talk. His bones did cease to grow. His hair is all fell out, no one rightly knows what age he is though he has been seen with wolves & bears, he has been spotted at the tops of trees & dipping his paw in the nests of eagles & owls.

I did not know where these wicked words come from, it was as if Jim Coyne had had this story in his head waiting for his chance to tell it.

I had heard too many cruel words said about me to count but these was the first what made me feel like I truly was not even human.

If yis would like yer chance to see him, he said, then yis must do it now. It will cost yis a mere 10 cents, a single dime, for the privilege. Now for them who is brave enough to see him if yis would form a line then yis will be give yer time to witness one of the queerest designs God ever chose to make.

For 2 hours then I shuddered in the cold of my cage as face after face come mooning in at me. They breathed their stink at me & some even paid twice to see me again & the second time they was not content to look but took the sticks from their childs & set to poking at me so I had to shrink myself up like a spider what in death turns its legs in on itself & begins to pick & tear at its own body.

Jim Coyne stood to one side, I could peer up & see his face, it was flushed with the thrill of them coins what was dropped in his beaver-skin hat. He did not stop them words of his flowing out, embroidering that Tall Tale until it become the tallest in the land, until them people become feverish with excitement.

Elsewhere Forrest & Benjamin Quick played their fiddles & I heard the sweet voices of the Challip twins as they sung but they was attractions for folk to enjoy only after they had had their fill of me.

When it come to an end I did look down to see my arms & legs was broke & bloodied, them jabbing sticks had tore through my skin, they ached & stung as if I had run bare-limbed through a briar patch.

Jim Coyne crouched by my cage, I seen his wicked face split again, he held out his beaverskin hat, it was filled with glittering coins. He shook it at me in his greedy hands.

Well done, young Yip, said he. Yis is a fine new addition to the family.

74

THE WILDLING

THE NEXT NIGHT WE WAS in a different town, now I did not ride on the box-seat beside Jim Coyne but was Bolted & Locked inside the wagon where I beat against them walls until my knuckles run red with blood.

Let me say here that I never knowed how long I was a part of that Traveling Show, such was the Rush & Blur of them horrid moments that it could have been a whole yr, I did not only lose track of time but of myself & who I was before such Cruel Misery was heaped upon me.

My own clothes was left to me in a bundle in the corner, buttons was now missing from my shirt & the soles of my boots come flapping off where I had kicked to try & escape. But in the pocket of my britches there did remain that single piece of chalk what I held & turned in my fingers, how it did keep my heart beating to see the white dust on my fingertips & the thought that I would one day set it to slate again.

Of course I had woke the morning after my First Performance & there was no sight of them reams of paper he had sworn to, Jim Coyne had no intention of giving me back my voice, he wanted to keep me trapped in my silence like a fish in a barrel.

He had Joseph sleep next to me & stay by my side every waking moment, my only relief was that I did not have to bed down with Miss

Vivian Ray. I did no longer have no Leash fastened about my chest but I might as well have done, I felt something tight about my neck, Joseph's cold pale eyes was like a noose, they did never seem to close.

I only ever seen Miss Vivian Ray's Act the one time, it come from an old & dusty legend of a little girl born with no human face like most but a pig's. Like me she was not cut from the same cloth but she had a mighty rich mama & daddy, they did try to marry her off with a dowry every penny as much as a king's ransom. But no suitor ever seen beyond her grunts & groans & now here she was.

Jim Coyne took a table & very sturdy chair, they was arranged for her which she did miraculously take her seat at the table like a Graceful Lady. Jim Coyne would then take a stick & crawl under that table, his devious rear hid by the tablecloth hanging down.

Them people lined up then & would ask their foolish questions & Jim Coyne would then poke Miss Vivian Ray with his stick, her grunts was took for her pleas to be wed to a handsome man.

What folk did see in that shaved face was often not what I seen, O I did think it was a woeful sight indeed & I noted Joseph never watched her Act neither, he turned his back to it & smoked his long pipe.

Again Jim Coyne told me I would be rewarded with reams of paper & this time he promised me a Turkey Quill of the highest quality but he did not have to tell me them lies no more. I knowed I had been tricked, I could not help the tears come shining in my eyes & running down my cheeks.

No need for the cryin, said Jim Coyne, yis will have your paper soon enough & I've been askin around for that friend of yours, Dan Carper, but there is no sign of him here I am afraid to say, young Yip.

He shook his head sadly as if his efforts was real & not Maggoty Lies.

But there's every chance he will be in the next town. Hope is a fine thing, young Yip, & I'm sure yis won't give up on him yet. Will yis?

I would not look at him but he demanded it, he pinched the skin at the back of my neck & made me face him.

Will yis?

I shook my head.

Yis is a good boy.

He give me that wink & oily smile, he run his hands through his greasy hair & tied it in that scrap of ribband.

Now yis had best get to it, said he.

So this is how my life went on. We traveled during the days & normally come to a town by late afternoon. Sometimes we did not come upon any & made a camp beneath the stars. Only in these times was I allowed out of the wagon to sit by the fire. I would stare at them flames & think of my Mama & of being sit in the warmth of our parlor. I wondered if she had looked for me or if she had heard I was a murderer & had disowned me for good.

I soon realized that first bowl of stew Jim Coyne ever give me was from his own Personal Pot what Joseph cooked separate & thickened with more vegetables & meat. This he would only share with the Challip twins for they did claim to possess very sophisticated palates & they was like to become awkward with Jim if they was not properly tret like Ladies.

When I had finished the thin & watery stew what was from the larger pot Joseph would take me back to the dark of the wagon & it brung me no shame to say I did cry myself to sleep each night, I had never knowed a loneliness like it, only Sad Thoughts come into my head, they could not be stopped. I would roll that single bit of chalk left me through my fingers, it did seem to live in my mind as my only bit of Hope.

Jim Coyne would not ever let me take off that hat he had bought me, he wished to keep my baldness a secret to any what might be spying on us, he considered it my Vital Asset.

But my scalp growed so dry & itchy it begun to crack & bleed, I am afraid when Jim Coyne seen this development his smile stretched wide as a toad's, he then worked this sorry detail into his speech.

I was The Wildling he favored me to be, I would now crawl into my cage & through all Miss Vivian Ray's woeful droppings, I did not have to be forced. That old bear would come trudging out & I would go straight in, I begun to see in her eyes a Great Sorrow not just for herself but for me also, we was locked in this wicked loop together.

If I could have made a sound I believe I would have grunted & groaned just like Miss Vivian Ray, they was cries to have her sorry life come to an end. O before them days I would never have claimed myself fluent in beartalk but I come to think I understood that tongue, it did articulate Pain & Misery just like any other.

But if Miss Vivian Ray's Showdays was coming to an end, mine was only just begun, Jim Coyne had come to demand that I chew on sticks & spit out stones at the audience. He ordered that I try to bite any fingers what come curling around my cage.

Worst of all he come up with what he called a way to turn my act more Authentic. After he had et his feed by the fire, he would take 1 of them twigs what burned a feverish red at the edge of the flames. I would then hear them clasps & bolts unlocked & he would stand there with its glowing tip.

Now it does not hurt, young Yip. Yis must remember when we come upon another town I will get yis what yis need. Yis will have that pen & paper soon enough.

Joseph would then hold me down, I did feel their cruel weight in the bones of my arms & legs, on my chest so I could not breathe. I would thrash & squirm but it was no use, Jim Coyne did brand my hands & forearms & legs & feet also, them marks rose up in terrible red sores & I come to know well the stink of Burning Flesh, it is a queerly sweet aroma what fast turns your guts to water.

O how them Silent Roars & Silent Howls come back now, I have them scars still but they is not like them innocent 3 milkwhite spots on my cheek, they is angry & purpled & pain smolders in them on bitter cold days.

But what hurt more was them lies, I was so sick of hearing them filthy promises, they come to drip like poison in my ear like Claudius done to the sleeping King.

Jim Coyne would then lower the lantern to my cage.

See the scars! he would cry. See how the yrs of tearing through the hard scrub of wood & brush have left his hands & feet! See how he longs to Whimper & Wail but he cannot for so long has he lived Out There that his tongue is growed dead!

Each time he would become more inventive with his narrative until some people would believe his every word, they did see in my face no Performer but the reality he had summoned.

Some crying childs hid their faces in their mamas' dresses, they could not bear to look at me.

Whenever my performance was over Jim Coyne took me back to the wagon & plied me with whiskey, he thought me numbed to all that Pain & Misery.

It is best yis stay in here, young Yip. Yis are proving a fine little earner. We don't want word getting around that yis is no Wild Boy but sittin around a fire with a spoon in yer hand. Word travels fast in this business. Faster than we can move, young Yip.

He give me his Sickly Smile.

It is a wonder yis have only just decided to enter into the business, he crowed.

I had not decided nothing & he knowed it but he was a man what was bereft of any thread of good. I had thought myself saved from Solus but Jim Coyne was no savior, I was his prisoner of that there had come to be no doubt. I could not imagine how I would ever find my way out of his service, for it was clear as day he did not ever plan to let me speak again.

75

A NEW VOICE

LIGHT SNOWS BEGUN TO FALL as we clumb higher into them old Appalachians. A second mule was took from the wagon behind to help assist Mr. Johnson on them steeper roads. The air was growed thinner now & he wheezed & hacked his way up, I had not ever wished ill on any animal & have not since but I will say I did not mind to hear the suffering of that Wretched Beast.

The wagon rocked & jumped, I was wrapped in a heap of blankets, my beaverskin pulled low over my ears for warmth even though it did pick & irritate them sad scabs atop my scalp.

I had took to sit in that chair nailed to the floor but let me tell you there was times I was shook off by that winding trail we took & all them wounds of mine was opened up & the slow work of healing was undone & dark blood & bright pus did run free as creeks.

It was in this chair what sometimes 1 of the Challip twins would sit when they was pretending to be them Living Dolls. The other would stand or sit somewhere near. Their eyes growed like glass, they would not move, their cheeks was rosy, somehow they had trained theirselves to remain so still they would not move an inch for an hour at a time.

People was not allowed to touch them but they could get awful close &
some did leave not believing blood run through their veins.

Now I could hear Jim Coyne singing on his box-seat, his voice was
low & muffled. He sung many songs but this must have been his favorite,
he sung it over & over again. Many of them tunes he told me his daddy
had teached to him back in his old country which I had come to understand was Ireland. How or why he had come over here he never said but
they was always a faraway look in his eye when he spoke of his home.

But this one he told me he had made up himself, he was awful proud
of it, he called it The Calling Man.

Warm up them feet,
Turn back them sheets,
Listen out if you can.
Over the hill,
On past the mill,
Here come the Calling Man!

What does he bring,
What will he sing,
Was ever a man so grand?
Pull up them drawers,
Come out of your doors,
Here come the Calling Man!

All gather round,
The whole of the town,
Here does Dominion stand.
The girls braid their hair,
The men pay him fair,
Here come the Calling Man!

Now lower your eyes
And don't tell no lies,
He's off to that other land.
What you just seen
Is best kept between
You and the Calling Man!

The smell of his tobaccy then come drifting through the slats. I remembered that first night I had heard him sing beside Solus in that stinking old wagon. I had come to realize that night it was Jim Coyne who got Solus & his sister caught & strung up like that. To think I had once thought his voice a precious thing to behold, now it made me sick to hear it.

Only the light what come through the chinks lit that wagon, I was for the most part kept in darkness. Occasionally that old tea chest slid about, it was not nailed down like them others.

I put my eye against 1 of them cracks & seen the snow come falling down. I had not been give any water for some time, my throat was so dry I tried to thread my tongue through the gap & catch 1 of them flakes.

Jim Coyne had started up on another song but I could not hear it so well, we had hit a particularly rocky stretch of road & the wagon tossed this way & that, them frames clacking away with their chatter, it was an awful racket, I could not hear myself think.

But it was not so loud I did not notice when Jim Coyne quit his singing, that was such a constant in my ears I knowed its absence well. There come then the sound of another voice & the sound of more hoofs upon the ground, there was someone come riding alongside him.

Jim Coyne did not hardly ever like to stop once we was back on the road, it was forbid for anyone from the wagon behind to do so & so I knowed it was some other traveler.

Them 2 voices talked for a good while, I could only hear the occasional word here & there but I knowed for sure that voice did not belong to Joseph nor Forrest or Benjamin Quick. This fellow Traveler did sound very well spoke as if he come from money & learning. Two words then found my ears & they stuck fast, I thought I heard someone say the name Henry Brooks.

Did I not know a Henry Brooks? I was sure I heard that name somewheres before, I turned it over in my brain but could not put a face to it.

I then heard them hoofs go thundering off & Jim Coyne begun singing to himself again. The conversation was obviously come to an end but still my mind worked very busy.

Through that long day I watched the light change from the cold bright of morning to the dim grays of afternoon, that snow did not stop its falling. I could not rid myself of that name. I pulled them old blankets around my shoulders I was so lonely & so bitter cold I did not think it so far off that my mind would get lost in itself, I begun to think myself gone queer in the head.

It was near dark when Jim Coyne stopped the wagon, I seen his eye staring at me through the chink. His beaverskin hat was askew, his features bitten red by the cold.

We have kindly been give some news of a hotel opened up down the way, said he. A fine Gentleman does request old Jim's company for a drink & to converse on matters of business.

I could tell he thought himself very important.

Yis has best be on your best behaviors, young Yip, I won't have none of yer moping now. Yis must keep up that Hope, this could be the town yis find yer friend.

He could not help himself a little chuckle, if I had had the strength I would have beat that wagon open with my fist.

76

MRS. BLUM

IT WAS DARK BY THE time we arrived in the next town. The snow had stopped, the roofs of them houses & the earth was well covered, the wind had blowed it into small drifts banked outside each door.

The towns had growed smaller & smaller the farther we clumb, this one was an assemblage of low cabins nestled between 2 hills like a pendant fit snug between 2 large & accommodating bosoms. But it did boast a large new building what was 3 times the size of every other around it, its sign was on a post drove into the earth, it read MASON HILL HOTEL.

Jim Coyne was in very high spirits, his eyes was bright, the prospect of a drink & whatever Matters of Business did await him was a great cheer to his soul.

Now have yis ever seen so welcoming a domiciliary? he asked.

He did not receive the enthusiasm he had hoped for, we was all of us tired to the bone.

We then seen a broad-hipped & bustling woman come out onto the porch of the hotel. She ordered a young black-haired boy to take care of our consignment. Joseph went with him & so too did the Quick brothers, they would no doubt be setting poor old Miss Vivian Ray up in a cold damp stable somewheres.

She then motioned for me & Jim Coyne & the Challip twins to come inside.

Them twins was complaining bitterly of the cold, their hearts was steeped in drama, they said they longed for spring. Jim Coyne told them spring was no further than just around the corner but for now if they would kindly keep their mouths shut, they must endure the winter like good girls with Pluck & Fortitude.

The twins turned their little button noses up, I knowed now they would be most uncooperative in their dealings with Jim Coyne, they would refuse to do as he bid until he had made his Reparations.

It was a well-lit hall we entered, the wood polished & gleaming in firelight, the smell of oils & all things fresh & new was in abundance. That woman who had come out onto the porch was now ensconced behind a low counter, she had put her needlework to one side to attend us. She had a plump & ample figure, her head was uncommon small with a sharp chin & nose & straight thin hair what poked like straw from beneath her bonnet.

Welcome to the Mason Hill Hotel, said she.

He accent was most unusual, I later found out she was a Hessian woman. Her eyes was very round & she did not appear to blink as she stared at us.

I trust yis are the owner of this fine establishment, Mrs.? asked Jim Coyne, he took off his hat & shook out his hair.

Mrs. Blum, said the woman, pursing her lips importantly. My husband is outside, he chop the wood.

We heard it loud & clear, Mrs. Blum, there is no sound more pleasing to the ear on such a cold night, said Jim Coyne. My name is Mr. Coyne & these here with me are artists One & All: singers, dancers, actors & the like. I trust it will be alright if I took from you 2 rooms for the evening? These 2 lovely girls will have 1 & the other will be for me & my boy here & there are 2 more gentlemen tending to our livestock outside. Joseph can take the stable.

Mrs. Blum did not blink, her eyes hopped from 1 of us to the next & then to the door as if she could see the others.

And I trust you understand, Mr. Coyne, that you will be paying for more than 2 rooms with so many guests. I have some straw ticks available that we keep that can be brung up to your room.

That will do nicely, Mrs. Blum. We have some bedding of our own that the girls here – since they have their own room – will gladly go & fetch.

Jim Coyne looked at the Challip twins & smiled.

The tea chest, girls. Go & fetch it for old Jim would yis?

The Challip twins stared at each other in dismay but they could not deny they had been give their own room & so they left without complaint.

And since yis have been so very accommodating, Mrs. Blum, said Jim Coyne, I would like to put on some Entertainment for yis tonight & for anyone else who might care to come & join. I shan't be askin yis to pay of course though it might be worth mentioning to other guests that a contribution would not go unwelcome.

77

THAT NAME AGAIN

IT WAS AWFUL CRAMPED IN them rooms at the Mason Hill Hotel. The Challip twins had the luxury of their own but in the other was me & Jim Coyne & Forrest & Benjamin Quick. It was the first time I had been let out of Joseph's sight, I did feel myself a little freer for it.

The room was very sparsely decorated with a bed & small table beside it but once Mr. Blum – a full-bearded man with dark green eyes who did not say a word – had dragged up 2 straw ticks then there was not much floor left to stand on.

Mrs. Blum brung us up a flavorsome soup, there was plenty chunks of tender meat ready for the chewing. Her mien was growed a deal sunnier since Jim Coyne had mentioned the prospect of Entertainment, I could well imagine that the Notion of Jollity was rare enough in these parts. She had spread word to the other town members & she claimed they was most enthusiastic.

Jim Coyne was all smiles as he held his bowl of steaming soup.

We thank yis for the fine hospitality yis have showed us, Mrs. Blum. You & Mr. Blum is as fine a pair of hosts as I has ever seen.

He paused & smelt the juicy vapors come drifting from his bowl. That thin nose of his was still bit red by cold, he had not shaved for several days, his chin was growed stubbly with them first few flecks of gray & silver poking through.

A man couldn't hope for more, said he.

Mrs. Blum smiled & nodded, she thought it all the Pinnacle of Excitement. But just before she was to return downstairs, Jim Coyne cleared his throat to have her attention.

Dear good Mrs. Blum, said he, I trust yis have a bar somewheres down the stairs there? Yis know how we performers like to have ourselves a little nip before setting foot before an audience, a little warmth to put courage in the Stomach & Heart.

Mrs. Blum nodded very eager, she said downstairs there was a Communal parlor of sorts where guests was served drinks by Mr. Blum & encouraged to consort.

People should, said Mrs. Blum, they should not be strangers.

That's exactly right. If yis aren't makin friends in this life then yis'll be mighty lonely in the next, that's what I say, Mrs. Blum. We will be down with you directly.

Mrs. Blum was about to close the door when Jim Coyne once more brung her to a halt.

O, Mrs. Blum, said he, I forget to ask.

He give his Oily Smile & shook his head in that self-admonishing way of his.

I don't suppose yis have a guest going by the name of Henry Brooks?

There was that name again, I had managed to forget all about it.

Mrs. Blum thought for a moment & then nodded, slowly at first & then a little quicker.

He is the fancy dressed one, no?

Jim Coyne smiled & pressed his palms together.

That would be him, Mrs. Blum. Mr. Brooks & I is firm friends, in fact it was he who recommended this fine establishment to me. Tell him I will be down to enjoy that drink he so generously offered.

Mrs. Blum nodded & left, her short little steps ringing out down the hall.

78

HENRY BROOKS

BY THE TIME WE HAD come downstairs it appeared that whole
town had turned out. The parlor was certainly a note more opulent than
the bare walls of them bedrooms. There was 2 giant bear pelts laid out
as rugs on the floor & the wood of the walls was not rough but dark &
smooth, I could well imagine the stern & humorless Mr. Blum at work
sanding & polishing in the cold dawn light.

Indeed there was Mr. Blum now resolutely stationed behind a bar, it
was a damn sight finer than Tom Peeper's with rows of sparkling glasses
& bottles filled up with honey-colored liquor. Lanterns with tasseled
shades was burning around the room & there was a great fire also, them
flames licked out so many had took off their hats to make the most of
the warmth, faces was shining bright & red.

It was dark outside now but I could see the flakes of snow was falling again against the panes.

I searched all them new faces & seen Jim Coyne doing the same,
we was both looking for Henry Brooks. Forrest & Benjamin Quick then
begun to play their fiddles, it was a very sweet tune & with no announce-
ment the Challip twins begun to sing along & everyone was turned to

watch, their faces lit with warmth & cheer, even Mr. Blum's eyes did seem to soften from behind the bar.

It was awful crowded in there, I could not see now I was led through all them legs & rears in my face. But if I was uncomfortable this was no bad thing, Plots & Plans then come winging my way, they was charming visitors in such Dark Times. A room filled to the rafters with so many merry souls is a fine place for a boy to do some sneaking, how easily I might fix a trick & have myself saved was my thinking.

In my pocket I did then feel my faithful knurl of chalk, I had knowed well enough it would serve me in my hour of need. These bright & shining floors polished by Mr. Blum himself was smooth as slate, how perfect they was to write on. O Mr. Blum would be moved to fury when he seen but I did not care for that more than I did my own Sweet Freedom, I would crouch & write like the wind a message for all these faces to see that I was no performer but a boy stole from his rightful liberty & made to live in serfdom.

But just as I was about to I heard over the music Jim Coyne then shout out & his hand clamp down awful fierce on my shoulder.

Ah, Mr. Brooks! cried he.

He raised up his hand in greeting then & moved toward the bar, dragging me along behind. My opportunity was flung onto the flames, I could do nothing then but watch as them bodies what was still eyeing the twins begun to part & I seen first Mr. Brooks's feet & legs. It is true that even in my dejection I seen they was very handsomely attired in calfskin boots & finely wove britches the like I had never seen. He had also a finely tooled leather belt with a brace of pistols tucked in either side, their handles was decorated with swirls like the top of a very fine Wedding Cake. Then I seen he wore a starched shirt & blue checkered waistcoat, a silver timepiece on a heavy chain tucked into its pocket. I thought this man must be mighty rich, I had been right to imagine him as very learned.

Finally the last body did move away & Henry Brooks was revealed in full, I could not have imagined who I then seen sit before me. He was clean shaved, his hair had been chopped & oiled & combed, it was a moment before I stared into them small gray eyes & realized it was Dud Carter himself.

I felt I had not seen that face for yrs, I took in now every line around his eyes, his great nose was itself like an old friend, I seen then he had even give his teeth a clean, they was not so mossy as before. But I also seen he did his best to hide all them holes where his teeth had once been, they was not befitting of a Gentleman of his stature now.

I was about to leap at him when he suddenly stood up to shake the hand of Jim Coyne & knocked me to the floor.

He still had some bruising about his face but this he did seem to wear with pride, his nose also was bent awry, this he gently caressed with his finger like it was proof of some Family Distinguishment.

Dear me, said he looking down, I did not know you kept a dog, Mr. Coyne.

That is no dog, Mr. Brooks, this here is my own nephew.

Dud Carter squinted down at me & pulled a disgusted face as if he had swallowed a cup of seawater but I swore I just then seen him wink, I knowed I was to trust him.

You say it is a boy, Mr. Coyne?

Dud Carter was talking as if his nose was stuffed with cotton bolls, his mouth worked much slower than usual, his lips sticking out very pompous, he wrinkled his nose again.

He don't look much like one yis is right, Mr. Brooks, but a boy he is. My poor aul sis, she couldn't care for such a creature as this, I am such a soft-hearted sort I could do nothing else but take him under my wing.

Now Jim Coyne bent his long legs & grabbed me by the collar of my coat & hauled me onto my feet.

Does he always stare so insolently at a new acquaintance? Surely he is a little too warm to be requiring the benefits of such a crude hat-piece, is he not, Mr. Coyne?

Dud Carter then extended his hand to remove my hat but Jim Coyne very quick reached out & took him by the wrist.

Dud Carter looked down where he was held.

What is this? he cried, most indignant. I am being manhandled!

My sincerest apologies, Mr. Brooks, but the boy don't like to be interfered with. Yis see, he hasn't the use of his tongue, Mr. Brooks, so yis might forgive his staring.

Dud Carter looked down at me again.

What an Unfortunate Creature, said he. Does he not have his letters?

Not a one, said Jim Coyne. Can't even write his own name, it is most sad to say. If there's a brain between his ears then yis would do well to find it, I expect it is no bigger than a Walnut.

What an Unfortunate Creature, said Dud Carter again.

So convincing was this new character I found myself questioning whether it was Dud Carter at all, but he could not ever lose that mischief at play in his eyes, I could see he was enjoying himself. O yes it was like them first days we set out, it did make my bruised heart sing to see it.

Well, Mr. Coyne, said he. Enough talk. I believe I promised you a drink.

That you did, Mr. Brooks, yis have found me a very thirsty man.

Forrest & Benjamin Quick played a great medley of tunes, some was slow & sweet & some was so lively the whole room was dancing. Mrs. Blum was very red in the cheeks, she was the Belle of the Ball.

Jim Coyne & Dud Carter did not stop talking, Dud had acquired a whole flask of whiskey from Mr. Blum, I could see he was very liberal with his coinage & they drunk copious amounts, I never heard Dud talk so much Gibberish in all my days, if only Jim Coyne knowed every single word what come out of his mouth was a Dog's Lie.

They sit theirselves at 2 stools away from the merriment, Jim Coyne had offered me a stool for myself but this Henry Brooks was a very Cruel Man, he declared it most improper to have such a *grotesque* as me sit beside such Worthy Gentlemen.

Yis is quite right, Mr. Brooks, I don't know what I was thinkin. I would send him away but I would worry he would do himself an injury. Yis see he don't have the sense to keep himself away from harm.

Jim Coyne was now made suitably loose with whiskey, his words was begun to slur, his eyes a little misty. But he was a man who could hold his drink I knowed that, if it was Dud Carter's plan to sink him this way then it would be a Long Night.

But Jim Coyne was in a Talking Mood, he was made awful verbose.

What do yis think of them fiddle players of mine, Mr. Brooks? Ain't they the finest yis has ever heard?

Tolerable, said Dud Carter.

Jim Coyne raised his brows.

Yis is not much of a one for praisin are yis, Mr. Brooks?

Dud Carter tilted back his head very imperious indeed, he showed the dark of his nostrils like they did breathe in a different quality of air.

I am not one for praising things that are at their essence Mediocre.

Mediocre? cried Jim Coyne. What about them girlies? Ain't they got the sweetest set of pipes on them you ever heard?

Bearable, said Dud Carter.

Bearable! cried Jim Coyne again. Yis is a very harsh critic, Mr. Brooks. And what with them lookin so very pretty as well?

Middling, said Dud Carter.

Middling! cried Jim Coyne. Surely yis must think that together – the fiddles & the voices – they sound like they could be heard up in heaven & God & all the Angels would be clappin their blessed hearts out.

Dud Carter's face expressed nothing, it was cold & flat, who could have guessed he knowed so many long & cumbersome words? The old devil must have read himself more books than I thought, I suppose I should not have been surprised no more by his Wily Ways.

Dissonant, said Dud Carter.

Jim Coyne was now Well Riled, he stood up from his stool & wagged his finger in Dud Carter's face.

Now yis can listen to me, Mr. Brooks, I have traveled the length of this country & I had every manner of fella clap their hands in appreciation. I don't know what it is makes you think yis ears are so much better than everyone else's.

He then realized his temper, he calmed himself down.

I don't mean to insult yis, Mr. Brooks, I know yis is a very learned man. But how about I sing a song of my own & if yis aren't happy to clap after that then I may have to concede we is somewhat out of touch.

Dud Carter said nothing, he only nodded. Jim Coyne smiled & then downed his drink, he went shambling off through the crowd, he had all but forgot about me.

It was now Dud Carter looked down at me & for the first time we was able to smile at one another but still I could not embrace him as I so desperately wished.

Evening, Old Salt, said he, ain't you happy to see me?

He did not have no idea how happy I was, all the darkness what had clouded my skull was suddenly lifted.

You ain't lookin too well, said Dud, eyeing me with considerable alarm.

I had all but forgot how sorry I must have looked, I had come to think like the Wildling Jim Coyne so wanted me to be. My clothes was filthy, they had not been washed for weeks, Dud had not yet seen them welts & burns what run along my arms & legs but he could see clear enough them dark rings around my eyes & the ghosts what surely did reside inside them.

I was so pleased to see him I could barely keep from crying, Dud Carter seen the tears what threatened to come pouring down my cheeks.

Now don't you be gettin like that, Old Salt, said he. You jus got to keep on playin Dumb & we will be out of here tonight. That won't be so hard for you.

He could not help telling a joke, he smiled again & stared off toward the crowd.

Now look here, we don't want him figurin anythin out, I have strung him along about as far as he will go, he ain't so stupid that I can treat him like a fool. Now, Old Salt, you jus got to look out for our chance & when you think you see it you let me know & I'll be right behind you.

We then heard Jim Coyne interrupt the song what was being played & now he stomped his bootheel down on the wooden boards so that all them dancers come to an abrupt halt. A last screeching note of the fiddles come yowling out & Mrs. Blum held a chubby hand up to her heaving bosom as she did try to catch her breath.

Had Jim Coyne not stood himself plum in front of the door we might have been able to make our escape there & then but we could not.

Ladies & Gentlemen, cried Jim Coyne. My name is Jim Coyne & these here is my Loyal Performers. If yis have enjoyed their playin so far then please do put your hands together & give them a fine ovation.

There was a great eruption of clapping hands & whistles from the crowd, they was most appreciative.

Jim Coyne looked over at Dud Carter & raised his brows before he continued.

But we have had a special request from a most Distinguished Gentleman that I myself sing yis a little song. I admit I ain't took to the stage for a while but I do consider it my home & it would be a great honor to treat yis to a song.

He walked over to Forrest & Benjamin Quick & whispered something in their ears. They nodded quickly & then with their bows angled & at the ready they started up, it was at first a tune filled with yearning & longing until it dipped into a lively number, their arms sawing back & forth until Mrs. Blum was dancing again & Jim Coyne singing out his heart.

Who is it that sails
'Cross them old ocean waves
Who is it that sails to see me?

Who is it that sails
Spared the dark of them graves
Who is it that sails to see me?

She tells to me her name
Mary is my name, she says
She tells to me her name
It's Mary
She tells to me her name
I won't never forget, Mary
Mary, I won't never forget you

And so Jim Coyne went on through every verse until he had every soul, Mr. Blum included, in a feverish sweat, they was all of them singing. As you know I did hate every bone in his body but I could not deny his showmanship & the way that song come alive with flesh & blood & dripping with sweat.

After he had finished his hair was damp & come loose from its ribband, he took a long bow & received the thunderous applause with glittering eyes before he made his way back over to me & Dud Carter at the bar.

Well, Mr. Brooks, said Jim Coyne. What did yis make of that?

For a good long while Dud Carter stayed silent, he looked Jim Coyne in the eye. I thought him about to pronounce it Sufferable or some other such thing but slowly he begun to clap.

Jim Coyne took another long bow.

That was a fine performance, Mr. Coyne, I cannot deny it, said Dud Carter.

I thought that might have yis change yer mind, Mr. Brooks.

Consider it changed, Mr. Coyne.

How about a drink to celebrate the settlin of a difference between 2 old friends, said Jim Coyne.

He caught a hold of Mr. Blum's sleeve & ordered yet another flask of whiskey. Mr. Blum did not like being touched, he did not say nothing but his face was like a dark cloud as he planted that fresh flask down.

Jim Coyne took no notice, he raised his glass.

Here's to changin yer tune! cried he.

His glass was halfway to his mouth when Dud Carter raised up his hand to stop him. Jim Coyne gawped at him.

I must admit to there being one issue with your performance, Mr. Coyne, said Dud Carter.

Jim Coyne's face dropped, his eyes growed suddenly wide with disbelief.

I did admire your spirit & your starch, said Dud Carter, stroking at his chin, but I have always been of the opinion that a Performer should be raised above those he performs to if he is to achieve Greatness.

Jim Coyne was listening very hard, his brow was deeply furrowed.

Yis mean a stage of some description, Mr. Brooks?

Exactly, said Dud Carter.

Here Jim Coyne paused, his eyes bore into Dud Carter's.

Yis is a very demanding man, Mr. Brooks.

Jim Coyne's tongue went rooting around his back teeth. He poured himself another great measure & swilled it down immediately. The sweat still run down his face, he smiled but there was a sour edge to it now, I was familiar with that Dark Look.

I demand the best of everyone, Mr. Coyne.

Have yis ever demanded a little too much & found yerself lookin at a man with nothin but a bitter taste left in his mouth?

Dud Carter shuffled on his stool.

Let me tell you, Mr. Coyne, I've a great deal of money & if I were to see a performance in here on a stage like the one I have just witnessed, I might be persuaded to part with some of it. To make myself a Backer, if you will. As you know, Mr. Coyne, I am an Investor & a good Investor is always on the lookout for Success.

Now Jim Coyne's eyes near popped out his head, the flames of his greed was well fanned. His demeanor changed very quick, he leaned in toward Dud Carter with his head obsequiously cocked.

We do carry with us an old tea chest, Mr. Brooks. It is a good height & might serve for the time being. Do yis think it would do the trick?

Perhaps, said Dud Carter, his face deadly serious as he stared at Jim Coyne.

I knowed the tea chest was upstairs, the Challip twins had brung it up.

Yis need say no more, Mr. Brooks, said Jim Coyne. Stay right where yis are.

He begun patting at Dud Carter, dusting off his shoulders & straightening the lapels of his frockcoat.

He turned then & headed toward the door but soon he come hurrying back, a Pleading & Inquiring look upon his face.

Would it be a large investment yis was thinking, Mr. Brooks?

Substantial, said Dud Carter.

Jim Coyne nodded & looked down at me.

Then the boy is your property as well as mine now & yis would do well to keep him safe whilst I go & fetch the old chest. He is not so useless as he looks if you catch my drift, Mr. Brooks.

He winked & then hurried off toward the stairs. He announced to the audience that there would be a brief interval followed by more festivities. Some adjustments must be made, he said, at which point he looked over & inclined his head conspiratorially again toward Dud Carter.

He then took Forrest & Benjamin Quick & the Challip twins in tow, he was no doubt cooking up the show of his life. He did leave our escape so easy we seen we could simply walk out & that is exactly what we did.

Don't act like you is goin anywheres in particular, Old Salt, said Dud Carter, though he was still talking in that slow & fancy drawl of Henry Brooks.

Dud placed a proprietary hand atop my head as if I was his own charge, he gently steered me through that lively crowd. Drink & dance had give them a rowdy bite to their business, they did not care to look where they trod & I was knocked between legs & rumps & ale & whiskey was spilt down me, it did regrettably remind me of that Wicked Cage.

But O my freedom was near, I could not ever go back with Jim Coyne, we was coming up to the door. I turned & seen Dud Carter acting very poised & calm & incurious to all them rambunctious goings on, he took out his pocket watch & brung its face close for his inspection but he did not rush, I felt his hand steady & solid on my skull.

Then we was out of that room & the heat was sloughed off & the chatter dimmed & so too did the light as we made our way through that dark hall toward the porch. There was my Freedom, I could smell the Cold Outdoors & as we paused to open that last door I swore we could hear also Jim Coyne's excited cries from above, his boots stamping like they had been above me in that wagon long ago it seemed, they was the cries of a man who thought himself king of all the world but even kings can be robbed of their Great Prize.

79

ESCAPE

GUSSIE WAS WAITING IN THE stables behind the hotel, she lifted her head when we come bursting in, it was not the first time she had been disturbed like this, we was now Old Hands. O I was glad to see that faithful beast, that sleek coat & impatient rustle of her black tail, the soft clop of her nimble hoofs I would have knowed anywhere. She feigned a sulk but I knowed she was glad to see me, she could not keep it from her dark & shining eyes.

And there in the stable next to her was Mr. Johnson, he bared his teeth when he seen me, he begun to bray & shake his head. I swear that old mule was the Devil himself, I hope he is long in the ground.

Dud lifted me back up into my old saddle & there we was again with him sit behind me, there was no better feeling, the smell of his hair oil was rich in my nose as he reached over me to take the reins. But it could not mask that other smell I was now become so familiar with.

God Almighty, said Dud Carter, they is an evil stink in here.

I suddenly seen then a stirring from the corner, it was Miss Vivian Ray. She had buried herself beneath a heap of straw & hay to warm herself, her sniffling snout pressed up against that cruel wire I had spent my own good time behind. And there beside her was Joseph, he held in his hand a length of timber, he made as if to bar our way.

Only later would Dud Carter inquire after the queer beast he seen residing in that cage but for now his mind could not be distracted from our flight.

Move out the way, said Dud Carter.

Joseph did not move, I thought he was set to attack but I seen then he was shivering with the cold, I seen his pale eyes was growed so very milky with age. Joseph had throwed me in that cage each night & I had thought him pleased to do it but now I seen there was no thought of Violence in his head, he did drag himself very slow over to the stable door & hold it open, a squall of snow come blowing in & he closed his eyes to endure the fierce chill what ripped through his body.

Go on, said he, go on.

Them was the only words I ever heard him speak, his voice worn to no more than a whisper by the yrs gone by.

Dud Carter steered Gussie on past him, I turned to see that old man & the tilted snout of Miss Vivian Ray staring out after us, she let out a faint groan as the snow set to gathering on Joseph's shoulders until he turned back to her & no doubt set to whispering some sweet consolations.

I did not think no pang of Guilt or Remorse would ever have visited my heart but to leave them 2 behind was to suffer a loss of some strange kind, I was too young to know it then but you do not have to love something to feel its absence, you do not have to have gained nothing to feel a Loss. I do hope old Joseph did not suffer no more than he had to for the rest of his days but I know hope don't make no good ingredient in a world run by the likes of Jim Coyne, you got to hold on to something a little firmer.

The snow was indeed falling thick & fast now, the ground was covered & so Gussie's charging hoofs was muted as we sped out of the yard & spied that little raven-haired boy whose dark hair was whipped from one side of his forehead to the other as he held open the gate for us.

All the lights of the Mason Hill Hotel was blazing, we could still hear the voices & cheers come from the parlor travel across the stillness of that night.

I knowed Jim Coyne was not the type of man to suffer such indignity, I had seen his temper & it was as foul as they come. Soon he would be after us but as I have said before the snow is a fine Secret-Keeper, the prints of Gussie's hoofs was already beginning to be covered.

Dud Carter cried out again into the night as he had once done when we left Heron's Creek, it did seem like a lifetime ago.

Get thee behind me, Satan!

He could not help himself, we was back together again. He reached down & took from his saddlebag something wrapped in dark cloth. I did not have to unravel it to know what it was.

I suppose you will be wanting this back, Old Salt, said he.

80

BENEATH THE POPLARS

MANY YEARS LATER I COME across a playbill tacked to the wall of
a bank nearest to where me & my dear wife was living at the time. It was
before we was blessed with our 3 childs, we was still young & enjoying
the many pleasures of New Love. It was a time I finally did feel happy
after all what would soon happen to me & Dud in them days & weeks
since we broke free from the Mason Hill Hotel.

But I was stopped to see that poster & here is what it read:

JIM COYNE'S
WILD WEST SHOW
Featuring:
Larry Simms and his Wild Lariat

Bill the Bandit

Lloyd Gibbons and The Gadfly

Them other names escape me but you get the gist, if indeed it was the
same Jim Coyne I cannot be sure but I don't know how many other Jim
Coynes was in that business. Them Acts was changed since I had been

with him – gone was the Challip twins & gone was Forrest & Benjamin Quick. I seen then Joseph's old face & pale eyes in my mind as he looked when he held open that stable door with the snow gathering on his hunched shoulders, him & the blighted Miss Vivian Ray must both have been long dead by then, may their poor souls Rest in Peace.

If I had run into Jim Coyne who knows what would have happened. But it did not worry me, it only brung back to my mind that night me & Dud Carter was riding through the snow & the pair of us shook up with laughter at the tricksy Henry Brooks. How good it was to be back by Dud Carter's side, we thought we was a pair now what could never be Broke Apart.

Looking back I dare say we could have stole me a horse from them stables but I think we was both glad to be riding off together, we had started this journey on Gussie & we was like one person in that saddle now, I knowed that same feeling did flood Dud Carter as it then did me, it was the greatest pleasure to be reunited in this way.

Old Henry has helped us out twice now, Old Salt, I suppose we should be thankin him, said Dud Carter.

Of course that was where I had heard that name before, Henry Brooks had talked his way around Charles Eder, he had a silken tongue that was for sure.

I could not imagine how Dud Carter knowed where we was going, that snow come down so thick we could barely see. I was sure we must be headed for some town he knowed but I was wrong.

There ain't no chance that galoot will find us where we is goin, Old Salt. I made myself some friends while you was away. Let's hope there is some dinner on the boil for us, I must admit I is hungry as a horse.

Soon Gussie had worked up a sweat, her flanks begun to steam & I caught a whiff of that damp smell of her coat what come rising up. I did not know how I had missed it.

We come occasionally upon some slopes so steep that Dud Carter had to slow Gussie down & hold on to the back of my coat so's I weren't pitched over the pommel. I did yearn to throw that beaverskin hat away but I was glad I had it now, it was mighty cold, my nose & lips was near froze, they had gone so numb they felt like another person's stuck on my face.

But still Dud continued to talk over all what had happened to him, he told me of how Gussie had bolted & when he had come back he had seen my slate in the scrub & that boy laid dead in the road. We had vanished & at first the folk of that town thought he was to blame but he told them of Solus & he followed them into the woods in pursuit.

But of course he could not find me, he said he spent every day since searching & only when a man in a saloon told him he had seen a small bald creature in a cage the previous night did he know he was on my trail.

He then stopped talking, that snow did swirl around us.

This was not the way we had come by I knowed that for sure, suddenly Dud Carter brung Gussie to a stop by a grove of poplars, their branches was laden with snow & bowed down. Dud clumb down & took Gussie by the reins & begun walking her into the trees.

Mind your head up there, Old Salt. We is nearly here now, said Dud Carter.

81

ONACONA

DUD CARTER TOOK US DOWN a narrow track, once we was under them old tulip trees the snow come down lighter & there was that silence very particular what only comes when it snows. As for the finer qualities of that silence you would do well to list them, it is only a feeling that things dropped from the heavens should surely make some sound but when that snow don't breathe a whisper you is left with a wondrous Hollow Feeling as if all the world was quieted only for you.

It was not so much a clearing we come upon then but a stand of birch trees at the center of which glowed a home of sorts. The snow did not cling to it for long, it was much like that queer design Dud Carter had made for himself back in Heron's Creek only it was a good deal bigger & a more shapely & sophisticated-looking thing on the whole.

It was wove with saplings & plastered with mud or clay & roofed with poplar bark what had no doubt been stripped from them very trees we just passed through.

Dud Carter led Gussie into a small corral & a stable, a black horse poked its head over the gate shut with leather hinges. Dud Carter did act like it was his own home. I was glad Gussie would have company for the warmth though she was not the most sociable of creatures when it come to sharing her quarters.

Just then the door of that house opened up & there stood a Cherokee Indian. His dark hair was wrapped up in a turban of sorts, a large mantle tucked around his thin shoulders, though beneath this he wore an old trade coat & britches & leather boots like what any white man would. His face did not look so much old as tired, his large eyes was very dark, his nose slightly flattened at the tip, his ear lobes weighted with a queer array of hoops & feathers.

I had seen me a good many Cherokee in Heron's Creek before, they sometimes come down from the far hills to trade, their mounts laden with parcels of deer meat & wild turkeys. But I had not ever entered one of their homes.

This here is Onacona, said Dud Carter. He's a fine friend of mine & he would be glad to have us.

Onacona looked at me, I had thought him in a somber mood but suddenly he become very excited to see me, he took my hand in his own papery palm & begun to work his tongue with them queer sounds what pass for words & to my great surprise Dud Carter answered him in that same tongue.

I did not know what it was they talked about as we went inside but Dud was doing a lot of listening as Onacona gabbed on, only later when we was in Blue Run would Dud Carter inform me that all them Cherokees did believe in a race of kindly immortal spirits what was thought to be holed up in underground townhouses throughout the mighty Appalachians & would make theirselves visible to the Cherokee in the form of little child-sized people.

You can well imagine Dud Carter thought this all very amusing, O yes it was one of these spirits what Onacona had took me for, it took some time for him to be convinced I was no immortal spirit but flesh & blood, he did have to keep touching me to make himself believe it.

Onacona was a small man himself but still he loomed over me as I walked in his hut, he smelt very strong of pipesmoke, he could not stop from smiling down at me.

Of course I had heard them rumors that Dud had spent some time in the Cherokees' company as a boy but I did not know he had gone so far as to learn the subtleties of their speech.

There was a fine blaze in the middle of the room, a circular hole was cut in the roof where the smoke was sucked out, the snow come drifting in at the top before it was lost in the heat. There was a good many pelts heaped about & hanging from the walls & near all of his wares was made of copper what shined bright in the flames.

Onacona did sit himself down by the fire on a heap of buffalo calfskins. There looked to be the beginnings of a smile on his face as he watched Dud Carter bend his long shanks & take a seat.

There was a large pot bubbling away over the fire.

That would be *conee-banee*, said Dud Carter. Squash, corn & beans never tasted so good, Old Salt. Even your mama's cookin won't hold up to Onacona's conee-banee here.

Onacona stared at me intently, I seen no hostility or fear in his eyes but only curiosity. Them hoops in his ear also shined bright with the fire, them feathers waved very gentle.

He turned then & said something to Dud Carter.

That sounds like a mighty fine idea, said Dud Carter, rubbing his hands together & scooting closer to the fire.

I seen now he had brung one of his saddlebags inside & he now took it onto his lap.

While old Onacona here gets us a nice helpin of his delicious stew I got a few things to show you, Old Salt, said he.

He went rummaging about then in the bag & soon took out a book, I knowed it immediately for the one he had kept in his old riding jacket. I seen the cover now, it was *Gulliver's Travels* by Jonathan Swift. I had

not ever read it but I have since many times & I believe I come to understand why Dud Carter held it in such high esteem.

But he did not want to talk about no *Gulliver's Travels*. He opened
up the pages & out come a great many Newspaper Cuttings. He laid them
all out in front of me. My eyes could not focus until Dud Carter pointed
his finger, in every title I seen then the word **GOLD** writ in bold letters.

Looks like we wasn't the only ones, said Dud Carter. Some been discovered up in Virginia & North Carolina. Turned out they wasn't much
there but it was enough to whet the appetite of many a man.

I thought then of Jim Coyne & the Gold he had said he was after
in Virginny.

Onacona then come round with our 2 steaming wooden bowls. Dud
Carter thanked him & I took my bowl from him, the heat made my hands
burn after all that cold, they was only just thawing out.

Dud Carter took a mouthful & nodded his appreciation. He pointed
with his spoon at Onacona.

Onacona tells me he knowed about Gold for as long as he can
remember. He says it is damn near all over these hills. He remembers
been jus a little boy & findin a big old chunk of it & takin it back to his
mama & her shushin him right up.

He tapped his finger down on the dirt floor.

You see, Old Salt, plenty of this Gold is on Cherokee soil & she
knowed as well as any that if the white man got a hold of news like that
there'd be no stopping em.

Dud Carter now looked over at the old Cherokee.

But Onacona here knows his secret ain't safe no more. It's out in
the world & there ain't a thing any of us can do about it.

I looked at Onacona then, I was not sure if he could understand
Dud Carter's words but his face looked suddenly drawn & tired. I was
well used to searching in eyes for Answers if words could not be used,
I seen in them a frightful misery, he knowed these Developments for
what they was.

Dud Carter shoveled some more of the conee-banee into his mouth. We had both been give what looked like very shallow spoons carved out of bone. The stew was still too hot & he chased them beans around his mouth until he could swallow them down, mine did still lie steaming by my side.

No, there won't be any stoppin every damn man comin this way from every damn corner.

He pointed then to a particular clipping by my foot.

Take a read of this, Old Salt.

Here is what it said:

GOLD – A gentleman of the first respectability by the name of Edgar Soppet writes us thus under date of 6th of December:

'Gold has been discovered in the town of Heron's Creek by a free-flowing body of water by the name of Simmerstone Creek.'

I had never seen them words of my hometown in print, I always thought it a separate world in itself. I looked at Dud Carter & I seen him wince as if he had some creaking wound beneath his clothes. He took another spoonful of the conee-banee & spoke with his mouth all filled up & running with juices.

He said, We got to get back to Heron's Creek. Ain't no way around it. This Soppet fellow has done it now, that place will be busier than an ants' nest in a couple of weeks. If we don't get back there, we will lose out, Old Salt, there ain't no doubt about that.

I took out my slate, it did feel so good to have it back in my hands. I still had kept that knurl of chalk safe in my pocket all this time.

We can't go back, I said.

Dud Carter put down his bowl.

Well, Old Salt, I must disagree with you there. There is now a number of reasons as I think you know. That article was writ weeks ago now, folk will already be on the move. I reckon these roads will busy up faster than you know it. We got to get back.

He looked at me then I knowed he was thinking about my Mama as well as that Gold. With all that had happened I had not had chance to think on it but let me say that notion was no more appealing to me now than it was way back before Solus come out from them pines.

Dud Carter could not see my Anguish, he suddenly shuffled over closer to me.

And I am sure you wouldn't mind hornin in on some of that Gold for ourselves. You & me would partner up, Old Salt. Even old Onacona here could come along if he wanted.

I seen his eyes was lit up now, he had forgot all that Danger what awaited us & he had dreamed up what he must have been thinking about since he first seen it in the Stranger's hand.

Imagine it, Old Salt.

He pointed at the newspaper clipping writ by Edgar Soppet.

We already know a spot where that Gold is ready & waiting. You put an end to that fellow what took us there. Poor Burl bless his soul is dead & now you & me is the only ones who know. We would have that whole stretch to ourselves & we would only have to go pannin maybe for a few weeks before we struck ourselves a fortune.

What about the other man? I asked.

Dud Carter did not look at me, he reached over & ladled some more conee-banee into Onacona's bowl & then his own. He did sit himself back down.

Onacona ate with his head bowed, he did not look at us.

The fellow with the feather? said Dud Carter.

I nodded.

We can't go back, I said.

Well we can't be hidin away for the rest of our days neither, said Dud.

He was suddenly very het up, his face turned red, his eyes ablaze. He pushed his conee-banee to one side & stood up & begun to pace around the hut.

You know, Old Salt, I fancy myself a life where I ain't always got to be livin low or been somebody else's sucker, said he. I seen my own daddy live like that all his life an it ain't a pretty way to be I can tell you that. And then before you know it you is in the ground & we is meant to be thankin God for the blessed time we had on His earth.

Dud Carter stopped & breathed in heavy through his nose as he watched me write.

You was the one who told me that if we go back there we'll end up in the ground.

Well I ain't so sure about that now, snapped Dud Carter. Look at how we handled ourselves since we been away, Old Salt. We got ourselves in all manner of scrapes, we seen blood & guts & death galore. We ain't the same 2 boys what run away cowerin into the night, now I reckon we'd be comin back as Men.

I shook my head, I thought he was talking Rot. I rubbed my slate clean & was about to set to writing again but now Dud Carter was more worked up than ever.

You listen to me, Old Salt, I know that man & he ain't nobody we ought to be too worried about. He probly done vanished right after he seen his partner get his head knocked open. And even if it was to come down to them Final Moments, you ain't never seen how quick these fingers of mine can work a trigger.

Dud Carter raised up his hand like it was something Holy sent down by God Himself, he did admire his own waggling fingers as they cast a shadow on the wall of the hut.

I ain't lying when I say there ain't a man in this world who can beat me, Old Salt. Not with this fine new piece here on my hip, they would need a miracle to claim their victory.

Dud was right, I never witnessed his gunskills but I heard enough of his smug talk, I seen then we could have argued all day & I reckon I would have tried to give him another serving of sense if I had not then become distracted by something else he said. I spit on my hand & rubbed my slate clean again.

What do you mean you know him? I asked.

Know who?

You just said you knowed that man.

Dud Carter took up his bowl again & begun spooning more stew into his mouth, his eyes was lowered, I seen in him that Churlishness what I seen when I first met him & he was so prone to them Seasons of Despondency. He did not look like the Man he claimed to be but the Boy I still reckoned him for. I throwed my slate down in front of him so's he would have to look at my words again.

82

WAY BACK WHEN

YOU GOT YOURSELF ANY MEMORIES? asked Dud Carter. He did not look at my slate but right into the flames of the fire.

I shrugged & told him I supposed I had as many as anybody else.

He nodded his head. The firelight lit the fine hairs scudding his long jaw & glowed them red as embers.

I got me some, said he. The way I see it they come at you & you ain't got no choice whether you want to look at em or not. They just come & you got to sit & look it over. Don't matter if you seen em a thousand times afore, you just got to see em again an again an again.

I got aplenty like that, I said.

He read my slate in the flickering light & nodded.

There's some, he said, that you don't even know if they real. You mighta just made em up. Then there's some that come at you realer than you & me sittin here now. You know they real cus you got them burned into your eyes & whatever else they is to get em burned into.

I could not guess why he was so took with this notion of Old Memories. Surely we had ourselves more important things to discuss, I was growed awful impatient with all this Lazy Talk & I asked him where this conversation was headed.

Well, said he, rubbing at the hairs along his jaw, I admit I had me a queer feelin since we was first at Simmerstone Creek all that time ago. Seems like it could have been 10 yrs don't it, Old Salt?

I had to agree with him there, that did seem a different world back then we was living in.

He went on.

I told you I thought I knowed that man, the man what kilt Burl & then I told myself I didn't know him. I told myself I got my guts all shook up for nothin. I sit down & I said: Dud Carter, you ought not to think too hard. You think so hard on some things you ain't got no room to think on anythin that's starin you right back in the face.

He paused & leaned back on one elbow & picked something up from the dirt floor & turned it in his hands. The shadows of them long fingers of his turned also, we are always looking for patterns in this world, I thought perhaps some message might be revealed in their movements.

I never got chance to tell you, Old Salt, but that man you done for & the one with the hair & the feather & that ugly stain on his face, I seen em before.

Dud Carter rubbed his face & shook his head a little & made a low whistling sound as if whatever he wanted to say was trapped so deep inside him he had to coax it out. He placed his bowl down on the dirt floor.

They been on my mind for a while now & maybe I ought to have told you earlier but I dint see no clear reason to. But now I reckon it's different. If we is going back to Heron's Creek then you ought to know what—

He seen me pick up my slate then to contest him some more but he leaned over & placed his hand very gentle on top of mine.

Just give me a little time here, said he.

He looked over at Onacona.

You see Onacona here takes me back to that night also. His old face seem to got my own old memories hid away in it.

I did not know what night he spoke of but Dud Carter's eyes had took on a queer shine.

You know, Old Salt, I spent a good deal of time with the Cherokee over the yrs, I knowed plenty of em & got them down plumb as some of the finest folk in this land. But it's awful strange to say that the face I remember most I did never know, I seen her just the once.

Here Dud Carter did trail off again, I did not know what was come over him. Something was eating away at him, he turned & spoke them strange words to Onacona then, they did appear to agree on something, I did not know what.

He turned then back to me.

You see, Old Salt, he said, my daddy used to take hisself off each yr, just when the leaves was beginning to brown & nights are darkenin before them first cold licks of winter come down it was & leave me wherever it was we was stayin. He'd up & leave without no word of where it was he was headed & that would be that. I'd just have to get on an keep livin. He didn't leave no note or no little basket of vittles to keep me from starvation.

Sometimes I wouldn't mind so much. I got to go about where & when I damn well pleased. No one tellin me what & what not to do. I had me plenty of time to do what I pleased.

He spat in the dirt & rubbed at it with his elbow. I did not know if Onacona was listening, his head was bowed, I could not see his face. But Dud Carter had a far-off look in his eyes, he was not with us but wrist-deep & digging through the Past.

He continued, Then this one time he went off for near a week. That was longern I was used to & I thunk he might well of got himself kilt. We was stayin not far from Heron's Creek, just up in them hills what clumb up over near your mama's store.

Well, I don't know how old I was, maybe 6 or 7, but I hadn't had no food for long enough that my mouth got that dry & Godawful taste in it & my head feeled as if it was about to float off from my neck. I was seein stars even when it was daytime, they was shinin all around me an sparklin in my eyes.

Here Dud Carter paused & took out from his saddlebag a tin flask. He unstoppered it & took a long swig & then handed it to me. I took a swig & then I passed it to Onacona. He took a long glug himself before putting it down beside him.

So's I go out grubbin for roots, continued Dud, an berries an anythin I can git my hands on. I go through the shallows of a creek I come across & try to catch myself a trout but before I knowed it night was comin down & I done walked myself halfway up that mountain over there.

And there was a mist had fallen all over so thick I could not see where it was I was goin. I might as well have been blind. My daddy had left me an old goatskin coat so's I weren't so cold as I coulda been but I weren't exactly warm let me tell you.

He paused to gesture for the flask. Onacona took another swig what made his eyes water before he handed it back round. Dud took a long pull before he started again.

Then I started hearin some voices. I thought maybe I was goin mad but I followed them farther on up through them pines & then I seen a fire flickerin away through the trees & I seen men gathered about it like they will on them cold nights.

I didn't fancy bin seen myself, you understand I was awful nervous around people back then, I was happy enough on my own even if I was growed hungry again from them berries, they give me that feelin what made me hungriern anythin.

So's I clumb up one of them great big pines & found myself perched up there like an owl, like you was up over the creek that night, Old Salt, an I was lookin down on them in this clearin with the fire & the snow fallin all around.

He paused & looked at me.

What you think I done seen next, Old Salt?

I told him I did not know.

Well I'll tell you what I seen. Them young eyes of mine had seen moren most but they widened a damn good bit when they took in what come along next.

Turned out them 4 men had got theirselves 2 prisoners, 1 was trussed up like a bird, a young girl already laid in the snow beneath the fronds of a pine. Not a moment later I seen a man slung across 2 different horses on the other side of the camp. I can't never be sure how they come to be in this fix, them prisoners was perfect strangers to each other of that I am sure but their fates was the same. But now here was this girl I told you of earlier, Old Salt. Have never forgot her & won't for as long as I live.

Well this girl's skin was darkern any white girl, I knowed right off she was a Cherokee they done snatched from somewheres, looked like she was no older than 18 yrs. She had on a wraparound skirt covered with them brass runners & fastened with a leather belt, a calico waistcoat, her dark hair clubbed with all them beautiful ribbands of red & yellow they like to dress theirselves in.

As them men come closer she begins to struggle, thrashing & bucking like a balking mare she was. Her hands was still bound fast but she manages to shift her weight so she falls heavy onto the snow. She reaches for her ankles but they is trussed also, she can do little but squirm about in the dirt.

I tell you, Old Salt, I never seen a more sorry sight & then 2 of them men come over & I seen 1 got a hatchet—

Here Dud did pause to look at me. I picked up my chalk & wrote.

The same hatchet?

Dud nodded.

It had them dark hairs hanging from the handle, it was the same hatchet no doubt. So then I seen the older git down on his haunches & start pawing at her, he ain't got no hatchet or no knife & he's goin at her bonds so's he can git at her. He pulls the last knot loose & the girl's hands are freed & the old fellow just sits back with a big ole grin on his face. But he don't see the girl reach into her skirts & quick as you like she brings out this curved blade with a bone handle & she don't waste no time sticking it into the side of the old man's head.

Well, Old Salt, you know the sound of a skull being split, it is as ugly as they come. That old boy was dead as dead can be & that fierce girl was fixin to loosen them bonds around her ankles but now our other man is too quick, he reaches into his trouser band & takes out that hatchet we seen him with & I got to watch as half her skull leaps away from the rest of her face, just about all of her brain come spillin out as he hacks away at her.

Dud Carter shook his head, he looked down at the floor & scooped out some of that fine dirt & let it sift through his fingers.

It was a gruesome tale but I knowed it was not finished. Dud Carter heard the scrape & whine of my chalk, he looked up to see my question.

The man still trussed up? I don't remember him so well. He was young hisself, maybe a little older than the Cherokee girl, tall & thin but I do recall very well he wore hisself a Red Kerchief tied around his neck. If you had seen how pale he was gone, that kerchief did look bright red against his skin. He was so scared I could see his poor frame shakin away. I dint hear no names but for that one with the feather in his hat, they called him Mr. Coombs.

Dud Carter shook his head again.

Let me tell you I ain't seen the likes of such gore, her blood was all about & I was froze to that branch up there, so shocked & scared I couldn't move. I just kept on lookin an that's when they turned on the man.

Now Dud Carter stood up so he could better act out his tale.

The branch I was perched on weren't too strong & now it snaps clean beneath me & I goes tumblin down makin a right commotion. I was lucky they was another branch just below it I landed real clean on otherwise I would have been done for.

But them 2 heard it an sure enough our man with the hatchet come runnin into the trees below me tryin to sniff me out. But he didn't think to look up so I was safe enough up there still. He run off somewheres else & I was left to watch as that man with the feather, Mr. Coombs, as he starts goin to work on that poor man. He's talkin away about something, I reckon he's after findin out where he lives or somethin & then he starts circlin him like a dog before it's about to shit & before I know what's happened he's gone an slit his throat & more blood is leapin out onto the snow, I tell you now, Old Salt, there was no tellin the difference between the blood & that Red Kerchief he got on.

83

REVELATIONS

YOU WILL BY NOW HAVE remembered it was my daddy who always wore a Red Kerchief. You will remember it was just as them dark nights was coming in when I was born & he never come back, the very same time Dud Carter said he went off into them pines.

O yes it was that Cold Knowledge I had always held in my own self, there was then no doubt in my mind it was my daddy what had been killed by that man with the feather Mr. Coombs & it was Dud Carter who had knowed all along, he had seen him murdered all them yrs ago. I realized me & Dud had been bound together longer than we ever knowed, he knowed The Truth & now it was out in the world.

I had not moved since Dud Carter had finished his tale, he did have no idea about them Revelations lit & burning in my brain. He was now spooning more stew into his mouth, he looked up at me, some was dribbling down his chin.

Well? What do you have to say about that, Old Salt? There was me thinkin you would be scribblin away, accusing me of keepin secrets & what not. But here you is lookin at me like a damn fish.

Still I could not move, I turned to see Onacona eyeing me very close, he had seen something in me was greatly disturbed. But Dud Carter was suddenly in a Fury.

You tell me you don't want to be goin back to Heron's Creek. You tell me you is too scared. But I'll tell you somethin, Old Salt. You got to learn to stand up for yourself sometimes. I can't come rescuing you every time you need some helpin out. I dint have much of a daddy but he taught me a few things & one was that a Man has to stand up for himself.

He jabbed his finger at me, he would not stop his talk of being a Man.

We ought to go back to Heron's Creek & if that Mr. Coombs is there we ought to tell him it's our claim. It's our Gold. We ought to show we ain't scared of nobody, we got as much right to it as him & if he don't like it then he will have to deal with Us.

I tried then to write but my hand shook too much to hold the chalk, it spilled from my grip & rolled into the dancing shadows of the fire.

What is it, Old Salt? asked Dud Carter, he seen my face gone deathly pale, he was worried to see me so shook.

He picked up my chalk & handed it back to me.

I ain't tryin to fright you, Old Salt. What I is trying to say is that I ain't feared of no one no more. I ain't worried about no man waitin for us. And neither should you be, we both seen enough now.

I took up my slate then & found I could write.

I revealed to him what I now knowed & held it up for him to read.

He read them words & then looked at me.

I don't grasp your meanin, he said.

I held it up & thrust it closer to his face, I would not lower it until he understood.

What is it you is tellin me, Old Salt?

He begun to smirk, he thought me mad.

You mean to say that man I seen get kilt when I was a boy was your daddy?

I nodded my head.

Now he laughed plain in my face.

And how do you know all this?

I explained I was born around that time just when he was talking about & that my daddy had gone missing that very day I was born. I told him that I knowed my daddy had always wore a Red Kerchief around his neck, my Mama had told me so, he did never take it off. He had disappeared & never come back & now I knowed for sure he had been killed.

When Dud Carter had finished reading my words, the smile was gone, his eyes was lit like I had never seen them. He stayed quiet, he got up & walked around, then he come back to sit & read them words again.

If what you is tellin me is Truth, Old Salt, then we ain't got a choice but to go back. Jesus! he cried.

He leapt up to his feet.

That son of a bitch killed your daddy, Old Salt!

I still sit there & looked up at him.

You can't just sit there!

Dud Carter kicked my bowl of stew & skittered it across the room. Onacona seen that bowl & stew dashed across the floor, more sorrow come to his eyes but Dud Carter did not care. He come right up close to me then, he put his arm around me & whispered in my ear.

He said, To me belongeth vengeance, & recompense; their foot shall slide in due time: for the day of their calamity is at hand, & the things that shall come upon them make haste.

I knowed his words for the words of God & here they found me in my Time of Need. I thought then of them wretched weeks with old Jim Coyne & how the pain & misery brung me to this here very moment. I took my slate up in my hands, they was suddenly steady, my grip was so very strong & fierce.

I guess we both got our reasons to head back to Heron's Creek, I said.

84

BLUE RUN

I THINK NOW OF MYSELF SIT there by that fire, I see myself still no more than a Boy but hearing words what was too big even for most Men. I wish that boy knowed to open his eyes a little wider & see beyond them first thoughts of Glory & Foolish Honor what come racing into his head.

So often a man believes he has nothing to lose not because it is true but because he can't yet see all there is to lose, all them things might not be present now but waiting in the yrs to come. Just because he has not found them yet does not mean he cannot lose them.

We spent just that one night beneath Onacona's hut, Dud paid him very handsome with them coins what Solus had stole & Dud had kept. They had been in Gussie's saddlebag when she bolted after that gun was fired & Dud Carter had took full advantage of them. They was what bought him them new clothes & now I seen he looked me up & down, he winced at the stinking rags Jim Coyne had left me with.

We cannot go back to Heron's Creek right away, said Dud Carter. Ain't no need for no detour, we'll be ridin right past a place I know but we cannot have you returning home to attend such important business looking like this, Old Salt, it will not do. Mark my words. I seen the Man in you now & I knows once you is all dressed up you will have the Fire

in you to go back & put an end to what we begun. We need to fix you up
& I reckon I know just the place.

It was Dud Carter's plan for us to ride out through the snow to a
town what called itself Blue Run, for in the spring its roads & fields was
lined with them nodding heads of Toadflax. Dud said they had there a
good many haberdashers & a damn fine Social Scene with a tavern what
was Legendary for the Ale & Liquor it did produce. It would not hurt
us one bit, he said, if we was to celebrate our being reunited with a jar.
Some good corn liquor will put fire in your belly as much as fine clothes
on your back. After that, we would be on our way.

This was the extent of our Plan, we was now too buoyed on thoughts
of Gold & Glory to think much else, we thought we seen our future
Bright & Clear.

Blue Run is no longer standing, it did sit at the bottom of a great
slope & it suffered one storm too many & that slope come tumbling down
some yrs ago. I do not know who it was thought it a good idea to start
building there but they did pay a High Price, a good many was buried
alive, they suddenly found theirselves in the dark of their graves & was
not dug out until that was where they then belonged.

But it was back then a fine little town & Onacona waved us off, the
sky was blue, the branches dripping & the snow breathing out its fresh
scent. I did feel myself to be prepared for anything what come my way,
no nothing could have stopped me.

The face of the old Indian always seemed to tell a tale I could not
read, I thought he looked as if we wrenched a part of him with us. I have
thought about him over the yrs, I hope he was not drove away like so
many but clung on in that little hut and kept his peace.

We arrived in Blue Run at midday.

We had kept our eyes peeled for Jim Coyne & his Traveling Show
but they was nowheres to be seen, perhaps he was still shut up in the
Mason Hill Hotel & lamenting the loss of his Little Earner. I thought
about Joseph & knowed he would surely be punished but them times

was already growed distant with these new Important Days ushered in their place.

Dud Carter was right, Blue Run was indeed a picture of a place, the snow heaped up & that white slope it leaned against sparkling in the sun like quartz. Dud jingled them coins in his saddlebag as we wove by some stores. The thoroughfare was very quiet but that was not to be mistook, I never knowed a town stay so quiet in the day & come to life at night.

Without delay we went about our business with the sort of fervor only men who believe theirselves Wronged & are on a course to set things Right can have. It was a trick of course, nobody can know what the future does have in store but I had convinced myself I was beyond the Natural Order.

In my head it was no Simple Act of Vengeance, I thought it more than that, it come to appear to me in them days as a chance to resolve all them torments of my past. I could not have told you in what ways I thought that the case but it circled in my mind & would not quit. But I thought Dud Carter was right, I thought I must learn to look after myself & what finer opportunity was there to prove my worth?

That very afternoon Dud Carter kitted me out with a fine new outfit, the tailor was at first most alarmed by my dimensions but he seen our money & he quickly become most obliging, he did compliment me on my Compact Frame & the shapeliness of my limbs.

From that point on I will put it very plain, we was 2 young fellows in very high spirits & once we had ourselves a drink there was no end to our debauchery. Even them thoughts of Gold & Revenge could not tear us away from the tavern, our resolve was not so strong as we thought. I wore new boots & britches, a new blue shirt & weskit & a black slouch hat what fit my head like a glove. Them scabs on my head had finally quit their running & begun to heal over nice but I did not fancy no girls eyeing them up & so I was glad to keep it firm atop my head.

Our vanity knowed no limits, no window we walked past would not be used for us to examine ourselves & see how very dashing & handsome we looked. A man can become addicted to the look of his own face & how I did love to see myself in them new clothes, fresh corduroy britches & shirt & boots & a very fine hat. Dud had also give me a new pistol, its cool handle did poke out of the fresh fragrant leather of its holster. It embarrasses me to say it but I did even name it Justice, I thought myself the Height of Elegance.

I had left that old beaver hat Jim Coyne give me with Onacona as a parting gift, he did not know how glad I was to be rid of it even if it was still bitter cold. O yes now I was feeling like a new man entire, I was on my way to becoming That Man I had always hoped I would become.

85

FARO

LET ME SAY IT PLAIN that it took no stretch before that money begun to run dry, all of Mr. Eder's coins only brung us so far. We slept that first night heaped up on the floor of the tavern amongst all them other men snoring & farting like cattle & when we woke we had just a few coins to our name. But Dud Carter always seemed to have something up his sleeve, I seen his fingers slyly interwove with a Cunning Plan a-dawning on him.

We was holed up in the sour gloom of that tavern & you would think us eager to get home with all that had come to light but our heads was in the clouds, these excesses was owed us, Dud claimed we must gather up our strength if we was to be at our best.

I admit I did not need much persuading, I had swore to avenge my daddy on God's word but there was no harm in staying a little while. We had been in the tavern for a goodly spell when I seen that old devil Dud was eyeing up a table on the far side with candles lit & 6 or 7 men sit around it in Silent Contemplation. They might have been at prayer they was so still & quiet but Dud knowed well enough what they was up to.

It has been a great pleasure to spend that old goat's money, said Dud.

He then held out the old bundle what we had first picked up from Solus & jiggled the few remaining coins left. His eyes was still on that table, I seen in them that Old Mischief.

But as you can see, Old Salt, it will not take us all the way down this Road of Pleasure we is embarked upon. And so there is only one thing for it.

He looked down at me, I was already so drunk I could see 2 of him swaying before me. He did rest his hand on my shoulder to steady me.

You just wait on here, Old Salt. Ain't nothin you got to worry about. Dud will make us a Big Killing in this wolf-trap over here & sort this little problem of ours no bother.

He walked off then toward that table, he did grip onto the back of chairs to stop himself from stumbling, I thought he was surely too drunk to do any good. More likely I thought he would end up with a bloody nose but I had underestimated my old friend too many times before not to feel a shim of hope.

Them men was of course in the thick of a Game of Cards, Dud Carter did later tell me it was Faro they was playing. I never knowed the first thing about cards or Faro or anything of the sort but Dud Carter had always been the more Worldly of our pairing.

I seen him sit himself down at that table, he made his back very straight & set about introducing himself, perhaps he was Henry Brooks once more I could not hear.

There was a man standing beside the dealer, his beady eyes was watching out for trickery. But the game did commence & I did try to keep my eyes on that table & on the watch for any signs of our victory but all them men's faces was like Closed Doors, they did not smile or cry out or nothing of the sorts.

O I do not deny it is quite possible I did fall asleep for it did not seem so long to me before Dud Carter was standing again before me. He held out the sack & dumped it on the bar so that coins spilt out shimmering along it just as they once had across that moonstruck road.

You look like you might have regained your thirst, Old Salt, said he.

I found I could not write a word, I was so shocked. He ordered us 2 more shots of whiskey & when I looked over toward that table he had sit at I seen a great many Aggrieved Faces staring over at us.

He give me a wink. Don't you mind them, Old Salt, they is just sore losers. Dud here won fair & square & if this ain't a sign that we got all the Luck in the world on our side at the moment then I don't know what is.

86

FIRST EXPERIENCE

AS DUD HAD PROMISED THE tavern in Blue Run was never empty, now our pockets was full again we did think there was no harm in staying one more night before our Grand Return.

And as Dud had talked way back when we was bathing in that creek, he was quite a Charmer with the ladies. This did not surprise me no more, I had seen evidence enough of his Silky Talk to know it for truth.

O yes let me not delay, I did enjoy my first Experience with a woman in Blue Run, I am not so proud of it now as I was back then. No it was not Love but I was young & filled with desires I thought Too Important to be ignored.

It become Dud Carter's habit whenever we got to talking with a woman he did bill me as a Silent Mysterious Type, he was very careful not to spook no one, he knowed my looks could often do that. He warned against me using my slate, he said words when they was writ down would likely scare a girl right away.

Best to play it like you got things to say but you just decide to keep em to yourself, said Dud, nodding like the Great Sage he thought himself.

And so when we did get to talking with a woman Dud Carter would introduce himself & then me but before I even got to shake their hand or kiss their cheek, he would lean in & set to whispering.

You won't get no words out of him, he would say. He seen hisself too many Things to talk on.

Like what Things?

That ain't for me to tell. But he got a story for every day of the year.

Then why don't he tell none of em?

Maybe he will, Dud Carter would say. But only when he's Good & Ready. He got to trust a person before he starts to work his tongue.

Here Dud Carter would often wink, there was some wordplay at work, I do believe it is called Innuendo but I knowed nothing of the sort back then.

Them girls was always very skeptical at first, they thought it all a Pack of Lies. Their eyes did look me up & down.

Ain't he a bit young? they would say.

Young? Dud would cry. He ain't young. Not if you look into them eyes of his he won't seem so damn young. Why that is a insult to a man who has lived as hard & as long as he.

I didn't mean no insult, I was just—

Just know he's plenty older than you'd expect, Dud Carter would say. And don't worry none about that insult, he also happens to be saintly in his appreciation of Forgiveness.

While Dud went about all this talk, he had urged me to look as Aloof & Unruffled as possible, even if my palms was sweating with nerves & I had never been more afeared of making a fool out of myself.

You look on over elsewhere, said Dud, like you don't give a fig. Like you got bigger things on your mind. But when the time come you got to go to work with them big ole eyes of yours. God blessed you with a pair of blinkers what I have at times envied myself. Pin them on a girl an she'll be yours.

I did not know what quality my eyes possessed but I did as I was told. And sometimes a girl took a liking to me & sometimes she did not. Dud warned you can't take no rejections to heart, every woman has her appetites just like us men & it is only natural some will not care for you right away.

I admit it is rare for me to be shunned but believe it or not it has happened, said he, shaking his head sadly.

But many of them girls did seem to like me, all I had imagined they would dislike was what they did appreciate. Some even took off my hat & stroked my bald head, them scabs was now Badges of Bravery from my travels.

The girl I did spend that night with was called Elizabeth. She was herself small, she had long dark hair, dark eyes, very narrow about the waist, I thought her a veritable Beauty.

Dud Carter had done his part, he claimed he had other engagements & moved off but Elizabeth did stay behind, she looked into my eyes & then took my hand in hers, with the bridge of her thumb she did begin to stroke my own.

So you seen a lot of Things? said she.

I done as Dud said, my heart was beating very fast but I nodded slow & looked elsewhere.

I sure would like to hear about them, she said.

I turned then to look at her, I made sure she looked deep into my eyes, I hoped they told all them stories Dud Carter had hinted at.

Well let me say Elizabeth did seem to grow very Amorous after that, she did seem perfectly content with my silence. We drank into the night & she was no slouch, she matched me with every one until she begun to fiddle with them buttons at the neck of her dress, she undid 3 or 4 & promised me more if I would just follow her. I did not have to be asked twice, my nerves was vanished, I was very gentlemanly & helped her down from her stool.

Once we was down from our stools I only come up to the top of her breasts but that did not bother her none, she was a most Liberal Soul. I turned & seen Dud Carter in the corner, he did salute me as we was on our way out the door. Elizabeth led me to her little cabin & her warm bed & that is where I will stop, them details is not for sharing now.

87

TRUE MEN

ON THAT FIRST NIGHT WE had spent I had begun to note that after Dud Carter had set me up he never partook in none of the Afters, he would retire to a quiet corner to smoke his pipe & sip away at his drink. We did not talk about it but I knowed he was saving himself for my Mama, I suppose I could not help but be impressed.

One night I did decide to put my own feelings to one side, we had not ever got no chance to speak about how he truly felt. Naturally we was both emboldened by drink, there was nothing we could not discuss. I asked him & he told me he was in love & no man had ever loved my Mama as much as he, not even my daddy, said Dud, God rest his soul.

He had then cried in front of me, he said he had bared his heart & if I could not see it was Love what come pouring out of him then I was blind.

Well soon enough we was both crying & I give him my blessing, I said there was no man I'd rather see paired up with my Mama. Of course I was drunk as a mule, I did not know what I was saying but it was too late for that, the next day Dud Carter thought me a Hero Amongst Men, he claimed me for his Brother although he did admit he would in all truth be my Father if his wishes was to come true.

In them fleeting moments when I was sober, I did begin to think
on my Mama & how she had always been alone when I had knowed her.
Perhaps she had longed for a companion on them lonely nights, I had
not ever thought until now. The prospect of Dud Carter being that man
was still a queer one but I begun to think it might give her some Happiness what she had always been missing.

Of course women was not all me & Dud talked about through them
2 long days & nights, we also spent many a hour on Gold & what sort
of life we might carve out for ourselves. We reckoned we would be rich
beyond our Wildest Dreams, Dud said he would buy my Mama anything her heart desired.

And if we talked about that Mr. Coombs we made no plans as to
how or when we might kill him if we had to, our Youth & the Drink did
warp our imaginations, we could only see Success Ahead.

O no it did not take much to convince ourselves he was no threat
to us. Perhaps we neither of us truly believed he would be there when
we was returned. We thought he would have been frighted off somewheres after what he had seen happen to his friend in Peeper's tavern.
The truth is we had come to believe all kind of things about ourselves
in that period, there was nothing we could not do. We was now Men &
True Men will do as they please.

How we then did need an old wise head to set us straight. If only
Shelby Stubbs had been there he would have knocked our fool heads
together but there was no one & so we could not be stopped. Even just
the sight of his pate of white curls & his lively blue eyes darting behind his
eyeglasses I reckon would have been enough to bring me to my Senses.
But there was no one in Blue Run who was likely to act that part, we
was on our own & left to them Grand Enterprises such young hearts is
all too likely to conjure.

88

A LONG PROCESSION

DUD CARTER'S WORDS IN ONACONA'S hut was true enough, we woke bleary-eyed the next morn on the tavern floor to hear the churn of footsteps outside & that's when we seen a Slow Procession of men & women & scraggy-clad childs come through the town.

I did not know what it was but Dud Carter certainly did.

What did I tell you, Old Salt, said he.

We could not take our eyes from it, even in them first few hours we must have seen a hundred men of all kinds come plodding by, they was whites & negroes & Indians & half-breeds. Some was dressed in no more than filthy rags & carried what they could on their backs & some come in fancy wagons with a glistening horse & a wagon bed filled with every tool Under the Sun.

We looked at each other & grinned.

At around noon we still had not left the tavern & one of them men from the procession, a rangy fellow with a thick mustache & all his appurtenances lashed to his back did peel off & come up to the bar for his refreshment.

It was not common practice to introduce yourself in them days unless you was to play a game of Faro or some such but this fellow could not help himself, he had that mild look of surprisement always on his face, he did need to make a friend wherever he went.

My name is Rawley Gibbs, said he.

He did extend his dirty hand.

Dud Carter could not help himself, there was no need but still he did give himself another new name of Walker Tilson, he was in a High Mood so he give me the queer title of Budge Needham.

Pleasure to meet you both, said Rawley Gibbs, he took a tentative sip of his whiskey, he was no seasoned drinker that was clear.

You boys on your way to the Gold?

What Gold? said Dud Carter.

What Gold? said Rawley Gibbs, he did nearly spit out his drink. Ain't you heard?

Heard what? said Dud Carter.

Hell, said Rawley Gibbs, looking about him in astonishment. He pointed out the door to the line of men still trudging past.

What do you reckon all these folk is coming by for, Mr. Tilson? Ain't you give a thought to the Why of it all?

I'm afraid I ain't, said Dud Carter.

He was never happier than when he was playing with somebody, the look in his eye did take me back to that night with Jim Coyne.

Well hell, said Rawley Gibbs. Ain't you give a thought to it, Mr. Needham?

I shook my head, we was both barely containing our smiles.

Well look down here.

Rawley Gibbs pointed at his feet, he had a poke where he had stashed his pan & pick & other such necessaries.

Some fellow discovered Gold down in a little town a ways away, they call it Heron's Creek. They reckon they's enough for every man to have his fill.

Is that so? said Dud.

It certainly is, said Rawley Gibbs who took another sip of his whiskey. I reckon you boys should come on down & join the rest of us. Get yourself some Gold before he all runs out.

Maybe we will, said Dud Carter. What do you reckon, Budge?

I nodded, I thought it did sound a fine idea.

Well that settles it, said Rawley Gibbs.

He slammed down his empty glass & picked up his wares.

I'll be seein you boys down there.

Then he waved his merry goodbyes & joined that line again.

I reckon we best be going, said Dud Carter as he watched him go. You go on & fetch Gussie & then we will have one more drink before we leave.

Any other time & it would have been a great wrench to leave but we knowed our pockets would soon be filled with Gold & I did have my murdered daddy now firm on my mind to avenge, so me & Dud Carter had our final drink & then give up our Lordly Reign in Blue Run to join the end of that long line of rattling pans & dreaming men what would not stop until it reached Heron's Creek.

89

A SILHOUETTE

JUST BEFORE WE WAS SET to leave Dud Carter's eye was took by a man busy at some mysterious craft. We had seen him many times before, he was a large fellow always sit & hunched over a barrel opposite the tavern, a pair of what looked like little gold scissors glinting in his great big hand.

We had always had other things on our mind when we seen him but now Dud walked over to him, he was suddenly most intrigued.

We got plenty of time, said Dud. I just got me a little hunch this man could be of use to me.

We wove between the trudging prospectors of the procession & seen him then at work on some small scrap of paper, them fingers of his was very dextrous for their size, he did manage to work their tips very neat & delicate around the scrap.

What you workin on there, friend? asked Dud Carter, leaning over him so he blocked the morning sun & shade fell over the man's practice.

The man looked up, his jowls was stubbled, his eyes very rheumy, like the rest of Blue Run he was evidently no stranger to a drink. But his was a kindly face, he stood himself up straight & introduced himself.

Degory Samuels, said he.

Awful nice to meet you, said Dud Carter. I come over to see what you was up to.

Well, said Degory Samuels, it is my aim to help any man after winning a woman's heart.

Dud Carter looked down at me.

You have won enough I reckon, Old Salt.

He looked back then at Degory Samuels.

You got my interest pretty much piqued, Mr. Samuels. What is it exactly that you do here?

How's about I show you & if you got a likin for the results then perhaps you might part with a few coins & we will both be the happier for it?

That seems fair to me, said Dud Carter. Go on right ahead.

All I ask, said Degory Samuels, is that you stand here & look on down the road that way so that I got a good look at the side of your face.

Dud did as he was told.

Like this?

That's it. That's just right.

Mr. Samuels then set to his work, Dud stood very proud, his chin raised up, his hat well adjusted, his long nose pointed like a weathervane to the west. You might have thought him off to war.

With them tiny golden scissors Mr. Samuels then set to peering up at Dud & very slow & careful snipping out the outline of Dud's head, I watched him do it very close & I must admit he captured it perfect, no line was gone to wrong or gone to waste. It was Dud Carter alright, there was no doubt.

When he was done, Mr. Samuels then reached into the pocket of his coat, he brung out then a box what held an assortment of pendants, their chains shined dully in the sun. They was all of them well used but pretty enough, he did open one of them lockets & popped in the image of Dud's profile.

The man handed it now to Dud.

For your sweetheart, said he.

Dud Carter opened up the locket & studied the tiny image of his own head. He nodded with approval.

This will do nicely, he said.

90

A NEW TOWN

YOU COULD NOT HAVE PREPARED us for what we seen when we arrived back in our old town. We had not been away so long but our quaint little town was changed beyond all recognition.

It was December still but it was like some Queer Spring the way tents & shacks & hotels had come up from the ground. We seen 3 new taverns before we even reached the main street, they was awful ramshackle, they did look like a strong gust might blow them over but each had its share of patrons, they was all men black with dirt, their beards growed long & their eyes rimed with rivermud.

O & what a noise! Many was hammering & sawing & calling out to each other & foundations was getting dug & timbers dragged through the mud & there was no end to their activity, it did bring to my mind a hive or nest of critters in the service of their Queen.

It was late afternoon & the sun already dipped behind the mountains but our eyes was still stunned, we seen what seemed like dozens of stalls selling mining equipment & other goods & necessities, there was even a Dentist set up, he wore an apron smeared dark with blood, he waved drunkenly in his hand what I took for clamps of some description, whether they was to hold his patients' heads still or wrench out the offending tooth I did not know & I would not be finding out.

O it was not just them sounds what rung out, I had always been able to smell Nature's sweet scents come wafting & riding them mountain winds but there was no such aromas now, they was the Harsh Stink of dung & damp cloth & dirty bodies not washed or scrubbed but left to dry in the sun, for all our journey home that sun had not stopped its shining, we was still in the thick of winter but you would have thought it spring to see that cloudless sky. That snow was become a distant memory & here in Heron's Creek the earth was dry & the air crisp, a wind come whipping through & set them tents to rippling & them men to holding on to their sweat-soaked hats.

O yes me & Dud Carter was in a trance, we was lost in our own home. But it was Dud what snapped out of his reverie first.

Keep your eyes peeled, Old Salt. He might be here somewheres & it is up to you to set the score.

Following that long line of Prospectors & Fortune Seekers home he had continued to talk about Revenge as if it was the only healing power in the world, no other would have brung me peace or indeed him any peace for my battles was his battles, my injury his injury, his loyalty to me was so great that our hearts did seem to pound with the same blood.

Of course we had barely put a thought into all them other scenarios, if he seen us first or how we would explain ourselves if indeed we did kill him. O we was no more than childs at play, how quick we would soon find them waters we thought a stream would reveal theirselves to be a river & sweep our feet from under us.

We had thought Peeper's tavern might have been burned to the ground, that night I had done for the Stranger did seem Long Ago. I thought then how I had seen the man Mr. Coombs stalking through the smoke of that blaze, I seen his feather singed & aglow like that of the great Phoenix. My eyes did scan then for that same feather, I thought I might find him still standing there but the porch was empty.

Though some of its wood was well charred it had been repaired in places with fresh lengths of timber, only now it was flanked on either side by a launders & a queer little hut even more decrepit than most others, there was a tow-headed man what sit on a cane chair & he did claim himself a Doctor of Miners' Maladies.

O yes he had a great list of them painted on a ripped sheet & blowing in the wind so's you could barely read the damn thing. But he did sit there proud enough, he did wear no shirt, his hairy belly was cradled by 2 bony knees.

MINER'S COUGH
MINER'S LUNG
MINER'S FOOT
MINER'S SCALP
MINER'S LIVER

The list did go on, he had a cure for all or so he said, he seen us approach & tried to hail us down but Dud Carter shooed him away.

Gussie's old stable still remained but it looked now like there was a family living in there, a little boy was sit & looking down at us from the roof Tom Peeper had once mended. Gussie seen her old dwellings newly occupied & tossed her head in Disgust.

Perhaps we should say Hello to old Tom, said Dud Carter. No doubt he'll be able to tell us on a few things what has bin happenin around here.

We did not bother to tie Gussie up but rode her right on up them old porch steps.

Dud did climb down & knocked at the door. He waited a full minute but there was no answer.

Strange, said Dud Carter. I ain't never knocked on Tom Peeper's door & not had an answer.

Maybe he's out panning, I suggested.

That is possible, said Dud, looking around him again. Every other bastard looks to be.

He begun then to look through the windows. He turned to me & stroked at them wispy hairs he had let grow on his chin again. Henry Brooks would not have wore them ugly whiskers but now he was Dud Carter again through & through.

Don't look so homely in there no more. Awful dark & cold like it ain't seen a customer for a goodly spell. You know as well as me, Old Salt, how precious this place was to him. Seems odd he would let it fall so cold & quiet.

There then come a sound from inside. Dud Carter pressed his face to the window again.

That you, Tom? It's your old friend Dud Carter out here. I come back & I have little Yip Tolroy with me as well. We sure could do with wettin our lips with some of your famous liquor. You wouldn't believe the swill we been drinkin on the road.

There come no reply.

Tom? Tom Peeper? We heard you in there, Tom!

But still there come no reply.

Dud Carter tucked his thumbs in his soft leather belt & stood back looking most puzzled.

Well, I dare say he's probly drunkern all hell in there. Best leave him steady hisself a little & we'll come back tonight to do some celebratin. This town might rival old Blue Run for a good time by the looks of it.

91

MAMA

THE ROAD TO MY MAMA'S store was so busy me & Dud Carter could not believe our goddamn eyes. We was so shocked we did not speak, I felt like I had never seen so many people in my life, we was strangers in our own home.

Dust come roiling up from the earth with all them feet treading & carts rolling, the noise of chatter & of more men selling their wares was near deafening, I had not never seen so many people in one place, they was swarming all around, their hot breath billowed up like a moth-eaten sail. It did not seem like a one of them was clean shaved or had washed in all their lives, their hands & faces was black with dirt, their boots clot with mud. Some of them men seen us dressed very smart & set to whispering amongst theirselves, I know we both did enjoy their Envious Looks.

O no that whole road to my Mama's store was not the quiet & peaceful ride it once had been, some of them old cottonwoods had been cut down to make way for them crude little shacks & ugly canvas tents.

Men did sit in the dark of their windowless huts or had brung with them chairs to sit outside & smoke their pipes, all their equipment was laid out drying in the pink & bowing sun, their filthy clothes was hung up & giving off a Foul Reek. Some had brung with them their families, their wives was doing their best to keep order, childs was running around & screaming, they did know no better.

Them shacks was pressed right up to one another, a cat could not have fit between some of them, God alone knowed where they was doing their Dirty Business, I would later smell a latrine dug deep but them things can never be dug deep enough, the stink was Ungovernable.

Of course we should have been looking out for that man Mr. Coombs but our minds was elsewhere, after all that time spent thinking on my Revenge I had neglected to think about my Mama.

Dud Carter had talked about her some on our journey back but I had seemed to keep her at the back of my mind. Why this was I do not know but now as we growed closer to her, I begun to think on all that had changed me since I seen her. I did not know with what kind of eyes she would see me, I never knowed her next move back then & I certainly did not now.

But there was a part of me what hoped she would see me in my new clothes & believe I had growed into a Man she could be proud of. Perhaps she would also see the weight of the Knowledge I did keep in my head, I knowed the fate of her husband all them yrs ago. I will not lie there was something I savored in knowing something she did not, how I would tell her I did not know, I thought we would soon see.

When we reached the store we seen a great line outside. There was my blessed old tree, I had missed it like it did itself have a beating heart. I seen its old scarred trunk, its crooked branches, I could not help a tear coming to my eye. O it was mine & I had always thought it mine but now I seen 4 men was sit beneath it & smoking their pipes, my trusty stool was nowhere to be seen. I had spent more time there than any other, I longed to beat them men away & take my Rightful Place but Time was moved on. To imagine myself there & waiting for old Shelby Stubbs now seemed near impossible. For anyone who has returned to the place they did their growing & found it changed they will know how it unsettles the Head & Heart, you do not know what was real & what was not, your memories have been took.

Well, said Dud Carter, looks like your mama is doing some fine business.

I seen then 2 boys had made theirselves their own fire near one of the shacks next to my Mama's store, they was poking at it with sticks. Their mama was nowhere to be seen, their daddy was sit right near them with that fire at his feet, he drunk from a flask of liquor in his hand, he stared into them little flames with bald & unblinking eyes.

I could not imagine my Mama had took to all these intrusions on her plot but Dud Carter was right, you could not deny she was doing some Fine Business, if I knowed her then she would have stocked up on the finest equipment in town & would have them Prospectors fighting over it.

There was no room at the hitching rail & so we walked Gussie round the back of the store & tied her up. We would have to find her a new stable, for now we would have to plead with old Tom Langston that she could be put up in one of his.

Dud Carter took off his hat & run his hands through his oiled hair.

How do I look, Old Salt?

I did not like to say he looked well but I had to confess he looked a damned sight better than he used to.

Well? he said. My heart is beating like a damn drum.

He took out that necklace & opened it up & looked at the little silhouette of his own face. I had found him holding it a lot on our journey back, now he could not keep still, he was a Bag of Nerves. He leaned over me, very eager to read my words.

You look just fine, I said.

Just fine? I do not like the sound of that, Old Salt. Handsome. Dashing. Spectacular. These was words I was hopin for & you come up with 'Just Fine'.

I rubbed my slate & wrote again.

You look handsome, dashing & spectacular.

How very droll of you, Old Salt, said Dud Carter. I am so pleased you have my back.

The rear door was open, it led straight into the parlor. Nothing had changed in there, the light come sweeping in & the table & chairs was all where they had been & my Mama's seat by the fire where I had so many times imagined her sit.

Now we could hear all the noise through the wall from the store, all them boots scuffling across the boards & then we did hear my Mama's voice, keeping them Mannerless Men in order.

You first, cried she. You will be served first!

I turned & seen Dud Carter smiling.

Before I could stop him he begun to walk toward the door what opened up into the store. I knowed just then how we would find her. She would be in her gray dress, some of her fiery curls would have escaped their pins, her head would turn & her green eyes would find me.

Dud Carter did open that door then & she turned to look at us just as I thought, she looked suddenly weak on her feet. The color left her cheeks & she then come blundering over to me & fell to her knees.

I nearly did trip back myself from shock or her grasping hands I did not know, I felt then the warm wetness of her tears as she burrowed her face into mine & begun to sob.

No I could not ever remember being so close to her, now I could smell her hair, I could smell her breath & when she pulled back her face to look into my own I could see the fine lines around her eyes & the tears stream down her cheeks.

All them customers was silenced, their bearded & dirt-streaked faces turned upon the scene before them. She suddenly become aware of them, she did not say a word, perhaps out of some awkwardness she then embraced Dud Carter.

I seen then his cheeks growed rosy with pleasure, he could not keep a smile from playing across his lips, I can still see that smile now as I write, I do like to think on how happy he was then.

My Mama then turned to go back to her counter but before she did she turned & looked at me one last time, I seen something in her face then what I had not seen before.

She did reach out then & I felt the dry curve of her thumb stroke my cheek & her fingers wrap warm around my chin. She had not touched me like that for so many yrs, I did stare back into her eyes & it was like them times we had had before I could write, our eyes was locked & we was talking through them, she did not need to open her mouth.

I have been so worried about you, she said. I am so pleased you are home. I must work now but soon we can talk & I will hold you tighter than I ever did before.

92

BY SIMMERSTONE CREEK

WE LEFT MY MAMA TO her work & walked back out the store.

Well, Old Salt, you must have seen how she took me in her arms at the end there. Every man has his doubts but that has gone some way to dispelling them. She loves me. Not every one of them tears was for you, you must have knowed that.

He took out the pendant & begun to thread the links of the chain through his fingers.

I should have foreseed it that her emotions would get the better of her when she seen me. It is best I give this to her when she has calmed otherwise I fear she might do herself an injury. It is not uncommon for a woman to take a queer turn if she is the recipient of the attentions of such a man as myself.

He nodded at his own sapience but I was still too stunned by my Mama's greeting to listen to his ramblings. He continued to wax on & on but I could not stop from thinking how my own cheeks was dry with the salt of her tears, she had squeezed me so hard my ribs felt bruised.

Even now as I write my skin is raised & all a-tingle at the thought of that look & touch she give me & all it did seem to say of our past & all it seemed to say of what we thought was to come.

I think this calls for a celebration, Old Salt, said Dud Carter. It seems clear to me that old Mr. Coombs has not stuck around, I told you he took a great fright & has hightailed it off. Now how's about we head back down to old Tom Peeper's place & see if he's roused himself yet. We will partake in a few jars of his famous brew & then we will return here & you can see your mama & I will see Ellen.

He sniffed the air loudly & rubbed his hands, he was very pleased with this Distinction he had made.

We had mounted Gussie & Dud was about to turn us back toward town when I held up my slate. I reckoned it wise we go & check on where we would be making our Fortune.

Dud read my words & nodded.

I suppose you is right there, Old Salt. Old Dud is getting ahead of himself. We do make ourselves a fine team, what with you orderin me about all the time.

He winked at me & turned Gussie round again, her ears was besieged by flies in this uncommon warm weather we was having.

I reckon we'll find everything as it should be, said Dud, but there ain't no harm in checkin. Best we claim it for ourselves before some fool comes & takes what's rightful ours from under our noses.

We made our way toward the woods, down that same road we had come all them nights ago in the rain. I took then the chance to bring up something else we had discussed on the journey home. I had claimed we was dutybound to find & bury Burl but now I mentioned it again & Dud sighed his disapproval.

It is almost as if you like the stink of a rotted body, Old Salt.

He deserves to be put to rest, I said.

I ain't sayin that's not the case. I just reckon Nature might have done Her work on Burl already, Old Salt. We can't be sure how much will be left of him.

Then we'll bury what is left of him, I said.

Dud dropped the reins & held up his hands in surrender.

So be it, Old Salt. I don't want no arguments with you now. This is a great day for the both of us & we ought not to be bickerin like a pair of old maids about their needlework.

We plodded on in silence then. The sun was dipping & we could see more fires was getting lit, the air was bitter with the smoke what was carried by them sere winds. I had rode in the same saddle as Dud Carter for long enough now to know when he was deep in thought, his fingers begun to fidget & he sniffed very regular behind me. It was a minute later when he finally spoke up.

It will be a long while until my time comes, said he, but I knows no doubt I would like to be left out for the Elements to do their honest work. Ain't no use in putting ole Dud Carter in the ground, Death got to do his dance with me first & I don't reckon he got hisself a quick enough step.

He sniffed & looked up at the sky.

It is getting dark & it will be grisly work, said he.

He nipped Gussie with his bootheels so she edged into a lively trot.

Best we get ourselves a move on, Old Salt.

93

PITIFUL CREATURES

MORE TENTS & SHACKS WAS scattered across that old cornfield what led to the woods & beyond toward Simmerstone Creek. Some men was beginning to light little fires outside their homes & cook theirselves up a sorry-looking dinner. Darkness was nearly upon us.

Them woods what used to be so quiet was now alive with the footfall of returning miners & all the rattle & jangle what accompanies their wares. They did not look at us as we went by, I seen their britches was often sodden & so was their sleeves, they did look the Picture of Exhaustion.

Dud Carter looked at them as they went by.

They is pitiful creatures ain't they, Old Salt?

I had to agree they was.

That won't be us, said Dud. Wait till you see our Spot. We won't hardly have to do none of that grubbin around. We seen what we got already, 1 scoop of our hand in them waters & up come a palmful of Gold.

Dud kept on his talk as Gussie walked on. She was not so relaxed as us, she knowed this place, it had never give her no bounty of Good Memories before so she did not know why it would now. Her ears was pricked but we did not take no heed of her, Dud pulled harshly on her reins.

When we finally come upon the first bend of the creek we seen men still hunkered low in the waters & turning their pans up to the failing light to see what they found.

Dud Carter tutted again, he did think the lot of them fools.

We followed it round farther into them woods until the men begun to thin in their numbers & that familiar quiet I had heard all them long nights ago come back to me.

What did I tell you, Old Salt? said Dud Carter. I told you no one would have come this far yet, they is all too eager.

He shook his head, there was nothing he did not think he knowed.

They see that first bit of water & they go divin straight in, they don't know the business is all about knowin the Secrets.

Finally we seen that old stand of willows in the distance.

There they are, said Dud. Remember that first night we was here, Old Salt? Remember how you was up in that tree like a damn owl? Look at us now, we come back to claim what is ours.

It was then I seen a man crouched beneath them willow fronds, I snatched the reins from Dud Carter's hands & pulled Gussie to a halt. We could not see his face, he was turned away from us. I turned to look at Dud Carter, his eyes was wide.

Hold up, Old Salt, whispered Dud Carter. This here looks like our man. Should have knowed he'd be holed up right on our patch.

Both our pistols was loaded, Dud clumb down from Gussie ever so quiet, he did not wait for me to but picked me up & placed me on the ground like I was a precious vase on a mantel.

Dud Carter looked into Gussie's eyes, he brung his finger up to his lips, she knowed she must keep as quiet as us.

The man was still crouched & busy with his find as we begun to creep through them river birch toward him. The light was growed very dim, we could see that dark hair poked out from his hat & he was humming some tune to himself. He thought himself very smug on our claim, we would soon show him.

I seen what looked like that feather & I know Dud Carter seen it too for he brung his finger up to his lips again & steadied his pistol.

O yes we moved so quiet he never heard a thing, we was near right behind him when Dud Carter made his move.

Don't move! cried he.

But the man spun round right away, he held in his hands something dark & aimed it right for us, we took it for a pistol.

There was then the flare & crack from Dud Carter's pistol & we seen too late Tom Peeper's stricken face as he toppled to his side.

Dud Carter did not move, his face was aghast, he could do nothing but stare as I run toward the felled body of our friend.

Poor Tom was face down in the dirt, I could not bear to turn him & see his lifeless eyes, I had had my fill of Death & did want no more to do with it. Now Dud Carter come walking slowly over, his face was pale as the moon, his eyes was streaming tears. He crouched on the other side of Tom & rolled him onto his back.

We was both expecting blood & gore but Tom Peeper was no more dead than us, that bullet was passed straight through the crown of his hat like a railroad tunnel blown into a mountain. There was no sign of Cold Death in his eyes, they was burning with rage instead, he swung a punch straight for Dud Carter & did nearly crack him square on the jaw.

What in hell's name you shooting at me for? cried Tom.

He took off his hat & poked a finger through the still-smoking hole. You near blowed my head off, said he.

Them familiar eyes of his was wide with indignation, his dark beard was flecked with more gray than I remembered it.

We're awful sorry, Tom, said Dud, we thought you was—

What? A goddamn turkey?

Tom Peeper shook his head, he could not take his eyes off that hole in his hat. If you have ever cheat Death so close as that, you will know that you got to get used to being alive again.

Dud Carter wiped the tears from his face with the sleeve of his coat. He looked down at the pistol what gleamed in his shaking hand. I thought perhaps all his talk of gunskills back in Onacona's hut was not idle boasts & he was indeed mighty sharp on the trigger.

We sure is sorry, Tom. We got a little jumpy & thought you meant to do us some harm. We thought you was out to get us.

I ain't out here to get nothin but the Gold what God seen fit to run down this creek, he said. I did not expect to be gettin shot at for it.

I got to admit that is our mistake, Tom. I am awful glad you ain't got a hole in your head right about now. We're just about as sorry as any folk could be.

Tom Peeper picked up his hat again & looked through it like they was keyholes in a door. He shook his head in wonder & then reached into his pocket & produced an old rusted canteen of his own brewed corn whiskey. He swigged long & hard.

I guess you didn't mean nothin by it, he said, wiping his mouth with the back of his muddied hand.

That's right, said Dud, nodding like he never heard nothing more agreeable in all his days. We dint mean nothin by it. We just let ourselves get a little jumpy.

Tom Peeper might have all them scalps on his wall but he could be very forgiving to his own kind. For a long while he stared down at the ground before he looked up at us & said, I don't reckon I seen you 2 boys for some time. Where you been hidin out at? You just upped—

We ain't been nowhere, said Dud Carter very sharp. We just been ridin here & there & now we come back to see what's new.

Well I don't blame you for comin back now, said Tom. God done us a lucky turn in these parts & every man who still got a pair of hands is out digging for their fortune.

So we hear, said Dud.

Tom Peeper took himself another quick swig, then eyed us both & give us a crooked smile.

You done well to pair up like you has, he said. I done got myself a partner also. Best way to do it I reckon, if you got the trust between you. Reason I took a liking to my partner is he told me he found Burl alive & well. Says he was a friend of his daddy's & that Burl had found hisself another woman in Ohio. Don't know how he got there but I was awful pleased to hear it. I been worried about him for a long old time.

He laughed again & then offered up the canteen, its rusted neck dripping with liquor.

You boys let me know if you fancy wettin your gullets. So where is it you boys been doing your gallivantin? You sure is dressed up all fancy. You been up near—

I made to reach for it, all this pother had rightly give me a bit of a thirst but Dud Carter was suddenly leaning in awful close.

What partner? asked Dud.

Say what?

What partner you got yourself? asked Dud Carter, leaning in a little closer still.

Tom Peeper stared very quizzical at Dud for a moment, he could not figure why Dud was suddenly turned so intent on interrupting him.

I asked you what partner you got yourself, said Dud Carter again, whose tears was now well dried & his eyes turned hard & glaring.

I heard what you said & I don't mind tellin you if you give me a goddamn chance, Carter.

Dud held up his hands & lowered his eyes.

We're awful sorry, Tom. We just got ourselves a little het up is all.

Well I don't reckon you got much cause to be no hothead so how's about you just take that sharp edge off of your tongue?

Dud Carter raised up his hands again & nodded.

You're right there, Tom. I got myself all worked up & there ain't no need for it.

Dud kept his head lowered until Tom started up talking again.

He come along some weeks back, said he. We got to talkin & struck ourselves up a deal. He's a cordial enough fellow. Some reckon he got hisself a queer manner but I never seen nothin to give me no concerns. Sometimes he comes out pannin & I stay at the tavern. Sometimes it's the other ways around. Depends on who's feelin luckiest.

He laughed that deep old rumble what we had both heard shake the timbers of the tavern.

That's the thing when you is comin out here with your pick & your pan. You got to be workin off of them feelins in your gut. You got to be payin very close attention to them or you might find yourself losin out to another man & that's a mistake less easy to reckon with than you 2 boys near puttin me in the ground.

Tom chuckled to himself some more & swigged again from his canteen.

Nearly got my head blowed off, he said.

Dud Carter looked at me then, the sky was growed darker & I could just make out the glim of his eyes. He turned back to Tom Peeper.

Who is he? asked Dud Carter.

Who? said Tom.

Your partner, said Dud. Who is he?

Like I said, I ain't seen him before too long ago. Quiet sort he is. Goes by the name of Bill Addington, though I heard him called Coobs or Cooves or some other such title. I reckon it for a sobriquet, such is his character. Wears hisself a fancy hat. Now a hat don't need no adornments in my view but this fellow got a feather of some kind in his, I reckon he looks a damn fool myself but I ain't bout to quibble with him over it. You don't need no arguments getting stirred up over nothin.

He laughed again & then offered up the canteen, its rusted neck dripping with liquor.

You boys don't fancy a drink? asked he.

I don't reckon we got the time, said Dud. You say this partner of yours is at the tavern, Tom?

Tom Peeper looked up at him.

That's what I said. Sometimes I goes out & he stays there. I reckon he'll be there now.

Dud Carter nodded & then give me a nudge with his boot. I knowed as well as him what we got to do.

Come on now, Old Salt. I reckon we caused poor old Peeper enough of a scare here. We best be goin.

Tom Peeper made as if to rise but he must have had more liquor than we seen him drink just then, for he rocked back onto his scrawny rump.

I ain't seen you boys in a good while, said he. You dint even tell me where you got to. You never told me—

We'll have ourselves a good ole talk soon enough, Tom, said Dud over his shoulder. We just got ourselves a few things to tend to for now & then we'll be seein you directly. We is awful sorry for earlier.

I turned & watched as Tom Peeper took up his hat again & fingered the hole left by Dud Carter's bullet, he was mighty puzzled by what had just come to pass no doubt.

94

A BLAZE

THERE WAS A STORM OF thought behind them eyes of Dud Carter now. I could not keep up with him as he marched back toward Gussie, I seen he still held his pistol gripped tight in his hand.

Hurry yourself up, Old Salt. We got him now. You heard old Tom, that's him alright. We know where he is & he don't know where we is. In my mind that adds up to a damn Good Advantage.

I cannot help but see these moments pass before my eyes now so very slow, O it is here I do find my fingers seek to interleave in prayer but I know as well as any that Sacred Act is reserved for them instances as yet unpassed & cannot provide to alter the Been & Gone.

We found Gussie in Agitated Spirits, she had got her bridle twisted, her teeth was bared & her dark lips flecked white with spittle. I had never seen her so irked but the reasons behind her behavior was not left a mystery long. O yes that is when we heard it, a Wild Chorus of distant cries come from the camp of miners beyond the trees. They did sound like crows in that creeping darkness the way they repeated that same word over & over but we could not hear it clear enough yet.

We waited still as stones, them cries kept coming, echoing through the woods. They did grow louder & louder, O that same word come carried on Black & Wasted Wings until it hovered above us.

Fire.

Dud Carter's face whipped round to face mine & I seen his eyes & all I knowed of him seemed now lost to me. You surely must have seen it yourselves before, a person you know so very well took away by Fear & Panic, their eyes you seen so many times now changed in a way you could never say how, only the word Emptiness might come to mind.

Now Dud was hauling Gussie toward him, she bucked & snapped but Dud was soon in the saddle & reaching down his hand to me.

I looked up at him then & I seen that hand stretched out, O if I had knowed where we was headed perhaps I would never have took it but take it I did & we was off.

Flickering through the dark limbs of the trees we could see the sky was turned a queer shade, it was as if hell was opened up, oranges & pinks & reds did stain the firmament.

Dud Carter beat at Gussie's flanks with the flat of his palm, fronds whipped at us, I tried to pull at Gussie's reins but Dud Carter pinned my arms to my sides with 1 wiry arm, he would not slow even for a second.

We seen then as them trees begun to thin Black Smoke pluming thick & bilious toward the heavens. Dud Carter did not say he knowed it, I now think that perhaps in his heart he somehow did, even from that moment we heard them cries of Fire. I remember how his hands was gripping the reins & how I could then smell that smoke what we both seen blowed from the direction of my Mama's store.

The camp of tents & shacks in the field was all but empty, we wove between them unwatched fires & Gussie dashed through a good many others, sparks went flying off her hoofs.

We could see now a great crowd of men headed toward a terrible streak of flame what stretched the length of the road & was headed toward town. How quick we seen it move, that dry & fierce wind was blowing it & encouraging it, it did move like a riderless chariot with no hand to steer it.

Dud Carter cried out for them men to scatter their sorry selves, Gussie's eyes was bright & tinged orange with them approaching flames. Them men had no choice but to dive to the ground or be trampled, they did curse us with Foul & Ungodly words.

At first as we come down the road & by some trick of the smoke I thought the store remained untouched & only them shacks beside it was ablaze. But as we come closer that smoke did part & I seen flames licking their way up each wall of my Mama's store, it was surrounded like you seen a pack of wolves circling a lame buffalo.

The crowd was so thick we was forced to jump down from Gussie, we did leave her untied, her ribs was heaving, her dark eyes filled with them flames & shooting embers hungry for their freedom.

I held on to the back of Dud Carter's coat as he pushed his way through them people. I was knocked about, I tripped & fell, Dud did drag me between the legs of who I did not know, there was so many of them, they did rise up then like a Great Wood.

We both did search them faces for my Mama but near all was men, some was drunk & cheering them flames on, others did stand in Dreamy Silence & others was throwing pots of water what was only swallowed up by the blaze.

I had seen them 2 boys what had been poking at their fire, their eyes was wide, they could not believe how big it was growed. There come a sharp shriek, it was the glass begun to crack & squeal, the heat what come gusting out, we could not get no closer.

Where is she? cried Dud Carter. Where is she?

Still Dud Carter pushed on, the stink of all them britches my face rubbed past as we come closer to the store, our arms was raised against that Wicked Heat.

It was then I seen some movement up in the window of my Mama's room. I pointed & Dud Carter seen it also, it was a glim of white what flashed through the darkness.

All went black again until a moment later we seen a pair of hands press against the glass. But that glass was scalding hot & them hands soon went darting back into the dark.

Is it her? said Dud but his voice was no more than a whisper beneath all that clamor.

Is it her? He did scream it now looking down at me but my hands did not once reach for my slate, they was froze by my sides, I knowed it was my Mama & so did he but we could not let that Dark Thought into our hearts.

Then there come something flying through the window, it landed by my feet, I seen it was my Mama's Bible, them pages was glowing at their edges. God forgive me I had to stamp on them Holy Pages so they did not go up in flames, I picked up that book & held it to my chest, only later was it I realized it had burned a book-shaped hole in my shirt.

When I looked up a jagged hole was broke in the glass, smoke billowed out & it was then we seen my Mama's pale face as she tried to suck the air. I turned & seen Dud, his eyes was wide, his mouth agape. The heat of the fire was so fierce my eyes was streaming, we watched as she begun then to scream & cry out, I never heard her make such a noise in all my life, I admit I had not ever imagined her capable of it.

Dud Carter then rushed toward them flames, I knowed he was going to try & get in the store & rescue my Mama but he never got no chance, suddenly the whole room was lit behind her, my Mama's dress was now alight & there come a cracking sound like you never heard, no Thunder or Shipwreck could ever match it. The floor give way beneath her & she disappeared in a hellish rush of Spark & Flame as the roof broke open & my Mama's soul was carried up into the night sky & beyond into them Heavenly Plains what reach out for all Starry Eternity.

95

TO GOD KNOWS WHERE

DUD CARTER DID NOT WAIT before he run back into that crowd & returned with Gussie. She reared up & people was scattering everywhere as Dud Carter fired his pistol into the air.

Out of the way! cried he. Out of the way!

I have since that moment set foot on a battlefield & been led to war by a bloodied & maddened Captain & now in my memory that is how I reckon Dud Carter did look. Gone was all reason & gone was all sense. It is the case with some men that when they do lose what they love most their own life is give over to gusts of Senseless Blood, it does run too hot for their veins.

I seen behind Dud them 2 boys again, they looked at all around them, I have thought often of their striped & sooted faces since & wondered if they could know the Destruction they did cause that night.

But Dud Carter did not see them, he looked down at me & now he did not reach out his hand. His mind was gone blank with Grief & Pain, O how I longed to see them old eyes of his alive with Mischief & Cunning, but such innocence was vanquished & in their place was a longing to find Coombs. In his poor & broke mind he knowed he must deliver some measure of Justice in this burning world.

I could see his lips was moving but I could not hear no words over all them screams & howls, the snare drum of them flames. It was then as if he did not see no fire nor no Yip Tolroy standing before him. That Pact we once made was cinders, his lips kept on moving like he was uttering some Secret Chant of his own design, no I could not hear them but I come to read them clear just as easy all them yrs before sit on my stool.

It's him, said he. It's him.

I reached into my Slate-Sling but I was too slow, no words could ever be writ quick enough, he spun & turned Gussie round & galloped off toward Peeper's tavern. I dropped my knurl of chalk, I did grind it into the hot earth, I have not ever wanted a Voice more than in that moment, O I would have cried his name so loud he would have had no choice but to stop & turn. But I could not do a thing, I seen his pistol still raised in the air before he vanished beyond the smoke.

I would like to say I stayed to heap buckets of water onto the flames & sift through the remains of the store & find my poor Mama's wrecked & smoking bones. But I knowed this night was not yet done, that look in Dud Carter's eye told me so. I could not save my Mama but I might yet stop Dud Carter from committing whatever he had convinced himself he ought to do.

So I begun then to run back toward town, these poor legs of mine never took me nowhere quick, I cursed them as that Wall of Fire worked its way along them huts, tearing at a speed I never seen. Men had tried to knock down them shacks & halt it but still it was cunning as a snake, it moved too quick for any human hand or mind, you would swear it had been wronged & was come back to wreak vengeance.

It clumb so high it lapped at the branches of the old cottonwoods what was left & the base of one was indeed in flames, I seen people scatter as it begun to fall, it come down like a great guillotine of old & shook the ground.

I did have no time to think about my Mama or them last looks she had give me, all that pain was waiting for me, but now I did pelt through the Blistering Heat, ash come raining down like snow, it was in my eyes & in my mouth, sometimes I can still taste them bitter notes now.

All them people I passed looked mad & wild but their cries & curses I did not listen to, their words was become meaningless to me beneath the crackle of the flames.

I thought then of my Mama's hands pressed so brief against that glass & then her Bible what still smoldered in my pocket. I do have it now beside me, its pages still black & charred, some will crumble in your hands if you is not careful. O they is days when I cannot read it without hearing them cries of hers come shrieking out at me, I must shut it & turn away, the only words what could give me comfort made to make me sick.

A hundred yds before the town the fire had took a devious turn, it had split itself in many parts, a branch of flaming river what had worked itself around the town though not yet touched the main street.

I did not know where Dud Carter was gone, there was no sign of him. I seen Amos Seagrave without his brother Ned, he was just staring dumbly at the flames what approached the town, there was nothing he could do.

I seen then Tom Peeper's tavern, the door was come off its hinges, it had been kicked & throwed down the porch steps where it lay against the earth like it might occasion some dark entrance into the Underworld said to have once teemed with the Dead & the Doomed.

The fire still raged behind me but it was far enough away now that the cool of the night reached my skin. The sky was filled with stars, that wind did keep the smoke drifting like dark clouds.

I took out my pistol & edged inside.

All was silent & dark in there, I seen them horses carved by Tom Peeper staring down at me. I seen the grate was filled with cold ashes, them tables & chairs was all overturned.

I never knowed a place to be so cold then or since, I remember how I was begun to shiver. I held that pistol out before me but my hand did shake, my heart had never beat so fast. I had not noticed but I then tasted salt, tears was falling down my cheeks.

I searched behind the bar, I searched out the back, I even found myself looking beneath tables & chairs as if Dud Carter might suddenly appear there.

There was no sign of him, there was no sign of Gussie neither.

Out on the porch I seen that fire growed closer, it had reached the first stores of the town, I could feel its Evil Heat.

A weariness come over me then, I did sit down & thought I might wait for them flames to come & turn me to cinders.

That was when I heard the first gunshot.

Beyond the town along that pitch-dark length of road Dud Carter had took us as we escaped all them weeks ago I seen the flash of a muzzle in the meadow.

I tumbled down them steps & into the Deepening Dark away from them flames & into the Sudden Silence.

I stared out into the black of the meadow where I had seen the shot fired. There come the whispering grasses & the dark mountains was risen up beyond them & if I had turned I would have seen the glow of that fire rip through the town.

And then I seen another muzzle flash bright in the darkness & the echo & then the wind come rushing & the whispering grasses again.

Behind me the glare of that fire growed ever closer but spread before me was darkness & the shadowed hills beyond it & only them 2 pistols flaring Bright & Sharp now 1 after the other, the crack running up & down the hills until there come no more shots & the echoes did die & I find that my legs is carrying me & I am running toward them with my own pistol held out before me.

I come to 2 dark shapes, 1 is laid out on the ground & the other standing. I cannot see no faces, there is only starlight & the creeping glow of the fire to go by.

O I want it to be Dud Carter who is there standing, I want to see his small gray eyes & I want him to say, I have got him, Old Salt, I have got him. But instead that dark shape stays silent & then the muzzle flares again & them echoes still reach me now & there is a shooting pain through my hand & arm as my gun is flung into darkness & 2 of my fingers shot clean off.

Warm blood runs from that wound but I do not feel no pain now, I am on my knees & that Dark Shape is still standing, O I know he is, he is looking at me. The stars wheel above us, they stare blindly down at this Strange Game played out beneath them but still he does not say nothing & it is a silence I have never knowed before or since as he only stands there, the dark outline of him, faceless but watching me & breathing very slow.

And that other shape laid so Still & Quiet.

Then I hear that shape come walking toward me, the grasses brushing against his britches. I can hear him breathing, he keeps walking, come so close now & I know he will place that cold metal against my skull & I too will leave this world behind.

But he does not.

He walks past me so close that the hem of his coat touches my ear & a shiver goes through me & I can smell the smoke trapped in its weave & I can smell blood & liquor & then I can see that Feather in his hat as he walks away, it is flickering ever so gentle like it was still in the wing of a bird & it might suddenly lift him into the sky.

96

MY BROTHER

I CRAWLED OVER TO THAT BODY laid on the ground, I knowed Dud Carter was dead from the moment I touched him. Still it did not stop me from shaking him until my arms ached, for though I knowed he would not come back to me I had never believed so much it was in my power to raise him up.

And so I shook & tried to drag him & beat against his chest until I could no more, that is how much I wanted him back. O that is how much I loved him.

I stayed by Dud Carter's side until the light of dawn begun to creep into the sky. The fire had burned through the night & growed so fierce that I felt its warmth & still that ash found me & come drifting down soft as snow.

I had heard the cries of people, I had watched them from afar with that Distracted Gaze I seen in my own boy's eyes as he acts out his Tyranny on a nest of ants.

But how could I have cared for them when I held Dud Carter in my arms?

I had wanted to see his face but when that sliver of gray light finally worked itself above the hills I seen he had been shot through the eye, his face black with the blood that had only hours ago run through his veins as we talked & laughed & planned all what lay ahead of us.

I will not deny it I could not bear to see him, to see that person I had knowed who was so filled with Life now emptied of it. It does strike me now as Cowardice, I wish I had looked full & bold at that face, I wish I had pressed my own to it but I was sick with grief for him & my Mama & all the world for allowing these things to happen.

I closed my eyes then & I seen Dud Carter as he was when I first met him, with his crooked hair & his long nose & them gray eyes staring down at me. And I seen the length of whipcord what held up his old britches & I seen him sit drunk & laughing across from me & I felt his arms around me as we rode Gussie & after I seen all of it I could not figure what it was had brung us to this point.

Stories do so often come to us fully formed & it is up to us how we read them. Me & Dud Carter read it wrong. We thought we knowed every line but we didn't know none of them, we was Boys at play in a Deadly Game.

And so I stood up & I left Dud Carter where he lay to the elements just as he had said he wanted. I walked past my 2 fingers strewed in the grasses & I walked through the smoldering ruins what was Heron's Creek & I walked by the store where my Mama's bones still glowed hot beneath the timbers & I kept on walking & I did not stop.

97

FRESH PAGES

OVER ALL THEM YRS WHAT have passed since that bitter day I have discovered the comfort what comes from the knowing of your own Inconsequence. O but then there is a biting need to have your own particular song heard & understood by all the world.

I got to say I never knowed which of these God hoped us to feel. They is times when the world does seem a Cruel & Violent place with Him hid behind His fretwork of stars, up above making Pronouncements what we cannot hear for the Rumblings of the Devil down below. He never did care to make it easy for us & I don't reckon He's got plans to now. I don't think I'm mistook to suppose He'd argue that's just the way it should be.

Not a day does drift by when I do not turn & look back over my shoulder at all that has Been & Gone. I imagine my poor daddy. I see Dud Carter with all them looks of well-set swagger & boyish hurt. I see my Mama behind her counter, her wild hair broke free of all them pins & nodding in the breeze. Did I do all I could in them days to live a Good & Honest life? How did I come to suffer the loss of all them I loved most?

Such thoughts as these could divide a man in 2 but you is no use to no one halved up like a apple, you got to keep yourself whole & be who it was you was set here to be.

You got to consider how you is in the Now but I will tell you they is times when I do find it hard to credit how I come to be here. I turn & see the bed where each night my wife does dream away & I do lie & look & listen to her breathe in the air she chose to share with me. Perhaps I ought to divulge now this dear woman closest to my heart is the very same girl what so long ago come sit in the snow beside my stool & the very same girl no less what me & Dud Carter seen rollicking along in her wagon before Fate was to take us our separate ways. It sure is queer how Life got a knack for gathering up a Loose End but I reckon how it all come to be is a Different Story for a Different Time.

Now I see my old Slate-Sling, worn soft & smoke-sweet hanging down from the hook in the wall. I see all my old treasures, that dear locket what holds the face of my old friend & beside it my Mama's pins & burnt-edged Bible, all of them spread out on my desk & staring back at me. People don't count on such things being Alive but I know they is, they was all once touched & that touch is a Wondrous Stain what don't ever leave.

O I did wend my way down an awful lot of roads to find myself in such a Quiet & Peaceful spot. Strange how peace only likes to let itself be knowed after you done near had thunder coming out your ears. Out the window I see the heavens is opening up, big old feathers of snow come drifting down in a dance with no 2 steps the same.

ACKNOWLEDGMENTS

ABOVE ALL, THANKS ARE DUE to my parents, for always encouraging me to follow what I love. This book is the very least I could give them in return. My siblings, Tom and Olivia, and my cousins, Joel and Alex – to have grown up alongside you is a gift that I could never articulate, though I hope something of it might be glimpsed at times in these pages. And to the rest of my family – too numerous to name but no less important – I am blessed to be one of you.

For her brilliant understanding of this story and her fierce eye for detail, I want to thank my agent, Zoe Waldie, as well as all those at Rogers, Coleridge and White who worked with this book.

For their warmth, support and invaluable input, I wish to thank all those at Doubleday who helped bring this book to life and into the world: Larry Finlay, my editor Suzanne Bridson, Tabitha Pelly, Jane Lawson, Alison Barrow, Kate Samano, Kirsty Dunseath, Irene Martinez, Lilly Cox.

For those at The Overlook Press, who embraced this book with such enthusiasm and dedication: Editorial Director Tracy Carns, Andrew Gibeley, Kevin Callahan, Mamie VanLangen, Eli Mock, and Lisa Silverman.

I reserve special gratitude for one dear friend: Erica Wagner not only believed in this book from the very first sentence, but she helped shape it until the very last. She is a true wonder, and without her expert knowledge, guidance and love for the characters in this story, I fear I would still be writing it now. I thank her for all her tireless work, but most importantly, I thank her for her friendship